KT-492-220

A *vision filled Ivypool's eyes. Warriors* swarmed from the shores and spilled into the forest. Torn-eared and scarred, their eyes gleamed with hate. Shrieks echoed and Ivypool heard the thud of muscle against rock as the world shook in the claws of the Dark Forest warriors.

As the vision faded she could still taste the tang of blood and fear. Ivypool realized that she was shaking, and her pads were sweating. All the battle skills in the Place of No Stars would not be enough to stop that unrelenting tide of death.

WARRIORS

THE NEW PROPHECY

POWER OF THREE

OMEN OF THE STARS

DAWN OF THE CLANS

EXPLORE THE
WARRIORS WORLD

Warriors Super Edition: Firestar's Quest

Warriors Super Edition: Bluestar's Prophecy

Warriors Super Edition: SkyClan's Destiny

Warriors Super Edition: Crookedstar's Promise

Warriors Super Edition: Yellowfang's Secret

Warriors Field Guide: Secrets of the Clans

Warriors: Cats of the Clans

Warriors: Code of the Clans

Warriors: Battles of the Clans

Warriors: Enter the Clans

MANGA

The Lost Warrior

Warrior's Refuge

Warrior's Return

The Rise of Scourge

Tigerstar and Sasha #1: Into the Woods

Tigerstar and Sasha #2: Escape from the Forest

Tigerstar and Sasha #3: Return to the Clans

Ravenpaw's Path #1: Shattered Peace

Ravenpaw's Path #2: A Clan in Need

Ravenpaw's Path #3: The Heart of a Warrior

SkyClan and the Stranger #1: The Rescue

SkyClan and the Stranger #2: Beyond the Code

SkyClan and the Stranger #3: After the Flood

NOVELLAS

Hollyleaf's Story

Mistystar's Omen

Cloudstar's Journey

Also by Erin Hunter

SEEKERS

RETURN TO THE WILD

MANGA

Toklo's Story
Kallik's Adventure

OMEN OF THE STARS

WARRIORS

THE LAST HOPE

ERIN
HUNTER

HARPER

An Imprint of HarperCollinsPublishers

Special thanks to Kate Cary

For Dan, in hope

The Last Hope
Copyright © 2012 by Working Partners Limited
Series created by Working Partners Limited
Warriors Adventure Game © 2012 by Working Partners Limited
"Looking for Newleaf" © 2012 by Working Partners Limited

All rights reserved. Printed in the United States of America. No part of
this book may be used or reproduced in any manner whatsoever without
written permission except in the case of brief quotations embodied in
critical articles and reviews. For information address HarperCollins
Children's Books, a division of HarperCollins Publishers,
195 Broadway, New York, NY 10007.
www.harpercollinschildrens.com

Library of Congress Cataloging-in-Publication Data
Hunter, Erin.
    The last hope / Erin Hunter. — 1st ed.
        p.   cm. — (Warriors, omen of the stars ; bk. 6)
    Includes instructions for "Warriors adventure game."
    ISBN 978-0-06-155529-9 (pbk. bdg.)
    [1. Cats—Fiction. 2. Prophecies—Fiction. 3. Adventure and
adventurers—Fiction. 4. Fantasy.] I. Title.
PZ7.H916625Laj   2012   2011052409
  [Fic]—dc23   CIP
                                                                      AC

Typography by Hilary Zarycky
14 15   CG/OPM   10 9 8 7 6   :
❖
First paperback edition, 2013

ALLEGIANCES

THUNDERCLAN

LEADER   **FIRESTAR**—ginger tom with a flame-colored pelt

DEPUTY   **BRAMBLECLAW**—dark brown tabby tom with amber eyes

MEDICINE CAT   **JAYFEATHER**—gray tabby tom with blind blue eyes

WARRIORS   (toms and she-cats without kits)

GRAYSTRIPE—long-haired gray tom

DUSTPELT—dark brown tabby tom

SANDSTORM—pale ginger she-cat with green eyes

BRACKENFUR—golden brown tabby tom

CLOUDTAIL—long-haired white tom with blue eyes

BRIGHTHEART—white she-cat with ginger patches

MILLIE—striped gray tabby she-cat with blue eyes

THORNCLAW—golden brown tabby tom

SQUIRRELFLIGHT—dark ginger she-cat with green eyes

LEAFPOOL—light brown tabby she-cat with amber eyes, former medicine cat

SPIDERLEG—long-limbed black tom with brown underbelly and amber eyes

BIRCHFALL—light brown tabby tom

WHITEWING—white she-cat with green eyes

BERRYNOSE—cream-colored tom

HAZELTAIL—small gray-and-white she-cat

MOUSEWHISKER—gray-and-white tom

CINDERHEART—gray tabby she-cat

LIONBLAZE—golden tabby tom with amber eyes

FOXLEAP—reddish tabby tom

ICECLOUD—white she-cat

TOADSTEP—black-and-white tom

ROSEPETAL—dark cream she-cat

BRIARLIGHT—dark brown she-cat

BLOSSOMFALL—tortoiseshell and white she-cat

BUMBLESTRIPE—very pale gray tom with black stripes

DOVEWING—pale gray she-cat with blue eyes

IVYPOOL—silver-and-white tabby she-cat with dark blue eyes

HOLLYLEAF—black she-cat with green eyes

QUEENS (she-cats expecting or nursing kits)

SORRELTAIL—tortoiseshell-and-white she-cat with amber eyes (mother to Lilykit, a dark tabby she-kit with white patches, and Seedkit, a very pale ginger she-kit)

FERNCLOUD—pale gray (with darker flecks) she-cat with green eyes

DAISY—cream long-furred cat from the horseplace

POPPYFROST—tortoiseshell she-cat (mother to Cherrykit, a ginger she-cat, and Molekit, a brown-and-cream tom)

ELDERS (former warriors and queens, now retired)

MOUSEFUR—small dusky brown she-cat

PURDY—plump tabby former loner with a gray muzzle

SHADOWCLAN

LEADER **BLACKSTAR**—large white tom with one jet-black forepaw

DEPUTY **ROWANCLAW**—ginger tom

MEDICINE CAT **LITTLECLOUD**—very small tabby tom

WARRIORS **OAKFUR**—small brown tom

SMOKEFOOT—black tom

TOADFOOT—dark brown tom

APPLEFUR—mottled brown she-cat

CROWFROST—black-and-white tom

RATSCAR—brown tom with long scar across his back

SNOWBIRD—pure-white she-cat

TAWNYPELT—tortoiseshell she-cat with green eyes

OLIVENOSE—tortoiseshell she-cat

OWLCLAW—light brown tabby tom

SHREWFOOT—gray she-cat with black feet

SCORCHFUR—dark gray tom

REDWILLOW—mottled brown-and-ginger tom

TIGERHEART—dark brown tabby tom

DAWNPELT—cream-furred she-cat

PINENOSE—black she-cat

FERRETCLAW—cream-and-gray tom

STARLINGWING—ginger tom

QUEENS   **KINKFUR**—tabby she-cat, with long fur that sticks out at all angles

IVYTAIL—black, white, and tortoiseshell she-cat

ELDERS   **CEDARHEART**—dark gray tom

TALLPOPPY—long-legged light brown tabby she-cat

SNAKETAIL—dark brown tom with tabby-striped tail

WHITEWATER—white she-cat with long fur, blind in one eye

WINDCLAN

LEADER   **ONESTAR**—brown tabby tom

DEPUTY   **ASHFOOT**—gray she-cat

MEDICINE CAT   **KESTRELFLIGHT**—mottled gray tom

WARRIORS   **CROWFEATHER**—dark gray tom

OWLWHISKER—light brown tabby tom

APPRENTICE, WHISKERPAW (light brown tom)

WHITETAIL—small white she-cat

NIGHTCLOUD—black she-cat

GORSETAIL—very pale gray-and-white tom with blue eyes

WEASELFUR—ginger tom with white paws

HARESPRING—brown-and-white tom

LEAFTAIL—dark tabby tom, amber eyes

ANTPELT—brown tom with one black ear

EMBERFOOT—gray tom with two dark paws

HEATHERTAIL—light brown tabby she-cat with blue eyes

    APPRENTICE, FURZEPAW (gray-and-white she-cat)

BREEZEPELT—black tom with amber eyes

    APPRENTICE, BOULDERPAW (large pale gray tom)

SEDGEWHISKER—light brown tabby she-cat

SWALLOWTAIL—dark gray she-cat

SUNSTRIKE—tortoiseshell she-cat with large white mark on her forehead

ELDERS
    WEBFOOT—dark gray tabby tom

    TORNEAR—tabby tom

RIVERCLAN

LEADER
    MISTYSTAR—gray she-cat with blue eyes

DEPUTY
    REEDWHISKER—black tom
    APPRENTICE, HOLLOWPAW (dark brown tabby tom)

MEDICINE CAT
    MOTHWING—dappled golden she-cat
    APPRENTICE, WILLOWSHINE (gray tabby she-cat)

WARRIORS

GRAYMIST—pale gray tabby she-cat
    APPRENTICE, TROUTPAW (pale gray tabby she-cat)

MINTFUR—light gray tabby tom

ICEWING—white she-cat with blue eyes

MINNOWTAIL—dark gray she-cat
    APPRENTICE, MOSSYPAW (brown-and-white she-cat)

PEBBLEFOOT—mottled gray tom
    APPRENTICE, RUSHPAW (light brown tabby tom)

MALLOWNOSE—light brown tabby tom

ROBINWING—tortoiseshell-and-white tom

BEETLEWHISKER—brown-and-white tabby tom

PETALFUR—gray-and-white she-cat

GRASSPELT—light brown tom

QUEENS

DUSKFUR—brown tabby she-cat

MOSSPELT—tortoiseshell she-cat with blue eyes

ELDERS

DAPPLENOSE—mottled gray she-cat

POUNCETAIL—ginger-and-white tom

CATS OUTSIDE THE CLANS

SMOKY—muscular gray-and-white tom who lives in a barn at the horseplace

FLOSS—small gray-and-white she-cat who lives at the horseplace

OTHER ANIMALS

MIDNIGHT—a star-gazing badger who lives by the sea

Hareview Campsite

Sanctuary Cottage

Sadler Woods

Littlepine Road

Littlepine Sailing Center

Littlepine Island

River Alba

Whitchurch Road

PROLOGUE

❧

A *jagged ridge sliced across the* horizon, piercing the black sky with its peaks. Four shapes, their pelts flecked by starlight, crouched on the silvered granite where the highest summit pushed into ice-cold wind.

"We have come." The white she-cat hunched down harder against the chill reaching for her bones. "Just as you asked us to."

Her companion dipped his head to the cats who had been waiting for them. "Greetings, Owl Feather, Broken Shadow."

"Greetings, Slant." Broken Shadow spiked her thick fur, muffling the stone-cold air. Her eyes reflected the rushing stars as she met the white cat's gaze. "It is good to meet you again, Half Moon." As she spoke, two more pelts moved like shadow over the stone.

"Bluestar, Spottedleaf, I'm glad to see you." Half Moon welcomed the StarClan warriors as they settled beside the four Ancients.

Bluestar curled her tail over her paws. "We have come to prepare for the end," she meowed solemnly.

Owl Feather narrowed her yellow eyes. "And to believe what we have to tell you?"

Spottedleaf let out a low growl. "Bluestar has always believed! It is the others we need to convince."

"We're running out of time!" Slant snapped.

The sky spun around them, its stars racing until they blurred into silver streaks—but the mountaintop seemed caught in stillness, like a warrior before the final pounce.

Bluestar's eyes glistened. "The Clans will make their own choices. I can do no more."

Slant leaned closer. "But the prophecies helped, didn't they?"

"Yes." Bluestar glanced at her medicine cat. "Spottedleaf recognized the flaming star that led me to Firestar."

Owl Feather acknowledged Spottedleaf with a blink. "She used her gift well. All along, it has been Firestar's kin who hold the last hope of the Clans in their paws."

"What about the fourth?" Slant leaned forward, anxiety pricking his gaze. "When will they find the fourth cat?"

"The fourth must be found soon," fretted Broken Shadow. "There is so little time left."

Owl Feather's tail twitched. "Are you sure we've done enough?"

"We have done everything we could." Half Moon's amber gaze flicked toward two figures clambering over the rocks toward them. "Midnight, is that you?"

"I come with Rock." The great she-badger lumbered onto the smooth granite. Rock stepped out behind her, his furless body pale in the moonlight.

Broken Shadow shifted her paws. "Greetings, Midnight. I . . . I didn't realize that you knew Rock."

"Since the dawn of your time, we have known each other," Midnight rumbled, turning her wide, striped head. "Since first cat put paw beside water."

Rock sat down on the cold stone. His blind blue eyes were round and white as moons. "We watched the first sunrise over the lake."

"It burst water into flame," Midnight recalled. "And in fiery reflection we see future of all cats: Tribe of Rushing Water, five Clan, four Clan, forest, and lake."

"We saw your whole journey, from lake to forest and back." Rock tipped his head as if watching the cats process in front of him. "The prophecies all came from that first reflected sunrise—the cat with a pelt of flame that would save the Clans, the silver cat who would save the Tribe of Rushing Water, and finally the four who would carry the last hope, not just of the Clans, but of light itself."

Midnight's claws scratched the granite. "Now we fear we see a final sunset that ends your story."

Half Moon stepped forward. "But the four? They will save us, surely?"

"They came as we saw they would and, when they came, they lit the darkest fires." Midnight gazed at the Ancient cats, her beady black eyes intent. "So you and all long-dead cats burn like stars once more."

"But evil is coming," Rock warned.

Midnight cut in. "Darkness we saw born like littermate alongside the light. Now all must stand and fight."

As the other cats shivered, Rock moved his blind gaze over them. "Thank you for safeguarding the prophecies for so long, and for passing them down from cats forgotten now and vanished."

Broken Shadow sighed. "So many lives lost."

"All lives are brief," Rock reminded her.

"My son's was too brief!" Her eyes flashed accusingly. "Why couldn't you save Fallen Leaves?"

"It was never my duty to save anyone!" Rock flashed back at her. "What is the point of a life held in the paws of another? There must be choice. There must be freedom. I can point the way but every cat walks on its own paws."

Slant narrowed his eyes. "Do the Clans walk alone into the final battle?"

Half Moon flattened her ears. "Never alone!" She lifted her chin. "I will fight alongside Jayfeather."

Broken Shadow unsheathed her claws. "And I will fight alongside my son."

"I will fight beside Jagged Lightning and my kits to defeat this darkness." Owl Feather's eyes sparked.

Bluestar thrashed her tail. "And I will die a tenth time to defend ThunderClan!"

"These cats will never stand alone," Half Moon declared. "We are with them just as we have always been."

"Light against dark," Midnight growled. "This is the end of all things—this is the last sunrise."

Rock touched her flank lightly with the tip of his tail. "It is what we have been waiting for, my friend."

CHAPTER 1

Someone's bleeding!

Ivypool stiffened as the memory of Antpelt's death flooded her mind, just as it always did when the scent of blood hit her. She could still feel his flesh tearing beneath her claws, still see his final agonized spasm before he stopped moving forever. She'd been forced to kill the WindClan warrior to convince Tigerstar of her loyalty. It had earned her the grim honor of training Dark Forest warriors, but she knew she would never wash the scent of his blood from her paws.

"Stop!" she yowled.

Birchfall froze mid-lunge and stared at her. "What's wrong?"

"I smell blood," she snapped. "We're only training. I don't want any injuries."

Birchfall blinked at her, puzzled.

Redwillow scrambled up from underneath Birchfall's paws. "It's just a nick," the ShadowClan warrior meowed. He showed Ivypool his ear. Blood welled from a thin scratch at the tip.

"Just be careful," Ivypool cautioned.

"Be careful?" Hawkfrost's snarl made her spin around.

"There's a war coming and it won't be won with sheathed claws." Hawkfrost curled his lip and stared at Ivypool. "I thought you were helping to train our recruits to fight like real warriors, not soft Clan cats."

Birchfall bristled. "Clan cats aren't soft!"

"Then why do you come here?" Hawkfrost challenged.

Redwillow whisked his tail. "Our Clans need us to be the best warriors we can be. You told us that, remember?"

Hawkfrost nodded slowly. "And you can only learn the skills you need *here*." He flicked his nose toward Birchfall. "Attack Redwillow again," he ordered. "This time don't stop at the first scent of blood." He narrowed his eyes at Ivypool.

Ivypool swallowed, terrified she'd given herself away. No Dark Forest cat could ever know that she came here to spy for Dovewing, Jayfeather, and Lionblaze. Growling, she lifted her chin and barged past Birchfall. "Do it like this," she told him. With a hiss she hurled herself at Redwillow, ducking away from his claws, and grasped his forepaw between her jaws. Using his weight to unbalance him, she snapped her head around and twisted him deftly onto his back. He landed with a thump, which she knew sounded more painful than it felt. She'd hardly pierced his fur with her teeth and her jerk was so well-timed it had knocked him off his feet without wrenching his leg.

She glanced back at Hawkfrost, relieved to see approval glinting in his eyes. He'd only seen the flash of fur and claw and heard the smack of muscle against the slippery earth.

"Hawkfrost!"

Birchfall and Redwillow stared wide-eyed as Applefur appeared from the mist. The ShadowClan she-cat's eyes were bright, her mottled brown pelt pulsing with heat from training. "Blossomfall and Hollowflight want to fight *Dark Forest* warriors."

Applefur's apprentices padded out of the shadows. "We can fight Clan cats anytime," Blossomfall complained.

Hollowflight nodded. "We come here to learn skills we can't learn anywhere else." The RiverClan tom's pelt was matted with blood. Clumps of fur stuck out along his spine.

Haven't you had enough? Ivypool glanced at Hawkfrost. "Are there any Dark Forest warriors close by?" she ventured, praying there weren't.

"Of course." Hawkfrost tasted the air.

The screech of fighting cats echoed through the mist. It had become like birdsong to Ivypool—filling the forest, so familiar that she only heard it when she listened for it. "Why aren't we training with them tonight?" she asked. Most nights, the Dark Forest warriors couldn't wait to share their cruel skills with the Clan cats.

Hawkfrost wove between Blossomfall and Applefur. "I want you to learn how other Clans fight."

Ivypool shivered.

"You may be fighting side by side one day," Hawkfrost went on.

Liar!

"You need to know your allies' moves so you can match them, claw for claw."

No, you're training them to destroy one another in the final battle.

A husky growl echoed from the trees. "Four Clans will unite as one when it matters most." Tigerstar padded from the shadows, his wide tabby head held high. "This is the law of the Dark Forest. Remember it."

Birchfall nodded solemnly. "Four Clans will unite as one when it matters most," he echoed.

"When will that be?" Blossomfall's eyes were round.

"You'll know when the time comes." Mapleshade slunk from the trees. Her tortoiseshell pelt was so transparent now that the white patches showed the forest behind. Ivypool flinched at the reminder that she too would fade from every memory one day.

"Tigerstar?" Blossomfall was staring at the dark warrior. "Are we training for something special?"

Ivypool flinched. "Not yet," she meowed quickly, one eye on Tigerstar. He nodded and she went on. "But you never know." She remembered the vicious battle with WindClan in the tunnels only a quarter moon earlier. "There may be more cats like Sol ready to lead one Clan against another."

Applefur stepped forward. "Next time a rogue tries to drive us apart, I'll stand beside ThunderClan, not against them!"

Ivypool shifted her paws. *These cats believe their loyalty to the Clans is being strengthened.* She glanced at Birchfall. *But who will they be loyal to when the final battle comes? Their Clanmates or the Dark Forest warriors?*

Tigerstar flicked his tail. "Go back to your nests," he ordered the Clan cats.

Hollowflight tipped his head. "But it's early."

"The senior warriors have a meeting." Tigerstar nodded to Mapleshade and Hawkfrost.

"Can I come?" Ivypool asked.

Mapleshade narrowed her eyes. "No."

"I'm a mentor now," Ivypool pressed. She had to find out when the Dark Forest cats were planning to attack the Clans by the lake.

"While you still have the taste of living prey on your tongue, you're not truly one of us," Mapleshade snarled.

Tigerstar nodded. "Go back to your Clan and rest," he ordered. "You'll need your strength tomorrow night." He turned and stalked into the shadows, Mapleshade hurrying after.

Blossomfall shrugged. "I guess we can practice our new moves in the forest as well as here," she told Birchfall. Closing her eyes, she began to fade.

Ivypool watched her Clanmate vanish from the forest. *She'll take her wounds with her. And the memory of what she's learned.* Ivypool's pelt pricked. She didn't want those memories, these vicious skills in ThunderClan!

"Are you coming?" Birchfall flicked his tail.

Ivypool twitched her ears to send him on his way. "I'll be right behind you."

Hollowflight, Applefur, and Redwillow were melting into the shadows as Birchfall disappeared. As soon as they had gone, Ivypool turned to Hawkfrost. "You trust me to train cats for the Dark Forest, but not to attend gatherings of the senior warriors?"

His eyes gleamed. "Do you really want to be there?"

Ivypool nodded.

Hawkfrost leaned closer. "Tough." He turned and padded after Tigerstar.

Ivypool flexed her claws. *I'm coming whether you want me to or not!* As Hawkfrost's pelt shimmered away between the trees, she darted forward and, heart racing, began to shadow him. Keeping just enough mist and bramble between them so that he was little more than a flicker at the edge of her vision, she matched his pawsteps.

"Snowtuft?" Hawkfrost suddenly slowed.

Ivypool halted and pricked her ears.

Hawkfrost greeted his Clanmate with a growl. "Are you heading for the meeting?"

"I wouldn't miss it for all the mice in the forest," Snowtuft rasped. "Where are the Clan cats?"

Hawkfrost snorted. "Tigerstar sent them back to their nests."

Snowtuft's claws scraped the earth. "Are you sure there won't be any hanging around the training rock?"

"Brokenstar will make sure there aren't," Hawkfrost growled.

The training rock! Ivypool flicked her tail. *They're meeting beside the river!* She knew the Dark Forest well enough now to find her way without being spotted by Hawkfrost. She only had to follow the old stream to the hollow trunks, then aim for the riverbank.

Crouching, she slunk behind bushes until she could hear

the deep murmur of the senior warriors. She slid behind a trunk and peered around. The mist cleared where the river cut through the trees. A large boulder stuck out of the mud on the shore. Ivypool flattened her ears. She had shared her first training sessions with her Dark Forest Clanmates here. Now it was circled by heavily muscled warriors. Feeling the stirrings of fear in her belly, she pushed them away. *I am a warrior of the Dark Forest,* she reminded herself. *I am the equal of any of these cats!*

Brokenstar stood on the stone, his thick, dark pelt spiked with excitement. "The time is close," he growled.

Mapleshade lifted her fading white muzzle. "Good," she hissed. "I'd hate to miss it."

Hawkfrost sat and watched through narrowed eyes. Blue as ice, they followed Brokenstar's every move. Shredtail and Thistleclaw paced while Tigerstar stood stiff-legged, his tail lashing. "Where will we strike first?" he demanded.

Brokenstar slid from the boulder and scratched a line in the muddy earth. "This is where the lake meets the land."

Slash.

Slash.

Slash.

With deft claws he sliced more shapes into the ground. "We will come at them from here and here." He stabbed the ground. "And while they are fighting there, another patrol will strike here."

Ivypool stretched forward, desperate to see where he was pointing at, but Tigerstar and Shredtail blocked her view as they crowded close. Her heart pounding in her throat, Ivy-pool listened for clues instead.

"They'll be weaker where the hill slopes down to the brook," Brokenstar growled. "We can come at them from higher ground and drive them backward."

"What if we approach from here instead?" Tigerstar jabbed the map with a claw.

Ivypool jumped as Brokenstar's eyes lit up with interest. "At the very heart of the Clan!"

"Once the kits are dead, their mothers will have less to fight for," Mapleshade pointed out.

"You're right." Brokenstar sat back on his haunches. "It's decided, then."

Hawkfrost looked over his shoulder, his gaze grazing the tree where Ivypool was hiding. She flattened herself to the ground, relief swamping her as Hawkfrost's gaze swept past, missing her, and the Dark Forest warriors began to pad away from the river. As soon as the shore was deserted, she slid out from her hiding place and crept toward Brokenstar's map. Tense as a rabbit, she glimpsed lines scored in the mud.

Suddenly, paws shook her violently. She jerked around, hissing, and lashed out at her attacker.

"Ivypool!"

Dovewing's shocked mew brought her to her senses. Ivypool was in her nest. "You woke me up!" she snarled at her sister.

Dovewing stared at her, terror glittering in her eyes. "Ivy-pool? Are you okay?"

"I was dreaming!" Frustration tightened Ivypool's throat.

She was about to see Brokenstar's plans!

"You're awake now, though?" Dovewing asked uncertainly.

"Yes," Ivypool muttered. "I'm awake."

Dovewing met her gaze. "You never would have tried to shred me for waking you up before."

"You know what happens when I dream."

"That's why I woke you. Your fur was on end. I was scared something was . . ." Dovewing suddenly narrowed her eyes. "Did you want to *stay* in the Dark Forest?"

Ivypool lifted her chin. Here, in the safety of her nest, the terror that had sharpened her dreams ebbed away. But the sense of danger still thrilled beneath her pelt. "I was doing something important!"

Dovewing leaned closer. "What?"

Ivypool turned away. "It's too late now." Brokenstar's plans would be scuffed or washed away by tonight.

Dovewing suddenly wrinkled her nose. "You smell foul."

Ivypool glanced down at her muddy paws and tucked them tighter beneath her. "Don't worry. I'll wash."

"Good." Dovewing squeezed past her and headed out of the den.

Ivypool glanced at Molepaw's empty nest and Cherrypaw's beside it. They'd already left for apprentice duties. Flexing her claws, she shouldered her way out of the den.

"Ivypool!" Bumblestripe called from the fresh-kill pile. The well-muscled gray tom had a fat blackbird at his paws.

Ivypool ignored him and ducked through the thorn tunnel, into the forest. How could she stay in camp, confined by the hollow, trapped with her Clanmates while her head still spun with the scents and sounds of the Dark Forest?

She bounded up the slope toward the ridge. Strength surged through her body. The Dark Forest had given her that power. It had trained her to be a more skillful warrior than her Clanmates, given her tactics that she would use against the Dark Forest cats when the final battle came. Ivypool's claws sliced through brambles as she crested the slope and burst from the tree line. Below, the lake glittered beneath a pale dawn sky. Leaf-fall was beginning to tinge the treetops. The green haze that had enfolded the forests for moons was darkening to amber. Excitement surged beneath Ivypool's pelt. There was no prey she couldn't catch; no warrior she couldn't defeat. Her paws itched to prove it.

Out of nowhere, a vision filled her eyes. Warriors swarmed from the shores and spilled into the forest. Torn-eared and scarred, their eyes gleamed with hate. Ferns trembled, brambles shivered as the woods seemed to heave, suddenly alive with battle-hungry cats. Shrieks echoed and Ivypool heard the thud of muscle against rock as the world shook in the claws of the Dark Forest warriors.

As the vision faded she could still taste the tang of blood and fear. Ivypool realized that she was shaking, and her pads were sweating. All the battle skills in the Place of No Stars would not be enough to stop that unrelenting tide of death.

CHAPTER 2

Evening was creeping into the hollow and dew dampened his fur as Jayfeather took a mouse from the fresh-kill pile and settled beside the bramble to eat.

The half-moon would be hanging in a clear, pale sky. Would the other medicine cats obey the dire warnings from their ancestors and stay away from the other Clans? Or would they travel to the Moonpool to share their dreams with StarClan?

Should I go?

He felt the moon's tug deep beneath his fur. Ignoring it made his heart ache. But since Dawnpelt had stood at the Gathering and accused him of murdering Flametail, the Clans had ordered Jayfeather to give up his medicine-cat duties. Firestar had given him permission to continue helping his Clanmates as usual, but he had been forced to surrender all his responsibilities outside the Clan.

The moon tugged harder. The will of StarClan was stronger than any living cat. And according to the prophecy, Jayfeather was stronger than StarClan. Besides, he knew he was innocent. He'd tried to save Flametail when he fell through the ice. No other cat had tried to drag the ShadowClan medicine cat from the freezing depths of the lake. Angrily Jayfeather ripped a bite from his mouse.

The trailing brambles swished beside him as Briarlight hauled herself out of the medicine den. Her forepaws were so strong now, she could easily pull her crippled hind legs around the camp.

"Do you want some of this?" Jayfeather held up his mouse with a claw.

"No thanks." Briarlight paused beside him. "I'm in the mood for vole."

He felt the sleekness of her fur brush past him as she pulled herself toward the fresh-kill pile. She was the cleanest cat in ThunderClan, washing herself tirelessly, checking for ticks twice a day, and rooting out every flea. An infected bite would weaken her and she was determined to keep exercising until she was the strongest she could be, even without the use of her hind legs.

Jayfeather sensed her fizzing excitement as she rooted through the fresh-kill pile, and her tiny jab of pleasure as she grabbed a vole from the bottom and dragged it out with sharp teeth. Nimbly she crossed the grass and settled beside Jayfeather. "Aren't you hungry?" She poked his barely-touched mouse with her paw. "It's half-moon. You'll need your strength to travel to the Moonpool."

Jayfeather growled softly. "I've been banned, remember?"

Briarlight scooped up her vole and took a bite. "Since when would that stop you?" she asked with her mouth full.

Brightheart's paws scuffed the ground beside them. "Stop what?"

Jayfeather snorted. "None of your business."

"It's half-moon but Jayfeather isn't allowed to go to the Moonpool," Briarlight chipped in.

"Can't you share dreams with StarClan in your nest?" Brightheart stroked her tail along Jayfeather's spine.

He shook her off. "There's more to visiting the Moonpool than sharing dreams!"

Jayfeather marched across the clearing. He ducked through the camp entrance, hissing as a thorn snagged his ear tip, and stomped into the woods.

Paws padded swiftly after him. Jayfeather tasted Firestar's scent. The ThunderClan leader had followed him out of the hollow. "I know it's frustrating," Firestar began sympathetically.

Jayfeather turned on him. "Really? Do you think the Clans would believe Dawnpelt if I wasn't half-Clan?"

Firestar stopped.

"Or if Leafpool hadn't broken the medicine-cat code in kitting me?" He felt Firestar's surprise. "Had you forgotten?" Jayfeather demanded.

"I don't think about it." There was honesty in Firestar's mew.

Jayfeather blinked. "You don't think about it?" he echoed. Every time he saw Leafpool or Squirrelflight or Brambleclaw, Jayfeather felt the prick of betrayal. He'd believed he was pure ThunderClan, that his parents were Squirrelflight and Brambleclaw, until Hollyleaf had discovered that Leaf-pool was their mother and Crowfeather, a WindClan warrior, their father.

Firestar's tail whisked over the fallen leaves. "You're one of the Three. Your birth was meant to happen." He padded closer. "Does it matter how you came to be born?"

"Yes!" Lit by rage, Jayfeather paced around Firestar. "I'm cursed by Leafpool's mistake! Every cat thinks I'm unnatural because my birth broke two codes—the warrior code and the medicine-cat code! No wonder they're so eager to think I'm a murderer. They certainly can't think I'm blessed by StarClan."

Firestar shifted his paws. "But we both know you *are* blessed by StarClan. More than any other cat."

"No thanks to Leafpool!" Jayfeather clawed the ground. "Or Squirrelflight."

"Leafpool kept your secret," Firestar reminded him sternly. "She and Squirrelflight did the best they could for you and your littermates. It was Hollyleaf who told the truth. She believed she had to, and now what's done is done. Squirrelflight and your mother are not responsible for the prejudices of the other Clans. And neither are you."

"It's not fair. Why couldn't Leafpool have just followed the medicine-cat code?" Jayfeather pushed his way deeper into the trees. "It's not exactly complicated!"

"And if she had?" Firestar called after him. "What then? If she'd never fallen in love with Crowfeather, where would you be? Think of the prophecy!"

Jayfeather raked the leaf mulch with his claws. "Why can't

I think about *me* for once?" With a growl he stalked away, ducking through ferns and pacing over tree roots until he sensed dusk turn to dark around him. Suddenly he felt a wall of fur blocking his path. He leaped back. "Who is it?"

As he spoke, he recognized the foul stench of Yellowfang's breath. Her muzzle was less than a mouse-length from his nose. *"Why can't I think about me for once?"* she mimicked.

"Leave me alone!" Jayfeather backed away but her stinking muzzle followed him.

"*You're* not important!" the old cat hissed. "Only the survival of the Clan matters! You're one of the Three and you have to find the fourth to defeat the Dark Forest before it's too late!"

"What do you mean, I'm not important?" Jayfeather spat back. *How dare she?* "How do you know that I'm not the *most* important one?" His anger was pulsing so hard that the words flooded out of him. "If the Clans stop me from being a medicine cat, the whole prophecy might be wasted."

Yellowfang wreathed around him, her matted fur brushing roughly against his. "Do you think *herbs* are going to save the Clans from the Dark Forest?" she snapped.

"There's more to being a medicine cat than herbs!" Jayfeather tried to push past her but she blocked his way.

"Like what?"

"Like sharing dreams with StarClan!"

Yellowfang's tail swished the ferns. "What do you think you're doing now, mouse-brain?"

Jayfeather growled. "Why are you bugging me?"

"You need to find the fourth warrior!"

"We don't know it's a warrior!" Jayfeather snapped. "We don't know which Clan this cat is in. We don't even know it is a cat!"

"Stop making excuses! You haven't even told the others there *is* a fourth cat, have you?"

Jayfeather's ears twitched guiltily. Memory swept his mind clear and suddenly he was back on a dark, windswept mountaintop. The Tribe of Endless Hunting surrounded him, their eyes glowing with hope. Stonetellers from ages past whispered the words that still echoed in his thoughts.

The end of the stars draws near. Three must become four to challenge the darkness that lasts forever.

"You haven't told them," Yellowfang repeated.

"No." Jayfeather sat down. "I've been waiting for the right time."

"Really?" Yellowfang sounded unconvinced. "I think the truth is that you don't want there to be a fourth cat. You can't bear the thought that you need help."

"That's not true!" Jayfeather's pelt burned. *How did she guess?*

"Then why keep the Tribe's prophecy a secret when you know time is running out?"

Jayfeather closed his eyes, suddenly weary. "Aren't our powers enough to save the Clans?"

Yellowfang's pelt brushed his. "You're facing the Dark Forest! You need all the help you can get! Find the fourth cat!"

"Okay!" Jayfeather snapped. "But where do I look?"

"If I knew, I'd tell you." Yellowfang pushed away through the ferns.

"Wait!" Jayfeather dashed after her. A bramble tripped him and he stumbled. "I need you to do something for me."

"Haven't I done enough?" Yellowfang kept walking.

"I need you to find Flametail and tell him to visit Littlecloud." Jayfeather bounded after her. "Flametail's got to explain that I tried to save him from drowning, not murder him."

Yellowfang shook her head. "Sorry, Jayfeather. StarClan is divided. I can't cross Clan lines."

"But you used to be ShadowClan," Jayfeather reminded her.

She turned on him, and he felt her eyes blazing. "I am *ThunderClan!*" she hissed.

"But—" Jayfeather was pleading to empty air. Yellowfang had gone.

"Mouse dung!" Furious, Jayfeather broke into a run. Letting memory of his territory guide him, he raced up the slope till he broke free of the trees and felt the fresh, cold wind from the lake streaming over his pelt. He twitched his whiskers as he smelled another scent. "Leafpool?"

She padded out of the forest and stopped beside him. "Are you okay?"

Jayfeather tensed, ready to argue, but no words came. He felt hollow.

"Firestar seemed flustered when he came back to camp," Leafpool meowed softly. "I was worried about you."

Stop acting like my mother! It's too late for that!

Leafpool moved closer without touching him. "I know how

it feels, to lose your place as medicine cat."

"Firestar says I can keep treating my Clanmates," Jay-feather reminded her.

"Brightheart could treat the Clan," Leafpool pointed out. "But that doesn't make her a medicine cat." Anger suddenly sparked from her pelt. "You need to be able to visit StarClan and share with the other medicine cats and our ancestors."

Jayfeather jerked away from her, unnerved that she under-stood so clearly. "I don't care," he insisted. He wasn't going to be tricked into feeling close to her.

"Go to the Moonpool." Leafpool ignored his protest. "Share your dreams with StarClan. Find Flametail and make him tell the truth to his Clanmates."

Jayfeather flattened his ears. "How can I go? I'm not allowed to be a medicine cat outside ThunderClan!"

"No one can stop you from visiting the Moonpool," Leaf-pool argued. "Do you think any cat would risk displeasing StarClan by standing in your way? Go to them and *make* Flametail tell the truth!"

CHAPTER 3
❧

Jayfeather closed his eyes, listening to the leaves crunch as Leafpool padded away. He could sense starlight dancing on his pelt. Far below, tiny waves splashed at the shore. Though he hated to admit it, Leafpool was right.

When he reached the Moonpool, Jayfeather called out hopefully. "Is anyone there?"

His mew echoed back, unanswered. He was alone.

Pushing away disappointment, he followed the dimpled path that spiraled down into the heart of the hollow. The wind whined overhead, worrying at the encircling rock like an abandoned kit searching for its mother. Jayfeather longed to feel the pelts of long-dead cats that used to jostle and hurry him down to the water's edge. But there was no sign of the Ancients who had dented the stone with their pawsteps over so many generations. Jayfeather stopped alone at the water's edge, hollow with a loneliness he'd never felt before. Closing his eyes, he crouched beside the Moonpool and touched his nose to the water.

"Jayfeather."

Jayfeather sat up. He had expected to wake in the warm

meadows of StarClan. But he was still in the hollow.

"Jayfeather." A she-cat sat beside him.

He'd awoken into a vision; he could see her white pelt, spotted black along her flanks. Her pink nose stretched toward him, twitching as she sniffed.

Jayfeather blinked at her. "Who are you?"

"Brambleberry of RiverClan."

Brambleberry? Jayfeather suddenly recognized the pelt he'd seen often in StarClan's hunting grounds. This was the gentle RiverClan medicine cat who tended to her Clan in the days before Leopardstar and Mistystar.

"Did Willowshine send you?" Jayfeather felt a flash of hope. Perhaps the RiverClan medicine cat was trying to communicate with him despite the rift between Clans.

Brambleberry shook her head. "I came to appeal to your wisdom, not hers."

"But you're RiverClan."

"So?" Starlight twinkled in Brambleberry's round blue eyes. "The Clans are like honeysuckle. One tendril chokes the other to reach for the light, believing they grow from separate stems."

Jayfeather pricked his ears as she went on.

"When the sun shines, young leaves fight for its warmth. The struggle makes the bush strong, each branch seeking out the light and climbing ever higher." Brambleberry's eyes darkened. "But when there is no sun, when the leaves begin to fall and the branches wither one by one, the stem must look to its roots for nourishment."

"So instead of four branches, there is one root," Jayfeather murmured. "But how? The Clans have been divided since the beginning of time."

"You have created your own boundaries, setting them and patrolling them." Brambleberry tipped her head to one side. "But they exist only in your minds. Why else would you have to mark them each day with fresh scent?"

Was she saying they should live as one Clan? Jayfeather frowned. "But we need boundaries," he argued. "To grow strong. You said so."

"Perhaps," Brambleberry conceded. "When the sun shines." She leaned closer. "But a great darkness is coming."

Jayfeather shifted his paws. "But I don't want to become mixed up with ShadowClan, or WindClan, or RiverClan."

Brambleberry gazed at him softly. "You're already half-Clan."

Jayfeather's fur spiked. "I'm ThunderClan from nose to tail. And my heart is loyal only to them."

"It was you who fixed your heart on ThunderClan," Brambleberry insisted. "But you're half-WindClan, just as Graystripe and Silverstream's kits were half-RiverClan. And Stormfur's heart beats for the Tribe now. Who knows where Feathertail's loyalties would lie if she'd lived?" The old medicine cat dipped her head. "Loyalty makes Clan cats strong. But no Clan has pure blood running beneath every pelt."

"Why are you telling me this?" Jayfeather's tail twitched. "Being half-Clan isn't a sign of strength. It's what happens when cats are disloyal." He unsheathed his claws. "It's what happens when they betray the warrior code!"

Brambleberry's gaze hardened. "Are you listening to me?" she growled. "Or are you too busy worrying about whether your blood smells of forest or moorland?" She snorted. "The Clans must unite! Don't look for boundaries that aren't there. Look for the ones that are."

Wind spiraled down into the hollow and set the Moonpool rippling. Jayfeather turned and saw its surface color and change until it reflected a landscape. A circle of water shone at its center, surrounded by hills and trees.

"It's the lake!" he gasped. "And there's ThunderClan territory!" He gazed at the bright green forest. This must be how an eagle would see the Clans' territories. Jayfeather squinted, trying to make out more detail.

"Are you looking for the scent lines?" Brambleberry flicked her tail. "Can you see them?"

"It's too far away." Jayfeather could only see one landscape blending into another, the gentle slope of valleys and glittering trails cut by rivers and streams.

"This is how StarClan sees your home," Brambleberry explained. "We see the beauty of it and the richness. We don't see which tree belongs to which Clan. Don't look for boundaries that aren't there . . ."

". . . look for the boundaries that *are*." Jayfeather echoed her words, searching the landscape again. "But where are they?"

Brambleberry touched his cheek with her tail-tip, guiding his gaze back to her. "The only true borders lie between day and night, between life and death, between hope and loss."

Jayfeather stared at the medicine cat. "So why is StarClan telling us to stay inside our territories, to listen only to our Clanmates?" he asked.

Brambleberry shifted her paws. "We can't see your lands anymore," she confessed. Her gaze flashed toward the pool. "It's all dark to us now and we are frightened."

Jayfeather whisked his tail. "What can I do?"

"Make them see!"

"The Clans?"

"StarClan!"

"Why can't you do it?"

"I wasn't born with the power of the stars in my paws!" Brambleberry turned and began to follow the curving path out of the hollow. "Make them understand that the Clans must fight together or die divided."

"Wait!" Jayfeather dashed after her. "How can I convince them?"

Brambleberry glanced back. "You already know the answer." Her voice echoed as she reached the edge of the hollow. "Three must become four to save all the Clans."

Jayfeather stared as her white pelt vanished into the darkness. He glanced back at the Moonpool. It reflected only the starlit sky. Blinking, he tried to wake from his vision, and the hollow disappeared. Relieved, Jayfeather welcomed back his blindness.

Then something flashed at the edge of his vision.

I'm not blind! I'm still dreaming!

Shapes moved around him. Trees towered on every side.

Darkness clung to everything.

"You won't see us coming," a voice whispered in his ear.

Jayfeather jerked away. A pelt brushed against him from the other side. Terrified, he turned, trying to see who was there. But the shapes kept moving, too dark to make out.

A growl sounded behind him. "Your death will come slowly and painfully."

Jayfeather spun around, straining his eyes into the trees.

"There is nothing you can do to prevent it."

I know that voice! He tasted the air, the scent curling his tongue. He'd met this cat before, in the Dark Forest with Yellowfang. "Brokenstar?"

A shadow froze in front of him. Amber eyes gleamed from the darkness. Jayfeather jumped backward.

"Scared yet?" Brokenstar taunted.

Jayfeather lifted his chin. "We're ready for you!"

"Really?" The eyes blinked. "I think some of your Clanmates are more ready than you know."

"What do you mean?" Jayfeather stiffened against the shiver that clawed his spine.

"Listen."

Jayfeather pricked his ears.

"Line up!" Somewhere in the trees, a tom was hissing orders. "Unsheathe your claws and prepare to attack!"

"They're training," Brokenstar explained.

"Which attack move do we use?"

Jayfeather's fur bushed up as he recognized Blossomfall's mew.

"The throat grip might work." That was Birchfall!

"Not straight for the throat!" Breezepelt of WindClan snarled. "Death shouldn't come too quickly. We must terrify our enemies before we kill them."

"If we shred the cats in front it'll unnerve those behind," Tigerheart added.

"First scare them, then *scar* them."

"Nice one, Icewing." Beetlewhisker congratulated his Clanmate.

This was worse than Jayfeather had imagined. *We've lost so many to the darkness!* Jayfeather thought in horror. The Clans *must* fight as one, more fiercely than ever before, if they were going to defeat the Dark Forest army.

Pelts brushed bushes, fur snagging on thorns. Paws thrummed the ground. *They're coming!* Jayfeather unsheathed his claws as he heard cats approaching swiftly through the trees. Hawkfrost broke from the shadows first. Behind him raced ranks of warriors, lean and low to the ground. Jayfeather scanned their faces. He recognized no one. He saw only eyes glittering with cruelty. These were different cats, Dark Forest warriors. They streamed toward him, teeth bared.

Jayfeather tried to run but his paws were frozen. As the first wave flooded around him, buffeting him, growls rumbling from every throat, Jayfeather blinked open his eyes.

He was blind again. The Moonpool lapped at his nose. With relief he felt smooth rock beneath his paws. His pelt was drenched with stinking dew, his breath fast as he struggled to his feet.

A voice startled him. "Jayfeather?"

"Mothwing?" Still struggling to push away his vision, Jayfeather tasted the air. The cold stone tang of the hollow was warmed by the scent of the RiverClan medicine cat.

"Are you all right?" Her whiskers brushed his cheeks as she leaned close.

"I'm fine." Jayfeather shook his pelt and frowned. Why was Mothwing here? Although she was skilled with herbs and could treat any sickness, she had no connection with StarClan. She'd stopped coming to the half-moon Gatherings ages ago, letting her apprentice, Willowshine, share tongues with RiverClan's ancestors instead.

"Are you the only one who came?" she meowed.

Jayfeather sat down. "Yes."

"Willowshine refused." Mothwing padded to the edge of the pool and Jayfeather heard her sniffing the water. "What is going on with StarClan? Willowshine told me they'd ordered her to stay away from the other medicine cats." Her paws scuffed the stone as she turned to face Jayfeather. "It doesn't make sense. Our shared code helps the Clans fight sickness. In the past it's helped keep the peace."

Jayfeather fixed his blind gaze on her. "Our code is no longer enough. StarClan is frightened."

Surprise pulsed from Mothwing. "Of what?"

"The Dark Forest." Jayfeather wondered whether to share what he knew. If Mothwing didn't believe her ancestors lived on in the stars, she certainly wouldn't believe in a forest filled with wicked cats. And yet, perhaps her lack of belief might be helpful. She couldn't be touched by either StarClan or the Dark Forest warriors.

What if she's the fourth cat!

Mothwing padded around him. "Willowshine says there will be a battle between StarClan and the Dark Forest."

"She's right," Jayfeather meowed. "But when it comes, it won't be just in our dreams; it'll be *real*. It'll be fought between living warriors on Clan territory."

Mothwing halted. "How can that be?"

"The Dark Forest warriors have been training Clan cats as they sleep." Jayfeather waited for disbelief to cloud Mothwing's thoughts but, though fear sparked beneath her pelt, her mind was like a wide-open sky.

"Some of my Clanmates have been acting strange," she murmured. "Restless and argumentative."

Jayfeather pricked his ears. "Who?"

"Hollowflight, Icewing—"

"What about Beetlewhisker?"

Mothwing shifted her paws. "How did you know?"

Jayfeather ignored her question. There wasn't time. "We need to unite the Clans." He began to pace. "The battle won't be fought over boundaries this time. Our very survival will be at stake."

Mothwing's breath quickened. "What can I do to help?"

Her offer sent a rush of hope through Jayfeather, but he knew he had to be honest. "Hawkfrost is involved."

"My brother?" Mothwing's tail swished over the rock. "How?"

"He has chosen darkness over light."

Grief flared from Mothwing but she pushed it away. "I am not my brother," she declared. "I have always chosen a different path from him. My loyalty is to living Clanmates, not dead littermates."

"So you'd fight him if you had to?"

"Fight him? He's already dead!"

"But the living and dead are training together to destroy the Clans!" Jayfeather pictured his Clanmates training in the Dark Forest. *They can't know what they're doing, surely? No cat could persuade Birchfall or Blossomfall to harm their Clanmates!* "They are using our own Clanmates against us."

Mothwing's paws scuffed on the stone. "How will we know who to trust?"

Jayfeather let out a slow breath. "We won't until the battle begins. But if we can stop StarClan from driving the Clans apart, we stand a chance of winning."

"I can't help you change what dead cats do," Mothwing meowed. "But I might be able to help guide the living ones. I'll try to persuade Willowshine to visit the Moonpool again."

"Will she listen to you over StarClan?"

Mothwing paused. "I don't know. But I have to try." Jayfeather felt the RiverClan cat's determination tingling beneath her pelt. "And if I think of a way to make the other medicine cats listen, I'll come and find you." Her breath touched his muzzle as she leaned closer. "You're not alone anymore, Jayfeather." She turned and padded up the spiraling path out the hollow. "Are you coming?"

Jayfeather followed. Mothwing was the last cat he imagined would help him fight the Dark Forest. But perhaps she was the only cat who could.

CHAPTER 4

Bright sunshine lit the hollow. The Clan was resting after its morning patrols.

As Lionblaze took a halfhearted bite from the mouse lying at his paws, Millie settled beside the warriors' den.

"Bring me a shrew!" she called to Graystripe.

"There's plenty." Rosepetal was sharing a blackbird with Blossomfall. "We found a whole nestful."

Graystripe padded toward the fresh-kill pile. It was well stocked. Hunting patrols had been stepped up to fatten the Clan before leaf-bare. Firestar wanted to make sure they faced the coming moons as fit and strong as any Clan.

"Can I join you?" Hollyleaf crossed the clearing and dropped a thrush beside Lionblaze.

Lionblaze rolled his mouse underneath his paw. "If you want."

His sister settled beside him, nestling into the shade of the fallen beech. "Jayfeather's not back," she observed before taking a bite from her thrush.

"I know." Lionblaze plucked distractedly at the mouse.

"Why did he go to the Moonpool?" Hollyleaf's mew was

muffled by feathers. "Firestar told him to confine his medi-cine-cat duties to camp."

"I guess he had his reasons." Lionblaze twitched his ears uneasily. Jayfeather had been reckless to travel alone. What if a WindClan patrol found him? Would they show mercy to a cat they believed was a murderer?

Cinderheart padded over to them. Lionblaze focused on his mouse while she greeted his sister. "It's been a good morn-ing for hunting."

Hollyleaf brushed a feather from her muzzle. "I've never seen so much prey."

Lionblaze lifted his head to glance quickly at Cinderheart. Her soft gray pelt shone and her long tail was sleek and well groomed. His heart ached. Why was she hanging around here? Shouldn't she be in the medicine den? She wasn't really Cinderheart, the cat he'd fallen in love with; she was Cinder-pelt—an old medicine cat brought back by StarClan to fill some stupid destiny.

"Shut your mouth before your prey falls out," Hollyleaf whispered in his ear.

Lionblaze flinched, suddenly aware that he'd been staring. He looked away, heat flooding his fur. "What do you want?" he asked Cinderheart sharply.

"Brambleclaw wants us to take a hunting patrol to the lake."

"Don't you have medicine-cat duties?" He'd seen her duck-ing in and out of Jayfeather's den ever since her old knowledge of herbs and cures had flooded back.

"Why should I?" Cinderheart's pelt spiked along her back.

"Jayfeather's at the Moonpool."

"He'll be home soon."

"I hope so."

"Hollyleaf!" Brambleclaw called from beneath Highledge. "Take a patrol to the Twoleg meadow," the deputy ordered. "I heard a dog there last night and I want to know if it's tethered."

Hollyleaf glanced ruefully at her half-eaten thrush, then headed across the clearing. Lionblaze watched her go, acutely aware of Cinderheart lingering at his side. "Don't you want to go with her?" he suggested.

"We're leading a patrol, remember?" She sat down beside him. "Who should we take?"

Lionblaze scanned the clearing, relieved to see Cloudtail trotting toward them. "Hi, Cloudtail." He stood up. "Do you want to come hunting?"

"No, he doesn't!" Brightheart trotted after Cloudtail. "We've been hunting all morning and he promised to fetch me something from the fresh-kill pile." She nudged her mate. "Do you want me to go to the fresh-kill pile while you stay and gossip?" Her eyes flashed.

Cloudtail swished his thick white tail, purring. "I'm going!"

Lionblaze envied their easy familiarity. Once, he'd thought he and Cinderheart might be like that. But the return of her memories had changed everything. Now he felt as if he'd never known her at all.

Brightheart nodded to Cinderheart. "Have you checked on Briarlight this morning?"

"Was I supposed to?" Cinderheart looked up anxiously.

"No." Brightheart shrugged. "I just thought, with Jay-feather away—" Her gaze flashed toward the medicine den as the brambles trembled at the entrance. "She's coming out!" She hurried away to meet Briarlight as the crippled warrior dragged herself toward the fresh-kill pile.

"Wait for me!" Cloudtail trotted after her.

"That could have been us," Lionblaze muttered to Cinderheart. "We could have been happy together."

"I don't think happiness is part of our *destinies*," Cinderheart spat. Then her expression changed and she looked sadly at Lionblaze. "Let's not torture ourselves by wishing." She stood and stretched, arching her back. "Who do you want to hunt with?"

Lionblaze scanned the camp. Blossomfall had finished eating and was play fighting with Thornclaw beside the nursery. She spun around, steadying herself with her tail and dodging a well-aimed swipe. There was something relaxed and comfortable in the way they matched each other's moves. "What about them? Thornclaw!"

The golden tabby looked over his shoulder. "What is it?"

"We're hunting by the lake and we need extra paws."

Thornclaw lifted his tail happily. "Can Blossomfall come, too?"

When Lionblaze nodded, the two cats ran toward the thorn barrier. Cinderheart bounded after them. Lionblaze shoved his half-eaten mouse beside Hollyleaf's thrush and followed his Clanmates out of camp.

By the time he caught up, Thornclaw and Blossomfall were

already climbing the slope, zigzagging through the brambles as though they were playing catch-the-squirrel with each other's tails. Another season or two and Blossomfall would be nursing Thornclaw's kits. His tail drooped.

"Ow!" Blossomfall let out a squeal.

Lionblaze broke into a run, skidding to a halt beside the tortoiseshell warrior. "What happened?"

Blossomfall writhed on the ground, her foreleg tangled in a bramble and her face twisted with pain. Thornclaw crouched beside her, holding the bramble between his jaws as he gingerly unwrapped it from around her paw. "Hold still," he whispered. "Tugging will make last night's battle wound worse."

"Shhh!" Blossomfall hushed Thornclaw, her gaze glittering with guilt as it caught Lionblaze's.

Lionblaze froze. These cats weren't mates! They'd been training together in their dreams. Lionblaze felt the trees close around him. He struggled to take a deep breath. *They don't know what they're doing.*

Trembling, he watched Thornclaw pull the bramble away and help Blossomfall to her paws. If he couldn't trust his Clanmates, who *could* he trust? He glanced over his shoulder at Cinderheart as she hurried to check on her Clanmate. Was she training in the Dark Forest, too? Lionblaze's thoughts darted from one Clanmate to another. The familiar faces seemed suddenly strange and cold.

"Check her," he ordered Cinderheart, but Cinderheart was already sniffing Blossomfall's shoulder, then pressing gently with her paws.

"Does that hurt?"

Blossomfall let out a groan but shook her head. "Just a little."

"Can you put weight on it?" Cinderheart asked.

Blossomfall tested it, her face tensing, then relaxing as her pad pressed against the earth. "Yes," she breathed. "It's sore, but I can walk."

Cinderheart turned to Lionblaze. "There's no heat in her shoulder," she told him. "It's just a light sprain. She'll need to go easy—"

Lionblaze interrupted her. "Are you sure?"

Cinderheart's eyes flashed. "Of course I'm sure!"

Lionblaze narrowed his eyes. Did she resent having her skills questioned? Or did she object to being asked to act like a medicine cat? Before he could decide, Cinderheart started nudging Blossomfall up the slope.

Thornclaw followed anxiously. "Are you sure you're okay?"

"It'll be fine by the time we reach the lake," Blossomfall promised.

Cinderheart glanced over her shoulder, catching Lionblaze's eye. "Our apprentices have suffered worse injuries," she told him. "So long as she doesn't run or jump for a couple of days, she'll be fine."

"Should she go back to camp?" Lionblaze asked.

"No, I'll stay with you. Even if I can't chase prey I can help carry home the catch," Blossomfall called. She began to walk a little faster, as if to prove she was okay. With a sigh, Lionblaze trudged after them.

* * *

In the end, there was little fresh-kill to carry home. Thornclaw hunted clumsily, making so much noise that birds set up alarm calls all along the shoreline the first time he stumbled on the slippery pebbles. Lionblaze was distracted, tracking his Clanmates closely, listening for clues about their Dark Forest training. Cinderheart's thoughts seemed elsewhere and she let a mouse escape beneath her muzzle.

Lionblaze led them back into camp, a sparrow between his jaws. Firestar was dozing on Highledge beside Squirrelflight. Graystripe and Millie lay outside the nursery while Daisy and Ferncloud spread pawfuls of moss to dry in the sun.

At the entrance to the elders' den, Mousefur sat staring into space with Purdy beside her. The old tom's rumbling mew droned like distant honeybees.

Lionblaze headed for the fresh-kill pile with Cinderheart on his heels. Blossomfall limped after them, holding a shrew.

"Is that all you caught?" Bumblestripe bounced up to her. "It's not leaf-bare yet!"

Cinderheart nosed him away. "She hurt her leg." She sniffed at Blossomfall's sprained shoulder. "How is it feeling?"

Blossomfall jerked away. "I told you! I'm fine!"

Lionblaze saw hurt flash in Cinderheart's eyes. He dropped his sparrow. "Get some poppy seeds from Jayfeather if you think the pain will keep you awake tonight." He glanced at Bumblestripe. "Is Jayfeather back?"

Bumblestripe nodded. "He got back just after you left."

"Was he okay?"

Bumblestripe shrugged. "He snapped at Hazeltail for

getting in the way, hissed at Cherrypaw for trampling on Ferncloud's moss, and ordered Foxleap and Toadstep to fetch comfrey." He glanced warily over his shoulder. "So I guess he's fine."

The thorn barrier rustled. Lionblaze turned to see Hollyleaf wriggle out. Rosepetal, Berrynose, and Whitewing trotted after her. Berrynose, his head high, eyes shining, was carrying a plump pigeon.

On the Highledge, Firestar got to his paws. "Borders clear?"

"Yes." Hollyleaf halted beside the rock tumble. "And we remarked the scent line along the ShadowClan border. It was a bit stale."

"Good." Firestar bounded down into the clearing. "And you checked the tunnel entrances?"

Hollyleaf nodded. "No sign of invasion."

Graystripe padded across the clearing. "WindClan wouldn't dare come back after the shredding we gave them last time." His eyes lit up when he spotted Berrynose's pigeon. "Nice catch."

Firestar's whiskers twitched. "I think you'd better lead the next patrol." He looked pointedly at his old friend's round belly. "You could do with stretching your legs."

Graystripe widened his eyes in mock indignation. "It's all fur, you know." He sat back on his haunches, revealing a wide expanse of soft gray fluff.

Hollyleaf purred. "You look like the pigeon!"

Whitewing padded around Graystripe, studying him. "You'll certainly make it through leaf-bare."

Graystripe stood up and shook out his pelt. "A good warrior needs to stay strong."

Lionblaze stiffened, pelt pricking. *A good warrior needs to stay strong.* Was Graystripe training in the Dark Forest, too?

"Are you okay?" Hollyleaf murmured in his ear.

"Fine."

"Come on." Hollyleaf nudged him toward the entrance. "Let's go for a walk."

Outside camp, the early leaf-fall sun pierced the leaves with brittle shards of light. They dappled Hollyleaf's black pelt. Lionblaze followed her along the trail to the Ancient Oak.

"What's up?" Hollyleaf kept her eyes fixed on the trail.

"Nothing."

Hollyleaf flicked her tail. "You hardly spoke this morning."

"I've got a lot on my mind." Had she forgotten he was supposed to be stopping the Dark Forest single-pawed?

"I saw how you were looking at Cinderheart."

A mossy log blocked the trail here. Sunshine rippled over its crumbling bark. "So?" Lionblaze meowed.

"It bothers you, doesn't it?" Hollyleaf guessed.

Lionblaze stopped. "What does?"

"Cinderheart being Cinderpelt." Hollyleaf flicked her tail. "It worries me, too." She shifted her paws. "She was my best friend before I—" Her voice dipped for a moment. "Before I left. But now I don't know who I've come back to. Is she Cinderheart or Cinderpelt? Was she ever Cinderheart?"

Lionblaze wanted to reassure his sister, but he couldn't. "I don't know," he admitted. He sat down. "Is there a difference?

I mean, if she was born with Cinderpelt's spirit, then she's been Cinderpelt all along . . . ."

"Is it that simple?" Hollyleaf frowned. "Cinderpelt was a medicine cat. Cinderheart is a warrior. How can she be both?"

Lionblaze shook his head. "I don't think she knows."

Hollyleaf tilted her head to one side, thinking. "StarClan gave her a second chance," she meowed. "We should trust them and just deal with Cinderheart as she is now. Whether she's a medicine cat or a warrior, she's still our friend, right?"

"Yeah." *But if she's a medicine cat, she'll never take a mate.*

"Come on!" Hollyleaf nudged him. "You're getting too serious." She leaped onto the log. "Let's race to the oak!"

Lionblaze blinked at her. "I remember when you were too small to get over that. Squirrelflight had to nose you over."

Hollyleaf scampered along the trunk. "And you used to graze your belly on it when we were apprentices." She disappeared over the other side, her paws thrumming away along the trail beyond.

Lionblaze bounded after her, clearing the log without touching it. He spotted Hollyleaf's black pelt streaking between the trees and chased after the flickering shadow. He caught up and fell in beside her. They raced side by side, leaping over roots and swerving bushes, their pelts brushing.

As the Ancient Oak loomed ahead, the tips of its branches pushing high above the other trees, he scrambled to a halt. "It's like you never went away."

Hollyleaf swerved and stopped ahead of him. "I wish that were true." Her eyes shone suddenly dark. "So much has changed. You and Jayfeather have so much responsibility now. Not just because of the prophecy. You've changed. Become so much a part of the Clan. Everyone depends on you."

"You've done a lot for the Clan, too!"

"Like what?" Hollyleaf plucked at the ground. "While you were fighting and hunting for your Clanmates, I was hiding from all of you. Hiding from what I'd done." She stared at her paws.

"But you came back." Lionblaze padded closer and nudged her shoulder with his nose. "And I'm glad you did."

She lifted her gaze to meet his. "Don't pretend the past never happened, Lionblaze." She padded slowly toward the Ancient Oak. "It's like my shadow. Always following me."

The ferns behind them rustled and Lionblaze turned to see Jayfeather and Dovewing bound out onto the path.

"I told you they were here," Dovewing mewed.

"Okay, big ears," Jayfeather snapped. His blind gaze drifted toward Hollyleaf. "We need to talk."

Hollyleaf blinked. "With me?"

"*Without* you." Jayfeather's bluntness took Lionblaze by surprise. "I'm sorry, Hollyleaf." He shrugged. "But this is something only the Three can share."

Hollyleaf dipped her head. "Okay." She padded back down the trail. "I'll hunt by the lake." Her purr sounded forced. "I might be able to do better than that limp sparrow you brought back earlier, Lionblaze." She was trying to tease but her eyes glistened sadly.

Lionblaze trailed his tail along her spine. "You always were the best hunter."

"Thanks." She headed off the path and disappeared into the ferns.

Lionblaze turned his attention to Jayfeather. "What is it?" Was the Dark Forest ready to attack? He unsheathed his claws.

"I have a message from the Tribe of Endless Hunting," Jayfeather announced.

"The Tribe?" Dovewing weaved between Jayfeather and Lionblaze and sat down. "When did this happen?"

"When I was in the mountains." Jayfeather swished his tail impatiently.

"And you're only telling us now?" Dovewing mewed in surprise.

"Just listen, okay?" Jayfeather muttered. "They said we have to find the fourth cat."

Lionblaze tipped his head, puzzled. "The fourth cat?"

"In the prophecy," Jayfeather meowed.

Dovewing shifted her paws. "But the prophecy says *there will be three*."

"That was the StarClan prophecy," Jayfeather explained. "The Tribe of Endless Hunting told me something else: *The end of the stars draws near. Three must become four to challenge the darkness that lasts forever*."

Lionblaze felt his fur prick. "Don't they think we can manage by ourselves?"

Jayfeather flattened his ears. "Obviously not."

"Have we done something wrong?" Dovewing's eyes clouded with worry.

Jayfeather paced in front of them. "Who cares? We have to find the fourth cat."

Lionblaze tried to ignore the uneasiness in his belly. "Did they say who it is?"

Jayfeather halted. "If they did, I'd have told you!"

"It must be Ivypool!" Dovewing's eyes brightened. She stood up, tail-tip flicking. "She's the only ally we have among the Dark Forest warriors."

Jayfeather turned to face her. "Ivypool was recruited by the Dark Forest. She has no special powers." He started pacing again. "It could be a cat from another Clan."

A thought struck Lionblaze like a shaft of sunlight. "It's Hollyleaf! That's why she came back! To be the fourth cat."

"If it was someone inside the Clan, we'd have noticed their special power by now," Jayfeather objected.

"But it must be kin of Firestar's kin!" Dovewing argued.

"Well, Mothwing is Brambleclaw's kin and Brambleclaw was Squirrelflight's mate." Jayfeather lashed his tail. "That makes her kin, if you like."

"Mothwing?" Lionblaze stared at his brother in astonishment. "What special power does she have?"

"What special power does Hollyleaf have?" Jayfeather shot back.

"Ivypool can dream her way into the Dark Forest!" Dovewing insisted.

"So can a lot of Clan cats! I told you it was pointless arguing." Jayfeather headed away again. "We just have to hope that when the fourth cat is needed, we'll know who it is."

Lionblaze watched him go, his pelt pricking with irritation. How could Jayfeather be so stubborn? Hollyleaf should have been part of the prophecy all along. Of course she was the fourth cat.

Dovewing shifted beside him. "It's got to be Ivypool."

Lionblaze closed his eyes. "Whoever it is, how in the name of StarClan are we going to be sure?"

"Perhaps they'll send a sign," Dovewing mewed.

"They didn't even know about the fourth cat." The world shifted beneath Lionblaze's paws: Cinderheart wasn't Cinderheart; the Three were now four. How were they supposed to win a battle when nothing stayed the same?

His belly felt hollow. Did StarClan know what was happening? Nothing they said made sense, and now even their prophecy was wrong.

How could Lionblaze trust them with the fate of the Clans?

CHAPTER 5

Dovewing watched Jayfeather pad away.

There's a fourth cat. Her paws trembled. *Aren't I good enough?* Perhaps StarClan had hoped for more when they made her the third cat in the prophecy. So what if she could hear the Dark Forest warriors coming? It didn't mean she could defeat them.

She glanced at Lionblaze. "Are we going to hunt?"

"Go ahead without me."

Dovewing shifted her paws. Lionblaze had been her mentor. He was one of the strongest, bravest warriors in Thunder-Clan. Why did he seem so lost? "I'll see you later, then?"

"Okay." Lionblaze didn't look at her.

She trotted into the trees, snatching a glance over her shoulder, wishing he'd follow. But he stayed where he was.

She leaped a small stream and pushed deeper into the forest, soothed by the shade and relishing the musty scents of nettle and fern. The first fallen leaves of the season specked the forest floor. Surely Ivypool was the fourth cat? She risked her life every night fighting with the Dark Forest warriors. She *deserved* to be the fourth cat.

"Ow!" Dovewing squeaked as a thorn speared her pad. She'd been so lost in thought she'd stepped into a trailing bramble.

A sharp growl made her freeze. "Did you hear that?"

ShadowClan stench flooded Dovewing's nose. *I'm at the border!* She'd wandered up to the scent line like a mouse in a daze. She froze, ducking beside the bramble that spilled over the boundary. Holding her breath, she listened to the Shadow-Clan warriors prowling behind on the other side.

"Don't worry, Dovewing." A hiss sounded through the branches. "I'll get rid of them. Just stay still."

Tigerheart!

"It was just a rabbit," Tigerheart called to his Clanmates. "It's escaped into ThunderClan territory."

"I don't smell rabbit."

Dovewing recognized the growl of Ratscar. The bush rustled as he snuffled his way into the brambles. She caught sight of his fox-red pelt through the leaves. *StarClan, help me!* Her lungs ached for air but she didn't dare breathe.

"Come on!" Rowanclaw called to his warriors. "Blackstar wants us at the shore. A dog's running loose there. We need to scare it off before it decides to head into the forest."

Dovewing heard Ratscar give a dissatisfied growl. "But I can smell ThunderClan."

"I'll stay and check it out," Tigerheart offered.

"Okay, but stay this side of the border," Rowanclaw warned.

Ratscar growled again. "Let me stay too. If ThunderClan cats are sniffing about I want to make sure they know—"

"Tigerheart can check it out." Rowanclaw cut the warrior off. "We need to meet Blackstar. You can lead a patrol back here later to re-mark the borders."

Dovewing drew in a long, deep breath as the ShadowClan patrol pounded away toward the lake.

"Dovewing?" Tigerheart whispered through the thorns. "Were you looking for me?"

"Of course not!" Relief flared to fury. He must think she was a wide-eyed kit! And a traitor! "I heard you accuse Jayfeather of murder, don't forget!"

Tigerheart crawled out from underneath the bush. "I had to support Dawnpelt." He stared at her imploringly.

"Why?" Dovewing hissed. "She was lying!"

"She's my littermate." Tigerheart blinked at her. "And my Clanmate. What did you expect me to do?"

"You could have kept your mouth shut!" Dovewing lashed her tail. "Or do you believe her?"

Tigerheart's ears twitched. "I couldn't let her stand up alone. Not when she was making such a serious accusation." He moved closer, eyes round. "You'd have done the same for Ivypool, wouldn't you?"

"Not if I didn't think she was telling the truth."

Tigerheart narrowed his eyes. "And what if Ivypool had done something terrible? Would you abandon her?"

Dovewing's fur prickled. "Ivypool *couldn't* do anything terrible!" Tigerheart's tone unnerved her. "She *wouldn't*!"

"Really?" His eyes gleamed with a hint of a challenge.

"What do you mean?" she demanded. Dovewing knew he

and Ivypool both trained in the Dark Forest. Had something happened there, something Ivypool had kept secret?

Tigerheart dropped his gaze. "Nothing."

Dovewing lifted her chin. "This doesn't have anything to do with Ivypool. This is about Dawnpelt's dumb lie!"

"Dawnpelt believes what she said."

"Do you?" Dovewing arched her back.

"I miss you, Dovewing." Tigerheart's amber gaze pierced her. "Why do we have to argue?"

She flinched back in surprise as he leaned closer.

"Why can't we meet like we used to?" He sliced a bramble leaf with his claw and watched it flutter to the ground. "When it's just the two of us, everything's so much simpler."

Dovewing opened her mouth to argue. They were from different Clans. She shouldn't even be thinking about him, let alone talking to him. Not like this. "I—I don't know," she stammered.

"You do know!" He took a step forward until their muzzles were almost touching. "You feel the same way as I do. I can tell."

He trains in the Dark Forest! Dovewing tried to back away but his strength and warmth pulled her closer. For the first time in moons she felt safe, as though she could melt into him and never be afraid again. *Ivypool trains there too,* she reminded herself. *Perhaps Tigerheart is spying for his Clan, like she is.*

His breath was soft on her cheek. Just like it had been when they'd sat together in the old Twoleg place, away from Clan territory, alone beneath the moon.

"Tigerheart!" Ratscar's yowl made her jerk away. The ShadowClan warrior was on the other side of the brambles.

"Coming!" Tigerheart scrambled under the bush. "Meet me tonight!" he hissed at Dovewing. "I'll wait for you here."

Trembling, Dovewing turned and ran. *I can't meet him!* Her thoughts raced with her paws as she skimmed the drooping grass clumped between trees.

But why not? I'll just meet him once. If it still feels wrong I won't meet him again.

An orange pelt flashed in front of her. Skidding, Dovewing stumbled to a halt, missing Firestar by a whisker.

He reared back, surprised. "Dovewing!" Finding his paws, he stared at her. "Sorry. I was thinking about something. I didn't even hear you coming."

"I should have been looking where I was going."

He gazed at her sympathetically. "Were you worrying, too?"

Yes. About Tigerheart. "I w-was just . . ." As she stammered guiltily, Firestar interrupted.

". . . listening for danger?"

Dovewing bristled. *There's more to me than ears! I can hunt and fight as well!*

The ThunderClan leader shook his head. "It's hard knowing, isn't it?"

Dovewing frowned. "You mean, knowing about the Dark Forest?"

"Yes." Firestar stared deep into the forest. "The Clan feels it too, even if they don't know what the danger is. They know something's wrong. I ordered them to increase patrols and reinforce the dens. They're not mouse-brains. They sense danger." He suddenly turned toward her. "Are *you* okay?" His gaze was as green as the forest. "You're young to have so much responsibility."

Dovewing straightened. "I can handle it."

"I know." Firestar tipped his head. "But make sure you're getting enough prey and rest, and remember . . ." He paused, glancing into the trees once more. ". . . the final responsibility is mine. You don't hold the whole Clan in your paws. I just need you to do what you can." He lifted his chin. "I'll take care of the rest."

CHAPTER 6

Watery sunshine filtered through the den walls.

Ivypool yawned, arching her back till her legs trembled. She was aware of every muscle tensed beneath her skin, each one a little stronger after another night's training in the Dark Forest. Now that she was mentoring Birchfall and Redwillow, she woke with fewer wounds, but weary from the effort of demonstrating moves and running through them again and again. Redwillow was a quick learner and Birchfall was clearly hungry to prove that he was as good a Dark Forest warrior as he was a ThunderClan one. He'd picked up the rearing lunge she'd shown him on his first try and, though he was her father, not her kit, Ivypool had felt a fond rush of pride.

Dovewing yawned.

"You look tired." Ivypool could see weariness in her sister's blue eyes, and Dovewing's pelt was unkempt, dusted with fragments of leaf. Had she been out of the camp?

"The forest noises kept waking me."

Ivypool guessed it must be hard to sleep with ears that heard far beyond the walls of the den. "You could try stuffing them with moss."

Dovewing blinked, confused. "What?"

"Your ears." Ivypool frowned. Dovewing seemed like she was in another world.

Molepaw rolled over and struggled to sit up. "I wish I'd stuffed my ears with moss," he mewed sleepily. "Then I wouldn't be woken up by you two chattering like blackbirds."

Cherrypaw stretched. "It's dawn," she pointed out. "Time to wake up."

"But Rosepetal and Foxleap are practicing tree climbing with Spiderleg," Molepaw reminded her. "Which means no training for us."

Cherrypaw lifted her head. "Why can't we train with them?"

"Spiderleg thinks we're too small to jump off a branch." Molepaw lashed his tail. "I bet I could jump down from the Ancient Oak and land safely."

Ivypool cuffed his ear gently. "We can't risk any injuries." *Not with the Dark Forest getting ready to attack.* She ducked out of the den and padded over to where Brambleclaw was doling out morning duties.

"Prey is starting to go to ground," the ThunderClan deputy declared. "We must hunt while we can. But we can't forget battle training. The Clans are nervous. And nervous Clans are dangerous."

"Is that why WindClan tried to attack us through the tunnels?" Sorreltail called.

Cloudtail narrowed his eyes. "And why ShadowClan accused our medicine cat of murder?"

Firestar bounded down from Highledge and joined

Brambleclaw. "We mustn't be drawn into Clan squabbles. We have to concentrate on preparing for leaf-bare."

And the attack from the Dark Forest. Ivypool's tail twitched. Her Clanmates were fretting over the threat from their neighbors. They had no idea a far greater threat hung over the forest.

Brambleclaw padded forward. "Firestar's right. We must prepare for the cold moons, but keep training. Berrynose!" He looked up to a nest woven on top of the beech trunk. A wide, cream head poked out.

"Yes?"

Brambleclaw beckoned him with a flick of his tail. "I want you to help Spiderleg train Foxleap and Rosepetal in tree battle."

Berrynose slid out of his den and jumped into the clearing. He shook out his pelt, his muscled shoulders rippling. "Great!" His eyes shone. With claws as strong as an eagle's talons, he was one of the best climbers in the Clan. And he knew how to time a drop so that he could land squarely on any warrior passing underneath his branch.

Spiderleg looked expectantly at Brambleclaw and, when the ThunderClan deputy nodded, headed for the thorn tunnel. Rosepetal and Foxtail followed, Berrynose bounding after. Molepaw watched them go, his brown-and-cream pelt fluffed up along his spine.

Brambleclaw blinked at the apprentice. "You and Cherrypaw can train with Dovewing and Ivypool today."

Ivypool's tail drooped. She'd spent all night training apprentices in the Dark Forest.

"Did you hear that, Dovewing?" Cherrypaw hopped out of

her den, calling over her shoulder. "You're training us today."

Dovewing slid out, yawning.

Ivypool frowned. *Why is she so tired? I'm the one who's been up all night.* "Come on." She marched past Dovewing, heading for the entrance.

"Can we learn some battle moves?" Molepaw's wide amber gaze fixed on Ivypool. "Blossomfall said that you know some awesome attack moves."

"Let's concentrate on defense today." She'd taught enough killing moves in the Dark Forest last night.

"We can practice attacking if you like, Molepaw." Dovewing padded along the trail.

Ivypool stared after her. *Didn't you hear what I said?* She opened her mouth to argue but Cherrypaw and Molepaw were already haring toward the training hollow.

"Be careful!" Ivypool yowled after them. "I don't want any injuries. Keep your claws sheathed." *This isn't the Dark Forest.*

As the apprentices disappeared up the trail, Ivypool caught up with Dovewing. "What's up?"

"Nothing."

"Then why are you acting like you woke up in the wrong Clan?"

"I'm not." Dovewing stared ahead.

Ivypool was unconvinced. "What really kept you up last night?"

"I told you." Dovewing shrugged. "Noises."

They reached the training hollow and Ivypool jumped down the short, steep slope. Molepaw and Cherrypaw were already tussling on the smooth, sandy earth.

"Battle crouch!" Ivypool ordered.

The apprentices rolled away from each other and dropped to their bellies.

"Keep your tail still." Ivypool pressed the twitching tip of Molepaw's tail with a paw and turned to Cherrypaw. "Shoulders down and tuck your hindpaws in." She nosed Cherrypaw's haunches till the ginger she-cat drew her hind paws tighter beneath her. "It'll add power to your jump. Now practice your leap and see which one can reach the farthest."

She padded back to Dovewing, who had settled at the edge of the clearing. "Don't forget to stretch out your forepaws," she called back to the apprentices. "You want to meet your enemy clawfirst, not nosefirst." She sat beside her sister. "I know something's wrong," she hissed.

Molepaw and Cherrypaw launched themselves across the clearing, more like panicking rabbits than warriors.

"Try again," Ivypool suggested. "And keep trying till you've got it." She turned back to Dovewing. "Well?"

Dovewing's round, blue eyes glistened. "It's the prophecy," she whispered.

"What about it?"

"The Tribe of Endless Hunting told Jayfeather there's a fourth cat."

Ivypool's tail stiffened. "A *fourth* cat? Who?"

"Jayfeather thinks it's Mothwing." Dovewing's gaze drifted to a point on the far side of the clearing. "Lionblaze thinks it's Hollyleaf."

"Didn't the Tribe say who it was?" Ivypool flexed her claws. Why did the Ancient cats make everything so difficult?

"I don't think they know."

"What about StarClan?"

Dovewing shrugged.

"Who do *you* think the fourth cat is?" Ivypool murmured.

"You."

"Me?" Ivypool blinked. "Just because I'm your sister doesn't mean—"

Dovewing cut her off. "You risk your life every night in the Dark Forest."

"I'm just spying for you." Ivypool shook her head. "StarClan hasn't spoken to me."

Dovewing leaned closer. "Are you sure? Have you had any special dreams?"

Ivypool rolled her eyes. "I don't have time for special dreams," she pointed out. "I spend every night in the Dark Forest."

"Can we try swerves now?"

Ivypool swung around as Molepaw interrupted them. "Soon." She turned back to Dovewing. "Surely it's Hollyleaf?"

"What's Hollyleaf?" Cherrypaw padded toward them.

"Practice your leap," Ivypool ordered.

"But Molepaw's taking up the whole clearing!" Cherrypaw complained.

Ivypool glanced at the brown-and-white apprentice. "Molepaw! Keep to the edge and let your sister use the middle."

"But that's not fair—"

Ivypool growled. "Are you training to be a warrior or a kit?"

Muttering, Molepaw trailed to the edge of the clearing and hunkered down, ready to leap again. Cherrypaw lifted her tail defiantly and marched to the middle of the hollow.

Ivypool turned back to Dovewing. "Why else would Hollyleaf come back now?"

"If she was part of the prophecy, she wouldn't have gone away," Dovewing argued. "It has to be you!"

"I don't have any special power," Ivypool pointed out.

"You have courage," Dovewing mewed fiercely. "You spy every night on our greatest enemies. It *must* be you!"

A squawk made Ivypool spin around. Molepaw and Cherrypaw were fighting in the center of the clearing. Ivypool darted toward them and hauled Molepaw away. "What in the name of StarClan are you doing?"

"He kept jumping into my space!" Cherrypaw hissed.

"You're Clanmates!" Ivypool snapped. "What use will you be in battle if you end up fighting each other?" As she spoke, a well of despair seemed to open up in her chest. What horrors and betrayal lay ahead for her innocent Clanmates?

As the sun peaked over the camp, Ivypool padded to a pool of light beside the fallen beech and lay down. Her belly was full and her pelt was warm. Weary from the morning's training, she closed her eyes. *Am I really the fourth cat?* Dovewing's words echoed in her head. *You spy every night on our greatest enemies. It must be you!* Ivypool tried to push her sister's voice away.

I'd know if I was the fourth! I'd have a special power, wouldn't I?

"Ivypool!" Birchfall's hiss jerked her from her doze.

She sat up. "What?"

Her father was a dark shadow against the blazing sunlight. She blinked, adjusting to the brightness, and made out Mouse-whisker standing beside him. Ivypool's shoulders drooped. This was going to be about their Dark Forest training.

"We need to talk." Birchfall twitched his nose toward the camp entrance. "In private."

Ivypool gazed across the sunny camp. Poppyfrost and Leafpool were sharing a mouse outside the elders' den. Beside them, Mousefur rested her nose on her front paws, her eyes shut while Purdy washed her pelt with long strokes of his tongue. Cherrypaw and Molepaw were trying to outdistance each other, practicing their attack leaps beside the nursery.

"Come on, then." Wearily, Ivypool padded toward the entrance. She didn't meet Mousewhisker's eye in case he spotted her reluctance. She had never imagined that so many of her Clanmates would be taken in by Hawkfrost's lies.

I was. She'd been so eager to learn new battle techniques that she didn't care who taught her. And Hawkfrost had been so convincing, charming her into believing he was helping her to become the best warrior she could be. Why would Mouse-whisker be any wiser?

The forest was cool outside the hollow, shaded by leaves that swished in the soft breeze. Ivypool led Birchfall and Mousewhisker along the trail and stopped at the edge of the training hollow.

"We're going to meet up with the Dark Forest cats from the other Clans."

Birchfall's confession made Ivypool stiffen. "When?"

"Now."

Ivypool swallowed. "Why?"

"We need to practice fighting in daylight," Mousewhisker added.

Birchfall leaned forward, eyes bright. "If we can practice what we're learning in the Dark Forest, we can improve our skills."

"And we've got to think of a way for the Dark Forest warriors to get to our territory if we need their help."

Ivypool stifled a gasp. "Why would we need their help?" The thought of Hawkfrost and Tigerstar running freely beside the lake made her feel sick.

Birchfall blinked at her. "That way, if one Clan's threatened, we can all help them."

Do they really believe that? Ivypool stared at her Clanmates. Their eyes were wide and clear. *Everything's upside down!* The Clans were on edge, threatening one another's borders as their fear rose, while the warriors training in the Dark Forest grew closer and closer. She searched her father's gaze, desperate to confess what she knew and warn him that he was stalking wolves, not mice.

Her heart quickened. She couldn't tell them she was a spy. What if they betrayed her?

A sharp wind whisked through the branches overhead.

"So?" Mousewhisker demanded. "Are you coming?"

Ivypool shifted her paws. "Where?"

Birchfall flicked his tail excitedly. "We've arranged to meet Sunstrike at the border."

"She's bringing Larkpaw and Harespring," Mousewhisker added.

Ivypool fought to keep her fur smooth as horror surged through her. How mouse-brained were they? She stared at Birchfall. His light brown tabby pelt was glossy and smooth, his chest puffed up. He actually thought he was being loyal to his Clan by meeting WindClan warriors to share battle moves!

I have to stop this!

As Birchfall and Mousewhisker headed away through the trees, Ivypool stretched her ears, wishing she had her sister's hearing. She couldn't order them not to go because it would reveal too much about what she was doing in the Dark Forest. She had to keep spying as long as possible. She had to find out when and where Brokenstar planned to attack.

"Wait for me." She hurried after her Clanmates as they joined the trail that led to the WindClan border. Following the path upward, she scanned the forest. Birds flitted from branch to branch. A squirrel was skittering across the forest floor beyond the ferns. She suddenly spotted a fox-red pelt in the brambles beyond. Someone was stalking the squirrel.

Her heart lifted. "I'll catch up."

Birchfall looked back at her. "We're meeting at the stream," he mewed.

"Okay." Ivypool veered off the trail and ducked into the

ferns. Poking her head out the other side, she saw the squirrel run. The fox-red pelt darted after it, landing squarely on the squirrel and killing it with a bite.

"Foxleap!" Ivypool raced from the ferns.

The warrior turned, the squirrel dangling between his jaws. He dropped it. "What's up?"

Ivypool glanced over her shoulder. Mousewhisker and Birchfall had disappeared over the rise. "Bring a patrol to the WindClan border," she hissed. "Not this way. Follow the lake trail." She couldn't risk a ThunderClan patrol catching up with Birchfall and Mousewhisker and following them directly to the meeting place.

Foxleap tipped his head. "Why?"

"I smelled WindClan scent at the border," she lied. "I think patrols have been crossing the stream."

Foxleap frowned. "I'll fetch some others." Scooping up the squirrel in his jaws, he raced toward camp.

Ivypool rushed to catch up with Birchfall and Mousewhisker.

"Is everything okay?" Birchfall narrowed his eyes.

"Fine." Ivypool fell in beside him, lifting her chin. "I just had to make dirt."

Birchfall's gaze flicked back to the trail. Ivypool could see the trees lighten as they neared the edge of the forest. She slowed her pace. The stretch of grass beyond ran straight to the border. She had to give Foxleap time to fetch the patrol.

"I'm proud of you." Birchfall's pelt brushed hers as he murmured in her ear. "Seeing you in the Dark Forest makes me realize how much I've underestimated your skills in the past."

Would he be as proud of her if he knew she was lying to everyone? She should warn him about the dangerous path he was choosing. She should confess she was only in the Dark Forest to find out what Brokenstar was up to. But she couldn't. There was too much at stake.

They padded into the sunlight. Ahead, the ground sloped down toward the border stream. Beyond that, WindClan's smooth, grassy moor rose, stark against the brilliant blue sky. Ivypool scanned the heather for pelts, then glanced furtively toward the lake. There was no sign of WindClan or Foxleap's patrol. She spotted a gorse bush clinging to the slope, a few fox-lengths from the stream. "Let's hide there till they come."

Mousewhisker bristled. "Why should we hide?"

Ivypool marched past him. "You don't want everyone knowing about the Dark Forest, do you?" She ducked underneath the low branches of the gorse. Spikes tugged at her pelt as she squirmed as far in as she could. She wriggled around and hissed to her Clanmates. "Come on, there's plenty of room."

Birchfall and Mousewhisker squeezed in after her and she lay, hot and prickly, staring out at the moor. Her heart thumped against the ground. *Please, StarClan, don't let Birchfall and Mousewhisker smell my fear-scent.* What if Foxleap arrived first? Birchfall might guess she'd given them away. Ivypool peered into the heather beyond the stream, praying for pelts to appear.

Fresh ThunderClan scent seeped under the bush. *Foxleap!* Straining, she saw the young warrior climbing the slope from the lake. Brackenfur and Graystripe flanked him. As they neared the gorse bush, the heather on the far side of the stream swished and Harespring padded out, scanning the border. Larkpaw and Sunstrike followed.

"Any sign of them?" Sunstrike murmured to his Clanmates. He stared across the stream as they approached the border.

"Stay back!" Foxleap's yowl sounded from the slope. The ThunderClan patrol ran toward the border and skidded to a halt opposite the WindClan cats. "What are you doing here?"

"Checking the border." Sunstrike met his gaze. "Just like you."

"You've been trespassing!" Brackenfur accused.

"We haven't crossed the border!" Harespring hissed.

"Not this time," Foxleap growled. "But warriors have picked up WindClan scent this side of the stream."

Birchfall stiffened beside Ivypool. "Have they?" he whispered.

Ivypool shrugged. "I don't know," she lied.

Mousewhisker's tail flicked. "Why did Firestar have to send a patrol here now?" he grumbled.

Sunstrike stood on the edge of the small gorge cut by the stream. Foxleap faced her on the other side. Both warriors were bristling, ears flat.

Sunstrike bared her teeth. "No *WindClan* cat has crossed the border."

Graystripe lashed his tail. "Are you accusing ThunderClan of crossing the scent line?"

Brackenfur dropped into a crouch—the same one Ivypool had spent the morning teaching Molepaw and Cherrypaw. *Don't attack!* Guilt flooded through her. She didn't want to start a fight. She just wanted to save her Clanmates from making a terrible mistake.

Harespring met Brackenfur's gaze through narrowed eyes. "Onestar says we should challenge any cat we find on our land."

"This is our land." Brackenfur's hindquarters twitched as he bunched his muscles.

"Stop!" Birchfall shot out from the gorse.

Foxleap spun around, his eyes wide. "What are you doing here?"

"Guarding the border." Birchfall straightened up and signaled to Mousewhisker and Ivypool with his tail. Mousewhisker slid out from under the bush and, reluctantly, Ivypool followed.

Foxleap's eyes narrowed. "How do you guard from inside a bush?"

"We were waiting to see if they'd cross." Birchfall's gaze slipped toward Sunstrike. The WindClan cats began to back away. Graystripe shifted his paws.

"No one's crossed any borders," Birchfall announced. "Let's just all retreat."

Foxleap growled. "Not till I've checked for WindClan scent on our land."

Sunstrike's ears twitched. "You won't find any." She turned and led her Clanmates back into the heather.

Foxleap was pacing the border sniffing every clump of grass. "There's no sign of invasion." He glanced expectantly at Ivypool, since she was the one who'd told him about Wind-Clan cats crossing the border.

She looked away, relief flooding through her. "Not this time," she murmured.

Foxleap sniffed the gorse once more, then left a scent marker. "Come on, let's get back to camp."

Ivypool was first into the trees. Her paws were heavy as stone and she wished she was still asleep in the sun beside the fallen beech. A pelt brushed hers and she turned to see that Foxleap had caught up with her. "Did you know they'd be there?"

She flinched. "No."

"But there's no sign of WindClan crossing the border." Foxleap was frowning. "What made you call for a patrol? Did you overhear something in the tunnel battle?"

Ivypool shook her head. "It was just a hunch," she muttered. "You know how tense it's been between the Clans. I must have caught a whiff of WindClan scent while I was in the woods and I was just on edge—"

". . . and you overreacted." Foxleap finished her sentence.

"I suppose so." Ivypool's ear twitched.

"Well, it was a good guess."

Ivypool glanced at Foxleap, her belly tightening as she saw doubt shadowing his gaze. *He doesn't believe me.* Tail flicking with unease, Ivypool pushed harder against the ground and raced for home. Being a spy was forcing her to betray her own Clan after all.

How much longer will I have to live like this?

CHAPTER 7

❧

Jayfeather dropped the pebble a mouse-length away from Briarlight's nest. "Can you reach that?"

"Easy!" Briarlight leaned out, grabbed the pebble, and heaved it into her nest, the firm muscles in her shoulders curving under her pelt.

Jayfeather stuck his nose into her nest and picked up the pebble between his teeth. He strained to lift it out. He'd chosen a heavy one for today's exercise. He dropped it half a tail-length from her nest. "What about this?"

Briarlight stretched out with her forelegs again, puffing a little this time, but she still scooped the stone back into her nest with nimble paws.

"Let me check your spine." Jayfeather buried his muzzle into her pelt, feeling her muscles with gentle nips. They felt healthy and strong all the way down to the break. Beyond, they were lifeless and thin, but the fur covering them was sleek and shiny. "You've worked hard." Jayfeather sat up. "As long as we keep up with your exercises, you'll be fine."

Briarlight flung the pebble out of her nest and began reaching for it again. "I want to be able to climb trees using my forepaws alone," she puffed.

As she struggled to reach the stone, Jayfeather's attention drifted. He'd been worrying all morning about the fourth cat. Mothwing was the only one who'd offered any help fighting the Dark Forest. It must be her. He cast his mind out, as though releasing a bird, and let it skim across the lake toward RiverClan territory. As it reached the camp, he blocked out the clamor of emotions and probed for Mothwing. He sensed Willowshine, counting herbs, and felt Mothwing beside her, but as usual he could not penetrate the mist that swathed the medicine cat's thoughts like cobweb.

She has to be the fourth cat! She's the only cat whose dreams were safe from the Dark Forest. She couldn't be lured into their treacherous plans.

"Can you finish your exercises by yourself?" he asked Briarlight. "I need to go out."

"Of course I can."

Outside the den, the morning sunshine was warm on his pelt. Lionblaze and Whitewing were sharing a mouse beside the thorn barrier. Thornclaw and Sorreltail shared tongues at the edge of the clearing. Ferncloud and Daisy were gossiping outside the nursery, while Seedkit and Lilykit stalked fallen leaves in the shadow of the beech.

Lionblaze hopped out of the way as Jayfeather ducked into the entrance tunnel. "Where are you going?"

"To see Mothwing."

Alarm flared from Lionblaze. "I'll come with you."

"No, thanks." He didn't want his brother arguing all the way around the lake that Hollyleaf was the fourth cat.

"This is medicine-cat business."

"But you're not supposed to be a medicine cat anymore," Lionblaze called after him.

"StarClan will protect me." Jayfeather scooted through the tunnel, aware of his own lie. Brambleberry had told him that StarClan could no longer see the cats by the lake. For them, the darkness had fallen already. "Tell Firestar where I've gone." He listened for Lionblaze to follow, relieved when he heard only a sigh of resignation drifting through the thorns.

"If you're not back by dusk, I'm coming to look for you," Lionblaze called.

"You won't need to." *I hope!*

He headed for the shore. He'd follow it through WindClan territory. He opened his mouth to taste the air, checking the shore for WindClan warriors. There was a trace of familiar scent . . .

Onestar!

Jayfeather tensed. The WindClan leader was standing at the water's edge a few fox-lengths ahead.

Jayfeather approached cautiously. "Greetings, Onestar."

Onestar didn't move. "Jayfeather."

"I'm sorry for trespassing on WindClan land." Jayfeather dipped his head. "I'm on my way to speak with Mothwing." He tensed, expecting anger to flare from Onestar's pelt. But the WindClan leader's fur stayed unruffled.

"You may pass in peace," Onestar told him. "Although I thought the medicine cats no longer spoke to one another."

"That is StarClan's wish," Jayfeather meowed. "Not mine."

"You would go against StarClan?" Onestar sounded surprised.

"Yes." Jayfeather made no apology. "If it means keeping the peace between the Clans."

He heard pebbles shift as Onestar sat down. "The Clans have always fought, but this is the first time the medicine cats have been divided," the WindClan leader said heavily. "I feel as if something bad is coming." Onestar's gaze seared Jayfeather's pelt. "The water is calm," he murmured. "But currents pull beneath the surface. Though they can't be seen, they have the power to drag cats to their death."

"Not if you know where they lie." Jayfeather leaned forward. "Watch your borders, Onestar, but keep an eye on your own Clan, too."

Pebbles cracked as Onestar turned to face him. "Are you saying that my warriors aren't loyal?"

Jayfeather backed away. "Any cat can be tricked into disloyalty."

Onestar's breath billowed in Jayfeather's face. "Are you talking about Sol?"

"No." The threat from the Dark Forest was far more dangerous than a troublemaking loner. "Just look out for unusual behavior among your warriors."

Fury sparked from the WindClan leader's pelt. "I trust my Clan with my life!"

Jayfeather bent his head. "Forgive me." He slunk past Onestar and walked on toward the RiverClan border. His fur prickled as he felt Onestar's angry gaze follow him along the shore. *Perhaps I shouldn't have tried to warn him.*

The scent line at the RiverClan border reached down to the water's edge, marking the stones on the shore. Jayfeather crossed it.

"What are you doing here?"

Jayfeather spun around, claws unsheathed. He could smell the fierce scent of Beetlewhisker. Troutstream and Mintfur were bristling beside him.

Jayfeather lifted his tail. "I'm here to speak with Mothwing."

"You're not a medicine cat anymore." Beetlewhisker's fishy breath grazed Jayfeather's cheek.

Jayfeather stifled a shiver. He'd heard Beetlewhisker training in the Dark Forest. "ShadowClan doesn't make decisions for StarClan," he hissed. "Only StarClan can deny my power to heal."

Mintfur murmured to her Clanmate. "I think Mistystar should decide."

"I guess." Distrust edged Beetlewhisker's mew. Jayfeather suddenly wished Lionblaze was with him after all.

Troutstream strode forward. "Come on." The she-cat nosed him uphill and Mintfur and Beetlewhisker fell in beside them.

"There's a tree-bridge here." Troutstream's pelt brushed Jayfeather's whiskers as she leaped up ahead of him. Jayfeather smelled the stale sap of a fallen trunk. It must span the river that carved RiverClan's camp from the mainland. He scrambled up after her, digging his claws into the peeling bark, and followed her gingerly, his heart lurching as the log rocked under the weight of Mintfur and Beetlewhisker behind him. The river swished beneath him. It would wash him into the lake if he fell.

When he felt the trunk divide into brittle branches, he knew he'd reached the other side. He gathered his haunches under him and leaped forward, hoping to clear the top of the fallen tree. He landed clumsily among some trailing twigs but Troutstream steadied him.

"This way." She led Jayfeather through tall grass. River-Clan scent bathed him as they reached a clearing. He could sense shock flash around him from the cats in the camp.

"Why's *he* here?"

Heronpaw was silenced by Rushtail. "Listen and you might find out."

"Welcome, Jayfeather." Mistystar's pelt scraped against twigs as she squeezed out of her den. "Have you come to see Mothwing and Willowshine?"

Jayfeather dipped his head. "Yes, if I may."

"He's got no right!" Beetlewhisker snarled.

Jayfeather could feel warmth flooding from Mistystar. At least she was pleased to see him. "He has the right of StarClan," she cautioned her warrior. Her tail-tip touched Jayfeather's flank. "I'll take you to the medicine den."

He followed her across the camp, into a tunnel of grass that opened into a small clearing. Jayfeather inhaled the familiar scents of coltsfoot, borage, and watermint. Grass swished and paws scuffed the ground.

"Jayfeather?" Mothwing sounded surprised.

"Is everything okay?" Willowshine's tail brushed the soft earth.

Mistystar turned beside him, her pelt brushing his as she padded away. "I'll leave you to talk."

Willowshine was at his side in a moment. "What's the matter? Is someone sick?"

"I needed to talk to Mothwing," Jayfeather explained.

"But you're not a medicine cat anymore." Willowshine sounded puzzled. "Dawnpelt accused you of—"

Jayfeather interrupted her. "If ShadowClan told the river to stop flowing, would it?"

Willowshine stiffened. "It's not just ShadowClan!" she protested. "StarClan has shared dreams with me and they told me that medicine cats must stay away from one another."

Mothwing snorted. "They've said nothing to me, so you can go collect mallow while I talk to Jayfeather."

Jayfeather felt silence harden between the two medicine cats. Then Willowshine whipped her tail over the ground. "Okay." She stomped from the den.

Mothwing's tail twitched. "If StarClan told her to jump in the lake, she would!"

Jayfeather shrugged. "She can swim."

A growl rumbled in Mothwing's throat. "Don't joke. This is serious. It's you who told me we are facing a terrible battle."

How will I know if she's the fourth cat? He crouched beside her. "The Clans need to unite for the battle that is coming, but that's impossible while the medicine cats are divided."

Mothwing's claws scratched the earth. "It's so mouse-brained! Ignoring common sense just because some starry old cat tells you to." Her tail whisked past Jayfeather as she tucked it around her. "I'm sorry," she apologized. "I know you believe in StarClan and I respect that. Faith has helped to guide the Clans through difficult times before, but right now it seems to be getting in the way."

Jayfeather understood the frustration in her mew. StarClan was making the threat of the Dark Forest more dangerous by driving the Clans apart. "If only I could talk to Flametail, perhaps I would be able to persuade him to tell Littlecloud the truth."

"That would be a start." Mothwing shifted her paws. "The medicine cats are never going to come together while they think you're a murderer." She sat up. "I'll talk to Littlecloud and Kestrelflight. I might be able to persuade them to see that they're undermining the strength of the medicine-cat code."

"Would they listen to you over StarClan?"

Mothwing's claws scraped the earth. "I'm glad I don't have StarClan buzzing like bees in my brain! How can you think clearly with old cats muttering in your thoughts all the time?"

"Jayfeather?" Mistystar's mew sounded softly in the entrance tunnel. "You have to leave."

But I still need proof that Mothwing's the fourth cat!

"My senior warriors no longer see you as a medicine cat," Mistystar explained apologetically. "I have to respect their feelings. You can't stay here any longer."

Jayfeather could sense hostility prickling in the air outside the medicine den. "They think I'm a trespasser."

"I'm afraid so." Mistystar nudged him to his paws. "It would be best if you left now." He nodded to Mothwing and headed through the tunnel.

Beetlewhisker paced the camp, Hollowflight and Minnowtail flanking him. Reedfeather stepped forward. "We'll lead you to the border."

"Thank you." Jayfeather dipped his head to the RiverClan deputy. *Four warriors to escort me home?* He flattened his ears. *I've done nothing wrong!*

He felt Mothwing at his heels. "I'll come and tell you if I manage to persuade the others to see reason," she whispered.

"I think the Clans have *lost* their reason," Jayfeather hissed back. He could sense the RiverClan warriors flexing their muscles as though they were about to go into battle. *You're fighting the wrong enemy!* Forcing his pelt to stay smooth, he followed Reedfeather out of camp. Hollowflight and Beetlewhisker walked on either side, hurrying him up onto the fallen tree, while Minnowtail nudged him from behind.

"Do you want me to fall in?" Jayfeather hissed as his paw slipped off the trunk and dangled in thin air for a moment. The river splashed hungrily below.

"Hold tight, then," Beetlewhisker growled, nosing him onward.

Jayfeather dug his claws into the rotting bark, his heart lurching as he scrambled along the log. At the other end, he jumped down before Beetlewhisker could give him a shove. He held his tongue while his escorts steered him through the marsh grass. At last, he scented the WindClan border and crossed it without a word.

"If you want to come back, bring a patrol and be prepared to fight!" Hollowflight growled after him.

Lashing his tail, Jayfeather marched away from her. He tasted the air. *Where's the shore?* He could smell heather above him and hear water lapping below, but it was quiet, meaning he was too far inland. Turning his paws toward the lake, he weaved through the tall grass, the ground boggy beneath his paws.

Suddenly a chill touched his tail-tip and spread over him like a leaf-bare fog. It carried the stench of decaying prey. Jayfeather stopped and jerked around. Shapes swarmed around him like hornets, dark and cruel. His mind flooded with images of bloodstained pelts.

"Who's there?" Spinning the other way, he lashed out with a paw. Fear shot through him as his claws grazed hard flesh. "Who are you?"

A shoulder buffeted him. Claws scraped down his spine.

Jayfeather ran. Blind, he stumbled over the marshy earth, his paws sliding on the mud and plunging into puddles. Sharp as thorns, claws raked one side, then another. Pelts jostled him and hot, stinking breath scorched his ears. He tripped and fell sprawling into the mud, scrabbling to his paws, fighting the blurry shapes that jabbed from every side.

"Can't StarClan guide you?" Brokenstar's sneer made Jayfeather freeze in horror.

Have the Dark Forest cats broken through into the real world?

Hawkfrost pushed him from the other side. "We shall taste victory soon!"

Now Tigerstar blocked his path. Jayfeather lashed out but strong paws blocked his desperate swipes. "All the power of the stars in your paws?" Tigerstar's growl dripped with scorn. "I don't think so."

Jayfeather crouched, his body pulsing as his heart seemed to thump the ground beneath him. "You'll never win!" Terror exploded into fury. He sprang forward, claws stretched, and slashed at his shadowy attackers. Claws raked his muzzle and teeth sank into his tail.

Yowling with rage, Jayfeather fought harder. "You can kill me!" he screeched. "But that won't stop me. I'll find you beyond my death, and I'll stop you!"

"Jayfeather!" The call of a WindClan warrior made him stop in his tracks. The stench of the Dark Forest warriors faded and the scent of Owlwhisker, Nightcloud, and Gorsetail flowed around him, warm and familiar.

"Are you okay?" Owlwhisker leaned over him. "Did you fall into a thornbush?"

Jayfeather could smell his own blood as it welled in his stinging wounds. "Y-yes." He struggled to find his paws and felt Gorsetail's muzzle beneath his shoulder as he helped him up.

"What are you doing?" Jayfeather recognized Crouchpaw's mew. The WindClan apprentice sounded frightened. "That's the medicine cat who killed Flametail!"

"Murderer!" Nightcloud growled.

"Be quiet!" Gorsetail silenced them. "This is a Clan cat who needs our help."

"I—I'm okay." Jayfeather fought the tremor in his voice.

Owlwhisker brushed past him. "We'll escort you to the border." His mew was brisk.

"Can you walk that far?" Gorsetail asked.

Nightcloud growled. "If he can't, we'll drag him."

Owlwhisker ignored his Clanmate and sniffed Jayfeather's pelt. "It's just a few scratches." He headed down to the shore. "Come on."

Gingerly Jayfeather followed, testing out each paw. He was relieved to feel his scratches didn't reach too deep and he hadn't wrenched any muscles. He quickened his pace, using scent to follow Owlwhisker's pawsteps. Gorsetail padded behind him while Nightcloud and Crouchpaw hung back, distrust sparking from their pelts.

Jayfeather was still trembling from his vision. Surely it was a vision? The Dark Forest cats hadn't found a way to break through to the lake territories, had they? He pushed the thought away. *No.* Ivypool would have warned them. *Or StarClan . . .*

Despair washed through him. StarClan was useless. No Ancient cat had rushed to protect him from a vision that had been so real, it had left him scratched and battered. Where was Yellowfang, or Rock? Jayfeather's paws dragged on the pebbles. The Clans were going to face the Dark Forest warriors alone.

The familiar scent of ThunderClan touched his nose. They

had reached the border. "I can manage from here."

"We'd better see you to your camp," Owlwhisker told him.

"You seem a bit shaken up," Gorsetail added.

Jayfeather wanted to argue, but how could he reject their help? He'd been wishing the Clans would unite.

Owlwhisker called to Nightcloud and Crouchpaw, who were still trailing along the shore. "Go and hunt! We'll catch up with you later."

Jayfeather felt a prickle of relief, silently thanking Owlwhisker. At least he wouldn't be bringing an entire WindClan patrol onto ThunderClan territory. He led the way through the forest, the trail comfortingly familiar under his feet, until he reached the slope down to the camp.

"I can make it home by myself now," he told Owlwhisker.

"I know." Owlwhisker padded past him. "But I want to speak with Firestar."

Unhappily Jayfeather followed the WindClan warrior into camp, Gorsetail on his heels.

"Purdy!" Mousefur's alarmed mew sounded from the honeysuckle bush. "Is it an invasion?"

"I doubt it. There's only two of them," Purdy reassured the old she-cat.

Firestar jumped down from Highledge to meet them. "What's happened?" He sounded concerned as he sniffed Jayfeather's scratched muzzle.

Brambleclaw hurried from the warriors' den. "Are you okay?"

"He stumbled into a thornbush," Owlwhisker told the ThunderClan deputy.

"On our territory," Gorsetail added pointedly.

"You shouldn't have been there, Jayfeather." Firestar's mew was stern. "You are no longer a medicine cat!"

Jayfeather didn't argue. What else could Firestar say in front of the WindClan cats? "May I go to my nest?" he muttered.

"Yes." Firestar was simmering with fury. "And don't wander out of the territory again. I've got more important things to worry about."

Jayfeather padded to the medicine den, leaving Firestar to smooth the WindClan warriors' ruffled fur. He pushed through the brambles and headed for his nest.

"Are you okay?" Briarlight called from beside the pool. The pungent smell of horsetail filled the air.

"I'm fine." Jayfeather climbed into his nest. "What are you doing?"

"Cinderheart told me to soak herbs for Mousefur's tick," Briarlight explained. "She's put on a poultice but she wants a fresh one ready for the morning."

The brambles rustled at the den entrance. Jayfeather tasted the air. "Brightheart?"

For some reason, joy and anxiety were clouding the warrior's thoughts. Tired to his bones, Jayfeather ignored the buzz of emotions and began washing his stinging muzzle.

Brightheart padded to his nest. "Can I speak to you?"

"Can't it wait till the morning?" Jayfeather just wanted to sleep.

"It won't take long." Brightheart sat down heavily beside

his nest. "I'm expecting kits." Jayfeather heard a note of uncertainty in her voice. "They'll be okay, won't they? Even though I'm not as young as I used to be?"

Jayfeather sat up straight. Why would any cat bring kits into the world now? They would just be more lives to give up to the Dark Forest warriors! "What were you thinking?" he snapped. "Leaf-bare's on the way and we might starve without having extra mouths to feed!"

Brightheart reared back. "B-but—"

He didn't let her finish. "What a dumb time to have kits! Is everyone here a mouse-brain?"

Brightheart stood up. "How dare you speak to me like that?" Anger sparked from her pelt. "I never thought I'd have kits again, and they won't be the first to be born in leaf-bare. I thought you'd be pleased!"

"Kits!" Briarlight hauled herself quickly across the den. "That's great news!"

"Try telling that to Jayfeather," Brightheart growled.

"Why?" Briarlight sounded baffled.

"StarClan knows!" Brightheart stalked out of the den and Jayfeather sank into his nest.

"Well? What's up?" Briarlight prompted.

Jayfeather tucked his nose under his paw and ignored her. Weariness washed over him. How could he ever find enough strength to fight the Dark Forest?

CHAPTER 8

Lionblaze followed the moonlit trail back to camp. *Should I tell Hollyleaf she's the fourth cat?* The thought had been stuck like a burr in his mind since Jayfeather had told them about the Tribe's prophecy. *But what if she's not? She wanted to be one of the Three so much. Is it fair to raise her hopes again?*

Lionblaze tried to think about something else. Overhead the trees rustled in the breeze. The birds were quiet now that night had fallen. He glanced over his shoulder. Sorreltail and Squirrelflight padded behind him. They'd patrolled the borders. There was no sign of trouble. Now they were heading home.

Squirrelflight yawned. "I can't wait to get to my nest."

Sorreltail shook out her pelt. "It's not that late." She glanced up. "It's just getting dark earlier."

Squirrelflight shivered. "And chilly."

Why do we need a fourth cat? Lionblaze's mind started whirling again. *Doesn't StarClan believe in us?* A small pang jabbed his heart. *I was going to save the Clans. It was my destiny. But now . . .* Now the prophecy had changed. Lionblaze stared at his paws as they followed the well-worn trail down toward the hollow.

Has my destiny changed, too?

"Is everything quiet?" Firestar was waiting for them in the clearing. The camp looked deserted, the Clan tucked in their dens for the night.

"WindClan re-marked its border," Lionblaze reported. "ShadowClan seems to have been sniffing around the big bramble, but they haven't strayed into our territory."

Firestar's green gaze glittered in the dark. "Anything else?"

Lionblaze knew he was asking if there was any sign of the Dark Forest warriors. *Surely they couldn't break through from the Place of No Stars?* But Lionblaze had seen the wounds Ivypool carried back from her dreams. Those were real enough.

"Nothing," Lionblaze reported. He dipped his head to the ThunderClan leader and headed for the warriors' den. His nest was tucked near to the trunk of the fallen beech and he picked his way carefully among the sleeping warriors, settling eventually beside Cinderheart, asleep in her nest. He closed his eyes. But his mind kept churning.

"Hey!" Cinderheart jerked her head up. "Stop fidgeting!"

"Sorry." Lionblaze lifted his muzzle.

"Can't you sleep?" Cinderheart blinked at him.

"I'm not used to the early nights," he admitted.

Cinderheart heaved herself to her paws. "Come on." She hopped out of her nest. "Let's go for a walk."

Lionblaze watched her slide from the den. *Like we used to.* Hope flickered in his chest. He followed Cinderheart into the clearing. The moonlight turned her gray pelt silver.

"Don't look at me like that," she muttered, turning as he

reached her and stalking away toward the thorn barrier. Confused, Lionblaze followed as she led him up the slope and out of the forest. The lake glittered below them.

"Come on." Cinderheart raced away along the ridge.

Lionblaze bounded after her, speeding down the hillside, swerving around bushes, his paws skidding on the grass. At the bottom, he leaped the short, steep drop onto the beach.

Cinderheart was already waiting at the water's edge. "When I see the lake like this, it feels like nothing could ever go wrong. Not for us, not for any of the Clans."

Lionblaze followed her gaze toward the distant shore. The marshlands of RiverClan glowed beneath the moon, rippling in the starlight as wind stirred the reeds. He could feel Cinderheart's pelt brushing his.

"It's never going to happen, is it?" Cinderheart turned her sad, blue gaze on him. "No matter how much we want it to."

"What's never going to happen?" Suddenly Lionblaze wished he hadn't spoken. He knew what she meant, and he didn't want to hear her answer.

She turned back toward the lake. "We have to stop fighting our destinies."

"I'm not fighting mine."

"Really?" Cinderheart rested against him for a moment. "Then why did you follow me here?"

"How do I know you're not part of my destiny?"

Cinderheart pointed her muzzle toward the stars. "You're closer to them than you are to me."

"That's not true!"

"But StarClan has chosen *you* to protect the Clans." Pebbles crunched beneath her paws. "I can't get in the way of something so important."

"Don't *I* get to choose?" Lionblaze argued.

Cinderheart looked at him. "It's not that simple. I need to figure out my own destiny, too. I have to find out if I'm supposed to be a medicine cat or a warrior. And I can't do that if I take a mate."

Lionblaze bristled. "So you wouldn't choose me over your destiny?"

"Do you want me to make the same mistake Leafpool did?"

Her words sliced through his heart. "That's not fair!"

"None of this is fair." Cinderheart turned and headed for the slope. "We have to make the right choice. Lives depend on it." She glanced back. "Are you coming?"

Lionblaze ignored her. The lake reflected his face, dark against the starry sky. He stared down, losing himself in the image he saw there. *Is that really me?*

Jerking back, Lionblaze growled, "I can't do this anymore." He turned, hoping to see Cinderheart's warm gaze, but she'd gone. Suddenly weary, he sank onto the stones and closed his eyes.

Lionblaze woke feeling stiff and cold. Water lapped at the pebbles a whisker from his nose. Dew soaked his pelt. Above the moor, a streak of pale dawn lit the sky. Wincing, he stumbled to his paws and shook out his fur. *I'll show Cinderheart we don't have to be ruled by our destinies.* Numb with cold, he headed up the hillside and into the trees.

A gray pelt was moving between the bushes down below. *Graystripe.* Lionblaze tasted the air. *Cloudtail, Squirrelflight, and Millie too.* It must be the dawn patrol. Plunging down the slope, he raced to catch up.

"Can I join you?" He skidded to a halt behind Squirrelflight.

She spun to face him, her eyes wide. "Lionblaze!"

Graystripe turned. "Were you out all night?" His gaze swept along Lionblaze's damp pelt.

"I slept by the lake," Lionblaze murmured.

Cloudtail tipped his head. "Are you okay?"

"Of course." Lionblaze paced around his Clanmates. "Where are we heading?"

Millie crunched over the leaves and stood beside him. "The ShadowClan border."

"Good." Lionblaze ducked beneath an arching fern and nosed his way into a swath of bracken. His paws itched for trouble.

Graystripe pushed past him, bending the brown stalks to take the lead. Lionblaze fell back. Fresh warrior scents were drifting on the wind. He called to Graystripe, "Can you smell that?"

"Smells like Ratscar," Graystripe growled. The gray warrior quickened his pace. Lionblaze speeded into a trot, pelt pricking with excitement.

Graystripe bristled. "I can see them!"

Six ShadowClan warriors moved along the border.

Lionblaze's fur rippled along his spine. He opened his mouth, the scents of ShadowClan so strong they soured his tongue. Cloudtail unsheathed his claws and let them sink into the soft earth as if he was imagining a ShadowClan pelt beneath his paws. Millie halted beside the white warrior, her tail bushed up. Squirrelflight arched her back.

A growl rumbled in Millie's throat. "Are they planning an invasion?"

Lionblaze flattened his ears. "They wouldn't dare."

Sniffing trees and ferns, the ShadowClan warriors seemed to be searching for something.

"Come on!" Lionblaze surged forward.

Graystripe chased after him with Squirrelflight and Millie pounding behind. Cloudtail swung wide, protecting the patrol's flank. The ShadowClan warriors froze as the ThunderClan warriors skidded to a halt at the border. Lionblaze recognized Ratscar, Smokefoot, and Stoatpaw. With a growl he spotted Dawnpelt behind them, Snowbird and Olivenose beside her.

"What are you doing here?" He scanned the ground on the ThunderClan side of the border, looking for claw marks or leaves disturbed by ShadowClan paws.

"Don't bother!" Ratscar squared his shoulders, hissing. "We haven't crossed the scent line."

Smokefoot stepped forward. "Which is more than you can say."

Cloudtail stiffened. "What are you talking about?"

Stoatpaw darted to the boundary and hissed. "A

ThunderClan cat has been on our land!"

Lionblaze tasted the air again. *Dovewing!* Her scent hit his nose, fresher than the ShadowClan stench pouring across the border. *She must have been spying.*

Dawnpelt barged past Ratscar and leaned across the border, spitting, "So you're trespassers as well as murderers!"

"Let me check." He strode across the border, tail whipping behind him. He sniffed out Dovewing's scent in a moment and stood squarely on it, masking it with his own. "I smell nothing."

Ratscar glared at him. "Get off our land."

Lionblaze flexed his claws as the ShadowClan warriors closed in. This was the perfect chance to show Cinderheart he shaped his *own* future.

"Get back here!" Graystripe ordered.

"What's the matter?" Lionblaze looked slowly around at the ShadowClan cats. "Are you scared I'll hurt someone?"

"Get back, Lionblaze!" Graystripe growled. "We didn't come here to start a fight."

Lionblaze lifted his chin. "Perhaps we got here just in time to stop one," he growled.

Ratscar backed away. "Is he crazy?" He eyed Graystripe nervously.

Graystripe watched Lionblaze through narrowed eyes. "Are you sure you want to do this?"

Squirrelflight's eyes widened. "Come back, Lionblaze!"

Lionblaze flicked his tail toward her. "They claimed a ThunderClan cat had been on their land," he snarled. "I'm just giving them proof." He spat at Ratscar. "Happy now?"

Ratscar narrowed his eyes. "Stoatpaw," he murmured. "You wanted a chance to practice your attack moves." He nodded toward Lionblaze. "Go on. Try them."

Stoatpaw's whiskers twitched and the skinny ginger apprentice dropped into an attack crouch. *Not him!* Lionblaze bristled with frustration as the ShadowClan cat hurled himself forward. He reared up and batted Stoatpaw away. *Who's going to believe I was beaten by an apprentice?* While Stoatpaw scrambled to his paws, Lionblaze glared at Ratscar. "Does ShadowClan send its apprentices into battle first?"

Ratscar drew back his lips, showing stained, yellow teeth.

Lionblaze pressed harder. "Do you want me to finish him off before I start on you?"

With a screech, Ratscar lunged toward Lionblaze.

"Help him!" Squirrelflight darted forward but Graystripe trapped her tail under one of his front paws.

"He started this fight," the warrior growled. "Let him finish it."

"No!" Lionblaze yowled as Ratscar hit him. Lionblaze lifted his paws to shield his face from the worst of the blows, but he didn't attempt to strike back; they rained hard and fast and Lionblaze could feel clumps of fur being ripped from his cheeks and shoulders and flanks as he ducked down. *Don't fight back! Don't fight back!*

When he could feel blood running through his fur, he rolled over and thrust Ratscar away with his hind paws. *They mustn't think I let him win.* Aware of his Clanmates watching in horror,

Lionblaze swept out a paw and hooked Ratscar's paws from under him in a classic battle move. But Ratscar was no fool. He leaped in time and Lionblaze caught nothing but leaves.

Claws pierced his pelt, reaching deep until Lionblaze screeched out loud. *Is this what it feels like for other cats?*

"Get off our land." With a mighty heave, Ratscar shoved Lionblaze backward, sending him staggering over the border.

Teeth grabbed his scruff. "Enough!" Graystripe was pinning him to the ground. "Hold him!" he ordered Squirrelflight and Cloudtail.

Lionblaze felt their paws press him down. His muzzle scraped leaves as he struggled to see what was happening.

"I'm sorry." Graystripe faced Ratscar. "We had no orders to cross into your territory."

"Don't ThunderClan warriors understand discipline?" Ratscar scolded. His eyes flashed with satisfaction.

"Tensions are running high in all the Clans," Graystripe reminded him.

Dawnpelt flexed her claws. "In that case, you should go home."

Stoatpaw paced the border, fur bushed. "Unless you really want a battle."

Graystripe backed away with his ears flat. "Come on," he growled to his patrol. "Let's go."

Lionblaze felt the paws lift from his spine and he jumped up. Pain seared beneath his pelt. It filled him with satisfaction. *I don't have to be invincible!* Limping, he followed his Clanmates away from the border. *I can choose my destiny!*

"Tell Firestar that there will be a real battle if any more ThunderClan cats cross the border!" Ratscar yowled after them.

Graystripe stiffened, but kept his eyes fixed ahead. Lionblaze glanced sideways and caught Squirrelflight's shocked gaze. *They must think I've turned hare-brained.* He lifted his chin and padded silently after his Clanmates.

"What in the name of StarClan did you think you were doing?" Graystripe suddenly turned on Lionblaze.

Squirrelflight wove between them. "He crossed the border deliberately." She searched Lionblaze's gaze. "Didn't you? You were covering up a ThunderClan scent, weren't you?"

Graystripe nosed Squirrelflight away. "He didn't have to start a fight."

Lionblaze pushed past the gray warrior. "I'm sorry, okay?"

Graystripe growled. "Let's see what Firestar's got to say."

The patrol walked on in silence, tails twitching. Lionblaze winced with each paw step. Blood dripped into his eyes.

Cloudtail padded beside him. "Lean on me," he murmured.

Lionblaze shook his head and quickened his pace. He was first back in camp.

"Lionblaze!" Sandstorm's shocked mew greeted him as he wriggled through the thorns.

"What happened?" Spiderleg bounded across the clearing. Berrynose and Poppyfrost crowded around.

"ShadowClan patrol," Lionblaze muttered.

Poppyfrost stared at him in amazement. "But you're our best warrior." She blinked as the rest of the patrol emerged from the barrier. "The ShadowClan patrol must have put up quite a fight."

"Lionblaze?" Cinderheart's mew made him turn to the fresh-kill pile, where she had been depositing a thrush. Lionblaze blinked the blood from his eyes and gazed at her.

"What have you done? You're not supposed to get hurt! What happened?" Cinderheart was at his side in a couple of paces, lapping the blood from his muzzle. Then she stiffened. "There's only one way this could have happened. You did this on purpose." Her words were no more than a breath in his ear. "Tell me you didn't." She backed away, staring at him.

"You told me we could choose our destiny," he reminded her, feeling a stone of fear in his belly. "I chose to be an ordinary warrior for once."

Cinderheart blinked. "I told you we had to make the *right* choice!"

"How do you know I didn't?"

"Look at yourself!" she hissed, gesturing with one paw at his wounds.

Lionblaze's heart seemed to split as Cinderheart turned and walked away, the fur bristling along her spine. A flash of gray fur caught his eye.

"Come on." Jayfeather was beside him, nosing him gently toward the medicine den. Lionblaze braced himself for another lecture. He was ready to be told he was a mouse-brain. A traitor, even, because he had rejected the prophecy. But Jayfeather just guided him through the brambles into his den.

Briarlight was lying in her nest, propped up on her forelegs.

"What happened?" she gasped as she caught sight of Lionblaze.

"Go and get some fresh-kill," Jayfeather told her.

"But—"

Jayfeather flicked his tail. "Now."

Hauling herself over the edge of her nest, Briarlight dragged her hind legs out through the entrance.

Jayfeather padded to the crack in the rock at the back of the den. "Sit down." He stuck his head into the shadows and pulled out a wad of leaves. Crouching, he began to chew them into a poultice.

The brambles swished at the mouth of the den. "Are you going to explain to me what just happened?" Firestar stood in the entrance, green eyes sharp with rage. "Graystripe told me that you started a fight with a ShadowClan patrol!" His ears twitched as he studied Lionblaze. "Why did you let them do that to you?"

Lionblaze stiffened. "Do I have to win every fight?"

"Yes!" Firestar thrust his muzzle into Lionblaze's face. "That's your destiny! That's what the prophecy has decided!"

Lionblaze growled. "So I don't get a choice?"

"No! You don't get a choice!" Firestar flexed his claws. "You have to follow your destiny."

Fury swept through Lionblaze like wildfire. "I wish I didn't! I never asked for it! You can't make me do anything I don't want to do!"

Firestar stared at him a moment, then took a step back. "You're right." His mew was weary. "I can't force you to follow the path StarClan has chosen for you, Lionblaze." His tail brushed the ground as he turned. "It's a destiny you must choose for yourself."

Lionblaze watched his leader disappear through the brambles. "So?" He turned on Jayfeather. "Aren't you going to tell me how dumb I am, too? Go on!" he goaded. "Remind me *again* how the prophecy is the most important thing in the world!"

Jayfeather picked up a mouthful of chewed leaves and padded to Lionblaze's side. He dropped the leaves and rolled them under his paw. "No."

Lionblaze blinked. *"What?"*

Jayfeather lapped up a tongueful of leaf pulp and licked it into a wound. Lionblaze gritted his teeth, shocked by the pain. "Whatever you want to say, get it over with!"

Jayfeather sat back on his haunches. "What *can* I say?" he murmured. "What if the prophecy isn't enough to save the Clans? What if it's just the last desperate hope of a Clan of fading ancestors?" He sniffed a long scratch on Lionblaze's cheek. "You can fight; Dovewing can hear; I can wander into thoughts and dreams. But does it make any difference? Are we any closer to defeating the Dark Forest? If we were, why would we need a fourth cat?"

"You think the prophecy won't save the Clans?" Lionblaze suddenly forgot the sting of his scratches.

"I don't know." Sighing, Jayfeather began working on the rest of Lionblaze's wounds.

Lionblaze lay back on the hard stone floor. Could his brother be right? Was the prophecy nothing more than StarClan's last hope?

CHAPTER 9

❧

"No, not like that!" Bumblestripe yowled.

Dovewing spun around to face him, gripping hard on the branch to stop herself from falling out of the tree. "You told me to climb, I'm climbing!" she snapped. *Can't I do anything right?*

"Not the *trunk*." Bumblestripe padded along the thick oak branch toward her. "In a battle, if *every* cat climbed the trunk, it'd be chaos." He tipped his nose up and focused on the branch two tail-lengths above his head. Crouching, he sprang and gripped it with his forepaws, then hauled himself up. "Your turn." He peered at her through the browning leaves.

Dovewing scowled. Hunkering down, she bunched her muscles, then leaped and dug her claws into the branch above. Flicking her tail, she landed nimbly beside Bumblestripe. "Is that better?" she sniffed.

Bumblestripe glanced at the leaves she'd sent fluttering to the ground. "You really need to aim for a bare bit of branch," he suggested. "The enemy's going to know you're here if you shower him with leaves every time you move."

Dovewing clamped her jaws together to stop herself from

snarling at the arrogant furball. *I can't believe I ever thought we might be more than just friends!* Seeing Tigerheart again made her realize what a dumb choice that would have been. *I only ever liked you because you're a ThunderClan cat.* Tigerheart wouldn't bother about whether she climbed the trunk or rustled too many leaves. He was a warrior, not a worrier!

They'd been practicing tree-battle all morning and Dovewing was hot and tired. "Why are we doing this?" she grumbled at Brambleclaw. "What cat is going to climb a tree to fight? There is no SquirrelClan!"

Bumblestripe flashed her a warning look. "Shut up!" he hissed.

But Brambleclaw was already bounding along the narrow rowan branch. It bounced under his weight, making Toadstep cling on with his fur spiked up. Brambleclaw jumped and cleared the space between the trees easily. The sturdy oak hardly trembled as he landed. "I know some cats don't like tree training," he meowed as he padded along the branch toward them. "But it gives us a strong advantage over the other Clans. If we can move through our territory and attack from above them, it's a great surprise."

Dovewing rolled her eyes. "I *know*. But Bumblestripe's acting like I've never been up a tree before. Every time I do something wrong he points it out like I hadn't already noticed."

Bumblestripe stared at his paws. "I was just trying to help."

Brambleclaw flicked his tail. "It's good of Bumblestripe to be so patient with you, Dovewing."

"*Patient?*" Dovewing retorted. He'd criticized every move.

"Can't we just move on to drop attacks and go hunting?"

"Is she ready for drop attacks?" Brambleclaw asked Bumblestripe.

"I guess." Bumblestripe's ear twitched. "Having seen her tree skills, I think she'd better practice falling out of them."

Dovewing glared at him. "Okay!" she snapped. "I'll practice climbing some more!" Bristling, she bounded onto a higher branch and kept jumping till Brambleclaw and Bumblestripe were nothing more than patches of fur far away through the leaves. Relieved to be away from Bumblestripe's fussing, she stared out across the forest. She hadn't been this high since her night with Tigerheart. She could see the wooded hillside they'd chased along. It looked a long way off. She could hardly believe they'd traveled so far in a single night.

Her ears pricked up. ShadowClan voices sounded at the border. Dovewing stiffened, listening harder.

"What's the point of visiting the ThunderClan camp?" She recognized Ratscar's growl. "Firestar will just make lame excuses."

Blackstar answered him. "He can make as many as he likes, as long as he gets the message."

"He should be grateful we didn't turn Lionblaze into crow-food," Ratscar muttered.

"ShadowClan!" Dovewing hissed down to her Clanmates.

Brambleclaw's gaze flashed up through the leaves. "Where?"

"Heading for our camp!" She scrambled down, slithering from branch to branch until she landed beside Brambleclaw and Bumblestripe.

Bumblestripe swiveled his ears. "I can't hear them."

"Too many leaves," Dovewing mewed quickly. "It sounds clearer up there."

Brambleclaw lashed his tail. "It must be an invasion!"

"No!" Dovewing thought fast. How could she explain that they were planning to talk to Firestar, not attack the camp, without giving away her secret power? "It's a small patrol by the sound of it, and they're not even trying to keep quiet."

Dovewing could hear the ShadowClan patrol heading past the Ancient Oak. "If we hurry, we'll get to camp before them."

"We should find them first," Toadstep growled. "And offer them an escort the rest of the way."

Dovewing flicked her tail toward camp. "Shouldn't we warn Firestar?"

Brambleclaw flexed his claws. "You're right." He glanced back into the forest. "Let them find their own way to the hollow." He bounded away, taking a trail that cut through a clearing and skirted the training hollow.

Dovewing listened harder. The ShadowClan patrol had stopped speaking but she could hear their paws scuffing the earth as they headed toward camp. She quickened her pace, following Brambleclaw's tail as it whipped between bushes ahead of her. Toadstep ran behind, his paws thrumming on the leaves.

Just as they made it into the hollow, Dovewing heard ferns swish behind them. She turned to see Ratscar and Tigerheart appear at the top of the slope. Stoatpaw stood at their side, his eyes glittering.

Blackstar padded from the rear and stared down at the ThunderClan warriors. "I'm here to speak with Firestar."

Brambleclaw dipped his head and signaled with his tail.

Firestar was waiting beneath Highledge, his head high and his pelt smooth. Dovewing scurried around the edge of the clearing to join her Clan leader. "They're coming to talk about the fight with Lionblaze," she whispered.

"Thanks, Dovewing." Firestar shifted his paws and lifted his chin higher as Blackstar halted in the center of the clearing. "Lionblaze!"

Lionblaze padded from the warriors' den, eyes narrowed. The wounds from his fight were still visible through his pelt. His muzzle was striped with dried blood. His gaze swept past Blackstar and met Firestar's. "What do they want?"

Blackstar growled. "You know what it's about!"

Firestar stepped forward. "Lionblaze crossed your border and provoked a fight."

Ratscar drew back his lip. "At least they admit it."

"ThunderClan warriors don't lie," Firestar told him evenly. "Nor do they make excuses for their mistakes." His green gaze flicked to Lionblaze.

Dovewing felt tension thicken the air. She fixed her gaze on Blackstar, trying not to look at Tigerheart, even though his dark, sleek pelt flashed temptingly at the edge of her vision.

Firestar's tail twitched as he frowned at Lionblaze. "Well?"

Lionblaze flexed his claws, then sheathed them again. "I'm sorry," he muttered.

Blackstar tipped his head to one side. "By the look of you,

I'm not surprised you're sorry." He turned back to Firestar. "Ratscar is a fine warrior, but he expected Lionblaze to be harder to beat."

"It was like fighting an apprentice," Ratscar scorned.

Lionblaze flattened his ears. Dovewing could hear a soft growl rumbling in the golden warrior's throat.

Blackstar circled his Clanmates. "Now is not a good time to be losing your edge," he snarled menacingly to Firestar.

Firestar stepped forward, fur spiking. "And it's not a good time to be making threats you can't back up." He met the ShadowClan leader's stare without flinching. "I think you should leave."

"Only when you've given your word that your warriors will stay off our land," Blackstar countered.

"I crossed the border *once*," Lionblaze hissed.

"There was another scent," Stoatpaw blurted out.

Dovewing gulped. *I must be more careful!* She sneaked a sly look at Tigerheart. He was staring at his paws.

Firestar's ear twitched. "Are you sure your Clanmates aren't mistaking rabbits for warriors?"

Blackstar's gaze flitted toward Lionblaze. "If we are, it's an easy mistake to make."

"Are you calling me a rabbit—"

Firestar cut Lionblaze off. "It's time you left," he ordered Blackstar. "Do you need an escort?"

"What about the trespassing?" Blackstar held his ground.

"No ThunderClan warrior will cross your border," Firestar told him.

Blackstar flicked his tail. "Good." He turned and headed for the barrier. "And don't bother with the escort. We can find our own way home."

Dovewing watched Tigerheart fall in behind the Shadow-Clan leader. As he passed her, his gaze caught hers. She looked away quickly, feeling hot.

Bumblestripe crossed the clearing as the ShadowClan patrol disappeared. "Do you still want to go hunting?"

Dovewing blinked at him. "What?"

"You said you wanted to go hunting after tree training."

"Did I?" Dovewing stared at the entrance. The thorns still trembling where Tigerheart had slid through.

Bumblestripe's pelt lifted along his spine. "And while we're out, we can make sure those ShadowClan cats have left our territory."

Dovewing dragged her gaze from the brambles. "Let's take Foxleap." She didn't want to hunt alone with Bumblestripe. He'd only fuss over her stalking technique. "Hey, Foxleap!"

The russet warrior was pacing by the entrance to the hollow, his tail twitching. "What?"

"We're going hunting," Dovewing called. "Do you want to come?"

Foxleap narrowed his eyes. "I want to make sure Blackstar's crossed the border."

Bumblestripe stretched his claws. "We can do that as well."

Blossomfall crossed the clearing. "I'm coming too," she growled. "While I still have the taste of ShadowClan on my tongue."

As Bumblestripe headed for the entrance, Blossomfall raced past him and slipped out of the camp first. Foxleap chased after them. Dovewing paused. The clearing still smelled of Tigerheart.

"Come on!" Foxleap beckoned her with his tail.

She hurried to catch up. By the time she ducked out of the thorns, Bumblestripe, Foxleap, and Blossomfall were racing up the slope.

"We're heading for the ShadowClan border," Bumblestripe called over his shoulder. "Are you coming?"

"I'll check the beeches, in case they've strayed deeper into the forest." Dovewing was glad of the chance to be alone.

"Pssst!" A hiss from an elderflower bush made her jump.

Dovewing tasted the air. "Tigerheart!" Heart lurching, she jerked around, scanning the forest for her Clanmates.

"It's okay." Tigerheart slid out from beneath the bush. "They're busy tracking Blackstar. I doubled back to find you."

"How did you know I'd be out of the hollow?"

His whiskers twitched. "Just a hunch."

She flattened her ears. "And you assumed I'd follow you?" she mewed indignantly.

"It's not every day I get an excuse to be in ThunderClan territory." Tigerheart shrugged. "We might as well make the most of it." His bright gaze softened. "I've missed you."

Dovewing nudged her head against his shoulder. "Me too."

"I can't stay long." Tigerheart glanced over the top of her head. "I told them I was just checking scents to see if I can match any to the one we found over the border."

Dovewing dropped her gaze. "We can't make that mistake again. It'd be even harder to see each other if the Clans were at war."

"Next time we'll meet outside the Clan borders."

"The Twoleg nest?"

Tigerheart nodded. "Can you come tonight?"

Dovewing rubbed her muzzle along his jaw, excitement fizzing in her paws. "I'll try to get there just before moon-high."

"Great." Tigerheart peeled away from her and began to head into the trees. "I can't wait." He looked back over his shoulder. His dark amber gaze made her heart swell.

Dovewing shivered with excitement as he bounded away between the trees.

"Can you smell ShadowClan?" The ferns beside her quivered and Bumblestripe padded out.

Dovewing tried not to look too startled. "Er, yes, I can." She shifted her paws. "They must have come this way."

Bumblestripe frowned. "I thought I'd tracked them to the border."

"Maybe they made a detour on the way and you didn't notice." Dovewing twitched her ears, trying to sound unconcerned. "They're gone now." She tasted the air, relishing the fading scent of Tigerheart. "The scent's stale already."

Bumblestripe wrinkled his nose. "Typical ShadowClan," he growled. "They never do anything straight. They only came to the camp to gloat about beating Lionblaze."

"ShadowClan cats have always been fox-hearted." Dovewing

stared at her paws. *And handsome.* She looked up, surprised to see Bumblestripe's eyes dark with worry.

"I'm sorry," he blurted out. His tail brushed the ground.

"What for?"

"About being so fussy about the tree training."

Dovewing had forgotten all about it. "Oh." She flicked his shoulder with her tail-tip. "That's okay. I was being a pain."

Bumblestripe brightened. "That's true."

"Hey!" Dovewing swiped him playfully with a paw.

Bumblestripe ducked, purring. "Should we get on with that hunt?"

"Okay." Tigerheart must have made it to the border by now. But just to be sure, Dovewing led Bumblestripe deeper into the forest, in the opposite direction. "Let's see what we can find near the beech copse."

"Come on!" Dovewing jumped down from the star-dappled ribs of the Twoleg nest. "Let's follow the beaver trail."

Tigerheart landed beside her. "Beaver trail?"

"The one we followed to the dam."

Tigerheart blinked. "That feels like a lifetime ago! I had only just been made a warrior. Now I feel like a different cat, but the same, if you know what I mean." His eyes narrowed thoughtfully.

Dovewing understood exactly how he felt. Back then, she'd just learned she was one of the Three. She didn't realize then how much it was going to shape her life. *Now the whole Clan's depending on me.* Her belly tightened. She pushed away the thought of the Dark Forest and the battle to come. She only wanted to be here, now, with Tigerheart. "Next leaf-fall you might be living in ThunderClan," she whispered. The idea made her warm. "We might have kits."

Cold air hit her pelt as Tigerheart drew away. "Whoa!" He glanced sideways at her, not breaking his pace. "That's not important right now, is it?" His mew was light, but his words felt like a claw-scratch on Dovewing's heart.

"O-of course not!" Why had she blurted out such nonsense? If Tigerheart wasn't ready, that was okay. *Just being a warrior is great!*

Her ears twitched. *Voices?* She listened harder. There were paw steps moving through ThunderClan territory, far away below them. *Perhaps Firestar has ordered a night patrol.* She tried to make out the voices, but they sounded unfamiliar. And they were edged with anger.

"Come on!" Tigerheart flicked her flank with his tail and shot off into the darkness. "Let's race!"

"You'll lose!" She bounded after him, her paws scattering leaves. The forest blurred around her as she ran, the earth thrumming beneath her paws. Tigerstar's pelt flashed between the trees a few tail-lengths ahead. "I'll catch you!" she yowled. Blood pounded in her ears, drowning out the murmuring from ThunderClan territory. It was probably nothing. Surely her Clanmates could cope without her for one night?

CHAPTER 10

♣

Ivypool shuddered. Mist swirled around her paws. The Dark Forest seemed colder than ever. Was it leaf-bare here, too? She glanced up at the trees, searching for browning leaves, but darkness swallowed their branches.

"Tonight will change everything."

Tigerstar's growl yanked her back to the present. The dark warrior stood on a fallen tree, his claws curling into the slimy moss. Shredtail, Hawkfrost, and Darkstripe stared up at him while Mapleshade hung back in the shadows with Sparrowfeather. Thistleclaw and Brokenstar watched through slitted eyes. Applefur, Hollowflight, and Redwillow clustered together, their fur spiked with excitement. Birchfall and Beetlewhisker were there too, as well as Tigerheart and Furzepelt. *How could so many cats have fallen for Tigerstar's lies?*

Tigerstar's eyes gleamed. "This mission will be the first of many."

Ivypool leaned closer to Blossomfall. "The first of many whats?" She hadn't been listening.

Blossomfall stuck her muzzle in Ivypool's ear. "Special patrols. Tigerstar's going to start taking us into Clan territories."

Ivypool felt sick. She stared at the dark warrior, his shoulders rippling in the eerie light.

"Knowledge is power." Tigerstar's amber gaze swung around and fixed on her.

Ivypool met his eyes, chin high, and held it as he went on.

"Knowledge of your battle territory will give you the greatest advantage imaginable because it will be the last thing your enemies expect. Most of you are unfamiliar with the territories beside the lake, so I will be taking you to visit each Clan—without them realizing, of course—and you can learn the best places to fight."

Redwillow stepped forward. "Where to lie in wait!"

Hollowflight clawed the earth. "Where to corner your enemy."

Thistleclaw swung his long, gray tail. "And where to chase your *prey*."

Prey? Ivypool dug her claws into the ground to stop her paws from shaking. *He means warriors.*

Blossomfall's breath stirred her ear. *"Four Clans will unite as one when it matters most."* She was quoting Tigerstar! "We'll be able to fight for whichever Clan needs our help."

Ivypool jerked her head around and stared at her Clanmate. *How can you be so dumb?* She turned back to Tigerstar. "Which territory will we start with?" she called.

Tigerstar's whiskers twitched. "ThunderClan."

"*I'd* like to see that." Mapleshade shambled forward.

"Me too!" Sparrowfeather bounded to the fading warrior's side.

Tigerstar narrowed his eyes. "Any other volunteers?"

Tigerheart and Furzepelt shouldered their way to the front.

Tigerstar nodded. "And from RiverClan?" His gaze stopped at Beetlewhisker. "You'll do. And Hollowflight."

Ivypool stared straight at Tigerstar. Was he only going to show ThunderClan's territory to the other Clans? She stepped forward. "What about *my* apprentices?" she challenged. "Birchfall and Redwillow deserve to go." Ivypool tipped her head toward Blossomfall. "And her." *Go on! Refuse!* If Tigerstar only showed ThunderClan territory to their enemies, *someone* must work out that he wasn't doing it for the good of the Clans but for his own twisted reasons. She willed Tigerstar to give himself away.

Tigerstar dipped his head. "Very well, Ivypool. They can come too."

"And me?" She stepped closer.

Tigerstar showed his teeth. "Of course," he murmured smoothly. "You can be our guide." The dark warrior nodded to Brokenstar. "I'll report back when we return." He leaped from the log and padded between the trees, signaling with his tail.

As Ivypool followed the patrol, she glanced over her shoulder, then scanned the trees and bushes they passed. If this route led from the Dark Forest to the lake territories, she wanted to remember it. They walked through gloomy glades, past foul-smelling bogs and across streams that were no more than muddy trickles. The earth beneath Ivypool's paws, at first slippery with moss, suddenly softened into grass. Ivypool looked up. She could see the branches of the trees above her head. The shadows had lifted and beyond them the moon shone in a wide, starry sky.

We've crossed over! She didn't recognize the slope that rose ahead of them. But as they climbed, brambles began to crowd the trail. The trunks of the trees suddenly became familiar, and the ferns spilling across their path were rich with ThunderClan scents.

Hollowflight wrinkled his nose. "How can you live with this stench?" he murmured to Ivypool.

Ivypool flicked the RiverClan warrior's ear with her tail. "If you put up with our scent, then I'll put up with yours when we visit RiverClan's territory," she teased.

Redwillow fell in beside them. "Thanks for getting me on the patrol," he whispered. "The more I learn, the sooner I'll be like a real Dark Forest warrior."

"A *real* Dark Forest warrior?" Ivypool jerked her head around and stared at him. "Don't you just want to be the best ShadowClan warrior you can be?"

"Dark Forest warriors are *way* stronger." Hollowflight nudged her. "And they don't worry about rules."

Redwillow nodded. "I feel like I'm training with kittypets when I'm with my Clanmates."

"Here, only the strongest survive," Hollowflight growled.

"It should be like that in the Clans," Redwillow added.

Ivypool stared at him. "Would you let your Clanmates die if they were weak?"

Alarm sparked in Redwillow's eyes as though he realized

he'd revealed too much. "O-of course not." His gaze flashed to Hollowflight. "We were just saying that we've got a lot to learn from the Dark Forest warriors, that's all. So we can be true warriors."

"Yeah." Ivypool kept walking, trying to stop her fur spiking in horror. "I guess that's what we're training for."

Tigerstar halted at the top of the slope, the trees behind him framing the lake below. "See how thick the tree trunks are." He nodded toward a sturdy beech. "That's why we teach you to climb in the Dark Forest. Here in ThunderClan territory you have to be prepared to fight in trees." His gaze sought out Blossomfall's. "Why don't you explain?"

Blossomfall pushed her way to the head of the patrol, her chest puffed out. "All ThunderClan cats are taught to climb so we can drop on enemies from above, and we can move through the forest by jumping from branch to branch without touching the ground."

"Like squirrels," Redwillow muttered.

Blossomfall flicked her tail. "We move like squirrels, but we fight like foxes!"

Ivypool's fur lifted along her spine. Blossomfall was giving away all of ThunderClan's secrets! "We hardly bother with tree-fighting now," she lied quickly.

"But Dovewing and Brambleclaw were practicing earlier!" Blossomfall blurted.

Ivypool caught Birchfall's gaze, relieved to see that his eyes were glittering with worry. *He understands the danger!*

"They don't have to know everything, Blossomfall,"

Birchfall cautioned.

Tigerstar shifted his paws. "Don't worry, Birchfall," he meowed. "We're among friends." He gazed around the patrol. "We're Clanmates now. Secrets aren't necessary."

Mapleshade padded heavily up the slope and stopped beside Tigerstar. "Perhaps Birchfall doesn't feel part of our Clan." There was menace in her mew.

"Of course he does!" Ivypool growled, stepping in front of her father.

"Then why doesn't *he* tell us something about Thunder-Clan territory?" Tigerstar invited.

"I-it's all woods," Birchfall began. Ivypool could tell he was feeling uncomfortable from the way the tip of his tail quivered. "Except for the slopes down to the shore and to the WindClan border."

"And is it better to fight in woodland or the open?" Tiger-star pressed.

Birchfall's gaze darted nervously toward Furzepelt. "Thun-derClan fights better in the woods, I guess," he admitted. "We can use the undergrowth to trap our enemies."

We're giving everything away! Ivypool padded to the top of the slope and stared across the lake toward RiverClan. "Why don't you tell us about your territory, Beetlewhisker?"

Beetlewhisker lifted his tail. "We have pine trees, not oaks," he began.

Brambles swished at the bottom of the slope. Ivypool stiffened. "Someone's coming!" Spiderleg's pelt was moving through the undergrowth below them. Brambleclaw was following him.

"Are you sure you heard voices?" Brambleclaw asked.

"I was guarding the entrance and I heard paw steps." Spiderleg faltered. "I wasn't sure at first if they *were* paw steps, to be honest. I thought I'd imagined them. But then I heard voices coming from this direction."

"It'd better not be another WindClan invasion." Brambleclaw growled. "We should check the tunnel entrances."

"But the voices came from here." Spiderleg's pelt disappeared under ferns as he headed up the slope.

Blood pounded in Ivypool's ears. "We've got to get out of here!" she hissed to Tigerstar.

"And miss a chance to practice our battle skills?" Tigerstar spat back.

"You can't!" Fear shot through Ivypool. "Take us back now!"

"Are you scared of your Clanmates?" Tigerstar's murmur was no more than a breath in her ear.

They mustn't find out I'm visiting the Dark Forest! The brambles shivered below them. Ivypool felt panic rising. "If they find us here," she whispered, "they'll start sending out night patrols." Hope flickered in her belly as Tigerstar's ear twitched. "And when the final battle comes, we'll have lost the advantage of surprise."

Tigerstar narrowed his eyes. "Very well."

Relief rushed through Ivypool as the dark warrior signaled with his tail and led the patrol quickly and silently along the crest of the slope. Swallowed by brambles and creeping

juniper, Ivypool kept low and followed Tigerstar, checking behind to see that the rest of the patrol was keeping up.
The undergrowth grew darker and when she looked up, the
moon had disappeared. The ground turned slimy once more
beneath her paws and ferns gave way to tangled thorn bushes.
Ivypool wrinkled her nose as the air soured with the stench of
decay. They were back in the Dark Forest.

As the patrol broke from a thicket of sticky brambles,
Tigerstar halted.

Mapleshade paced around him. "Why didn't we stay and
fight?"

Blossomfall lifted her muzzle. "We went there to learn, not
to fight."

Redwillow sat down. "I've never been so deep into ThunderClan territory." He ran a paw over his whiskers. "Wait till
you see ShadowClan's forests. They're totally different."

"So is RiverClan territory," Hollowflight chimed in. "The
reed beds make great places for ambushes."

Sparrowfeather flexed his claws. "I'm looking forward to
learning all your territories."

Why can't they see the menace in his eyes? As Ivypool glanced nervously at the Dark Forest warrior, claws pierced her shoulder.

"Don't ever challenge me like that again." Tigerstar thrust
her to the ground, eyes blazing.

Buckling under the pain, Ivypool glared up at him. "I was
only trying to protect the patrol!"

Birchfall's eyes widened with alarm. *Be careful!* Ivypool
stiffened as Birchfall padded toward Tigerstar. *Don't defend me!*

You'll make it worse for both of us.

Birchfall faced Tigerstar. "What exactly was the point of visiting the lake?"

He's trying to distract him. Ivypool felt a flood of relief and gratitude. She winced as Tigerstar's claws sunk deeper into her shoulder. "Why don't you explain it to your Clanmate, Ivypool?" the old warrior snarled.

Ivypool swallowed. "The more we know, the better warriors we can be," she gasped.

Tigerstar loosened his grip.

"We all follow the warrior code," Ivypool continued. She wriggled away from Tigerstar and stood beside her father. "Knowing all the territories like they are our own will help us to help one another." She hated lying to defend Tigerstar but there was no other way to hide her treachery against the Dark Forest.

A growl sounded behind Tigerstar. "How did it go?" Brokenstar padded into the clearing. Behind him, Dark Forest warriors swarmed like rats, their eyes bright with curiosity.

"What was it like?" Shredtail growled.

"Did you see the *stars*?" Darkstripe snarled mockingly.

Ivypool gazed around the ranks of scarred, scowling faces and thought of her Clanmates sleeping peacefully back in the hollow. *They have no idea of the danger they're in.* Her heart ached with pity. *But I promise I'll protect you, right to my very last breath.*

CHAPTER 11

☙

The sun slid behind the trees, washing the hollow with shadow. Sitting outside the medicine den, Jayfeather felt the light disappear and shivered as his Clanmates shared tongues around him.

"They must have been rogues." Brambleclaw's tail flicked against the ground beneath Highledge.

"But Spiderleg said there were *Clan* scents among them," Firestar pointed out.

Sandstorm shifted beside her mate. "Have the other Clans formed an alliance against us?"

"Why would they?" Jayfeather heard tension in the ThunderClan leader's growl.

Graystripe must have heard it too. "It's something we should be prepared for," he cautioned gently.

Despair pressed at the edges of Firestar's thoughts. Jayfeather felt him push it away. "Then we will be prepared." Firestar shifted his paws. "Brambleclaw, organize more patrols in the daytime. And make sure the borders are checked at moonhigh."

Surprise sparked from Brambleclaw's pelt. "You want the whole Clan to get involved in night patrols? Won't that alarm them?"

"If the Clan faces danger, it should know." Firestar's tone was grim.

Jayfeather let his attention drift away and sweep the rest of the Clan. He felt a stab of pain prick from his brother's pelt. Lionblaze was eating a mouse, flinching with every mouthful as the wounds on his cheek stung. *You chose to get hurt!* But Jayfeather's irritation with Lionblaze's decision faded in a flash. He understood why his brother had tried to veer from the path he'd been given.

Claws scraped the ground. Briarlight was hauling herself toward him, her powerful forepaws digging hard into the earth. "I'm going to my nest," she told Jayfeather as she passed.

She's very tired. With a prickle of concern, he sensed weariness in her broken body. "I'll come, too."

Irritation flashed from her pelt. "I can manage!"

"I know," Jayfeather replied. "But I'm sleepy."

He nosed into the medicine den after her. "Why are you so tired?" He tried to hide concern from his mew.

"Millie thought of a new exercise for me." Briarlight yawned. "She and Whitewing hoisted me up to a low branch sticking out of the beech and I hung on with my forepaws for as long as I could."

"That sounds tough." Jayfeather was impressed.

"It was good to feel the breeze on my belly," Briarlight mewed.

"If you keep trying, you may be able to haul yourself right up onto the branch."

"I'm going to practice until I can." Briarlight tipped herself over the edge of her nest and slithered inside.

Jayfeather crossed the den, stopping when he felt the twigs

of her nest poke his forelegs. "Comfortable?" He leaned down and tugged moss up around her, secretly feeling for any fever with his muzzle. She felt cool, her muscles limp with fatigue. Satisfied, he leaned back. "Sleep well, Briarlight."

"Are you okay?" Briarlight's question surprised him. "It seems like there's something on your mind."

"It's nothing," he lied. "I'm just tired." He turned away and padded to his nest. He felt Briarlight watching him for a moment, then heard her rustle deeper into her bed. Climbing into his own pile of soft moss, Jayfeather circled down and tucked his tail over his nose.

The Dark Forest flashed in his mind. Eyes blinked from the shadows. He imagined the army massing beyond his vision.

Borage leaves cure fever. Catmint cures greencough. He began listing remedies in his head to block out the nightmarish thoughts. *Dock soothes scratches. Feverfew cools fever.*

"Can't StarClan guide you?"

Mapleshade's sneer flooded his thoughts. *Comfrey mends broken bones.*

"We shall taste victory soon!"

He could still feel where Hawkfrost had shoved him into the mud. *Mouse bile treats ticks.*

"All the power of the stars in your paws?"

Jayfeather flattened his ears as though he could block out the memory of Tigerstar's jibe.

Marigold stops infection. Coltsfoot eases breathing. Poppy seed soothes pain and shock and brings sleep. Jayfeather fixed his thoughts on the neatly stacked herbs lining the wall of his store, repeating their names over and over until the words grew hazy and jumbled and he slipped into sleep.

When he blinked open his eyes, he could see dense green forest crowded around him, thick with familiar scents. *I'm dreaming.* Birchfall and Spiderleg's musky odor still clung to the bushes they must have passed on patrol. This was Thunder-Clan territory. Jayfeather looked up and saw stars twinkling beyond the canopy of leaves. An owl screeched nearby and branches shivered as it swooped through the forest.

The ferns behind Jayfeather rustled. He turned, tasting the air. "Dovewing? Is that you?"

The young gray she-cat slid out from between the fronds.

"Dovewing?" A second mew echoed Jayfeather's. Lionblaze was padding along the trail toward him.

The three cats stared at one another uncertainly.

"How did I get here?" Dovewing glanced at the trees. "I was in my nest."

"Me too." Lionblaze halted beside Jayfeather.

"We're dreaming," Jayfeather explained.

Lionblaze frowned. "So you're in my dream?"

"We're sharing one."

"Why?" Dovewing peered through the shadows.

Jayfeather nodded toward the short steep slope beside them. A hole yawned in the earth, and the scent of stone and water, of endless dark tunnels, drifted out. "I think we're supposed to go down there."

"Are you sure?" Lionblaze sounded doubtful.

Dovewing padded forward and sniffed the tunnel entrance. "Why else would our dream bring us to this part of the forest?" She padded inside and was swallowed up by the shadows.

"Wait." Lionblaze was staring hard at Jayfeather. "You looked at the tunnel like you could actually see it."

"I can," Jayfeather answered evenly.

"How?" Lionblaze's eyes widened.

"I always see in dreams."

"So you know what I look like?" The idea seemed to shock the golden warrior.

Jayfeather narrowed his eyes. "You looked better when you weren't covered in scratches."

Lionblaze flicked his tail. "I'll heal." He ducked into the hole after Dovewing.

Jayfeather darted after them, pushing past his Clanmates in the crowded space. "I'll lead," he told them. "I'm used to the dark." The floor of the tunnel was damp and muddy beneath his paws. It turned to freezing stone as he headed deeper into blackness. His pads began to ache with cold. He let his whiskers guide him along the twists of the jagged walls. "Are you two okay?" he called over his shoulder.

"Fine." Lionblaze's mew echoed from the stone. "Dovewing?"

"I'm right on your heels," she answered.

Lionblaze's muzzle touched Jayfeather's tail-tip. "Do you know where you're going?"

"No." But Jayfeather felt sure-pawed as he led them farther into the tunnels. Curiosity was tempting him onward. Behind him, he heard Lionblaze tasting the air, his tongue flicking against his lips. The warrior's mind was crowding with images of claws and blood.

"There are no WindClan cats here this time," Jayfeather promised.

"Listen!" Dovewing halted. Fear flashed from her pelt.

Jayfeather pricked his ears. The sound of water rippled ahead of them, echoing around stone walls. Jayfeather felt his brother's pelt slide past him as Lionblaze rushed ahead.

"I know where we are!" Lionblaze called.

Jayfeather caught up to him. Light silhouetted the warrior's broad shoulders as the narrow tunnel beyond him opened into a wide cavern. Moonlight was seeping through a hole overhead, lighting the tall stone walls and glinting on the fast-flowing stream that cut the wide, sandy floor in two.

Dovewing padded out of the tunnel, blinking. She stopped at the edge of the stream and touched it with one paw. The black water flowed around her claws.

"You came."

She leaped back as a voice rasped from high above them. Jayfeather jerked his head up to the ledge that jutted from the wall of the cavern. The moon illuminated a grotesque tom crouching on the stone, hairless and white-eyed, his pale skin wrinkled, his blind eyes bulging.

"What is it?" Dovewing squeaked.

Jayfeather flicked his tail. "It's Rock." He gazed up at the Ancient cat. After such a long silence, why had he summoned them now? Anger flared in his belly. The last time Rock had appeared, it had been to tell him to let Flametail drown. Jayfeather glared up at Rock, ears flat.

"You made me leave Flametail in the lake! Did you want the other Clans to think I was a murderer?"

Rock met his gaze boldly, almost as though he could see Jayfeather's bristling pelt. "What does it matter?" he hissed.

"I couldn't let you die trying to change another cat's destiny!" The ugly cat curled his lip, his sightless gaze taking in all three of them. "Why do you keep straying from the paths we laid down for you?" Rage cracked his mew.

Jayfeather's paws trembled. What did Rock mean?

"Who is this?" Lionblaze whispered.

Dovewing was staring up at Rock, frozen in horror. "Is he from StarClan?"

Rock growled. "Not StarClan! This was my home before StarClan was ever dreamed of."

Jayfeather could feel confusion sparking from his brother. "How do you know this cat?" Lionblaze murmured as he peered up at Rock.

Rock leaned over the lip of the ledge, his head weaving from side to side like a snake about to strike. "Jayfeather and I have known each other for moons," he snarled.

"Can he see us?" Dovewing's gaze fixed on Rock's bloated, white eyes.

Rock straightened up, his tail flicking ominously. "I never realized your companions were so mouse-brained. I summon them in a dream and they stand around asking questions like kits on their first day out of the nursery."

Jayfeather stepped forward. "You *summoned* us?"

Rock blinked at him. "Did you think you were the only cat with power over other cats' dreams?" Sneering, he showed his teeth. "You idiots!" Suddenly stretching onto his paw tips, Rock arched his back, spitting.

Lionblaze drew himself up in response, his tail bushing up, claws scraping against the rock.

"Just listen to him," Jayfeather warned in a whisper.

"This is all your fault!" Rock yowled. "You are the Three. If you had never been born, the Dark Forest would not have risen!"

Jayfeather stiffened in shock. "We never asked to be born!"

"But you were!" Rock spat. "You fulfilled a prophecy written at the beginning of time and gave power to enemies who should long since have faded from the memories of all cats!" He paced the tiny ledge, twisting like a cornered rat, back and forth, his skin rippling with anger. "Now, because of your existence, the Clans face their darkest moment." He froze suddenly, leaning forward from the ledge. "You Clan cats hold memories too long! You remember dead warriors and dwell on old enemies, passing on stories of battles that should be left behind, not picked over like rotting carcasses!"

Jayfeather swallowed, bristling with indignation that Rock should scorn the Clan's heritage.

"The Clans have brought this battle upon themselves," Rock snarled. "You bear grudges too long and refuse to let go of cats so cruel and unnatural they deserve to be forgotten! You keep them alive in your memories and let them find kindred spirits at the edges of StarClan where no star dares shine." He shook his head, his spine softening. "Why couldn't you just let them fade into the past?"

"Like you?" Dovewing stepped forward, hackles up. "Do you wish you'd been left to fade?"

Jayfeather tried to hook her back with a paw, but Dovewing pushed past him, her claws curling over the edge of the stream as she gazed unblinking up at Rock.

Rock sat down. "Even me," he croaked quietly.

Jayfeather felt a rush of indignation. How could Rock blame them? "We thought we were doing the right thing by honoring our ancestors."

"It was forged into the destiny of the Clans." Rock's shoulders drooped. "That you should remember those lost to you."

Lionblaze lifted his chin. "It has made us strong."

"And now it has become your greatest threat." Rock shook his head. "We always knew this moment would come. Without darkness there is no light, and now the darkness between the stars is rising up to banish the light forever." He thrust his muzzle forward, eyes widening once more. "You were our only hope, the Three joined with the fourth!"

Jayfeather swished his tail. "We still are!"

"Really?" Rock looked straight down at him, white eyes shining in the gloom. "Then why has each of you given up before the battle has begun?"

Dovewing flinched away from the stream and slunk back to join the others. Lionblaze dropped his gaze. Before he had time to guess what his Clanmates were thinking, guilt jabbed at Jayfeather's belly. "The Tribe of Endless Hunting told me that we weren't enough!" He flung the words at Rock. He hadn't lost faith without reason! "They told us we couldn't do it alone; that we needed a fourth cat."

"And have you found this fourth cat?" Rock hissed.

Jayfeather shrunk back. "We didn't know where to look."

Rock cut him off. "You've gossiped and guessed. There's no time for that! Find this cat! Choose your destiny! That is the Clan's last hope!"

The moonlight suddenly flickered as though clouds were

passing over the hole in the roof, and Jayfeather noticed eyes blinking from the darkness below Rock's ledge. Cats were crouched there, watching. Jayfeather crept closer to the stream and tasted the air. These weren't StarClan cats. The scent of endless sky and wind-scorched stone clung to their fur, as though they came from more ancient times. Were these Rock's Clanmates? Jayfeather stiffened as he tasted one scent among the others that made his heart quicken. *Half Moon!*

Now he could see her pale white pelt among the others. And then he noticed another shape, much larger than the others. A badger ambled forward out of the shadow.

Dovewing pressed against Jayfeather, her eyes sparking with surprise. "Is that Midnight?" she whispered. "From the nursery stories?"

Jayfeather nodded.

Lionblaze nudged his shoulder. "Who are the others?"

Jayfeather gazed at Half Moon. "They are Ancient cats." Looking closer, he recognized Broken Shadow and Owl Feather among less familiar pelts. "Some are from the Tribe from long ago."

"We have waited long." Midnight's rumbling growl sounded across the stream. The old badger's round, black eyes fixed on Dovewing. "Learn who to trust. It is heart that knows truth." She turned her wide, striped head toward Lionblaze. "Don't close eyes and wait for path to choose you. Choose path and follow it."

Jayfeather leaned forward, waiting to hear the words Midnight would share with him.

"You!" He flinched as her gaze pierced him. "When all cats

have closed eyes, we gave the gift of sight to the cat who is blind. You see more than most, but look inside, too. See your own strength."

Was that it? *See your own strength.* Frustration shot through Jayfeather. "Stop talking in riddles. Tell us how to save the Clans! At least, tell us who the fourth cat is!"

Rock growled from the ledge. "We have seen your weakness. Do you want us to make you weaker?" With a shove of his paw, he sent grit and stone showering down. Two pale shards—like broken bones—thudded onto the earth below. "You haven't tried hard enough!" he snapped.

Jayfeather hardly heard him. His attention was fixed on the pieces of wood that had fallen from the ledge. He darted forward and leaped over the stream, weaving between the Ancient cats until he was standing beside the scattering of debris.

My stick!

His heart quickened as he saw the twin halves of the ancient branch. In the watery moonlight, he could still see the scratches that had recorded the lives and deaths of so many cats lost in the tunnels countless moons ago.

"All those brave warriors!" Rock hissed down to him. "They took their chance in the darkness and found their way back to the light."

Jayfeather gazed at the half scratches etched in the wood. "Some didn't," he murmured. He felt Broken Shadow flinch beside him. Fallen Leaves's death was marked there.

More grit showered down as Rock peered over the ledge. "But they tried!"

Broken Shadow moved closer. "So many cats have waited for you," she whispered.

"Since before the dawn of the Clans!" Rock added.

Jayfeather looked up and saw Half Moon staring at him. "What gives you the right to abandon us?" she pleaded, and he saw many lifetimes of sorrow in her eyes. Jayfeather felt hackles rising around him. He backed away as growls rumbled in the throats of the Ancients. A screech rang around the cave.

"How dare you abandon us?"

Jayfeather sprang back across the stream and crouched beside Lionblaze. The Ancients were advancing on them, pelts bristling, eyes flaming.

"Would you let us all die again?" Rock screeched from the ledge.

Water washed Jayfeather's paws. He jerked back but only splashed deeper into wetness. Was the stream flooding? Panic rose as he looked down. The river had broken its banks and was washing the cave floor, but it wasn't black anymore. It was red.

Blood! It streamed around Jayfeather's paws, drenching his fur. He swallowed back a yowl of terror. *This is all my fault!* Jayfeather blinked open his eyes and found himself blind and awake. His pelt was spiked with fear; his heart pounded so hard it seemed to shake his whole body.

Find the fourth cat! Rock's voice wailed in his ear. *Find the fourth cat!*

CHAPTER 12

"Lionblaze! Quick!"

Lionblaze jerked his head as Jayfeather's hiss woke him. He sat up in his nest, blinking in the pale dawn light of the warriors' den. The dream was still vivid in his mind: the cavern, the blind tom, and the ghostly Ancients. He hauled himself out of his nest and padded, paws numb, out of the den. He shivered as he looked around for Jayfeather.

"Lionblaze." Jayfeather darted from beside the warriors' den. "We have to talk about the dream."

Lionblaze nodded toward the apprentices' den. "Is Dovewing awake?"

"I just woke her."

As Jayfeather spoke, Dovewing crept from the den, her eyes bleary with sleep.

"Come on." Jayfeather hurried toward the thorn tunnel with Dovewing close behind. Lionblaze scampered after them.

Jayfeather rounded a bend in the trail and stopped beside a bramble. Lionblaze halted beside him and glanced over his shoulder.

Dovewing's eyes were bright. She was fully awake now.

"So we *did* all share the dream?"

Jayfeather nodded.

Lionblaze narrowed his eyes. "And you've met those cats before?"

"Yes," Jayfeather snapped. "But that's not important."

Dovewing brushed past Lionblaze, pacing anxiously. "I can't believe that all those cats have been waiting for so long!"

Lionblaze curled his tail over his back. "Since before the dawn of the Clans!"

"We need to concentrate on what happens *now*!" Jayfeather insisted, flexing his claws. "We are here because the faith of our ancestors has brought us here."

"And the Dark Forest," Lionblaze reminded him grimly.

"Without faith, there would be no Dark Forest," Jayfeather snorted, echoing Rock's words. "But there is. And we have to find the fourth cat."

"It's not Ivypool." Dovewing twitched her tail. "I've asked her."

"Did you find out if it was Mothwing?" Lionblaze gazed at Jayfeather.

Jayfeather shook his head. "She's given no sign."

"Then it must be Hollyleaf!" Lionblaze was absolutely convinced. His sister had been part of this since the beginning. And she'd returned just in time to save ThunderClan from WindClan's attack.

Dovewing was frowning. "I think we're looking in the wrong place."

"What's the right place?" Jayfeather snorted.

"I don't know." Dovewing sighed. "It could be a warrior from another Clan."

"Why don't we ask Firestar to make an announcement at the next Gathering?" Jayfeather muttered sarcastically. "He could ask the fourth cat to stick their tail in the air so we know who it is."

Dovewing ignored him. "We must be missing something obvious."

"Yes." Lionblaze began to pace. "Hollyleaf!"

"But if it's *not* Hollyleaf," Dovewing ventured, "we need to start looking for a cat who was born with a special destiny, like we were."

Jayfeather narrowed his eyes. "A cat with the power of the stars in their paws."

"Breezepelt?" Dovewing suggested. "He's your half brother. Maybe he's special too."

"He's not kin of Firestar's kin," Jayfeather pointed out.

"That was the StarClan prophecy," Dovewing argued. "Perhaps the new prophecy doesn't care if it's kin."

Lionblaze swished his tail. "You can argue till the sun sets!" he snapped. "I'm going to try to find out." He turned and ran down the slope back to the hollow. If he could just spend some time alone with Hollyleaf, then he'd know.

The dens lay in shadow, even though sunlight was beginning to color the tips of the trees above the hollow. Below Highledge, Brambleclaw washed his face, swiping a heavy paw over his muzzle, his eyes still blurry with sleep. Spiderleg stopped to stretch as he emerged from the warriors' den. On the other side of the clearing, Ferncloud poked her head out of the nursery. Foxleap and Toadstep practiced battle moves while they waited for their Clanmates to gather.

Lionblaze fell in beside Cinderheart as she padded toward Brambleclaw.

"Are you okay?" she asked without looking at him.

He glanced at her. "Fine, why?"

She kept her eyes fixed ahead. "You were murmuring in your sleep. Bad dreams?"

"Just dreams."

When she didn't comment, he went on. "I made a mistake." He knew that he should never have tried to choose a different destiny. Too many lives depended on him following the path laid out for him. "It won't happen again."

He felt Cinderheart stiffen beside him. She knew what he really meant. *I won't be distracted by you anymore.*

She stopped and turned to face him, her eyes glistening. "Okay." Her mew was calm, but he could see sorrow in her gaze.

Lionblaze's heart twisted. *I'm sorry, Cinderheart.*

"The Clan comes first," she murmured softly.

"The Clan comes first." Lionblaze dipped his head and padded past her. He stopped in front of Brambleclaw. "Is it okay if I go hunting with Hollyleaf?"

Brambleclaw stopped washing. "Just the two of you?"

"Yes. I need to speak with her."

"Okay, if you wish." As Brambleclaw licked his paws and began once more to smooth his muzzle, Lionblaze headed for the warriors' den.

Hollyleaf was stretching at the entrance. The stiffening wind ruffled her fur.

"Come on." Lionblaze nudged her shoulder with his nose. "Let's go hunting."

Hollyleaf straightened up, stifling a yawn. "Who else is on the patrol?"

Lionblaze headed for the thorn barrier. "Just us."

Hollyleaf fell in beside him as they emerged outside the camp and headed up the slope. "I've caught up with all the new hunting techniques," she reassured him.

"I know." Lionblaze scrambled up a steep bank and skirted a bramble. "I thought we could hunt squirrels."

At the top of the slope, he broke from the trees, screwing up his eyes against the sunshine. Far below, the lake flashed shards of light as it rippled with the wind. Dying leaves swirled from the trees along the edge of the water and clouds thickened on the horizon. There would be rain before nightfall.

"Where should we start?" Hollyleaf caught up to him.

"Let's head along the stream," Lionblaze suggested. He could see the gully from here, running from the forest onto the shore.

"If we follow it to the beech copse," Hollyleaf prompted, "there'll be squirrels looking for nuts." She raced ahead, the wind lifting her fur as she flew down the slope.

Lionblaze felt an unexpected burst of joy. For a moment he was an apprentice again, out in the forest with his littermate, his thoughts on nothing but his first catch. He pushed hard against the grass, almost skidding as he hurtled after

Hollyleaf. Hollyleaf veered sideways as they reached the stream and leaped into the middle of the wide, shallow outlet, splashing through the water like an otter.

"Have you turned into a RiverClan cat?" Lionblaze yowled in surprise as she trotted confidently against the current.

Hollyleaf stopped and turned, whiskers twitching. "It could be the last sunny day of leaf-fall!" she called back. "We might as well enjoy it." She bounded onto the bank and shook out her pelt.

Lionblaze followed, surprised by how soothing the water felt as it flowed around his paws. Hopping onto the bank beside Hollyleaf, he purred, "Race you to the beeches!"

He sped away, weaving between the trees. Hollyleaf pounded after him. He could feel her breath on his tail and pushed harder. *How fast can you run?* Bushes blurred beside him as he ran at full-pelt. He glanced over his shoulder, hoping Hollyleaf might suddenly fly past, showing speed greater than any cat in the forest. That could be the sign that she was the fourth cat. But she was trailing, falling farther behind with each paw step.

Lionblaze pulled up. Hollyleaf slowed to a halt beside him, panting. "That was fun!" She fought to catch her breath, then glanced around, her eyes lighting up as she saw the first beech. She scrambled up the trunk and looked down from the lowest branch. "Come on, slow slug!"

Lionblaze hauled himself up the tree after her. "Let's see how high we can climb!" He was testing her again, letting her take every jump first, following the path she chose through the branches, watching every leap to see if it was lighter and stronger than their Clanmates. He spotted a wide gap between their tree and the beech beside it. "Look!"

Hollyleaf paused and followed his gaze. "What?"

"Do you think you could make that jump?"

"To the next tree?" Hollyleaf tipped her head, thoughtful, then raced along the branch and leaped from the end.

Lionblaze's heart skipped a beat as she glided through the air. He scrambled to the end of the branch, blood roaring in his ears as Hollyleaf stretched out for the next tree and caught hold of a branch tip. Her hind legs swung down as she gripped on with her forepaws.

"Be careful!" Lionblaze yelped as Hollyleaf swung perilously. A gust of wind made the trees swirl. "Hang on!"

"I'm okay!" Scrabbling with her hind legs, Hollyleaf dragged herself up onto the branch and stood triumphant, staring back at him. "Your turn."

Lionblaze gazed at the wide space between the trees, feeling sick. The gap yawned below him. He'd asked Hollyleaf to risk her life, just to prove he was right to believe she was the fourth cat. She'd made it, but only just. Would he be able to jump as far? "Let's—"

Before he could finish, Hollyleaf's gaze jerked up. The branches above her were trembling. *Squirrel.* She sprang upward and disappeared through the browning leaves, sending them fluttering down behind her. Lionblaze watched, stiff with fear, as the tree shuddered. Hollyleaf yowled once and then the leaves fell still.

"Hollyleaf?" he called.

There was no answer.

"Hollyleaf!" Lionblaze slithered down onto the next branch and raced for the trunk. Scrambling down backward, he zig-zagged around the jutting branches until he could see the ground beneath him. Unhooking his claws, he dropped and landed on the forest floor.

"Hollyleaf!" Had she fallen? He scanned the ground, fear coursing through every muscle. The branch above him rustled. Lionblaze looked up.

Hollyleaf poked her head through the leaves with a squirrel dangling from her jaws. Purring, she jumped down beside him and dropped her catch. "So?" There was a challenge in her gaze. "Did I pass the assessment?"

Lionblaze blinked in surprise. "It wasn't an assessment."

Hollyleaf tipped her head. "Then why race me through the forest and ask me to jump around the treetops like I've got wings?"

Lionblaze hesitated. The wind strengthened around them, swishing through the branches overhead. "It has to do with the prophecy," he confessed.

"Okay." Hollyleaf nodded. "What about it?"

"There's a fourth cat." Hollyleaf's ears pricked as Lionblaze went on. "I think it could be you."

Hollyleaf looked down at her paws. "No way."

"Why not?" Lionblaze leaned closer. "You've just proved that you're a great climber and hunter!"

"I'm a trained warrior!" she argued. "I'm supposed to be

able to climb and hunt. And I spent a long time taking care of myself."

Lionblaze ignored her. "But you'd do anything for your Clan! You had the courage and skill to fight WindClan in the tunnels." He searched her gaze. "Have you had any dreams? Has StarClan shared tongues with you? Or the Tribe of Endless Hunting?"

Hollyleaf stared at him. "I'm not a medicine cat!"

"But if you're part of the prophecy—"

"I'm *not* part of the prophecy!" Anger edged Hollyleaf's mew. "I killed a cat, remember?" She started to pace, her claws ripping leaves. "And not because I was being brave or noble. I killed Ashfur because I was angry that our birth had broken the warrior code!" She swung around, her eyes glittering with torment. "Ashfur died because I was so angry that I stopped caring about what was right!"

Anguish stabbed Lionblaze's belly. "It wasn't your fault!" He brushed around her, desperate to ease her grief. "Leafpool and Squirrelflight started it. You should blame them!"

Hollyleaf shook her head. "No, they made a mistake. They were just trying to make it better. No one should have died because Leafpool's heart led her along the wrong path." She fixed Lionblaze's gaze with hers. "Doesn't every cat do that sometime in their life?"

Lionblaze backed away. "I—I guess," he stammered. "But in the end *real* warriors do the right thing, don't they?"

"Yes." Hollyleaf sat down and wearily pawed the dead squirrel. "Which is why I'm doing everything I can to make it up to my Clan."

Hope flickered again in Lionblaze's heart. "Isn't that proof you're the fourth cat?"

"No." Hollyleaf looked up. "It's just proof I'm a warrior, like any other ThunderClan cat."

"But you caught a squirrel higher than any ThunderClan cat has ever hunted."

"I'm well trained."

"You fought in the tunnels better than any warrior."

"Those tunnels had been my home for a long time."

"You're loyal to the warrior code."

"So is every one of our Clanmates." Hollyleaf's gaze was unblinking.

Lionblaze's tail drooped. He couldn't argue anymore.

"You and Jayfeather and Dovewing are special," Hollyleaf went on. "If I have any destiny, it's to protect you three so you can fulfill yours." She padded closer until Lionblaze could feel her warm breath on his fur. "I've never had any special dreams or visions. Everything I've done, *any* warrior could do." Rain began to patter on the leaves above them. "I'm not the fourth cat," she murmured.

"I wish it was you," Lionblaze told her sadly. "You deserve to be part of the prophecy." His ears twitched. "We need to find the fourth cat or everything will be lost."

Hollyleaf pressed her shoulder against his as the rain fell harder. "Don't give up," she whispered. "Our ancestors have led us this far. They won't let us fail now."

CHAPTER 13

❦

Dovewing sat in the entrance and peered out of the den. The camp smelled of wet leaves. "It's stopped raining."

Ivypool stretched in her nest. "Is it clearing up?"

"Yes." Clouds still streaked the sky but a brisk wind was sweeping them away. "It'll be clear by the time we get there." Dovewing's whiskers twitched. There would be a Gathering after all. The past stormy days had left her restless. She hadn't seen Tigerheart since the last moonlit night. *StarClan, let him be at the Gathering.*

Bumblestripe padded from the fresh-kill pile, a mouse in his jaws. "Hi, Dovewing." He dropped it at her paws. "I thought you might be hungry."

She pushed the mouse away. "No, thanks."

Bumblestripe tipped his head. "Are you sure? It's a long way to the island. I'm starving already."

"Then go and eat something," Dovewing meowed. On the other side of the clearing, Firestar was emerging from his den. "We'll be leaving soon." Dovewing glanced at Ivypool. "You look better for your rest." At least the bad weather had meant the Clan had been confined to camp and Ivypool had been able to catch up on sleep. "Perhaps Brambleclaw will change his mind."

The ThunderClan deputy hadn't chosen Ivypool for the Gathering. When Dovewing had begged him to let her littermate join the patrol, he'd shaken his head. "She's been looking tired for moons. Perhaps Jayfeather should check her."

"She's fine," Dovewing had quickly reassured him.

Ivypool turned in her nest. "I'd rather stay here and sleep."

Dovewing blinked at her. Did she want to dream her way back into the Dark Forest already?

Ivypool's gaze flicked toward Blossomfall and Birchfall as the warriors passed the den entrance. Then she closed her eyes. "Brambleclaw's right," she murmured. "I *am* tired."

Dovewing ducked outside and crossed the clearing to where Lionblaze and Cloudtail were already waiting by the thorn tunnel. Foxleap sat beside them, while Cherrypaw patted playfully at Molepaw's twitching tail.

"Wait for me." Rosepetal hurried to catch up. "Bumblestripe's trying to cram in an extra mouse before we leave."

Dovewing snorted. "He'll be as fat as Graystripe if he keeps eating like that."

The pale gray warrior was rummaging through the fresh-kill pile, his black stripes like moon shadows across his pelt. Graystripe nosed in beside him. "Any good prey left?"

Bumblestripe hooked out a shrew and licked his lips. "This must have been hidden at the bottom."

"You'd better offer it to Mousefur first," Graystripe advised. "She loves shrew."

Bumblestripe looked across to the honeysuckle bush. Mousefur was outside, washing her ears with a trembling forepaw. Bumblestripe held out the shrew, letting it dangle from a claw. "Are you hungry, Mousefur?"

She looked up, whiskers twitching. "Not really. I wish I still had a warrior's appetite."

Beside her, Purdy rolled onto his back and stretched. "Do you ever miss hunting?" he asked.

"As much as you'd miss talking if your tongue fell out," Mousefur rasped.

Bumblestripe looked at the shrew, his eyes lighting up. "I guess it's mine, then."

Ferncloud marched from the nursery. "Brightheart would probably appreciate it more." She nipped the shrew from his claw and carried it back to where Brightheart lay resting, her belly round in the moonlight. Bumblestripe's tail drooped.

Dovewing purred and nudged Rosepetal. "Poor old Bumblestripe. Always first to the pile and last to get fed."

Firestar jumped down from Highledge and gazed at the rising moon. "We should leave." He glanced over his shoulder as Sandstorm landed beside him. "The break in the weather might not last long."

Brambleclaw stretched beside the warriors' den, then followed Firestar across the clearing. Cinderheart padded out of her den and stared wistfully at the thorn barrier.

Squirrelflight hopped out after her. "Are you going to the Gathering?"

Cinderheart shrugged. "Not tonight."

"What about Jayfeather?" Lionblaze met Firestar as the ThunderClan leader reached the camp entrance. "Is he coming with us?" Jayfeather stood in the entrance to the medicine den, brambles draping his spine.

Firestar shook his head.

"But no Clan goes to a Gathering without their medicine cat," Lionblaze objected.

Brambleclaw smoothed Lionblaze's ruffled fur with a flick of his tail. "He's not our medicine cat as far as the other Clans are concerned."

Lionblaze growled. "I don't like the other Clans telling us what to do."

"Nor do I." Firestar flexed his claws. "But this is not a battle worth fighting."

Rosepetal stepped forward. "Couldn't Cinderheart take his place? She used to be ThunderClan's medicine cat."

Cinderheart, still watching from the warriors' den, pricked her ears.

"No." Firestar dipped his head toward Cinderheart. "The Clans don't need to know Cinderheart's history until she decides for herself which path she must choose."

To Dovewing's surprise, Cinderheart looked relieved. Didn't she want to return to her old role as medicine cat?

A gust of wind rattled the thornbush. "Let's go." Firestar pushed into the brambles. "There's more rain coming. It may be a short Gathering."

The patrol pounded up the slope as Firestar followed the trail to the forest's edge. Pelts flashed between brambles.

Dovewing's paws slithered on wet leaves. As Blossomfall steadied her with a flick of her tail, a gray pelt caught the edge of her vision. Dovewing turned to see Bumblestripe fall in beside her, his feet skimming the ground as he matched her paw step for paw step. She pushed harder to pull ahead. The gray warrior seemed to be there every time she looked over her shoulder. She veered around a bramble, sliding across his path so he had to pull up and let her take the lead.

She reached the top of the slope before him and, breaking from the trees, stared down at the lake. *Please, StarClan, let Tigerheart be there.* The prayer pierced her heart, more an ache than a wish.

"Tired already?" Rosepetal pulled up beside her.

"*I'm* not!" Blossomfall mewed as she pelted past them, skidding down the slope after her Clanmates.

Bumblestripe scrambled to a halt beside Dovewing and Rosepetal. "You nearly ran me into a tree!"

"You should watch where you're going," Dovewing growled. "I nearly tripped over you." Muttering under her breath, she ran down the slope. "Clumsy mouse-brain."

"Why do you have to be so mean to him?" Rosepetal's whisper took Dovewing by surprise. "It's not a crime, you know!"

"What isn't?"

Rosepetal's gaze darkened meaningfully as Bumblestripe raced past them.

"What?" Dovewing repeated. Why did Rosepetal look so angry?

"It's obvious he likes you!" Rosepetal snapped. "You don't

have to keep biting his head off. He's your Clanmate, not prey!"

Dovewing flattened her ears. Why should she feel bad? "Why do I have to tiptoe around him just because he likes me? It's not my fault."

Rosepetal looked sideways at her. "Do you enjoy hurting his feelings?"

"Of course not!" Guilt flashed under Dovewing's pelt.

"Then apologize."

Dovewing winced. Rosepetal was right. If Bumblestripe had feelings for her, it wasn't fair to punish him for his attention. "Okay!" She pulled ahead, following Bumblestripe's tracks through the grass. She bounded down the short slope onto the shore, landing on the pebbles a moment after Bumblestripe. He glanced over his shoulder and kept running.

"Wait!" Dovewing panted, pebbles spraying out behind.

Bumblestripe eased his pace enough for her to catch up. "What?" he growled.

"Look." Dovewing tried to catch her breath but Bumblestripe was still running hard. "I'm sorry I snapped."

Bumblestripe turned his head to look at her, his gaze hard as ice. "I'm tired of being used as your scratching post," he hissed. "From now on sharpen your claws on someone else."

Dovewing's pelt pricked. "It's not my fault!"

"I *get* it, okay?" He didn't even look at her. He just kept running. "You don't like me the same way I like you. I'll get over it. I'm just disappointed you're not the cat I thought you were."

Dovewing bristled. How dare he say that to her? She gave everything to the Clan, and he wanted more! It wasn't fair. She slowed, letting Bumblestripe pull ahead.

"So?" Rosepetal caught up to her.

"Thanks a lot," Dovewing growled. "Next time I'll let you apologize."

"Is he angry?"

"Yes." Dovewing lashed her tail. "And he's not the only one."

She raced after the patrol, keeping her eyes fixed on the ground and flattening her ears to the gossip of her Clanmates until they reached the tree-bridge that spanned the water between the shore and the island. Hanging back, she let her Clanmates cross first. As they filed across, she opened her mouth, hoping to catch a taste of Tigerheart. But the air was thick with scents from every Clan.

Dovewing nosed her way out of the grass. The clearing was swarming with pelts. Faces turned as ThunderClan padded out from the grass.

"Did he come?" Dovewing heard a ShadowClan apprentice whispering to his denmate.

Ears twitched as eyes scanned ThunderClan.

"Can you see him?"

"He wouldn't dare!"

Dovewing stiffened. "Who are they talking about?" she whispered to Whitewing.

Whitewing lifted her chin and wove through a knot of warriors. "Jayfeather," she meowed.

Dovewing followed her mother past the staring faces and halted beside Blossomfall and Squirrelflight. Firestar shouldered his way through in front of them, heading for the Great Oak. Brambleclaw joined Reedwhisker, Rowanclaw, and Ashfoot at the bottom, while Molepaw and Cherrypaw trotted over to sit with a cluster of apprentices at the edge of the clearing. Dovewing scanned the rows of faces, looking for Tigerheart.

Three medicine cats, Littlecloud, Kestrelflight, and Willowshine, were gathered below the oak. Dawnpelt paced in front of them, lashing her tail.

Dovewing glanced at Whitewing. "She looks like she wants Jayfeather to come so she can start a fight."

She felt hot breath on her ear and turned to find Redwillow leaning close. "Murderers deserve to be punished!"

Dovewing turned on him, bristling. "Jayfeather is not a murderer!"

Pebblefoot stepped between them. "Why isn't he here, then?" he challenged Dovewing. "Too guilty to show his whiskers?"

Dovewing glared at him. "You told him not to—"

Whitewing barged Pebblefoot away with her shoulder. "Stay close to your Clanmates, Dovewing," she warned. "Some cats don't seem to realize there's a truce." She glanced up at the round full moon hanging over the island. A cloud hung across it like a smear of cobweb.

Dovewing turned her back on Redwillow and Pebblefoot. She wasn't going to be the one to make StarClan angry. "It's not fair," she hissed to Whitewing. "They tell Jayfeather not to come and then say it proves that he's guilty!"

Whitewing smoothed Dovewing's ruffled pelt with her tail. "They're just trying to provoke us."

"But why?" Didn't they care about the truce? As anger boiled in her belly, Dovewing caught sight of two dark ear tips on the far side of the clearing. Lifting herself onto her haunches, she peered over the other cats. *Tigerheart!*

"Can I squeeze past, please?" Dapplenose was nosing her way through a cluster of ShadowClan cats.

Dovewing shuffled to make room for the RiverClan elder. "You can sit here, if you want." She beckoned with a flick of her muzzle.

"Thank you." Dapplenose sat beside her.

Dovewing closed her mouth to block out the stink of fish rising from the old cat's pelt. "No problem," she muttered between clenched teeth.

Silence swept the Clan as Blackstar lifted his muzzle and yowled, "Let the Gathering begin." He gazed over the Clans from the wide, low branch of the Great Oak. "Thank you, Firestar." He dipped his head to the ThunderClan leader.

Firestar narrowed his eyes.

Blackstar went on, "You have followed the wishes of the Clans and kept Jayfeather confined to camp until we discover the truth about Flametail's death."

Dawnpelt's eyes flashed from beside Littlecloud, and she nodded importantly to show that she agreed.

Dovewing flexed her claws. *Who made you leader of everyone?*

Spiderleg rose on his haunches and called, "How will the

truth be known?"

Littlecloud stepped forward. "We are waiting for StarClan to speak." He glanced at Dawnpelt. "It's a difficult situation for us all."

Willowshine stood up. "None of us are comfortable with it."

Dovewing tried to see Tigerheart. Was he feeling uncomfortable?

"Don't stare!" Her mother's hiss made her jump. "We don't want to challenge ShadowClan!"

Flinching, Dovewing dragged her gaze back toward the leaders. Onestar had stepped forward, his tail curving over his back. "WindClan has had good hunting over the past moon. We are ready for the coming season."

Mistystar nodded. "We, too. Greenleaf filled the lake with fish and there has been no illness in RiverClan."

Firestar flicked his tail. "StarClan has blessed all the Clans this greenleaf."

Dovewing saw unease flicker in his gaze for a moment before he blinked it away. This might be the last greenleaf the Clans would see.

Mistystar interrupted her thoughts. "RiverClan has had only one concern." She tipped her head, her eyes questioning as she scanned the Clans. "There have been traces of rogues and loners appearing in our territory. No cat has been spotted, but there have been strange scents and paw prints."

Dovewing froze, remembering all the nights she'd roamed with Tigerheart beyond the bounds of Clan territory. Had their scents drifted into enemy territory?

Mistystar twitched her tail. "And yet we have found no trails across our scent lines. It's as if the cats simply appeared inside our territories."

Whitewing leaned closer to Dovewing. "Perhaps the tunnels reach into RiverClan territory, too," she whispered.

But Dovewing hardly heard her. *Don't let it be our scent!* She drew her paws tighter under her. Hadn't Spiderleg reported hearing strange cats on a night vigil? Brambleclaw had ordered moonhigh patrols. *Was that our fault, too?*

Firestar put his head on one side, his eyes sharp with interest. "We have also seen signs of rogue intruders." His tail trembled. "They've come at night and we've set up extra patrols, but no cat has actually been seen."

Onestar shifted his paws. "We've had strange scents, too," he admitted.

Blackstar hunched his shoulders. "There have been rogues in ShadowClan's forests as well."

Firestar leaned forward. "Have you actually *seen* anything?"

Blackstar shook his head. "Just scents, broken branch tips, tufts of fur."

Mistystar's fur lifted along her spine. "Whereabouts?"

"Deep in our territory," Blackstar replied.

Onestar nodded. "Same here. Nothing at the borders, but traces right at the heart of the moor."

Blackstar's claws scraped the bark. "Most scents have been found in areas perfect for ambushes."

"As though an enemy is scouting for an invasion," Firestar commented grimly.

Dovewing felt pelts bristling around her. Murmurs rippled through the Clans.

"I found orange fur on a gorse bush!" Heathertail called. "It smelled like no Clan cat I know."

Smokefoot lifted his muzzle. "There were paw prints near our training ground that had a foul scent." The ShadowClan warrior wrinkled his nose.

Dapplenose shifted beside Dovewing. "There was a trail of footprints tracking the river around our camp," she rasped.

Blossomfall raised her head above her Clanmates. "I don't think there's anything to worry about. Greenleaf has been warm and sunny," she called. "Kittypets, rogues, and loners always stray farther during fine weather."

Dovewing glanced at her Clanmate. Why was she so keen to dismiss the danger?

"These were no rogues! I smelled RiverClan among the other scents!" Rowanclaw yowled.

Brambleclaw nodded. "And there was definitely Shadow-Clan scent in ThunderClan territory."

Blackstar narrowed his eyes. "No ShadowClan warrior has trespassed across your border!"

A growl rumbled in Mistystar's throat. "RiverClan has no need to stray into other territories. We have everything we need in our own!"

Eyes glittered like tiny moons as the leaders flashed warning looks at one another. Dapplenose drew away from Dovewing, her gaze suddenly suspicious. Onestar's tail was lashing. Blackstar glared accusingly at Firestar.

"Listen to what you are saying!" Firestar hissed. His green gaze swept the restless crowd. "We haven't all been invading one another's territories!"

"Then how do you explain the scents?" Dawnpelt challenged from the bottom of the tree.

Firestar stepped forward to the end of his branch, his shoulders rippling beneath his pelt. "If rogues have been traveling across all the territories, they could have picked up scents and spread them like fleas in their path."

Mistystar's fur smoothed a little. "The scents *have* been confusing."

Onestar's eyes had narrowed to slits. "If rogues could carry scents from one territory to another, then so could a Clan patrol."

Firestar met his gaze. "Then we should all step up patrols and try to find these cats."

"Send out more patrols!" a ShadowClan tom called from the crowd.

"We must stay alert!" a RiverClan warrior yowled.

Firestar pressed on. "And if any Clan finds evidence, we must share it with the other Clans!"

Onestar bristled. "And warn them they've been found out? Never!"

Mistystar backed away from the other leaders. "I protect my own Clan," she growled. "No other."

Dovewing gasped as a WindClan cat barged past her, heading for his Clanmates farther down the clearing. All around her, warriors were weaving closer to their denmates.

Dovewing glanced over her shoulder. The knot of apprentices had broken up and Cherrypaw and Molepaw were scurrying back to the ThunderClan warriors.

Blackstar jumped down from the Great Oak. Mistystar slithered down the trunk next, while Onestar glared at Firestar before leaping into the clearing.

"Come on, Dovewing," Whitewing meowed. "There won't be any sharing tongues tonight."

Dovewing stretched her head up to find Tigerheart. There was no sign of him among the streaming pelts. "I'll catch up!" she called to Whitewing as her mother headed after Squirrelflight and Blossomfall. She felt buffeted like a leaf on a river as cats moved around her, heading for the tree-bridge, clustering close to their Clanmates.

"Dovewing?" A familiar mew sounded behind her.

She spun around, her heart leaping as she saw Tigerheart.

His tail was high. "I thought we'd been found out with all that talk of drifting scents!"

"Me too!" Dovewing saw relief in his gaze. "We have to be more careful from now on."

Tigerheart nodded. "There'll be more patrols." He stretched his muzzle close to her ear. "Let's meet outside the territories again tomorrow night," he whispered. "At the Twoleg nest."

As Dovewing nodded, she felt the fur bristle on the back of her neck. She looked past Tigerheart and saw Bumblestripe staring at her. Her heart missed a beat. "We were just discussing the intruders," she told her Clanmate quickly. "Tigerheart was asking if I'd noticed anything."

Bumblestripe's eyes widened.

"I thought it would be a good idea to talk to other patrols, to see if the scents have been picked up on the same nights." Dovewing realized she was chattering like a blackbird.

Bumblestripe shrugged. "You can talk to whoever you like," he meowed. "It's a Gathering." He began to follow the other cats toward the tree-bridge and disappeared into the long grass.

Dovewing turned back to Tigerheart. "I'd better go."

Tigerheart dipped his head. "Me too." He headed away, slipping between Rowanclaw and Dawnpelt as they passed.

Dovewing bounded after Whitewing, following her scent into the grass and catching up with her as she reached the shore. Whitewing glanced sideways at her as they waited for the other Clans to pass one by one over the fallen tree. "Are you okay?"

"Fine," Dovewing mewed as brightly as she could.

Whitewing didn't answer, but moved closer to her daughter till Dovewing felt her soft pelt brush her flank. Above them, clouds rolled across the sky and the wind lifted, sending waves scudding across the lake. Dovewing wished she could tell her mother everything: about Tigerheart and how much he meant to her; how heavy the prophecy seemed and how small she felt under its weight. But she couldn't talk about the prophecy to any cat beyond the ones already involved, and Whitewing would be devastated if she knew her daughter loved a cat from another Clan.

Whitewing pressed closer. "I'm always here if you need me."

Rain began to fleck Dovewing's pelt. Her vision blurred, and she told herself it was just raindrops. "Thanks, White-wing," she whispered.

"Come on." Whitewing nudged her toward a gap in the stream of cats. "We'll be home before you know it."

CHAPTER 14

"Are we all here?" Brokenstar's eyes gleamed in the darkness as he scanned the circle of cats.

Ivypool lifted her chin. Hawkfrost had told her about the Dark Forest Gathering the moment she'd woken into the Place of No Stars. She had to represent ThunderClan. Applefur, who had proved herself worthy of full warrior status here, stood for ShadowClan, while Breezepelt—WindClan's representative— shifted from one paw to another, eyeing Brokenstar warily.

"Beetlewhisker." Brokenstar greeted the RiverClan cat with a voice like ice as Beetlewhisker padded from the trees. "Did you have trouble finding your way?"

Ivypool tucked her tail tighter over her paws.

"I was at the Gathering." Beetlewhisker took his place beside Applefur. "I didn't get to my nest till well after moon-high."

Tigerstar padded around the edge of the circle. "You can't be in two Clans at once," he murmured, pausing in front of Beetlewhisker before sliding in between Mapleshade and Hawkfrost.

Thistleclaw dug his claws into the ground and tore out a

pawful of slimy grass. "Can we start now?"

Sparrowfeather sat down, ears twitching. "What's this meeting about?"

Darkstripe flashed him a warning look, then dipped his head to Brokenstar. "Sparrowfeather asks questions like a kit." He crossed the circle, blocking Brokenstar's view of the mottled tom. "I've told him already we've come to praise our brave recruits."

Brokenstar curled his lip.

"Our young warriors have practiced hard." Mapleshade took the center of the circle, shoving Darkstripe back to his place. "I've watched their training carefully. They can climb, run, swim, and fight." Her gaze slid toward Beetlewhisker. "Though not enough of them have learned to deal the killing blow."

Applefur frowned. "Warriors don't kill."

Mapleshade whipped around. "Clan cats don't kill but they're not real warriors," she hissed. "If they were, why weren't you satisfied with their training? Why did you seek us out?"

"I thought you sought me out." There was a note of uncertainty in Applefur's voice.

Shut up! Ivypool glared at her. *Why creep into a fox's den, then complain about the smell?*

Hawkfrost's blue eyes glinted in the half-light. "We recognized your need for better training. It led us to you."

Mapleshade's whiskers twitched. "That's right," she purred. "And you've learned a lot." Her gaze flitted from Applefur to

Breezepelt, then Beetlewhisker and Ivypool.

Ivypool met it, forcing her legs not to tremble. "You taught us well," she meowed with what she hoped was the right note of gratitude.

"You had more courage and strength than I imagined," Mapleshade conceded. "I'm proud of your progress."

Ivypool's heart quickened as Brokenstar padded forward. Muscles flexed like waves beneath his pelt, as though he was ready for battle. "Pride is not important." He waved Mapleshade away with a sweep of his tail. "Power is important, and the willingness to use it."

Breezepelt puffed out his chest. "I'm ready for anything!"

"Good." Brokenstar's whiskers twitched. "There are difficult times ahead but loyalty to the Dark Forest and hunger for victory will carry you through."

Ivypool swallowed. "Victory over what?" She had to find out exactly what these cats were planning.

Brokenstar jerked his head around and stared at her. His amber gaze blazed like a scorching sun. Ivypool narrowed her eyes against it.

"Our *enemies*," Brokenstar growled. "Our courage will be tested but we will be ready."

"Enemies?" Beetlewhisker stretched his muzzle forward, eyes puzzled. "What enemies?"

Mapleshade blinked at him. "Don't you know yet?" She flicked her tail. "Have your Clanmates never doubted you even though you were right? Has Mistystar never acted like a mouse-heart, siding with weaker cats while punishing the strong? Have your denmates never treated you like a kit when you are more skillful and dangerous than they could even imagine? I don't know how you can bear returning every sunrise to feed and protect such feeble creatures!"

Beetlewhisker bristled. "My Clanmates are not feeble or mouse-brained! Mistystar is noble. If she sides with the weak, it's because the weak need our protection!"

Tigerstar's eyes flashed. "The weak should be left to fend for themselves."

Beetlewhisker blinked. "But that's the opposite of everything the warrior code teaches us!"

Brokenstar lowered his head and spoke quietly. "The warrior code teaches you how to be weak."

"It teaches us how to be strong!" Beetlewhisker snapped. "I don't know what you're trying to do, but you'll never make me despise the warrior code, or my Clan!" He took a step toward Brokenstar. "My Clan thinks it's being targeted by rogues because of you. They're frightened by our nighttime visits to their territory. I don't want to be part of that." His voice softened. "I appreciate everything you've taught me, I really do. You've made me a stronger warrior than I could have ever dreamed of being, but I can't stay here. I must leave and protect my Clan. I won't be coming here again." He turned and padded away.

Ivypool's paws trembled as she watched Beetlewhisker shoulder his way past Hawkfrost and Applefur.

Brokenstar's ears flattened. "No cat leaves the Dark Forest unless I say so." He unsheathed his claws. "Your loyalty is to us now."

Run! Ivypool silently begged Beetlewhisker. *Run and don't look back!*

Beetlewhisker paused and glanced over his shoulder. "My loyalty is to RiverClan, just as it has always been," he meowed. "You promised me that coming here would make me stronger for my Clanmates. It has, and I'm grateful, but you must have known that I'd leave eventually."

Brokenstar's eyes glinted menacingly. "You really are dumb, aren't you?"

Beetlewhisker lashed his tail. "Not as dumb as you hoped! I'm going, and you can't stop me."

In a flash, Brokenstar shot from the circle and blocked Beetlewhisker's path. Ivypool started to move, but Thistle-claw's tail whipped her backward.

"Stay out of this," the dark tabby warned.

Applefur's tail trembled. "Don't go, Beetlewhisker. You've got friends here." Her mew was straining to be cheerful but Ivypool could see fear darkening her gaze.

"Thanks, Applefur." Beetlewhisker nodded to the ShadowClan she-cat. "But I have to go. This is the right time for me to leave."

"Really?" Brokenstar's growl started low and grew louder, sharpening into a screech. The Dark Forest warrior reared up until his shadow stretched right across the clearing. Then he dived toward Beetlewhisker with his forepaws stretched out and his teeth bared.

Beetlewhisker's eyes widened in horror. He put up his paws to fend off the vicious tom, but Brokenstar knocked him backward with a fierce swipe. Beetlewhisker staggered to his paws, blood spurting from his nose. "StarClan help me!"

"You think StarClan listens to what happens here?" Brokenstar hissed. He lunged again and clamped his jaws around Beetlewhisker's neck as though he were prey. Eyes shining, Brokenstar lifted his head, hauling Beetlewhisker by his throat until a crack split the air.

Ivypool felt sick as Beetlewhisker fell limp in Brokenstar's jaws. His body thumped to the ground as the Dark Forest warrior opened his mouth and let it fall.

"Would anyone else like to leave? Applefur?" Brokenstar challenged the ShadowClan she-cat. "Do you want to return to your Clan?"

"N-no." Applefur shifted her paws.

Ivypool could see her thoughts racing as she met Brokenstar's gaze. Ivypool pressed against her reassuringly. Every Clan cat must understand now. This place was evil. They had to get out!

"Breezepelt?" Brokenstar turned to the WindClan warrior, who was peering at Beetlewhisker's body through narrowed eyes.

"Did you hear me?" Brokenstar growled quietly.

"Why would I leave the strongest Clan?" Breezepelt lifted his head. "My Clan wastes too much time looking after the sick and old. If you led us, we'd never have to beg another Clan for help again."

Ivypool's chest tightened. How could he sympathize with these murderers?

Brokenstar stepped over Beetlewhisker's body. Ivypool held her ground as he strode back into the circle, though every muscle begged her to run. "You will all stay here," Brokenstar told them. "You will all be loyal to me. Or I will kill every one of you." He thrust his muzzle into Applefur's face. "Starting with you."

Applefur swallowed.

"Say nothing to any cat," Brokenstar ordered. "You will fight alongside us. And if I hear of any one of you spreading rumors and lies among your Dark Forest Clanmates, you will suffer beyond anything you have ever known." He turned his back and pushed his way between Tigerstar and Hawkfrost. "Go," he growled, disappearing into the shadow. "Train my warriors. The final battle is near."

Ivypool felt Tigerstar's questioning gaze pierce her through the gloom. Forcing herself to breathe steadily, she met his eyes. "My recruits will be ready when the battle comes," she vowed. "We're ready to kill every lake cat we meet." She ignored Applefur's wince of alarm beside her. *I promise I'm not evil! I'm doing this to save all of us.* Tigerstar watched her for a moment then turned away.

Hawkfrost nodded at Ivypool, his eyes glowing, before following his father. As he passed Beetlewhisker's blood-streaked body, he kicked it viciously. "I never trusted him anyway."

CHAPTER 15

Jayfeather wrinkled his nose as he swallowed a mouthful of herbs. The tansy tasted bitter and would sit like nettles in his belly till sunhigh, but he was determined not to catch any of the coughs and sneezes spreading through the Clan like fleas. He sniffed Briarlight. The tang of green leaves was fresh on her breath. "Have you eaten all of them?"

"Yes." Her fur brushed the floor as she crossed the medicine den and Jayfeather heard her lapping from the pool. "Why do herbs have to taste so bitter?" she complained.

"It stops the rabbits and mice from eating them," Jayfeather replied.

The days of rain since the Gathering—nearly a quarter moon ago—had brought with them the first real chill of leaffall. The Clan had been sheltering in their dens when they weren't patrolling, and every sniffle had been passed from nest to nest. Nothing serious, but the sound of coughing and wheezing made Jayfeather edgy.

He had turned Millie away yesterday when she'd come to visit Briarlight. "No cat is allowed in the medicine den except me."

Millie had tensed, her tail twitching with annoyance, but she hadn't argued. Jayfeather sensed worry pricking beneath her pelt. Millie wanted to keep Briarlight safe from infection as much as he did. Although Briarlight's forepaws were strong enough to haul herself onto the fallen beech now, Jayfeather couldn't predict how well she would fight sickness. The daily ritual of swallowing herbs was the best way he could think of for keeping them both safe from infection.

He pawed through the leaves he'd lined up outside the store. The stock of tansy was lower than he'd hoped. He reached instead for mallow. It should work just as well on Purdy's cough. He grabbed a wad of leaves between his jaws and headed for the entrance. "Stay in the den," he ordered Briarlight through clenched teeth. "And no visitors."

"What if Millie comes?" Briarlight asked hopefully.

"I've told her to stay away." As Jayfeather nosed his way through the trailing brambles, drizzle washed his face. He flattened his ears against it and headed toward the honeysuckle bush. Murmuring sounded from the dens, muffled by leaves that had been pawed into the woven walls to keep out the wind. Jayfeather ducked into the elders' den. The warm scents of Mousefur and Purdy filled his nose. Purdy was damp and the musky odor of fresh mouse hung in the air.

Jayfeather dropped the mallow beside Purdy's nest. "Have you been hunting?"

"Mousefur was hungry," Purdy rasped.

"Don't use me as an excuse!" Mousefur snapped. "He wanted to hunt," she told Jayfeather.

"We've been stuck inside for days," Purdy complained. "I needed to get out for a while."

Mousefur shifted in her nest. "Bored of my company?"

A purr rumbled in the old tom's throat. "I thought you could do with a break from my stories."

"Your stories are the only interesting thing that happens around here," she croaked.

Jayfeather picked up a few mallow leaves and dropped them beside the cantankerous elder. "Perhaps you could spend more time with Lilykit and Seedkit. They're getting to that restless age."

"Brightheart's kits are due soon," he added. "You'll be busy enough once they're bouncing around the clearing looking for trouble."

"I suppose." Mousefur sniffed. "No doubt it'll be up to me to teach them manners. Kits nowadays don't know how to show any respect."

Jayfeather's whiskers twitched with amusement.

"Don't you believe it," Purdy whispered. "She was teaching Lilykit and Seedkit how to reach under the wall of the warriors' den and catch stray tails yesterday."

"I heard that!" Mousefur snapped.

Jayfeather left the two old cats bickering and pushed through the honeysuckle into the rain. The nursery rustled on the other side of the clearing. Fur scraped thorns and Jayfeather smelled the scent of Cinderheart. She was squeezing into the bramble bush.

Jayfeather crossed the camp and poked his head inside. "Is

everything okay here?"

Brightheart shifted in her nest. "Ferncloud's under the weather," she puffed. Her belly was so round with kits that even sitting up to talk was an effort.

"She's got a bellyache." Cinderheart's mew sounded beside Ferncloud's nest. "I thought I'd check on her. You've got plenty to do."

Jayfeather hesitated, uncertain as usual whether he should let Cinderheart act as medicine cat or tell her to go back to her warrior duties. But it was a decision she needed to make for herself. "If you need herbs, let me know," he told her. "I'll leave them outside the medicine den for you."

Jayfeather withdrew, turning toward the apprentices' den, where he could hear Molepaw coughing.

"Cough again, Molepaw." Leafpool's mew surprised Jayfeather. She was already inside the den. Molepaw forced out a cough and Leafpool sat up. "It's not bubbling in his chest. Perhaps some honey will soothe his throat?" Jayfeather felt her gaze flit toward him.

There are more medicine cats than sick cats! Ruffled, Jayfeather pushed past Leafpool and listened to Molepaw's chest. She was right. It sounded clear. "I'll wrap some honey in a leaf and leave it outside my den." He turned and stomped from the den.

"That was quick." Briarlight greeted him as he pushed his way through the brambles and shook the rain from his pelt.

"Cinderheart and Leafpool are helping," Jayfeather muttered. He padded to the store, hauled out a lump of honeycomb, and folded it in a laurel leaf. Then he picked a few chervil roots for Ferncloud's bellyache. Grasping them between his jaws, he carried them to the den entrance, thrust his head out, and dropped them on the ground.

A familiar scent surprised him. *RiverClan.* As he slid out into the clearing, he tasted the air. Poppyfrost and Brackenfur were padding from the thorn tunnel. The two warriors smelled fresh from the forest. And there was a third cat behind them, walking into the clearing with hesitant steps. *Mothwing?*

Poppyfrost called to him. "Mothwing wants to speak with you."

"It's a RiverClan cat!" Squeaking excitedly, Lilykit dashed from behind the warriors' den.

"Why's she here?" Seedkit bounced after her sister.

Jayfeather waved them away with his tail and hurried to greet the RiverClan medicine cat. Nodding to Poppyfrost and Brackenfur, he steered Mothwing to the edge of the clearing.

Behind them, Spiderleg grumbled, "Why is she allowed to tramp across our territory when our medicine cat isn't even allowed at the Gathering?"

Jayfeather ignored him. "What is it?"

"You have to come with me," Mothwing told him.

Stones clattered as Firestar bounded down from his den. He skidded to a halt beside Mothwing. "Is anything wrong?"

"No," Mothwing meowed evenly. "There's just something I need to show Jayfeather."

Firestar shifted his paws. "Jayfeather can't leave Thunder-Clan territory."

Mothwing's pelt brushed Jayfeather's. "He can for this."

"What is it?" Firestar thrust his muzzle closer.

"Something only Jayfeather will understand." Mothwing headed away. "Are you coming?" she called to Jayfeather.

"I'd better go with her," Jayfeather meowed apologetically to Firestar. He ran after Mothwing as she vanished into the thorns. What was so important that she'd overrule a Clan leader?

Excitement sparked from Mothwing's pelt as she headed onto the narrow beach and followed the edge of the lake, crossing the WindClan border without even pausing to taste the air. Jayfeather followed, his pads pricking with curiosity. He hardly noticed the rain battering his face. Had Mothwing discovered proof she was the fourth cat? Hope flared in his chest.

A shout from the hillside made him jump. *Crowfeather.* The WindClan warrior was pelting toward them, yowling.

"He's leading a patrol," Mothwing warned. She shoved Jayfeather behind her and waited as the WindClan cats swished through the heather.

"What are you doing here?"

Jayfeather flinched as Crowfeather slowed to a halt in front of them. He tasted the scents of Whitetail and Owlwhisker as they joined their Clanmate.

"He's not allowed to cross Clan territory," Crowfeather growled.

Mothwing didn't move. "This is not your territory. We're within a tail-length of the water."

"It's not a full moon!" Crowfeather snarled. "There's no truce."

Jayfeather dug his claws into the pebbles. He couldn't believe this bad-tempered warrior was his father.

"We're medicine cats," Mothwing meowed calmly.

Crowfeather padded closer. "He's not."

Owlwhisker growled, "Let's escort him back to his border."

Whitetail shifted her paws. "He's not doing any harm," she meowed.

"He's a murderer!" Owlwhisker hissed.

"Do you believe *everything* ShadowClan says?" Whitetail snapped at her Clanmate.

Stones rattled beneath Mothwing's feet as she stepped closer to the WindClan patrol. "Let us pass," she insisted.

Crowfeather's tail lashed the air. "Jayfeather is trespassing."

"Do you want to fight me?" Mothwing challenged. "Because you'll have to if you lay a claw on him." There was a growl in her mew. "Would StarClan approve of you harming a medicine cat?"

Jayfeather felt frustration flare from Crowfeather's pelt. "You can pass." He leaned closer to Jayfeather. "But this is the second time we've caught you trespassing on our territory." His breath smelled of rabbit. "Make it the *last.*"

Mothwing's tail flicked past Jayfeather's nose. "He'll have to travel back," she pointed out. "Will I need to escort him? Does WindClan take pride in attacking blind cats?"

Jayfeather swallowed a hiss. He hated his blindness being

used as an excuse, but this was no time to let pride get in the way.

"Very well." Crowfeather backed away, his Clanmates retreating with him.

Shaking raindrops from her whiskers, Mothwing headed along the shore. Jayfeather trotted after her, impressed by her courage. "You should have been a warrior," he meowed as the WindClan patrol faded from earshot.

"Maybe, but I am a medicine cat," Mothwing replied in a tone that didn't invite further questions. She led him across the RiverClan border and into the reed beds. The ground grew boggy underpaw and marsh grass brushed Jayfeather's pelt as he followed the medicine cat along a twisting path.

"What's that?" Jayfeather stiffened as the faint smell of smoke touched his nose.

"That's what we're going to see." Mothwing kept going and Jayfeather hurried after her. "Duck," she warned as the marsh grass thickened.

Dripping fronds trailed over Jayfeather's nose, filling his muzzle with wet seeds that made him sneeze. Spluttering, he padded after Mothwing until suddenly she halted, and Jayfeather lost his footing in the mud as he tried to avoid crashing into her.

"Here," Mothwing announced.

The smell of smoke was even stronger. Why had she led him to a fire? "What is it?" he asked.

"One reed is smoldering," she told him. "It's been smoldering for days."

"In this rain?"

"The rest of the reed bed is soaked, but this one keeps burning," Mothwing explained. "It doesn't burn completely. The tip just glows with a tiny flame."

Jayfeather leaned close, the smoke making his eyes sting. Pain stung his nose as it touched the smoldering reed. He stepped backward. "How long has it been like this?"

"Three sunrises," Mothwing told him. "Ever since the Gathering."

"It's a sign!" Jayfeather turned to Mothwing. "You know it's a sign, don't you?"

She sat down. "For me, it's a trick of the marshes," she meowed. "But I knew you'd find an omen in it. That's why I showed you."

"Has Willowshine seen it?" Surely Mothwing would show it to her own Clanmate first?

"Willowshine isn't looking for signs," Mothwing told him. "Not like you."

Jayfeather leaned closer to the tiny flame. As its heat touched his nose again a vision flared in his mind. Fire shot like a stalk in front of him, spearing up toward the sky, glowing orange like a . . . Jayfeather's mind whirled . . . like a tail!

Flametail! StarClan was sending him a sign. *Find Flametail!*

He'd already been to the Moonpool in his search for the dead ShadowClan cat. But that time he hadn't even made it to StarClan's hunting grounds. Maybe StarClan was ready now.

"Thank you!" Jayfeather ran his tail gratefully over Mothwing's flank. Was he right about her being the fourth cat? *Maybe it's Flametail.* This sign changed everything! If he could talk to Flametail and persuade him to tell Littlecloud he drowned accidentally, the medicine cats could unite once more. And with the medicine cats working together, the Clans might join forces in time to face the Dark Forest.

"I have to get back."

Mothwing stilled him with a paw. "Do you know what it means?"

"I think so." It would take too long to tell her everything. Jayfeather wanted to get home, curl into his nest, and dream his way to StarClan's hunting grounds. "It means I can find Flametail now."

"But he's dead, right?" Mothwing asked uneasily.

"Not to me!"

Jayfeather felt sorrow flood Mothwing. "I envy your faith," she murmured. "You can always find hope, even in the darkest moments."

Jayfeather tipped his head. "If only that were true." A few sunrises ago he'd given up all trust in the prophecy and his power to fulfill his destiny. Now there seemed a tiny chink of light, but the darkness still loomed on every side.

"I'll always be here if you need me," Mothwing told him. "I may not share your faith, but I will always help you fight for what you believe in."

"Thank you." Jayfeather broke away, his paws itching for home.

"Do you want me to go with you?" Mothwing offered as he headed back along the trail.

"I'll be okay!" Running, he followed his own scent along the narrow path until he burst out onto the shore.

Mothwing's mew sounded from the reeds behind him. "I'll keep watching the flame!" she yowled. "If it goes out, I'll know you've found what you're looking for!"

CHAPTER 16

❧

Jayfeather shivered. A cold wind had woken him. He sat up, feeling rain spatter his pelt. *Where am I?* He'd awoken on a grassy hillside, the sky darkened by rainclouds and the dismal landscape patched together by dying trees and storm-battered meadows. Was he in the Dark Forest? StarClan had always seemed to exist in perpetual greenleaf, with only the lightest breeze to stir the prey-scented air. Jayfeather fluffed his pelt against the chill and headed for a cluster of trees lower down the slope. No bird sang, no creature moved. He strained to hear paw steps. Were there cats here?

Fur brushed bark. Heart thumping, Jayfeather ducked beneath a tangle of dripping bracken. He pressed his belly to the ground and peered out. Four muddy paws padded toward him. Was it a Dark Forest warrior? He scrabbled backward, deeper into the bush. A familiar scent bathed his tongue. *Spottedleaf!* Light-headed with relief, he dived out from under the bush.

Spottedleaf stopped. "Jayfeather! What are you doing here?"

"Are these StarClan's hunting grounds?" Jayfeather gazed up at the browning leaves.

Spottedleaf flicked her ears. "Yes."

"What's happened?"

"Leaf-fall." Spottedleaf hunched against the chilly wind. "The first StarClan has ever known." Her mew was flat. "And I can taste leaf-bare on the wind."

"Leaf-bare in StarClan? That's impossible!"

"Not anymore. The Dark Forest is rising," Spottedleaf shivered. "And StarClan could fall."

Jayfeather whisked his tail. "Not if I can help it!" He scanned the woodland, hoping to see more pelts. "I've come to speak with Flametail."

Spottedleaf looked surprised. "Why now?"

"I saw the sign," Jayfeather explained.

Spottedleaf stared at him blankly. "The sign?"

"The one StarClan sent. The burning reed."

"StarClan sent no signs." Spottedleaf tipped her head to one side. "We can't even *see* the lake."

"One of you must have!" Jayfeather shook rain from his pelt. "Last time I tried to find Flametail, I never made it past the Moonpool. But now I'm here!"

"StarClan sent no sign," Spottedleaf insisted.

Jayfeather padded past her and stared into the trees. "Well, someone did." *Was it Rock?* "I have to speak to Flametail. I have to reunite the medicine cats."

Spottedleaf glanced around warily. "You know StarClan is divided. You won't find Flametail. He'll be in ShadowClan's part of the hunting grounds."

Jayfeather snorted. "There are no borders here."

"There are now," Spottedleaf snapped.

"They're not real!" Why was she making this so difficult? "I'm going to find Flametail!"

Spottedleaf narrowed her eyes. "Things have changed!"

"The truth hasn't," Jayfeather spat. "And I'm going to make Flametail tell Littlecloud that I didn't kill him."

"It won't be as easy as you think," Spottedleaf warned. "ShadowClan won't let you cross their scent line."

Frustration surged through Jayfeather. "You don't have to help me!"

He flinched as Spottedleaf thrust her muzzle close. "I didn't say I wouldn't help you!" she hissed. "I'm just warning you it won't be easy. Yellowfang's been feeding StarClan's fears like a mother feeding her kits! The stupid old fleabag!"

Jayfeather backed away, startled by her anger. "Then you'll take me to Flametail?"

"Of course!" She began to head up the trail. "ShadowClan's territory is this way."

Jayfeather scurried after her.

"Did you actually think I'd abandon ThunderClan?" Spottedleaf muttered.

"This isn't just about ThunderClan," Jayfeather corrected her. "It's about all the Clans now."

They broke from the trees and crossed a meadow. The long grass was crushed, battered flat by wind. Jayfeather narrowed his eyes against the stinging rain, his paws squelching over rotting flowers. He heard the river ahead. As they reached the bank, his heart twisted. The water was brown and foaming, running in full flood, crashing over rocks and swirling between the muddy banks.

"Where is everyone?"

Spottedleaf flicked her tail toward a huddle of cats crouching upstream, beneath a rocky overhang. *Whitestorm?* Jayfeather hardly recognized the white warrior. His pelt clung to him, showing jutting ribs beneath the soaked fur.

"Prey's scarce now," Spottedleaf explained.

Longtail was sitting beside Whitestorm, staring out from the cramped cleft. His eyes were clear and bright, his eyesight restored, but his gaze was tinged with sadness.

Jayfeather broke away from Spottedleaf and headed toward his Clanmates. "Longtail!" He greeted the old tom with a purr.

Longtail dipped his head. "It's good to see you," he murmured.

A pelt flashed at the corner of Jayfeather's vision. Brindleface was picking her way down the steep bank edging the rocks. "Jayfeather? Is that you?" She broke into a trot as she drew near. "Something terrible has happened to StarClan! We can't see the Clans anymore."

"I know," Jayfeather mewed. "It's because of the Dark Forest."

"How is Firestar?" Whitestorm asked, standing up and circling Jayfeather.

"He's fine."

"What about Mousefur?" Longtail blinked anxiously at him.

"Grumpy." Jayfeather forced out a purr. He wanted to reassure them that nothing had changed in ThunderClan territory. "And Ferncloud rules the nursery as ferociously as any warrior."

"What about Briarlight?" Longtail asked. "Has she recovered?"

"She's doing well," Jayfeather promised. "And Brightheart's expecting kits."

Whitestorm's eyes gleamed. "That's great news!"

"Jayfeather!" Spottedleaf's mew called from behind. "We should get moving."

"Where are you going?" Longtail leaned forward.

"To find Flametail." Jayfeather's ear twitched.

Whitestorm's gaze darkened. "Don't cross the border," he warned.

"StarClan shouldn't have borders," Jayfeather growled.

Longtail lowered his head. "StarClan shouldn't have leaf-fall, either."

"I have to find Flametail." Jayfeather turned away.

Whitestorm whipped around him, blocking his path. "You can't go there!"

Spottedleaf ran her tail down the old warrior's spine. "We must," she mewed gently.

Whitestorm blinked at her, worry sparking in his gaze. "They'll force you back."

"They won't stop me." Jayfeather flattened his ears. "This is too important."

Whitestorm backed away, letting Jayfeather pass.

"Be careful!" Brindleface called as he followed Spottedleaf away from the rocks.

She led him downstream, following the river across the meadow till it turned and headed away toward a distant wood, finally stopping beside a tree stump. "We've reached the border."

Jayfeather could smell the washed-out scent of Shadow-Clan clinging to the dripping brambles that lined the path. He glanced nervously around. *This is StarClan!* he reminded himself. *All cats are safe here.*

"Get down!" Spottedleaf suddenly crouched, signaling to Jayfeather with a flick of her tail. Pawsteps sounded ahead. Spottedleaf's gaze darted from side to side. "We should hide," she warned.

"No! This is ridiculous." Lifting his chin, Jayfeather marched past her and stood in the center of the path. He lifted his tail as Russetfur rounded the corner and halted.

The ShadowClan deputy curled her lip to show sharp yellow teeth. "What are you doing here?"

Raggedpelt and Hollyflower appeared behind her. Raggedpelt hissed as he caught sight of Spottedleaf. "I thought we told you not to cross the border."

"This is StarClan!" Jayfeather hissed. "There should be no boundaries."

Spottedleaf weaved around him. "I know you think you're doing the right thing," she meowed. "But we have only come to speak with Flametail. Once we've done that, we'll leave."

Raggedpelt unsheathed his claws. "What do you want with Flametail?"

Jayfeather let his fur smooth and met the ShadowClan deputy's gaze. "I had a sign," he explained. "It told me I should talk with Flametail."

Hollyflower bristled. "StarClan sent no sign."

Jayfeather dipped his head. "With respect, given all these boundaries, how would you know?" he pointed out. "A cat from any Clan could have sent it. But it *was* a sign."

The brambles behind Russetfur shivered and Cedarheart stepped onto the trail. "Let them pass."

Russetfur bristled. "Why?"

Cedarheart tipped his head on one side. "What harm can it do to let them speak to Flametail?"

Hollyflower growled, "They crossed our border."

"And they'll cross it again to return to their own territory before long," Cedarheart told her.

Russetfur padded closer to Jayfeather. "What's the point of boundaries if we let any cat cross?"

Cedarheart didn't move. "Jayfeather isn't just any cat. You *know* that."

There was a pause. Then Russetfur lowered her head and took a step backward. "I guess we can make an exception," she muttered.

Jayfeather nodded. "Thank you." He padded past the ShadowClan patrol, feeling their gaze burn his fur. He glanced back for Spottedleaf. The ThunderClan medicine cat was following, eyeing the ShadowClan cats warily as she passed. Once they rounded the corner, Jayfeather picked up the pace. "Come on," he urged over his shoulder.

"Do you know where to look for him?"

"The vision was a burning reed," Jayfeather told her. "He

must be near reeds."

Spottedleaf looked doubtfully at the pine trees that loomed ahead. "Reeds? In ShadowClan territory? That sounds more like RiverClan."

It was a fair point. Jayfeather scanned the brambles, wondering if there was any water close by.

"Wait." Spottedleaf halted, her tail lifted. "The river runs through this part of the hunting grounds." She veered off the path and slid between the rambling bushes. Jayfeather followed, his fur snagging on thorns. Spottedleaf twisted between the stalks, seeking out gaps they could squeeze through. The ground sloped down beneath their paws and before long, Jayfeather heard the whispering of the river once more.

"There." Spottedleaf nodded to the muddy river swirling ahead. The slope flattened into reed beds at the river's edge. "ShadowClan claimed this land just to spite the RiverClan cats."

Jayfeather scanned the swath of pale stalks, hoping for a flash of orange. "Can you see him?" he asked Spottedleaf, but she was already bounding down the bank. As she slid between the reeds, Jayfeather raced after her. "Flametail?" He nosed his way into the thicket, shivering as cold water swallowed his paws.

He glimpsed Spottedleaf's tortoiseshell pelt through the reeds. "Any sign?" he called. Then he paused. A scent touched his nose. ShadowClan, definitely, and fresh. Could it be Flametail? He headed onward, the ground growing softer beneath his feet. Water brushed his belly fur and he began to struggle with every step as the spongy peat sucked him down. "Flametail?" He strained to see through the stalks. "Flametail!"

Jayfeather tried to take another step but his hind leg was stuck. He tugged, trying to pull it out of the black peat, but the mud sucked harder and he sank deeper. He stretched his shoulders, trying to pull out his forepaws, but they slid farther down until he was buried to his knees. "Spottedleaf! Help!" Panic flooded him. With every tug on one paw, another sank deeper. Wetness rose past his belly, soaking his flanks. He lifted his chin as mud began to climb his chest.

"Have you found him?" Spottedleaf poked her head through the reeds.

"Don't come any farther!" Jayfeather screeched. "I'm sinking!"

Spottedleaf lunged forward and tried to grasp Jayfeather's scruff in her jaws, but her teeth clacked shut beside his ear. She scrambled back onto firmer ground. "I can't reach!"

"Stay there!" Jayfeather hissed at her. "We can't both drown!"

Spottedleaf's eyes glittered. "Keep as still as you can! I'll find a stick. You can grab it with your teeth." She turned, her tail whipping past Jayfeather's nose as she hared away.

"You look as if you're in trouble." A voice sounded from the reeds. Jayfeather jerked his head around and saw an orange face peering at him through the stalks.

"Flametail!" The ShadowClan cat was watching him coldly. "Help me! I'm drowning!"

Flametail took a step forward, then stopped, his eyes burning. "I know how you feel."

"Can you reach me?" Jayfeather strained to see the ground behind him. Perhaps it was solid enough there to take Flametail's weight.

"Why should I?" Flametail's mew was icy. "You didn't save me."

"I tried!" Jayfeather felt his whiskers brush the surface of the mud. He tipped his head back, feeling the peat suck at his chin. "But I couldn't! It wasn't my time to die. I had to survive!"

Flametail hissed. "And I didn't?"

Jayfeather searched desperately for something to say to convince the ShadowClan cat that his death wasn't Jayfeather's fault, but bitter-tasting water was bubbling into the corners of his mouth.

"It wasn't fair," Flametail snarled. "It was such a stupid way to die!"

"But you still have a destiny to fulfill!" Jayfeather shook his head and spat out a mouthful of black water. "You are the only one who can save ShadowClan now! A darkness is coming that will wipe out all your Clanmates if you let it! I need you to unite the Clans. It's the only way we'll survive!" He coughed again as a lump of mud hit the back of his throat. "You have to tell Littlecloud I didn't drown you!"

"Why should I believe you?" Flametail spat. "ThunderClan is full of murderers! Even if you didn't drown me, your Clanmate tried to kill me as soon as I arrived here."

"Here?" Jayfeather struggled to speak. "Who?"

"Ivypool!" Flametail thrust his muzzle through the reeds. "I was looking for the path to StarClan and she tried to claw my throat out! She would have succeeded if Tigerheart hadn't stopped her! Now I'm going to let you die instead!"

Water flooded Jayfeather's mouth. He slammed his jaws shut, drawing air desperately through his nose as the mud seeped up around his cheeks.

"Flametail!" Spottedleaf's yowl cut through the air. "Stop making threats like a warrior! You're a medicine cat!" Flametail's gaze shot toward the tortoiseshell she-cat. She glared at him, a twisted branch at her paws. "You have more power than you ever dreamed of," she snarled. "You only need to tell the truth."

Flametail flattened his ears as if he didn't want to hear.

"Help the medicine cats work together again." Spottedleaf was begging now. "If our code is broken, the Clans will fall. We are the heartbeat of the Clans, not the warrior code. Think of the promises you made."

Water bubbling at his nose, Jayfeather watched Flametail shift his paws. Mud slid over his spine and he could no longer feel his legs. A strange peace had washed over him, as if he knew there was no point fighting anymore.

"Is it really in my power?" Flametail murmured.

Jayfeather tried to nod. *Yes! You have the power of the stars in your paws!* But his muscles wouldn't work and he closed his eyes, suddenly feeling more tired than he had ever felt in his life. He was dimly aware of a blur of movement in front of him, but it seemed a long way off.

Suddenly he felt something jabbing against his forepaws. Spottedleaf had pushed the branch deep into the mud and was prodding him with it. "Wake up, Jayfeather! Come on!" she hissed. "I will not let you die like this!"

There was a crackle of reeds and the sound of splashing as Flametail forced his way through the reeds to join her. He crouched down and held the end of the stick in his teeth, steadying it while Spottedleaf steered the other end closer to Jayfeather.

"Come *on!*" Spottedleaf yowled.

Jayfeather blinked. He couldn't give up. He had found Flametail! There was still hope! Fighting through the mud, he flailed his paws until he hooked a claw around the tip of the branch. Dragging it closer, he wrapped both front legs around it. Sodden peat splashed into his face, forcing his eyes to close and making him retch, but he didn't let go.

"Pull!" Spottedleaf gave the order and the two medicine cats began to heave on the branch.

Jayfeather felt himself being hauled forward and upward. He gasped as his mouth surfaced, gulping in air. Spottedleaf and Flametail grunted with effort as they slowly dragged him from the mud. Kicking out with his hind legs, Jay-feather managed to scrabble out of the bog. He collapsed, panting among the reeds, and felt Spottedleaf's paws massaging his chest.

"I'm okay," he gasped. "I only swallowed a bit." A hacking cough cut him off and he spewed up muddy water.

"We should go." Spottedleaf turned away. "There isn't much time."

Flametail nudged Jayfeather to his paws. "Time for what?"

"To speak to the medicine cats!" Spottedleaf called over her shoulder as she bounded up the slope. Flametail shot after her.

Not much time? Jayfeather pushed through the reeds and struggled up the slope. When he reached the top, he saw Spottedleaf and Flametail pelting toward the pines. He raced after them, gathering speed as the shock of his soaking began to fade. *What's the hurry?*

Then he remembered. *They'll be dreaming like I am. We must speak to them before they wake up!* He pushed harder against the ground, closing the gap on Flametail and Spottedleaf until he caught up with them at the edge of the pines.

Spottedleaf stopped and stared into the trees wild-eyed. "We have to find them!" she panted. "Before the sun rises."

Flametail's eyes widened. "Quick!" He hared along a trail that swerved among the pines. "I know where Littlecloud visits!"

Jayfeather pelted after him, Spottedleaf at his heels.

"Littlecloud!" Flametail called his Clanmate's name as they crested a low rise.

The ShadowClan medicine cat was standing in a hollow. He jerked around, blinking in surprise. "Flametail? *Jayfeather?*"

Jayfeather bounded down the slope toward him. "I know," he mewed quickly. "I'm not supposed to be a medicine cat anymore, but Flametail has something to tell you!"

Littlecloud's gaze flicked to the orange medicine cat. "Where have you been? I've been searching for you."

Flametail dipped his head. "I've been staying out of sight since I died," he meowed apologetically.

"But now I know you're safe with our ancestors." Little-cloud touched his Clanmate's cheek with his muzzle.

Spottedleaf nosed between them. "We can't stay here. We have to tell all the medicine cats while they're still sharing dreams with StarClan. Littlecloud, come with us." She turned to Flametail. "What's the quickest way to WindClan's part of the hunting grounds?"

"Out of the pines and head for the gorse." Spottedleaf nodded and raced away.

Jayfeather paused before following her. He held Flame-tail's bright blue gaze for several long heartbeats. There was so much he could say, but he had a feeling Flametail knew what it was already. "Thank you," he murmured.

Flametail nodded. "For the Clans," he meowed.

"For the Clans," Jayfeather echoed. Then he spun around and sent pine needles spraying behind him as he dashed after Spottedleaf. He heard Flametail and Littlecloud racing after him, their paws ringing hollow on the damp earth.

They broke from the pines onto a hillside crowded by heather; it rose toward a glowering, purple-gray sky. Spot-tedleaf plunged through a gap between the bushes and disappeared. Jayfeather raced after her, Flametail and Little-cloud at his heels. The path wound steeply upward, walled by prickly bushes on either side. Jayfeather sensed they were not alone: Pelts flashed between the stems, eyes shining in the shadows, but no cat stopped them.

As they neared the summit, a thick swath of gorse blocked their path. Zigzagging frantically, Jayfeather spotted an opening and darted through. He exploded out onto a rocky plateau.

Spottedleaf burst out after him. "There he is!" She raced toward a lone figure that sat at the edge of the rock. Kestrelflight turned to face them, his ears flat.

Spottedleaf scrambled to a halt beside him. "We need to talk to you!"

Jayfeather skidded on the smooth stone, gasping as he saw the ground drop away. He dug in his claws and stopped just in time. Kestrelflight's front paws were curled over the edge of a steep cliff. Far below, a wide valley rolled toward a distant horizon where it was swallowed by billowing cloud.

Kestrelflight frowned. "What's going on?"

"We need Willowshine!" As Littlecloud and Flametail caught up, Spottedleaf scanned the valley. "Is that RiverClan land down there?"

"There's no need to go there."

A voice sounded behind them. Willowshine was stalking across the hilltop toward them. "I saw you and wondered what you were doing." She stared at Jayfeather. "Are you here because of Mothwing? She said you'd visited RiverClan today."

"Yes." Jayfeather could hardly get his breath. "There was a sign for me."

Willowshine nodded. "That's why she told me to share

dreams with StarClan tonight. I thought it was strange. She doesn't usually mention StarClan."

Panic flashed through Jayfeather as he realized that the RiverClan medicine cat was beginning to fade. Willowshine was being pulled away from StarClan. Kestrelflight was growing paler, too. And Littlecloud. Jayfeather looked down at his front paws and saw gray stone where his toes should have been.

"The sun is rising over the lake! The medicine cats are leaving us." Spottedleaf gazed at Flametail. "Quick, tell them!"

"Jayfeather didn't kill me!" Flametail blurted out the truth. "I drowned. Jayfeather was trying to save me. But I was too heavy and the current was too strong. My death was not his fault!"

"Thank you, Flametail." Jayfeather dipped his head as the landscape around began to swirl. "You have fulfilled your destiny."

The flame-colored ShadowClan medicine cat lifted his head. *He must be the fourth cat.* Jayfeather looked around at the other medicine cats. They were almost transparent. "Let's meet at the Moonpool tomorrow."

"Yes!" Kestrelflight called.

"I'll be there!" Willowshine promised.

"Me too!" Littlecloud's mew was no more than a whisper as he disappeared.

Flametail's orange pelt burned against the fading rock. "How strange that I had to wait until I died to fulfill my destiny." He stared at Jayfeather. "Thank you for coming to find me." Peace flooded his gaze. "Whatever happens now, I'll stand side by side with the Clans. All of them."

"Jayfeather." As the world disappeared, Spottedleaf's breath brushed his ear fur. "He's not the fourth cat."

"He must be!" Jayfeather shifted in his nest.

"No! You have to keep looking!" Spottedleaf's voice echoed in his mind as Jayfeather woke, opening his eyes into blackness.

CHAPTER 17

Lionblaze paced the clearing. Rain dripped from the dens, though the clouds had cleared to reveal a clear dawn sky. The Clan was beginning to stir. Nests rustled and the honeysuckle shivered as Purdy padded yawning from the elders' den.

"You're up early, young 'un!" the old tom called across the clearing.

"I'm waiting for the dawn patrol," Lionblaze told him. His claws itched with worry. Would they return with news of more strange cat scents?

"You should be resting." Firestar bounded down from Highledge. "You were out on moonhigh patrol!"

Lionblaze halted. "So were you." They'd crossed the whole territory with Brackenfur and Sandstorm and found cat scent in every gully and hollow.

Sandstorm poked her head out of the leader's cave. "How can any cat sleep knowing the woods are filled with enemies!"

"Hush!" Firestar shot back at her, lashing his tail.

Sandstorm scrambled down the rock tumble and wove around her mate. "Sorry," she murmured. "But shouldn't the Clan know?"

Firestar dug his claws deep into the soil. "Not until I decide how we tackle this." His gaze met Lionblaze's.

How will he explain it to the Clan? Were they ready to know that the Dark Forest was preparing to launch an attack that could destroy all the Clans? Lionblaze shivered. It had been shocking to smell Ivypool's scent among the others. Had Firestar guessed that the young warrior had been with the Dark Forest cats? *He might just think it was stale scent from a hunting patrol.*

The brambles at the entrance to the medicine den trembled and Jayfeather pushed his way out. "Lionblaze." He trotted to his brother's side. "I shared dreams with StarClan," he whispered in Lionblaze's ear.

Lionblaze steered Jayfeather toward the far edge of the clearing. "Did they tell you anything?" he hissed.

"I found Flametail!" Jayfeather's sightless eyes were bright. "He told the other medicine cats the truth about his death. We're meeting at the Moonpool tonight."

"What if it's too late?" Lionblaze mewed grimly. If the Dark Forest cats were leaving scents so casually in the lakeside territories, the final battle must be near.

"We have to believe it's not!" Jayfeather hissed. "If the medicine cats are willing to join together once more, they might be able to get their leaders to do the same!"

"We still need to find the fourth cat," Lionblaze reminded him. What good was uniting if the prophecy was still unfulfilled?

"It's not Flametail," Jayfeather announced.

Lionblaze stared at his brother in surprise. "What made you think it was?"

"Mothwing showed me an omen," Jayfeather explained.

"A reed was burning with a flame that the rain couldn't put out. I thought it meant Flametail might be the fourth cat. But Spottedleaf told me he wasn't."

Lionblaze whisked his tail, frustrated. "I don't suppose she told you who it was?"

Jayfeather shook his head. "I don't think she knows." He paced around Lionblaze. "We have to find out for ourselves." He stopped.

Paw steps were thundering toward the thorn barrier. Lionblaze tasted the air. *Brambleclaw.* The dawn patrol was returning.

The barrier rustled as Brambleclaw exploded into the camp. "WindClan has reset the borders and put a permanent watch at the stream." Fur ruffled, he headed for Firestar. "We should do the same."

Graystripe and Millie followed the ThunderClan deputy into camp, with Molepaw, Rosepetal, and Dovewing right behind.

"I should have stayed at the border," Graystripe growled.

"What could you have done alone?" Millie argued.

Firestar narrowed his eyes. "Go back," he ordered Graystripe. "Don't start anything, but warn us if there's trouble."

Sorreltail poked her head out of the warriors' den. "Is WindClan planning to invade?"

"We're not sure," Firestar told her. "But it's better to be prepared." He signaled to Brambleclaw with his tail and the two warriors scrambled up the rocks to his cave.

Molepaw bounced around Rosepetal. "Can I go with

Graystripe?" he begged. "My hearing's sharper than his. I'll know if they're coming *way* before him."

Rosepetal gazed sternly at her apprentice. "Graystripe has the experience to know the difference between the sound of threat and the sound of action." She nudged him toward the fresh-kill pile. "We don't want any false alarms. Now go and eat."

As Molepaw stomped away, Dovewing joined Lionblaze and Jayfeather. "WindClan is furious," she warned. "They've found enemy scents all over the moorland, especially ThunderClan scent."

Has Ivypool been there too? Lionblaze's tail twitched.

Jayfeather narrowed his eyes. "At this rate the Dark Forest won't need to invade," he muttered. "The Clans will tear one another to pieces on their own."

"We have to find out exactly what Brokenstar's planning." Lionblaze leaned closer to Dovewing. "Get Ivypool. It's time she told us what's going on in the Dark Forest."

"She must be sleeping." Dovewing glanced at the apprentice den. "I don't like to wake her."

"I don't care," Lionblaze hissed. "Go get her!"

As Dovewing headed for the yew bush, Lionblaze nudged Jayfeather toward the fallen beech. Poppyfrost was stretching outside the warriors' den. Berrynose pushed past her and headed for the fresh-kill pile, where Foxleap and Toadstep were already rooting through yesterday's catch.

"Has Brambleclaw organized the patrols?" Foxleap hooked a shriveled shrew with his claw. "We're going to need something fresher than this."

"I should think so." Ferncloud padded from the nursery. "Brightheart's hungry and she won't want to eat stale mouse. With the kits coming soon, her appetite is fussier than ever."

"I'll go hunting!" Molepaw offered.

Rosepetal sat down. "We just got back from patrol!"

Foxleap rubbed his nose with his paw. "I'll take Molepaw and Cherrypaw out while you rest," he told the dark cream she-cat.

"Thanks," Rosepetal breathed.

The yew bush shivered and Dovewing emerged. Ivypool followed, her eyes bleary with sleep. Lionblaze signaled to them with his tail, huddling deeper into the shadow of the beech.

"What is it?" Ivypool yawned as she reached him.

Jayfeather shifted his paws. "You have to tell us what's happening in the Dark Forest," he hissed.

Lionblaze beckoned Ivypool closer with a flick of his muzzle. "There are Dark Forest scents all over Clan territory." He fixed her gaze with his. "And yours."

Ivypool flattened her ears. "I'm not the only Clan cat visiting the lake from the Dark Forest," she mewed defensively. "The others come too."

"Why?" Lionblaze lowered his voice.

Ivypool glanced over her shoulder to check no one was listening. "Brokenstar says we need to learn about each of the Clan's territories. So we can help one another if there's an emergency."

Anger pulsed through Lionblaze's paws. "Do the Clan cats actually believe that?"

Ivypool twitched one ear. "Most of them don't realize how evil he is."

"But some do?" Lionblaze tried to understand.

Ivypool's mew dropped to a whisper. "A few of them *want* the Dark Forest to win. They think their leaders have grown too soft."

Lionblaze's eyes widened. How could warriors turn on their own Clanmates? Didn't they believe in the warrior code? "Who are these cats?" he hissed.

Ivypool stared at her paws. "They may still change their minds, once the battle starts."

Lionblaze growled. "Tell us who these traitors are! We should warn their leaders."

Jayfeather padded between them. "Let's trust Ivypool on this," he cautioned. "They may decide to fight on the right side when the battle comes. If we condemn them now, we risk making them enemies for sure."

Ivypool flashed a grateful glance. "We have to do what Brokenstar says." Her tail quivered. "Or he says he'll kill us. And he means it. He killed Beetlewhisker."

Lionblaze gripped the ground with his claws. "Beetlewhisker?"

Dovewing was already pricking her ears. Ivypool nodded, staring round-eyed at her sister. Lionblaze knew the Dovewing was listening for signs of the young RiverClan warrior. He held his breath, praying Ivypool was wrong.

"Well?" Lionblaze couldn't bear the suspense.

"He's gone," Dovewing reported. "RiverClan can't find him. I can hear them calling for him but there's no sign."

Ivypool shrank back, trembling. "He'll lie in the Dark Forest forever."

"We know what we're up against," Jayfeather growled. "If Brokenstar is prepared to kill his own recruits before the battle has started, he must feel confident."

Lionblaze nodded. "And they're clearly scouting the territories for the best places to attack." He lifted his chin. "We have to tell Firestar." He padded from the shadow of the beech and crossed the clearing. "Come on, Ivypool!"

Dovewing started to follow but Lionblaze waved her back with his tail. "Stay with Jayfeather." Firestar's den would be crowded enough. "Give Ivypool some space."

He leaped up the tumble of rocks, showering Ivypool with grit as he reached the ledge. He waited for her to catch up, then nosed her into the den.

Brambleclaw looked up, surprised. "What are you doing here?" He was sitting beside Firestar.

Ivypool shifted from one paw to another.

"You need to know what's going on." Lionblaze could just make out Firestar's pelt in the shadows at the back of the cave. "Ivypool has been visiting the Dark Forest in her dreams." As Firestar stiffened, Lionblaze went on, "She's been spying for us."

Brambleclaw jerked his head up. "What in the name of StarClan is going on?"

Firestar's tail swished over the den floor. "The Dark Forest is rising, Brambleclaw." His eyes gleamed as he stared at Ivypool. "And I'm guessing these are the cats invading our territory each night."

Ivypool nodded. "Brokenstar and Tigerstar have convinced cats from every Clan that they're learning to be great warriors, and that training them together will make them stronger."

"Tigerstar?" Brambleclaw's eyes shone in the half-light. "What's he got to do with it?"

"He's one of the senior warriors in the Dark Forest," Lionblaze explained. "He's been recruiting cats from around the lake and training them in their dreams. Now he's found a way to bring his warriors onto our territory."

A growl rumbled in Brambleclaw's throat. "Will I never be free from my father?"

Firestar's eyes glazed, as though he was reaching for some distant memory. "This battle has been coming for a long time."

"What battle?" Leafpool's mew sounded at the mouth of the cave.

"Who are we fighting?" Squirrelflight peered, wide-eyed, over her sister's shoulder.

Firestar padded forward and leaned close to Lionblaze. "It's time you shared your destiny with your kin. They are here now. Tell them."

Lionblaze backed away. "It's none of their business!" Heart racing, he glanced from Brambleclaw to Leafpool. "And they're not my kin!"

Firestar's breath touched his muzzle. "Leafpool kitted you.

Squirrelflight and Brambleclaw raised you. Without them, the prophecy would never have been fulfilled."

It still hasn't been! How was any of this going to help find the fourth cat? Or fight the Dark Forest?

Brambleclaw got to his paws. "Come with me."

Lionblaze suddenly felt like a kit again. The warrior he'd known for so long as his father padded past him and left the cave. Quietly, Leafpool turned and followed, Squirrelflight on her tail.

"Tell them everything, Lionblaze," Firestar murmured. "They need to know." He sat down. "While you're gone, Ivypool can tell me what she's learned from her dreams."

Reluctantly, Lionblaze scrabbled down the rock tumble and followed Brambleclaw, Leafpool, and Squirrelflight toward the camp entrance.

Jayfeather darted over. "What's going on?"

"Firestar says I have to tell them about the prophecy," Lionblaze growled.

"I'll come with you." Jayfeather fell in beside him.

"Get Hollyleaf," Lionblaze meowed. "She's part of this."

"She's not part of the prophecy," Jayfeather reminded him.

"She's our littermate," Lionblaze insisted. "She knows as much as we do."

As Jayfeather headed back across the clearing, Lionblaze ducked through the tunnel. He snorted as Leafpool's tail trailed over his muzzle. By the time he emerged, thorns scraping his pelt, Brambleclaw was sitting in the shallow dip beyond the camp entrance. His tail was tucked over his paws while

Squirrelflight paced solemnly beside him. Leafpool settled a fox-length away.

"What's the matter?" Hollyleaf's mew sounded from the tunnel. She pushed her way out, blinking in surprise when she saw the cats gathered outside the camp.

Jayfeather crept out after her and nudged her forward. "We're going to tell them about the prophecy."

"Now?" Her ear twitched.

Yes, now. Lionblaze gripped the earth, dead leaves crackling beneath his claws. "A long time ago, Firestar was given a prophecy," he began. "He was told that three kits would be born with the power of the stars in their paws."

Brambleclaw stiffened. "You three?" His gaze flitted from Lionblaze to Jayfeather and Hollyleaf.

"Not me," Hollyleaf corrected him quickly.

Jayfeather moved closer to his sister. "Though we thought she was one of the Three at the beginning."

Squirrelflight leaned forward. "Who's the third cat?"

"Dovewing." Lionblaze pressed on. "We are destined to save the Clans from the Dark Forest."

Anger flared in Brambleclaw's eyes. "Why didn't you tell me? Was it because I'm not your true father?" He glared at Squirrelflight. "Did *you* know? Is that why you lied about them being your kits?"

Squirrelflight backed away, eyes widening. "No!"

Lionblaze walked between the two warriors. "None of you knew." He glanced at Leafpool. "Only Firestar and us."

Jayfeather took a step forward. "We had to fulfill our

destiny on our own."

"But we could have helped you." Leafpool's eyes clouded. "You didn't have to carry this burden alone."

Lionblaze growled at her. "We wouldn't have had to carry it at all if you hadn't broken your code!"

As hurt flashed across Leafpool's gaze, Squirrelflight darted in front of her sister. She glared at Lionblaze. "Would you rather have never been born?" she snapped. "Who would have saved us from the Dark Forest then?"

"We haven't saved you yet," Jayfeather muttered.

"But you will." Leafpool padded past Squirrelflight. Her gaze cleared. "You were born to save the Clans."

Brambleclaw's tail flicked angrily. "Did there have to be so many lies?" He was staring at Squirrelflight. "Couldn't you have told me the truth?"

Squirrelflight dipped her head. "It was never my secret to tell. Leafpool had so much to lose."

"She lost everything anyway," Brambleclaw snarled.

"No, I didn't." Leafpool lifted her muzzle. "I watched my kits grow into fine warriors, and I still serve my Clan with all my heart."

Lionblaze felt his heart prick. Perhaps this was the truth that was most important. Leafpool had sacrificed so much and, even though her kits rejected her time and again, she'd never stopped loving them. In his darkest moments, he couldn't deny that.

"Brambleclaw, I'm sorry." Squirrelflight moved closer to the ThunderClan deputy. Her voice was stronger now, as if she was tired of being punished for something she had believed to be right. "You have to understand that I never intended to hurt you. I loved you, and was proud to raise these kits with you. You were a wonderful father."

"But I wasn't their father!" Brambleclaw hissed.

"Yes, you were!" Squirrelflight thrust her muzzle close to Brambleclaw's. Her eyes blazed. "Don't throw away everything just because you are angry with me!"

Lionblaze swallowed. "I was so proud to be your son."

Brambleclaw looked at him in surprise, as if he'd forgotten Lionblaze was there. Something in the deputy's expression changed. "And I couldn't have asked for a better son. And you, Jayfeather. Or a better daughter, Hollyleaf." Hollyleaf opened her mouth as if to protest, but Brambleclaw spoke first. "You played no part in this deception, I know that. Whatever you did, it was because of the lies that had been told when you were born."

"It was my fault alone," Leafpool meowed quietly. "You are wrong to blame Squirrelflight. She was just being loyal to me. And now that we know about the prophecy, surely the only thing that matters is that these kits were accepted by their Clan? It's not about us, after all. It's about *them*. Their destinies shaped ours, right from the moment they were born."

Squirrelflight nodded. "Everything was meant to be."

Lionblaze looked down at his paws. If these cats could accept their destinies, then he had enough courage to accept his. *I am one of the Four.*

CHAPTER 18

❧

Jayfeather paced along the edge of the Moonpool. The stone felt icy beneath his paws and a cold wind moaned above his head. *Please, StarClan, let them come!* Last night, the medicine cats had promised to meet him here.

It seemed a moon away now. When Lionblaze had revealed the prophecy that afternoon, it felt as though he'd shaken the world between his claws. Leafpool's words echoed in his mind. *You were born to save the Clans.* Hope had sparked from her pelt, and the anger, which had been knotted around Squirrelflight and Brambleclaw for so long, finally began to unravel.

A pebble clattered beyond the lip of the hollow.

"Watch out!" Kestrelflight snapped.

"Sorry!" Fur brushed stone as a cat heaved her belly over the ridge.

Jayfeather padded forward, feeling the rock dimpling underpaw. "Willowshine, is that you?"

"We're here." The RiverClan medicine cat followed the spiraling path toward the Moonpool. "Mothwing sends good wishes."

"Why didn't you wait for us by the stream?" Kestrelflight

bounded down to join them.

"I wasn't sure you'd come." Jayfeather shifted his paws.

Littlecloud padded stiffly into the hollow, his old bones tired from the journey. "We told you we would be here."

"I've had to leave a camp full of sneezing warriors." Kestrelflight fluffed out his pelt. "The first cold of leaf-bare has brought sickness."

"Anything serious?" Littlecloud asked.

"Nothing more than runny noses and a cough or two," Kestrelflight told him with obvious relief. "I've left Whitetail in charge of the herb store. She knows how to treat a sore throat."

Willowshine's paws scuffed the stone. "Perhaps it's time you took on an apprentice?"

Jayfeather cut her off. "Kestrelflight won't need an apprentice if the Dark Forest destroys us!"

Willowshine's breath touched his nose. "What do you mean?"

"They've found a way of crossing over from the Place of No Stars," Jayfeather announced.

"Into *our* territory?" Willowshine whispered.

Littlecloud's claws scratched the rock. "It's been them all along!" Fear edged his mew. "It's been Dark Forest warriors sneaking into our territory!"

"Into all our territories," Jayfeather corrected him. "They're looking for the best places to fight. They could attack any day!"

Kestrelflight growled. "We can fight off a few mangy dead cats."

Jayfeather leaned forward, his heart pounding. "It's not just a few dead cats!" he hissed. "They've been training our Clanmates."

Willowshine gulped. "How?"

"In their dreams!" Jayfeather ignored the shock sparking from the pelts around him. They had to know the truth.

"WindClan wouldn't betray their own!" Kestrelflight snarled.

"Most of them don't understand what they're doing," Jayfeather explained. "They believe they're being loyal. They think Brokenstar and his Clanmates are teaching them to be better warriors so they can fight for their Clans."

"*Most* of them?" Willowshine echoed. "What about the others?"

Jayfeather faced her. "Some of them want the Dark Forest to win."

"We can handle a few traitors!" Littlecloud paced around Willowshine.

"I hope you're right," Jayfeather muttered darkly. "But Brokenstar has threatened the worst punishment to any cat who betrays him. And in the chaos of battle—with all four Clans under attack—do you really think the battle lines will be so clearly drawn?" Jayfeather stalked down to the water's edge. "Blood will flow from every Clan." He turned, widening his sightless eyes. "It's Tigerstar's destiny to destroy us all."

"What can we do?" Willowshine breathed.

He crouched beside the Moonpool. "It's my destiny to stop him."

"How?" Littlecloud padded closer.

Jayfeather hesitated. "I don't know." He'd warned the medicine cats. They could pass on his warning to their Clans. But would that be enough?

Willowshine shifted her paws. "StarClan will protect us."

"StarClan is divided," Kestrelflight reminded her.

Jayfeather gripped the rock with his claws, fighting back the fear that was turning his belly cold. "They're more scared than we are," he murmured.

Willowshine's breath quickened. "How can we fight the Dark Forest alone?"

When all cats have closed eyes, we gave the gift of sight to the cat who is blind. You see more than most. Midnight's words suddenly flooded back to him, and Brambleberry's mew echoed in his ears: *You already know the answer.*

Jayfeather lifted his chin. "Flametail united us," he declared. "Now I will unite StarClan."

"How?" Littlecloud's tail-tip whipped the stone.

"I'll let them see the danger for themselves!" Jayfeather turned and touched his nose tip to the Moonpool.

At once, the world opened around him and his blindness lifted. He was on a grassy hilltop, dark clouds skimming over-head. Wind-battered meadows stretched below him. Trees huddled in the valleys, stripped of leaves. StarClan's hunting grounds had slid deep into leaf-bare.

"Where's the sun gone?" Willowshine shimmered into view beside Jayfeather, her nose sparkling with water from the Moonpool.

Kestrelflight stalked from the long grass, eyes round as he adjusted to the gloom.

"Now what?" Littlecloud's pelt brushed his flank as the ShadowClan medicine cat joined them.

"Each of you must go to your own ancestors and bring them here."

Willowshine stared down to a muddy river flowing between the fields. Littlecloud faced the swath of dark forest spreading beside it while Kestrelflight fixed his gaze on the rolling moorland beyond.

"Can you do it?" From here Jayfeather could see the tops of the mighty oaks where ThunderClan sheltered beneath.

"I'll bring every cat that I find." Littlecloud headed down the hillside.

Kestrelflight broke into a run, streaking toward the moors.

"Willowshine?" Jayfeather saw the RiverClan medicine cat hesitate.

She whisked her tail. "Will the Dark Forest warriors come here, too?"

Jayfeather flattened his ears. "We won't let them."

Willowshine flashed him an anxious look and began to trot toward the river. Jayfeather headed down the hill and into the woods.

A white pelt moved at the edge of his vision. He snapped his head around. *Whitestorm!* The ThunderClan warrior was stalking prey. Tail down, muzzle low, he crept forward, his eyes fixed ahead. A mouse skittered over a tree root a tail-length away. Whitestorm sprang and landed on it squarely, killing it and sitting up with a purr rumbling in his throat.

Jayfeather padded out of the shadows. "I'm glad there's still prey here."

Whitestorm jerked around, blinking. The mouse dropped from his jaws. "Hi, Jayfeather."

"Follow me, Whitestorm. Please, it's important." He stared into the white warrior's eyes. "We need to gather StarClan."

Whitestorm tipped his head. "Everyone?"

"As many as we can." Jayfeather bounded forward and broke into a run.

Whitestorm chased after him. "But what about the boundaries?"

"The other medicine cats are helping me gather Shadow-Clan, WindClan, and RiverClan." He ducked just in time to avoid the prickly stem of a bramble.

"Didn't StarClan order you to stay away from the other medicine cats?"

"Yes." Jayfeather caught sight of a matted old tom snoozing in the shelter of a fern. "Goosefeather!"

The old ThunderClan medicine cat lifted his head, then hauled himself to his paws. "Is it half-moon already?"

"Come with us." Jayfeather flicked his tail. "We're gathering the Clan."

Goosefeather glanced at Whitestorm. "What's going on?"

Whitestorm shrugged.

"Come on!" Jayfeather raced away. He crested a rise to find Sunstar picking his way along an ivy-choked trail.

Jayfeather caught him up. "Follow us!" He didn't even

pause. There wasn't time to explain. The ground grew muddy underpaw and ferns gave way to bracken. "Frostfur!"

The white she-cat was reaching up into a cloud of tumbling leaves, batting at them with her paws. Her gaze widened as she saw Whitestorm, Goosefeather, and Sunstar on his tail. "Where are you going in such a hurry?"

"Join us!" Jayfeather called, racing past the she-cat and heading for a swath of brambles.

"Bluestar!"

The old ThunderClan leader was eating a vole in the shade of a withering juniper. She looked up in surprise.

"Follow us!" Jayfeather told her.

Bluestar glanced down at the vole, then bounded toward them, her eyes shining with excitement. "Where are we going?"

"Wait and see!" Jayfeather led the cats down a ravine that cut through the middle of the woods.

As they scrambled up the other side, Jayfeather glanced over his shoulder, surprised by the long line of cats trailing in their wake. Tawnyspots, Frostfur, Swiftbreeze, and Adder-fang had joined them. He reached the top of the ravine and caught sight of a thick, tangled pelt lurking in the shadows. "Yellowfang?" Her amber eyes narrowed as he called to her. "Come with us!" he urged.

She curled her lip. "What are you up to?"

Jayfeather stumbled to a halt. "I'm uniting StarClan!"

"Why would I follow fools?"

Jayfeather lashed his tail. "*Don't* come, then! Stay here in the dark. My words will be wasted on you anyway." He bounded forward, his Clanmates scrambling after him.

Pale light showed ahead and he pelted for the edge of the forest, breaking from the trees, tail high. The hill rose before him. Charging through ferns, he led his Clanmates onto the grassy slope. Cats were swarming from every direction, racing for the hill. He spotted Willowshine's gray pelt leading a horde of RiverClan warriors. Kestrelflight raced from the valley, warriors skimming over the grass behind him like a flock of starlings.

Jayfeather's paws ached from running but hope was swelling in his chest. At the crest of the hill, he stopped and turned, amazed by the ranks of StarClan cats crowding over the slopes below him.

Kestrelflight halted beside him. "Word must have spread."

Willowshine slowed, panting, and sat down.

As Jayfeather plucked at the grass, Littlecloud scrambled to the top of the hill and stopped beside him. His eyes stretched wide as an owl's as he saw the cats amassed below.

"Yellowfang came," Willowshine whispered in Jayfeather's ear. The mangy, old she-cat stood apart from the other cats, eyeing them distrustfully.

"StarClan!" Jayfeather stepped forward and lifted his chin. "Listen!"

"Why?" Yellowfang yowled. "We have the wisdom of ages. You have the stupidity of youth!"

Sunstar jerked around and hissed at her. "You can leave if you want to!"

Yellowfang flattened her ears but didn't move.

Jayfeather tried again. "You must listen to me!" he called. "Yellowfang's right. I'm younger than any of you."

Mosskit flicked her tail as she padded out from behind Snowfur.

"Younger than most of you," Jayfeather corrected himself. He unsheathed his claws. "There is a terrible threat to you all! And to the Clans you once lived in. You know the Dark Forest is rising. You can see it in the dead leaves that litter your hunting grounds, and the clouds that block out your sun." Jayfeather glanced up at the gray sky. "You must face the truth. And the truth is worse than you ever imagined." He gazed around the raised faces, hoping they understood. "The Dark Forest must be met and fought. You will not win by huddling together like families of mice. You must stand together or fall divided!"

"But how can we beat an enemy that can bring leaf-bare to StarClan?" Raggedstar called.

Darkflower's eyes glittered. "They have grown stronger than us."

Sunstar padded forward. "When we sent you the Prophecy of the Three, we didn't know the Dark Forest would grow so powerful."

"But now they are *Four*!" Bluestar pushed past her old leader. "The Ancients gave them an ally to make them strong enough to fight any enemy."

Jayfeather's pelt ruffled. "We don't know who it is yet."

Bluestar tipped her head. "Isn't it obvious?"

Jayfeather frowned.

"You are not the first cats guided by a prophecy," Bluestar prompted. "I was promised long ago that fire would save the Clan. It has never needed saving as much as it does now."

The fire in the reeds. Always fire.

Bluestar nodded, as if she could see into his thoughts. "Get him," she mewed softly. "He needs to know what is happening."

Jayfeather spun and darted away down the far side of the slope. Skidding to a halt, he closed his eyes. Forcing his thoughts into the minds of his Clanmates, tucked tight in their nests in the hollow, he searched their dreams for the cat who had always been destined to save his Clan.

"Surrender, you fox-hearts!"

"Never!"

Jayfeather crashed into a battle. He felt smooth rock beneath his paws. It stretched, flat and wide, toward a dark wall of pine trees. Jayfeather flinched as cats fought around him, throwing up dust from the sandstone as they reared and slashed at one another. A flame-colored pelt glowed at the heart of the battle.

"Firestar!"

The ThunderClan leader was wrestling with a dark-furred ShadowClan warrior. "Sunningrocks will never be yours!" With a sharp thrust of his hind paws, Firestar heaved the warrior away. His muscles flexed with the strength of a young cat, and his eyes were green and fierce.

"Firestar!" Jayfeather yowled again, dodging between the battling warriors.

Firestar froze, blinking at him.

Jayfeather halted in front of his leader. "Come with me."

Firestar pricked his ears. "Why?"

"The prophecy needs more than the Three. We need a fourth cat."

"What do you mean?"

Jayfeather twitched his tail impatiently. "When I went to the mountains, the Tribe of Endless Hunting told me that the prophecy could only be fulfilled if we found another cat. Mothwing showed me an omen, a fire in the reeds by River-Clan. It's *you*, Firestar. You are the fourth cat."

Firestar tipped his head to one side. "Yet again, fire will save the Clan," he murmured. "Very well. What do you need me to do?"

"Follow me." Jayfeather turned and dived between the battling cats, racing to the edge of the wide, flat rock.

Firestar quickly caught up. "Where are we going?"

"You'll see." Jayfeather drew in a breath and flung himself over the cliff, feeling a rush of air before his paws hit grass. Firestar landed beside him, eyes wide. They were on top of the hill beside the medicine cats. Below, StarClan was waiting.

"They needed to see you," Jayfeather explained.

"Why?"

"Because the prophecy makes you part of this. The life you have left will save the Clans." Jayfeather turned to face the ranks of StarClan. "You must follow me once more," he yowled. "You need to see for yourselves." Beckoning with his tail, he headed down the slope, not to Firestar's dream battlescape, but into a dingy forest where slimy bushes choked the roots of the trees and the sunshine turned to eerie half-light. Firestar's pelt brushed his as they crept deeper into the woods. Behind them, StarClan sparkled in the shadows, muttering.

"How can any warrior live in such darkness?"

"It smells foul."

Jayfeather heard a battle cry echo between the trees. "Look." He flicked his muzzle toward the shadows ahead. Dark pelts flitted through the slippery undergrowth. Agonized cries rose and fell in the darkness. Then one voice rasped louder than the others.

"Hook your claws into her spine and go for her throat!" Mapleshade loomed suddenly in front of them. Blind to the watching StarClan cats, she aimed a heavy blow at the ear of a scrawny tom and sent him reeling away.

Brokenstar stalked from the trees. "Hasn't Shredtail mastered the death blow yet?" He scowled at the tabby, who was wiping blood from his nose. Then he yanked the tortoiseshell to her paws, blood welling on her fur where his claws pierced her pelt. "If your opponent wasn't so useless, you'd be ripped to shreds by now. I want as many Clan cats dead as there are birds in the forest!"

"Where's the sun?" Mosskit's frightened whisper echoed in the darkness.

Snowfur wrapped her tail over his back. "Hush, little one!"

Creeping like prey, the StarClan cats headed back along the trail. Firestar walked heavily beside Jayfeather, his head low. "How can we fight such evil?" he murmured.

"The prophecy says we can win." Jayfeather felt daylight dapple his pelt. The trees had thinned and StarClan were flooding back into their hunting grounds.

"We're back!" Mosskit scampered onto the grassy slope. He turned, blinking, as StarClan streamed past him and stared at Jayfeather. "Why did you take us to see those horrible cats?"

Bluestar paused beside her kit and touched his head with her muzzle. "We have to know our enemy."

Firestar lifted his voice to the whole of StarClan. "Now that you have seen them, have heard what they are threatening our Clans with, are you afraid to fight?"

Raggedstar bristled. "Never!"

Jayfeather saw determination hardening the gazes of the StarClan warriors. "But will you fight together?" he questioned.

Bluestar swished her tail. "We can't fight such cruelty while we're divided."

Yellowfang stepped forward. "How will we know who to trust?"

"You can trust me." Firestar straightened up, his pelt bright. "And one another."

Raggedstar padded forward. "How could such horror have thrived?" he growled. "We should have been able to crush it before it grew so strong. After all, we have the power of the stars in our paws."

Jayfeather met his solemn gaze. "No," he meowed. "That is my destiny. Mine and Firestar's."

Beside him, Firestar nodded. "I am the fourth cat," he declared. "The prophecy has come true."

Jayfeather opened his eyes into blackness. The Moonpool rippled at his nose. Kestrelflight, Littlecloud, and Willowshine were waking, their pelts brushing the stone as they clambered to their paws.

Jayfeather felt blood welling on his pads. The long journey had left him grazed and aching. "StarClan is united. Now we must gather the Clans." He pushed himself up. "We must tell them everything."

Littlecloud's claws scraped the rock. "Let's bring them to the island."

"But we don't know which warriors to trust." Worry edged Willowshine's mew.

"We can trust the leaders, surely?" Kestrelflight's tail swished.

Jayfeather nodded. "I'll bring Firestar."

"And I'll bring Blackstar," Littlecloud promised.

"I'll bring Mistystar."

"I'll bring Onestar."

Jayfeather felt determination harden beneath their pelts. "Let's meet at sunhigh," he decided. "We have to make them realize that the only way to win this battle is to unite the Clans."

CHAPTER 19

"Brightheart has kitted!"

Poppyfrost's cry woke Dovewing. She jumped from her nest and darted into the clearing. The hollow sparkled with dew. Mist hung on the trees at the top of the hollow. The musty scents of leaf-fall laced the chilly air. Faces peered from dens, whiskers quivering, eyes bright.

Cloudtail was pacing outside the nursery while Mousefur hurried across the clearing on stiff legs. "How many?" the old she-cat rasped.

"Three." Cloudtail carried on pacing. "Two toms and a she-kit." He glanced anxiously at the bramble den as Jayfeather poked his head out of the entrance. "Is Brightheart okay?"

Dovewing's belly tightened as she crossed the clearing. Brightheart was old to be kitting.

"She's fine," Cinderheart purred. "Come and see."

Dovewing halted beside Mousefur. "It's the first good news we've had for a while."

The elder whisked her tail. "Perhaps Firestar should have sent her away to kit outside our territory." Her eyes were dark. "They'd be safer."

"Safer?" Graystripe padded toward them. "The safest place for any kit is at the heart of its Clan."

Lilykit slithered out of the nursery. "No one's sending me away!"

"Of course not." *And you shouldn't have been eavesdropping.* Dovewing wrapped her tail around the tiny tortoiseshell. "ThunderClan fights for its kits. They're the heart of the Clan." She nudged Lilykit toward the warriors' den. "Why don't you go and tell Sorreltail about Brightheart's kits?"

Firestar jumped down from Highledge, Sandstorm on his tail. He weaved past Dustpelt and Squirrelflight and stopped beside Graystripe. "How many?" he asked, stretching his muzzle to peer through the entrance.

"Three." Graystripe nudged his friend. "You always were softhearted over kits."

Sandstorm stopped beside them. "We should have had more," she murmured wistfully.

"It's a dark time to be born." Firestar narrowed his eyes. "The battle is near."

Graystripe looked at him sharply. "We can't be sure."

"It won't be long." Dovewing heard a growl in the ThunderClan leader's mew.

Graystripe's ear twitched. "How do you know? Have you had a sign?"

"I had a dream last night."

Before Graystripe could question him more, Cloudtail slid out of the nursery, bright-eyed. "They're lively!" he purred. "Fighting over who gets to be closest to their mother's belly."

The thorn barrier rustled and Jayfeather hurried into camp. The ThunderClan leader padded away, calling to Cloudtail over his shoulder. "Tell Brightheart I'll welcome her kits to the Clan later."

Mousefur shifted beside Dovewing. "I'm glad we have Firestar to lead us." She sat down heavily. "He has courage and strength enough for all of us."

Graystripe nudged her. "I remember when you argued with Bluestar about bringing him into the Clan."

Dovewing glanced at Firestar as he guided Jayfeather to the shadow of Highledge. Even though the whole Clan knew he had come from a Twoleg nest, it was hard to believe that the battle-scarred warrior used to be a pampered kittypet.

"I was wrong to argue." The old she-cat's eyes clouded. "I wonder if Bluestar knew that one day he would be our best hope for survival."

Graystripe glanced up at the sky. "She's probably watching now."

"Get Lionblaze." Dovewing jerked around as Firestar called to her. Heart racing, she leaped onto the beech trunk and padded to a den woven beneath a jagged stump. She stuck her nose inside. "Firestar wants us."

Lionblaze woke, jerking his head from beneath his paw. "What's happened?"

"Jayfeather just got back from the Moonpool and Firestar's acting like the battle's about to start."

Lionblaze shot out of his nest. He jumped down into the clearing and Dovewing followed.

As she reached Firestar, she noticed Jayfeather fighting a yawn. "Shouldn't you rest?"

"She's right," Firestar agreed. "There's time for you to sleep before sunhigh."

Lionblaze pricked his ears. "What happens at sunhigh?"

"We meet with the other leaders and medicine cats on the island," Firestar told him. "Jayfeather has united StarClan. Now I must unite the Clans."

"He's the fourth cat." Jayfeather's eyes shone.

Firestar! Dovewing blinked.

Lionblaze lifted his tail. "You were close, Dovewing, when you said we needed to start looking for a cat who was born with a special destiny."

Firestar's eyes darkened. "I just hope destiny is enough to save us."

Sunlight pierced the leaves and lit the forest floor.

Jayfeather was still yawning from his nap as Dovewing followed her Clanmates out of the hollow. Her belly churned. Suddenly the coming battle felt real. She could almost hear the screech of warriors and taste the stone tang of blood.

"Squirrel!" Lionblaze tasted the air a moment before a gray flash shot up a birch tree beside them.

"There'll be fresh-kill when we return," Firestar told him. "Brambleclaw's sending out extra hunting patrols. I want the pile fully stocked."

Dovewing followed her Clanmates through the woods,

swerving as she raced in their paw steps. The warm sun was driving mist from the lake, making the surface glitter like a fish. As Dovewing leaped from the bank and landed on the shore, she tasted the scents of forest and water mingling on her tongue. Pebbles scattered behind her as she charged onward. Firestar skirted the water's edge, his gaze fixed on the island. He slowed the pace and Dovewing, relieved, caught her breath. By the time they reached the tree-bridge, she was hardly panting. She pulled up beside Lionblaze as Firestar sprang onto the fallen tree and crossed the water. Jayfeather followed, landing neatly on the far shore.

"Go on." Lionblaze flicked his muzzle toward the tree and Dovewing jumped up, digging her claws into the rotting bark as she padded carefully across.

The island clearing was empty. Lionblaze paced, his tail twitching, while Jayfeather sat in the center beside Firestar. Dovewing padded nervously around them until the grass swished and Onestar slid out. Kestrelflight was at his side.

The WindClan leader circled the clearing, keeping his distance from the ThunderClan warriors. "It seems that our medicine cats are in charge of the Clans now."

Firestar dipped his head. "They know things we don't."

Kestrelflight crossed the clearing and sat beside Jayfeather. "We have seen our enemy," he explained to his leader. "You have not."

"Not *yet*," Firestar added grimly.

Lionblaze sniffed the undergrowth at the edge of the clearing, ears pricked. "There's some ShadowClan scent here."

Onestar glanced at him. "Probably left over from last full moon."

Lionblaze narrowed his eyes. "Probably." He padded back across the clearing.

Dovewing moved aside to let him sit beside Firestar. She pricked her ears and listened. Mistystar was coming, Willowshine and Mothwing beside her. Their paw steps crunched on the shore near the tree-bridge. Blackstar and Littlecloud were already rustling through the long grass on the island. Dovewing listened harder. The RiverClan camp buzzed like a beehive while ShadowClan chattered inside their bramble walls like starlings. She reached for WindClan and heard anxious whispers whipped away by the wind.

"They shouldn't have gone alone."

"What's Firestar up to this time?"

"It must be a trap."

"But Firestar is a noble warrior."

"Firestar wants to rule all the Clans. He always has."

They were scared of him! Dovewing twitched, surprised. *But he's your last hope!*

Blackstar emerged from the grass. Littlecloud padded after him, chin high.

The ShadowClan leader's gaze narrowed when he saw Lionblaze. "Why have you brought warriors?"

Firestar wrapped his tail over his paws. "I'll explain when Mistystar gets here."

Blackstar glanced over his shoulder at the trembling grass.

Mistystar padded out, leading Willowshine. "Willowshine

insisted I come," she growled. "She says the Dark Forest warriors are planning to invade Clan territory." Her eyes glittered with disbelief. "Has she gone mad?"

Mothwing nosed her way from the grass. "Willowshine has never been wrong before."

"But how can the dead threaten the living?" The RiverClan leader halted in the middle of the clearing.

Blackstar stayed near the edge. "Littlecloud told me they've learned to cross into our territories."

"That's impossible." Onestar circled his medicine cat.

Jayfeather's tail whipped from side to side. "How dare you question your medicine cat?" His gaze swept like fire over the leaders. "Do you think we'd lie?"

Mistystar shifted her paws. Onestar flattened his ears. Only Blackstar replied. "StarClan and the Dark Forest have always been beyond our reach. Now you tell us we are part of a war between them?"

"Not just between them," Firestar growled. "The Dark Forest has declared war on all the Clans. We must unite against them."

Onestar scowled. "Is that why you brought warriors with you? To force us to join you?"

"I brought them because they're part of a prophecy," Firestar explained. "Many moons ago I was told that the kin of my kin would be born with the power of the stars in their paws. For a long time I didn't know what that meant. Now I do." He nodded toward Lionblaze, Jayfeather, and Dovewing. "The time has come. These are the kin of my kin, and each has a special power that will lead them to fulfill the prophecy."

Blackstar leaned closer, flattening his ears. "What power?"

Lionblaze lifted his chin. "I cannot be defeated in battle."

"I can sense thoughts and walk in dreams," Jayfeather told him.

Dovewing's breath quickened as all four leaders turned to her. "I—I can hear things that are far away."

"What do you mean?" Mistystar demanded.

Dovewing felt her tail droop. This felt more like an admission of guilt. "I could hear your Clanmates now if I tried."

Mistystar's pelt bushed. "You're a spy!"

"I would never spy!"

Blackstar showed his teeth. "Really?"

Littlecloud darted forward. "You're missing the point!"

Jayfeather backed him up. "They were given powers to *save* the Clans, not harm them."

Blackstar wove around Lionblaze, a growl rumbling in his throat. "So you can never be defeated, eh?" He stopped and stared at the golden warrior. "Rowanclaw told me he shredded you."

"I *let* him!" Lionblaze snapped. The muscles beneath his shoulders rippled.

Blackstar backed away and looked at Firestar. "Suppose we believe you about this prophecy?" he growled. "What is it all for?"

"Why have you kept this secret from us until now?" Onestar put in.

"The time was not right before," Firestar snapped.

Blackstar flexed his claws. "And what makes it right now?"

Willowshine padded to Dovewing and touched her shoulder with her muzzle. "Can you hear as far as the Dark Forest?" she whispered.

Dovewing stiffened. "I—I don't know."

"Will you try?"

Dovewing nodded and stretched her ears till the tips ached.

Blackstar narrowed his eyes, staring at her. "What's she doing?"

Willowshine met his gaze. "She's showing you your enemy."

Dovewing's throat tightened. What if her power failed her? She reached out from the island, letting her hearing spread in every direction at once. The murmurings of the Clans swept over her; every movement and word crashed in like waves but she kept reaching farther, past the Clans and into the darkness at the edges. Slowing her breath, she forced herself to relax, opening her senses and letting whatever lay beyond the darkness seep in.

A distant yowl sounded from far away. Tensing, Dovewing focused her hearing on the cry and rushed toward it, every sense raw. She gasped as trees blurred at the edges of her vision. The sounds of the forest formed images in her mind, which sharpened and strengthened as she hunted deeper. Spindly undergrowth grew in tangled heaps. An eerie light glowed just strong enough to make them out. She glanced up and saw only darkness. *The Place of No Stars!*

"I've reached it!"

Onestar gasped. "You can actually hear what's going on there?"

Littlecloud meowed, "Don't disturb her."

"But do you really expect us to believe she can visit the Dark Forest in her thoughts?" Blackstar whispered.

Mothwing shook out her pelt, filling the air with the scent of herbs. "You believe that all the cats in StarClan can see beyond normal boundaries," she pointed out. "Why should one living cat not be able to do the same?"

"Hush!" Mistystar quieted them, and Dovewing concentrated harder.

A deep growl sounded beside her. "Dig your claws deeper into the muscle! He must feel fire touch his bones!"

Dovewing jerked her attention toward it. A scarred warrior, torn-eared and matted, loomed from the shadow. A tortured yowl screeched through the trees. Was this where Ivypool came every night? Dovewing's heart lurched. "They're training for battle," she breathed.

"They train every night," Jayfeather put in.

Willowshine twitched beside Dovewing. "They're as brutal as dogs."

"They have no warrior code," Littlecloud added.

A bloodcurdling shriek made Dovewing flinch. Instinctively she tried to snatch her thoughts away from the Dark Forest, but Willowshine pressed against her till she could feel the steady beating of her heart. "Keep going," she whispered.

She focused on the scarred warrior again, and this time she saw another tom beside him. Two more wrestled on the slimy ground ahead of them.

"We need to shred every Clan cat who ever lived."

Dovewing stared at the dark tabby who spoke. His shoulders were massive and his claws were longer than she'd ever seen.

"She's found Brokenstar," Jayfeather reported.

"How do you know?" Onestar gasped.

"I can see into her thoughts." Jayfeather's breath touched Dovewing's cheek. "He's talking to his Clanmates."

"What's he saying?" Blackstar demanded.

Dovewing began to quote Brokenstar's words. "Destroying the puny warriors who huddle like mice around the lake will be fun, but when we kill StarClan . . . that will be the final revenge." The growl in his throat suddenly turned into a wild purr, so loud it hurt Dovewing's ears. She shrank away, turning her ears to another part of the forest.

A white she-cat was slinking through the trees, complaining.

"Why do we have to train in this stinking forest?" Dovewing repeated the warrior's words. *"Why can't we train on our own land?"*

"Is that a *Clan* cat?" Mistystar exclaimed.

"Why would a Clan cat be in the Dark Forest?" Onestar snapped.

Dovewing focused harder, until she recognized the snowy pelt. *Icewing!* It was a RiverClan warrior. *I can't betray her!*

Dovewing shut off the sound, and pressed closer to Willowshine.

"Thank you, Dovewing." Firestar's gentle mew sounded in her ear. She opened her eyes, relieved to see the island clearing.

Mistystar was staring at her in dismay.

Onestar didn't move, his gaze leveled at Firestar. "How do we stop them?"

Firestar straightened up. "We fight."

"And we'll win!" Blackstar hissed. "They don't stand a chance on our territory. We know our own land like we know our own markings."

Dovewing got to her paws. "They know it, too," she ventured.

"What?" Blackstar turned on her.

"They've been sending patrols onto every Clan's territory to scout out the best places to ambush and fight," Dovewing told him.

"Have you heard them?" Blackstar hissed.

Lionblaze flattened his ears. "The scents you found?" he snapped. "They were from the Dark Forest. This enemy is better prepared and more deadly than any we've faced before."

Mistystar tipped her head. "There were Clan scents mixed with the rogue stench."

"They've recruited Clan cats," Lionblaze told her.

"Never!" Blackstar spat. "ThunderClan might have traitors among its warriors, but not ShadowClan!"

"They've been recruited from every Clan," Firestar told him grimly.

"You must have seen them!" Onestar challenged Dovewing. "Tell us who they are!"

Dovewing shifted her paws. "I—I can't say," she stammered.

Blackstar padded toward her. "Are you a traitor, too?"

"Of course she isn't!" Firestar stepped in front of her. "No one's a traitor yet. We don't know which side any cat will choose until the battle begins."

Onestar prickled. "But if we know who they are, we can be prepared."

For the first time Mistystar looked frightened. "Tell us who you've seen, Dovewing."

"They must be punished." Blackstar hissed.

Dovewing dug her claws into the earth. "I can't tell you," she meowed steadily. "Firestar's right. They haven't betrayed anyone yet."

Firestar flicked his tail. "They believe they are training for the sake of their Clan. They don't realize they are being prepared for our destruction."

"Then they're fools," Blackstar snarled.

Mistystar swished her tail. "They may be foolish, but Firestar is right. Until they turn their claws on their own Clanmates, we cannot condemn them."

"Some are only staying because Brokenstar has threatened to kill any cat who betrays him," Lionblaze explained. "You've had a glimpse of how ruthless the Dark Forest warriors are. Their recruits might be too scared to disobey their new leader. We must be ready to fight our own Clanmates."

Onestar tilted his head. "Or free them."

"So what do we do about the Dark Forest?" Blackstar demanded.

Lionblaze stepped forward. "We must stand together."

Blackstar backed away. Mistystar glanced at her paws.

"How can we trust one another?" Onestar asked quietly.

Firestar glanced at the medicine cats, then back to the leaders. "The time has come to fight our greatest enemy," he declared. "We can fight alone, or we can stand together. We're stronger side by side, as we were for the Great Journey. Uniting against the Dark Forest is our only hope."

Silence gripped the clearing, broken only by the fretful song of a sparrow high above them.

"Very well." Mistystar dipped her head. "RiverClan will join ThunderClan in this battle."

Dovewing suddenly realized she'd been holding her breath. She let it out, her chest aching.

"WindClan will join the alliance." Only Onestar's tail-tip moved, twitching as though caught by a breeze.

Firestar turned to Blackstar. "We will do what we can to defend you, even if you choose not to join."

Blackstar curled his lip. "My Clan will join." He began to pace around the others. "But there will be one condition."

"Very well." Firestar pricked his ears.

"On ShadowClan territory, ShadowClan is in charge of any warrior from any Clan." He scowled at Firestar. "Even a Clan leader."

Firestar nodded. "Okay."

Jayfeather sat down beside Kestrelflight. Willowshine, Littlecloud, and Mothwing gathered around them. "StarClan will be pleased," Jayfeather meowed as the other medicine cats murmured their approval.

Firestar faced the Clan leaders. "We need to make a battle plan."

"Where do you think the Dark Forest will attack first?" Mistystar asked.

Lionblaze shrugged. "It could be anywhere or everywhere at once."

"Patrols must move through all the territories night and day," Onestar suggested. "There must be no borders to block their way."

Blackstar's eyes glittered. "Enemy patrols moving freely through my territory?"

"We're not enemies now," Firestar reminded him. "I suggest there be one patrol in each territory made up of warriors from all four Clans. I'll send three warriors to each of your camps at dusk."

Mistystar stiffened. "So soon?"

"We must be prepared," Firestar insisted. "Will you each send three warriors to ThunderClan?"

Dovewing watched the leaders nod, their gaze shadowed. She felt cold to the bone.

"How do we know which cats we can trust?" Onestar narrowed his eyes. "Harespring keeps coming home with unexplained injuries."

"Troutstream has been bad-tempered lately," Mistystar admitted.

Onestar glared at her. "I don't want your traitors on my territory!"

"And I don't want *your* traitors on RiverClan land," Mistystar spat.

"We don't know that they *are* traitors!" Dovewing exclaimed. "We should be concentrating on the battle, not trying to guess who our enemies are."

Blackstar frowned. "But what if they tell our plans to their Dark Forest allies?"

"It's a risk we have to take," Firestar growled. "We must trust that enough Clan cats remain loyal to make our plans work." He began to pace. "Battle patrols must focus on protecting the camps of each Clan. Each camp must be defended by warriors from all four Clans. We must keep our kits and elders safe."

Onestar flexed his claws. "Once the camps are secure, then the patrol must draw the attackers away."

"We'll need messengers," Blackstar added. "To share news or offer reinforcement."

"The swiftest two cats from each Clan will be messengers," Firestar decided.

Onestar circled the ThunderClan leader. "They must swear not to be drawn into battle. They must only carry news. I don't want a camp lost because help doesn't arrive in time."

Blackstar nodded. "Agreed."

"Good." Firestar turned and stared through the trees, across the water. "Go home," he growled. "Prepare for battle. It will strike everywhere at once, but remember that we are fighting together. Not alone."

As he spoke, Dovewing saw the ferns at the far side of the clearing move. She froze as she spotted a pair of green eyes flash. *Tigerheart?* As Blackstar, Mistystar, and Onestar headed into the long grass, she glanced nervously at Firestar.

"Come on." The ThunderClan leader began to pad after Onestar. Lionblaze fell in beside him and Jayfeather followed, his eyes glazed with tiredness.

"I'll catch up!" Dovewing called.

As her Clanmates disappeared into the grass, she hared across the clearing and dived into the ferns. Tigerheart backed away, his eyes wide.

"What are you doing here?" Dovewing demanded.

"Did you really hear all the way to the Dark Forest?" Tigerheart's mew was barely a whisper.

"You know I did!" There wasn't time to explain. "I've told you about this before." Anger surged through her. He wasn't supposed to be here. Didn't he ever follow rules? Or take anything seriously?

"But I've never actually seen you use your powers." Tigerheart blinked. "It was great!" He moved closer, thrusting his muzzle toward her cheek.

Dovewing jerked away. "What are you doing?"

"What I always do!" Tigerheart protested. "What's the matter? Nothing's changed between us, has it?"

Doesn't he realize the Clans are on the verge of being destroyed? Or is he here to spy for the Dark Forest?

"I don't know." Dovewing's paws pricked.

"We can have one more night together, can't we?" Tigerheart pleaded.

"No, we can't." Pain stabbed at Dovewing's chest. "I have to concentrate on the prophecy! There's a battle coming." A lump rose in her throat. "I don't know who to trust anymore!"

Tigerheart shot to her side, pressing close. "You can always trust me." The warm scent of him made her shake. "I *love* you!" he breathed.

Dovewing wrenched herself away. "This isn't the time." She shook her head. "I have a battle to fight." She met his gaze. "So do you."

"What about afterward?" he murmured.

"There will be four Clans again." Dovewing shut her eyes tight. "You'll belong to ShadowClan and I'll belong to ThunderClan, and . . . and maybe that's how it should be."

Tigerheart stabbed the earth with his claws. "You can give me up so easily?"

Dovewing shook her head. "There's nothing easy about this," she hissed. "How can you be more worried about us, with everything that's going on? You know what's happening better than most cats!" It was as if she was looking at him for the first time: a ShadowClan cat, and a Dark Forest warrior. A cat who thought her powers were cool, but had no idea how important the prophecy was. *What am I doing?*

Spinning around, she crashed through the ferns and raced across the clearing. She heard Tigerheart call after her, but she didn't look back.

Her mind whirled. Tigerheart was training in the Dark Forest and he knew the Clans' battle plans. And now she had rejected him. What if the ShadowClan warrior decided to make her suffer in return?

CHAPTER 20

Lionblaze followed Firestar into camp, breathless after the race from the island. A cold wind had whipped them all the way home. He ducked through the thorn tunnel, Dovewing and Jayfeather on his tail.

"There's a battle coming," the ThunderClan leader growled.

Brambleclaw jerked around. Daisy thrust her head out of the nursery. "Battle?"

Outside the elders' den, Purdy wrapped his tail around Mousefur as Firestar crossed the clearing.

The ThunderClan leader leaped onto Highledge. "Let all cats old enough to catch their own prey gather to hear my words."

The Clan was already flooding the clearing, pelts pricking. Molepaw and Cherrypaw pressed together, their eyes round as they stared up at Firestar. Poppyfrost shuffled closer to Berrynose.

Cloudtail hurried to the nursery to find Brightheart. "Stay inside," he ordered his kits as they peered out like tiny owlets.

Lilykit popped her head out beside them. "I'll make sure

they stay in their nests," she promised earnestly.

"Me too," Seedkit squeaked from behind.

The brambles at the entrance to the medicine den rustled as Briarlight thrust out her muzzle. Jayfeather hurried toward her, Millie on his tail, while Blossomfall and Birchfall lingered at the edge of the crowd, glancing nervously at Mousewhisker as he settled beside them.

"Clanmates, we face an enemy stronger than we have ever known!" Firestar yowled. "The danger comes from dead cats as well as living. The Dark Forest has sworn to destroy the Clans."

"How can dead cats harm us?" Mousefur croaked.

Firestar looked steadily at the elder. "The warriors in the Place of No Stars have found a way to cross into Clan territory."

Ferncloud gasped.

"That's impossible!" Cloudtail growled.

"Oh, StarClan," Blossomfall whimpered to Birchfall.

He met her gaze, frozen until Mousewhisker murmured in his ear. Birchfall shook the young warrior away, eyes narrowing in disgust as though Mousewhisker had asked him to eat crow-food. Lionblaze watched Mousewhisker shrink away. What could the young warrior have said?

Firestar leaned over the lip of Highledge. "You've all smelled the scents and seen the paw prints in the forest."

"They're just rogues!" Dustpelt snarled.

Firestar returned the tabby tom's gaze. "Have you forgotten the scent of Tigerstar?"

Dustpelt stared at him. "I . . . I thought I imagined it."

Firestar went on. "A battle is coming that we have to win, for the sake of every warrior that ever lived. We must fight alongside the other Clans, because this enemy threatens us all. ShadowClan, WindClan, and RiverClan will each send three warriors here at dusk to join our patrols. We will send three warriors to their camps." He glanced down at his deputy. "Brambleclaw, you choose who will go."

Thornclaw's tail brushed the earth. "Won't ShadowClan just take advantage of this to steal our territory?"

"If they do, all will be lost," Firestar muttered darkly.

"How will I protect my kits?" Brightheart wailed.

Cloudtail pressed against her. "I won't let anything harm them!"

Ferncloud lashed her tail. "Nor will I!"

Sorreltail lifted her chin. "No one will hurt ThunderClan kits."

Ivypool walked to the front and turned to face her Clan. Lionblaze saw her take a breath and steady her trembling paws. "I know how they fight. I can teach their moves to the Clan."

Blossomfall huddled closer to Birchfall.

"How do you know?" Dustpelt hissed.

"I sent her to spy." Firestar leaped down the rock tumble and stood beside Ivypool. "She knows more about our enemy than any cat. Learn from her."

Mousewhisker gaped at her. "You were *spying* in the Dark Forest?"

Cherrypaw's eyes grew as round as moons. "You're so brave!"

Lionblaze narrowed his eyes. Had Firestar asked Ivypool who else had been training in the Dark Forest? He glanced around his Clanmates, searching faces for a glimmer of guilt. Some of them must have visited the Place of No Stars with Ivypool, trapped by Tigerstar's lies and Brokenstar's false promises. His claws sank into the wet ground and he felt the fur rise along his spine.

Firestar lashed his tail. "We will win this battle because we are fighting for our lives and the lives of our Clanmates. Our enemies are already dead. They fight only out of hate and that will be their weakness."

"We'll beat them!" Cloudtail yowled.

Molepaw reared up and raked the air with unsheathed claws. "I'll shred any Dark Forest warrior I lay my paws on!"

Firestar nodded. "Then let's start training. For victory!"

The Clan broke into clusters, murmuring like anxious pigeons. "We need to teach the elders and queens some defensive moves," Lionblaze told Brambleclaw. "I've already thought of some tactics Daisy can use even though she's never had warrior training."

"Good." Brambleclaw scanned the Clan. "Spiderleg can train Mousefur and Purdy. He's known them longest. They won't mind taking orders from him."

Spiderleg was huddled deep in conversation with Brackenfur. Lionblaze noticed for the first time that his black muzzle was flecked with gray. *He'll be moving into the elders' den before long.*

His pelt pricked. *If there's a den left.*

Brambleclaw flexed his claws. "We need to prepare for a new type of enemy."

"We have to learn to fight as viciously as Dark Forest warriors." Lionblaze swallowed the anger rising in his throat. "They're forcing us to break the warrior code."

"Defend your Clan above all things," Brambleclaw reminded him. "If that means fighting like rogues, then we must fight like rogues."

"I'll fight like Brokenstar if it means protecting the Clan."

"You may have to." Brambleclaw turned his dark gaze toward Spiderleg and called to the warrior. "I want you to teach Mousefur and Purdy some moves."

"Okay." Spiderleg headed for the elders' den.

"Hollyleaf!" Brambleclaw meowed. "Take Molepaw, Rosepetal, and Whitewing out of camp and practice every battle move you know. Ivypool will come and train with you next."

Sorreltail bounded toward the ThunderClan deputy. "Let me train with Ivypool first," she begged.

"If she shows us the Dark Forest's most deadly moves, we can figure out how to defend ourselves," Dustpelt added.

While Brambleclaw divided the Clan into training patrols, Lionblaze headed for the nursery. He padded past Daisy and stuck his head inside.

"My poor kits!" Brightheart was in her nest, curled around three squirming scraps of fur. Cloudtail crouched beside her, his pelt ruffled. Lilykit and Seedkit sat on the edge of their nest, chins high.

"We'll protect them," Seedkit declared.

"*You'll* stay hidden in your nests," Lionblaze ordered. He turned to Cloudtail. "Join your Clanmates. I'll teach Brightheart how to defend Snowkit, Amberkit, and Dewkit."

As Cloudtail slid out, Lionblaze hopped past him. "Come here, Daisy," he called. "I need you."

"What do you want me to do?" Daisy heaved her soft body inside. "I don't know any warrior moves."

"That doesn't matter," Lionblaze told her. "You and Brightheart are going to work together. You've got five kits to protect. Sorreltail will be needed on battle patrol so I'm relying on you to help defend the nursery. There is no cat more dangerous than a queen!" He flicked his nose toward Brightheart. "Stand up!"

Brightheart pushed herself to her paws. Lionblaze lunged toward her kits, teeth bared. Hissing, Brightheart lashed out as fast as lightning, her claws raking his nose.

Lionblaze pulled away. "See? All her instincts will protect her kits."

Daisy glared at Lionblaze. "How *dare* you attack her like that?"

"It's okay." Brightheart met Lionblaze's gaze, excited. "Let me practice another move."

Lionblaze flicked his tail toward Daisy. "You can learn this one, too." He moved backward, focusing on an imaginary attacker, then jabbed a forepaw high and swung his other one low. "It's easy to do and confuses your attacker."

"Let me try it on you!" Brightheart balanced on the edge of her nest. "Come at me."

Daisy hesitated, then darted toward Brightheart. Brightheart swiped high and Daisy instinctively looked at her paw. As she did, Brightheart used her other paw to scoop Daisy's forelegs out from under her. Daisy stumbled forward and bumped her muzzle on the den floor.

"If you work together, one can trip an enemy while the other attacks." He was relieved to see that the fear had faded from Brightheart's gaze. "Just make sure you always keep one eye on your kits." Dewkit, Amberkit, and Snowkit were clambering up the side of their nest, staring at their suddenly ferocious mother. "You three, stay in the nest. Right at the bottom," Lionblaze ordered.

Blinking at him, they slid down and huddled deep in the moss.

He turned back to Daisy and Brightheart. "Working together will make you as strong as the fittest warrior." He felt a rush of satisfaction. For the first time in a long while, he felt as if he was doing exactly what he should. He'd spent too much time worrying these past moons. Now he was ready to fight like the warrior he was born to be. Midnight's words echoed in his ears. *The journey you make is your choice.*

My choice! He froze, his heart leaping. *It's all my choice!*

"Can I leave you to practice?" he asked Brightheart.

"Can we work out some moves of our own?" she asked.

"Sure." Lionblaze stuck his head through the wall of the nursery and scanned the clearing. "I'll be back soon to watch them."

Where is she? He tasted the air and finally detected Cinderheart's scent mingled with Icecloud's and Leafpool's. He followed it across the clearing and out of the camp, breaking into a run as he headed up the slope. Leafpool and Icecloud were batting each other with their forepaws, practicing swipes while Cinderheart watched.

"You need to be quicker," Cinderheart told Icecloud. "Try using shorter blows."

"Cinderheart!" Lionblaze called from the bank.

She turned, ears pricked. "Lionblaze? What are you doing here?"

"I have to talk to you!"

She must have detected the urgency in his mew because she nodded to her Clanmates and hurried toward him. "What's the matter?" Worry pricked her gaze.

"Follow me." Lionblaze weaved past a clump of ferns and halted at the foot of a gnarled beech.

Cinderheart stared at him. "Is something wrong?"

Lionblaze took a deep breath. "You have a destiny," he began. "Just like every cat. But you also have a choice." *StarClan, let her understand!* "And so do I." Cinderheart leaned forward, opening her mouth, but before she could interrupt, he pressed on. "Our destinies guide our paws, but they don't shape every step. That's up to us. We walk the path we choose."

Cinderheart said nothing. Lionblaze persisted. "Whatever our destiny says, we still have to choose our own path, don't you see? We can walk side by side if we wish."

Cinderheart backed away, her gray pelt ruffling. "It's not that easy!"

Lionblaze padded after her. "It *is*!"

"My head is so full of memories!" Cinderheart wailed. "I

feel as though there are two lives inside me, not one. How can it be my choice to make? Doesn't Cinderpelt have a choice? I can't make her be a warrior! She was a medicine cat!"

Lionblaze pressed his muzzle closer. "She chose you," he murmured. "She gave *you* the choice."

Cinderheart began to tremble. Lionblaze could sense her mind whirling. "You can only live one life, Cinderheart. It's your choice! This is *your* destiny, not Cinderpelt's. She lived her own life."

Cinderheart gasped. Then her pelt smoothed. She lifted her chin. "Then I choose the life of a warrior." Her blue eyes shone. "And I choose you."

A breeze stirred the ferns. Lionblaze glimpsed a pale gray shape appear like a shadow beside Cinderheart. Stepping back in surprise, he saw it peel away from her and drift up like a cobweb carried by the wind. A soft voice whispered, *Thank you.*

Lionblaze's fur stood on end. "Did you see that?"

Cinderheart was watching the shadow disappear into the trees. "It was Cinderpelt," she breathed. "I've set her free."

Lionblaze purred loudly. "Will you fight alongside me?"

Cinderheart pressed her muzzle fiercely against his. "Always."

CHAPTER 21

♣

Ferns scraped Jayfeather's spine as he gathered comfrey from the patch near the camp entrance. Dew was already beading on the soft leaves. Dusk was drawing nearer. The patrols from WindClan, ShadowClan, and RiverClan would be here before long. He shook out his paws. They ached from gathering herbs all afternoon while the warriors trained.

Muscle thumped against earth behind him. "Don't forget what Ivypool taught us!" Squirrelflight called to Dustpelt. "Dark Forest warriors will go for your throat. Make sure you're always ready to fend off a killing bite."

Dustpelt's fur brushed the ground as he struggled out from under Graystripe. "How can I attack properly if I have to defend myself all the time?"

Graystripe was panting. "What about leading more with your shoulders and keeping your head low?"

Jayfeather plucked a final leaf and stacked it with the rest. Bundling them between his jaws, he headed back into camp. He ducked through the tunnel and hurried around the edge of the clearing, skirting Rosepetal and Molepaw as they practiced a tricky battle move.

"Never turn your back on a Dark Forest warrior!" Ivypool yowled.

"Can we try it next?" Leafpool paced restlessly while Cloudtail plucked at the sandy earth, anticipation pricking from his pelt.

Brambleclaw sat beneath Highledge with Lionblaze and Squirrelflight. "Sorreltail, Thornclaw, and Spiderleg should go to ShadowClan," he meowed.

"Whitewing, Berrynose, and Hazeltail could go to Wind-Clan," Squirrelflight suggested.

Jayfeather dropped the herbs beside his den and joined them. "Do you think we'll be ready in time?"

"We'll have to be," Brambleclaw growled.

Jayfeather tasted the air. "Where's Firestar?"

"He's setting traps with Sandstorm and Sorreltail," Dove-wing told him. "Stretching brambles across trails and hiding rabbit holes with nettles."

Ivypool's mew cut in. "Use your tail to balance, Rosepetal! You need to be able to fight on two paws as well as four! These warriors want to kill you!"

"How do we kill *them*?" Cloudtail called. "They're already dead!"

Jayfeather frowned. *Good question.* "I've seen StarClan warriors fade when there's no cat left to remember them," he recalled, raising his voice to reach Cloudtail. "If StarClan can fade, perhaps Dark Forest warriors can die." He stiffened as he sensed darkness suddenly engulf Ivypool. He reached into her mind and was plunged into the Dark Forest.

Antpelt was struggling beneath Ivypool's paws. Her claws ripped deeper into the warrior's throat as life ebbed out of him in a pool of blood. His shape began to fade until there was nothing left but a scarlet stain on the withered grass. Jayfeather recoiled, feeling sick. *She's killed a Dark Forest warrior!* He wondered if she'd tell Cloudtail that dead cats could vanish forever, but he felt her push the thought away.

Brambleclaw carried on planning. "I'm sending Foxleap, Toadstep, and Rosepetal to RiverClan," he decided. "They can share Ivypool's moves with Mistystar's warriors."

"I wonder who she'll send to us?" Jayfeather tried to imagine RiverClan warriors in the ThunderClan camp.

Anger flashed from Molepaw. "Are we expected to hunt for them and let them sleep in our dens till the battle begins?"

"Yes!" Brambleclaw turned on the apprentice. "If that's what Firestar wants. They're our allies now."

Cloudtail bristled. "I'm not sleeping next to a ShadowClan cat."

"Would you rather be in the patrol I send to fight alongside RiverClan?" Brambleclaw snapped. "There's no time to worry about Clan rivalries. We're facing the end of everything we know. We'll fight alongside the other Clans as though they are our Clanmates, and there will be no argument."

Lionblaze's tail whisked impatiently. "Firestar also wants two runners to pass messages between the Clan during the battle."

"Molepaw and Cherrypaw can do that," Brambleclaw meowed.

"But I want to *fight*!" Molepaw crossed the clearing. "It'll be my first battle."

"And you'll serve your Clan best as a messenger," Brambleclaw told him. "You're one of our fastest runners." The ThunderClan deputy dropped his voice to a whisper as he turned back to Lionblaze and Dovewing. "We need to find out which ThunderClan warriors the Dark Forest have recruited. We might be able to stop them."

"We could ask Ivypool." Jayfeather glanced toward the young warrior.

Dovewing was passing on her way to the elders' den with a piece of fresh-kill. She dropped it when she heard Jayfeather speak. "But Firestar said we didn't need to know who—"

Brambleclaw interrupted her. "It's better to find out who our enemy is now," he meowed. "Ivypool!" He waited for her to reach them. "Which ThunderClan cats are training with you in the Dark Forest?"

Ivypool backed away. "I can't betray them!" she gasped. Jayfeather felt fear pulsing beneath her pelt. "They d-don't realize what they're doing," she stammered. "When the battle comes, they'll make the right decision!"

"We can't punish them," Dovewing argued. "They've done nothing wrong yet."

"We're not punishing them," Brambleclaw meowed gently. "We're trying to save them."

"Tigerstar lied when he recruited them," Ivypool mewed.

"I know," Brambleclaw assured her.

"And Brokenstar threatened to kill them if they left."

"Then let us have a chance to protect them. Who's training in the Dark Forest?" Brambleclaw pressed softly.

"Birchfall," Ivypool whispered. "Blossomfall and Mouse-whisker."

"Cloudtail, Molepaw, Rosepetal!" Brambleclaw called to his Clanmates, firing orders. "Get Blossomfall. She's training in the sandy hollow. Birchfall and Mousewhisker are hunting. Find them and bring them back to camp."

As Cloudtail, Molepaw, and Rosepetal raced from the camp, Brambleclaw sat down. "We'll make them understand. They can be our allies in the Dark Forest. Like you, Ivypool."

Jayfeather let his fur smooth. After all the moons of waiting, it was a relief to face the danger head-on. He glanced toward his den. "I have to check my herb supplies." He headed across the clearing and picked up the bundle of comfrey. Pushing through the brambles, he padded into the den. Briarlight was fast asleep. He could hear her snoring as she lay among the herb stacks.

"Briarlight?" He touched her gently with his muzzle.

She jerked awake. "Sorry!" She heaved herself up. "All that counting made me sleepy. We're going to need more marigold and nettle."

"Go to your nest and rest properly," Jayfeather told her. "I'll keep going here."

"I can help," Briarlight argued.

"Rest," Jayfeather ordered.

"But—"

"Now!" He was going to need all her strength when the

battle began. Briarlight's nest rustled as she slid into it. Jay-feather pricked his ears, listening till her breathing deepened. Then he began gathering herbs from each pile and rolling them into bundles. Each bundle contained the herbs and cob-webs he'd need to treat a single injury. It would save time once the battle began.

"Jayfeather?"

Leafpool's mew surprised him. He looked up, heady from the smell of herbs.

"Can I help?" She slid through the brambles. "When the battle's finished, there are going to be a lot of injured war-riors." Her whiskers were trembling. "I—I'd like to help. Even if it's just carrying wet moss to thirsty patients."

"Moss?" Jayfeather frowned. *Moss! Of course!*

"I realize that I have no right to ask but—"

"I'd completely forgotten about moss." Jayfeather jumped to his paws. "We'll need pawfuls. I'll send a patrol out to find some." He brushed past Leafpool, heading for the entrance.

"Everyone's training or hunting," Leafpool reminded him. "Can I get some?"

Jayfeather paused. "Collect moss?" He felt her flinch, ready for rejection. "That would be a waste of your skills," he mewed briskly. "Molepaw and Cherrypaw can collect some when they get back. I need you working here."

"Really?" Shock sparked from Leafpool's pelt.

"You have as much experience as me," Jayfeather told her. "It'd be dumb not to use you. You said it yourself—there are going to be a lot of injured warriors. I'll need you to help treat them."

"B-but what about StarClan?" Leafpool stuttered. "They told me I was no longer a medicine cat."

Jayfeather growled. "Things have changed, Leafpool. We have to do what we think is right for the Clan. And if that means going against StarClan, then we must."

Leafpool padded closer. "Does this mean you've forgiven me?"

Jayfeather returned to bundling herbs. "There's nothing to forgive," he sniffed. "You did what you thought was best. No cat can blame you for that." He pushed a pile of borage toward her. "Start gathering herbs like I'm doing. I want plenty of cobweb in each bundle. And remind me to ask Molepaw and Cherrypaw to collect more when they go for moss."

Aching relief spilled from his mother as she sat beside him and began picking herbs from the piles. Jayfeather brushed against her as he reached for another pawful of marigold. He felt stone scrape beneath his claws. "We're running out."

Leafpool purred. "I'll remind you to ask Molepaw when he gets back."

They worked in silence until a yowl split the air outside the den. "They're gone!" Cloudtail pounded into camp. "We can't find them anywhere!"

Jayfeather scrambled out of his den. "Who?"

"Birchfall, Blossomfall, and Mousewhisker." Cloudtail was pacing in front of Brambleclaw. Molepaw and Rosepetal panted behind him.

"Are you sure you've looked everywhere?" Brambleclaw demanded.

"We've had the whole Clan scouring the forest," Cloudtail reported. "There's no sign of them."

Jayfeather crossed the clearing, his mind whirling. *Dovewing!* He tasted the air, searching for her. She was resting beside her den.

"Listen for them!" He hurried toward her. "Find out where they are."

She sat up, trembling. "Okay."

Jayfeather reached into Dovewing's mind as she stretched her senses across the forest. *Where are you?* His heart began to pound as Dovewing's hearing ranged beyond the lake and the forest and reached into darkness. She was venturing back into the Dark Forest.

"Has the battle begun?" Blossomfall's anxious mew sounded from the shadows. Dovewing focused in. The tortoiseshell warrior was following a twisting path through slimy bracken. Birchfall paced beside her.

Behind them, Mousewhisker stared into the trees. "How will we know when to attack?"

Blossomfall was shivering from cold or fear. "Don't worry, we'll know. Brokenstar promised, remember? There's no way he's going to let us escape from fighting alongside him."

The voices vanished as Dovewing's senses jerked back to the clearing. Reeling, Jayfeather straightened up.

"Where's Ivypool?" Dovewing wailed. "She has to go after them, bring them back before the battle starts."

Jayfeather shook his head. "There isn't time," he told her heavily. "They'll have to save themselves now." He turned his head, listening to the sounds of preparation for battle going on all around him.

It's all any of us can do, to defend ourselves against the vengeance of the Dark Forest.

CHAPTER 22

❧

They'll have to save themselves now.

Jayfeather's words turned Dovewing cold with fear. She tasted the air, searching for Ivypool, then darted to the apprentices' den. Ivypool was curled in her nest, eyes tight shut, ears twitching. *She's trying to dream herself into the Dark Forest to find Blossomfall, Birchfall, and Mousewhisker.*

Dovewing padded closer. *But they know she's a spy! What if they've already betrayed her to Tigerstar?* Suddenly, a voice sounded at the edge of her hearing.

"The time has come."

It was Brokenstar's rasping mew, ringing from the Dark Forest.

Cats crowed their approval, their yowls echoing through leafless branches. Dovewing closed her eyes and searched out the sound. She cast her senses between shadowy trees and heard the sluggish wash of water over slimy banks. A little farther along the river, a legion of cats jostled for position around a blackened tree stump.

"This is the last night you'll spend in this stinking forest!" Brokenstar declared from the stump. His amber eyes gleamed as he surveyed the sea of bristling pelts.

"What does he mean, *the last night?*"

Dovewing recognized Blossomfall's whisper. The tortoise-shell crouched at the edge of the crowd with Mousewhisker and Birchfall huddled beside her.

Tigerstar leaped onto the tree stump and nudged Broken-star aside. "Tonight we will sweep away the warrior code that has robbed the Clans of true honor for so long. For too many moons, the Clans have nurtured the weak and rejected the strong." He swung his broad head around to take in all the cats below him. "But tonight we will rage through the Clans like a storm until only the strong remain. We will build a new Clan where strength and victory are prized above weakness and failure!"

"No more warrior code!" yowled a battered tabby.

"The Dark Forest will rule the Clans!" Cries rose from the crowd.

"Follow me tonight!" Tigerstar lifted his voice. "And I promise you more power and freedom than you have ever known."

The Dark Forest warriors' cheers rang in Dovewing's ears. With a gasp, she spotted Sunstrike of WindClan and Min-nowtail from RiverClan. They were staring at Tigerstar, their eyes wide with shock. Not far away from them, Mousewhisker was backing toward the trees.

"The Clans have been flawed for too long." Hollowflight stretched up among the Dark Forest warriors. The River-Clan tom's eyes shone. "We have to show them that only the strongest will survive."

Dovewing felt sick. *How can a Clan cat believe in such cruelty?*

Icewing's white pelt flashed at the corner of her vision. The RiverClan she-cat nudged Mousewhisker back toward Blossomfall and Birchfall. With a flick of her tail, she beckoned Furzepelt and Harespring of WindClan closer. "Don't let Tigerstar see you're afraid," she hissed. "Keep quiet and do exactly what he says or you'll never see your home again."

Birchfall started to object but a ragged tortoiseshell turned to face him, eyes narrow. "I don't hear you cheering for our leader," she growled.

Icewing met her gaze. "We're planning our strategy, Mapleshade," she meowed. "Don't forget we have the edge when it comes to fighting the Clans. Our Clanmates *trust* us."

"Really?" Mapleshade sounded unconvinced. "Let's hope you're prepared for the battle of your lives." She leaned closer to Icewing. "Because fighting alongside us is the only way you'll survive."

A thin, black tabby tom pushed his way from the crowd and stopped beside Mapleshade. "How are our recruits doing?" he sneered.

"Darkstripe." Mapleshade greeted him with a curt nod. "They're scared as kits."

Darkstripe's gaze swept over the Clan cats. "Don't be," he snapped. "You're on my patrol and I'll make sure you fight like heroes." His eyes narrowed suddenly. "Where's Ivypool?"

"She's coming," meowed Blossomfall.

Darkstripe flexed his claws. "She should be here already." He glanced at Mapleshade. "I never trusted her," he growled.

"Always trying too hard to please Tigerstar. Sly as a Twoleg's dog."

Birchfall lashed his tail. "That's not true!"

Hawkfrost summoned them from the tree stump. He'd jumped up beside Tigerstar and Brokenstar, his pelt glossy in the eerie half-light. "Our warriors are ready," he yowled. "Death to the Clans!"

As the Dark Forest warriors picked up the chant, wind surged through the trees. It dragged at the branches, splintering bark and stripping shriveled, dead leaves. Lightning split the sky as thunder burst in Dovewing's ears.

She flinched, but kept watching as Tigerstar jumped down from the stump. The crowd parted to let him through and he raced for the trees, Brokenstar and Hawkfrost at his tail. The Dark Forest army surged after them.

"Death to the Clans!"

"Death to the Clans!"

The storm lit up the forest and tore at the trees. Battle cries ripped the air. Dovewing's breath caught in her throat as she heard countless paws thundering closer. *Oh, StarClan, help us! They're coming!*

She jabbed Ivypool with a paw.

Ivypool jerked up her head. "I was just starting to dream!"

"It's too late!" Dovewing nudged her sister to her feet. "The battle has begun. We have to tell Firestar." She darted from the den, then skidded to a halt at the edge of the clearing.

Around her, the Clan was watching Oakfur, Smokefoot, and Snowbird pad into camp.

"I can't believe this is happening," Cloudtail muttered.

"ShadowClan warriors in our camp."

"Welcome, Oakfur." Firestar hurried to meet them, flashing Cloudtail a warning look.

Brambleclaw caught up. "Smokefoot, Snowbird, it's good to see you."

"There's prey if you're hungry," Lionblaze offered.

"We'll catch our own if we need to," Smokefoot meowed stiffly.

Prey? Dovewing ran forward. "There's no time to worry about prey! They're coming!"

Firestar turned. "The Dark Forest cats?"

Dovewing pricked her ears and heard paws thundering over bare earth, then the sudden soft swish of ferns. "They're in the forest!"

The ShadowClan patrol faced the barrier, hackles high. Lionblaze unsheathed his claws and dropped into a battle crouch.

Hazeltail was staring at Dovewing. "How do you know?"

"She just does, okay?" Jayfeather bounded from the medicine den and stopped in front of Dovewing. "Which way are they heading?"

Brambles rustled and leaves crackled loud enough to make Dovewing's ear fur tremble. "I can't tell!"

Brambleclaw snapped his head up, scanning the tree line above. Dovewing stiffened as she realized that the paw steps were close enough for any cat to hear. Firestar swung his head around, meeting the panicked gaze of his Clanmates. Foxleap pushed between Berrynose and Hazeltail. Poppyfrost and

Cinderheart pressed close beside Rosepetal and Thornclaw. Millie lifted her chin, never more distant from her kittypet roots.

"It's time," Firestar meowed. "I trust you to do whatever you must to save our Clan." His gaze flicked to Smokefoot. "To save *all* the Clans."

Brambleclaw stepped forward. "Sorreltail, Thornclaw, and Spiderleg, go as fast as you can to ShadowClan," he ordered. "Fight like they're your own Clanmates. Whitewing, Berrynose, and Hazeltail, you must help WindClan." The warriors raced out of camp. Only Sorreltail hesitated, glancing toward the nursery.

"We'll keep Lilykit and Seedkit safe," Firestar promised her.

Sorreltail dipped her head and charged after her patrol.

Brambleclaw flicked his tail toward Foxleap.

The russet warrior was already running for the entrance with Toadstep and Rosepetal on his tail. "We'll get to RiverClan before the Dark Forest warriors," he called over his shoulder.

Cherrypaw and Molepaw dashed across the clearing and stood in front of Firestar. "Where should we go first?"

The ThunderClan leader nodded at the two eager runners. "Molepaw, head for WindClan and then RiverClan. Cherrypaw, go to ShadowClan. Bring back any news you can. We need to know where the Dark Forest strikes first."

Poppyfrost met her kits as they headed for the thorn barrier. "I know you'll be brave." She lifted her chin. "I'm very proud of you, remember that."

She stood aside and let them rush out, her eyes glistening. Berrynose padded to her side and pressed his cheek against hers. "They're *warriors* today," he murmured.

Dovewing glanced around the camp, shocked to find it so empty now that the patrols had left. Were there still enough cats here to defend it? Above, the sound of fur brushing undergrowth was so loud that she flattened her ears to muffle it. Jayfeather hurried toward the medicine den and grabbed a trailing bramble in his jaws. He hauled it across the entrance and Millie rushed to help him.

Briarlight called through to them from the den. "I've lined up the herb parcels and put moss to soak in the pool."

"Push the emergency supplies to the back of the store," Jayfeather told her, dragging another tendril to block the entrance.

Graystripe headed for the elders' den, where Purdy and Mousefur peered out. "Stay inside!" he ordered.

"What about the fighting moves Spiderleg taught us?" Purdy asked.

"Use them if you have to, but don't enter the battle until it finds you." The gray warrior nosed the elders back into the depths of the honeysuckle.

Daisy and Ferncloud paced outside the nursery, the fur on their spines sticking up like thorns. "Are Seedkit and Lilykit in your nest, Brightheart?" Daisy called through the bramble wall.

"They're all tucked in together," Brightheart answered.

"No cat will reach them," Ferncloud promised with a growl.

"We need to meet our enemy outside the hollow," Firestar decided. He nodded to Brambleclaw. "You stay in camp. Choose your patrol."

Brambleclaw turned to Squirrelflight first. "Will you fight beside me?"

Their eyes met for a long moment. "Always," she meowed.

"Good." Brambleclaw nodded. "Dustpelt, Bumblestripe, Cinderheart, Leafpool, and Graystripe, you'll help defend the hollow."

"Graystripe comes with me," Firestar put in, with a glance at his oldest friend.

Brambleclaw dipped his head. "Of course."

Lionblaze lashed his tail. "Where do I fight?"

"With me." Firestar faced his Clan. "Fight like rogues if you have to," he growled. "We're fighting for everything that matters. Whatever happens, no cat will forget that the Clans fought first with their hearts and then with their claws."

Smokefoot looked at the thorn barrier. "What about the WindClan and RiverClan patrols?"

Firestar pricked an ear toward the battle cries rising at the top of the hollow. "We don't have time to wait for them."

"Firestar," Sandstorm hissed. She walked over and stood between Firestar and his Clan. "This is your last life." Dovewing heard her whisper fiercely. "You can't risk losing it now. Your Clan needs you."

"They need me to fight," Firestar replied.

"But what will they do if you're killed?"

"They'll fight harder." Firestar's green eyes glowed. "My warriors have only one life, and they are willing to give it up for their Clanmates. I'm no different. My place is beside them."

Sandstorm pressed her cheek against Firestar's. "I love you," she breathed.

"I love you too," Firestar murmured. "Stay with Brambleclaw and guard the camp." He broke away and raced for the entrance. Lionblaze and Graystripe led the patrol after him, sweeping past Dovewing. She chased behind them, fear surging beneath her fur. *Where's Ivypool?* There was no sign of her sister's black pelt.

Heart pounding, she broke from the thorns. Firestar had scrambled to a halt outside the camp and was commanding silence with gleaming eyes. The patrol clustered around him, bristling. Above them, the forest shivered with movement. Dovewing held her breath. Firestar whispered in Graystripe's ear, then silent as an owl, flicked his tail one way, then the other, ordering the patrol to split in two. Dovewing shuffled toward Graystripe and found herself squeezed between Cloudtail and Snowbird. The ShadowClan she-cat smelled like pinesap, her fur sleek and the muscles beneath it like stone. Firestar nodded Graystripe toward the slope that circled one side of the hollow. Then he padded to the slope opposite, beckoning his half of the patrol to follow.

He wants us to climb up from both sides and trap the enemy at the top.

Dovewing waited for Firestar to give the order to charge, surprised when he summoned her forward with a jerk of his muzzle.

"Are they everywhere?" he hissed as she reached him.

She stretched her ears. A shriek rang out from beyond the ShadowClan border. On the moor, heather creaked as warriors pushed through and, beyond the lake, reeds snapped beneath paws. Her breath quickened. "Yes. They're attacking all the territories at once."

Firestar nodded. "We knew this would happen." His muzzle brushed hers. "Stay strong. Good luck." Eyes flashing at Graystripe, he lashed his tail.

It was the signal to begin fighting back. Dovewing took a deep breath. *This is it. The battle is here.*

May the powers of the stars truly be in my paws.

CHAPTER 23

♣

Dovewing swerved, feeling the patrol turn with her, and began to head up the slope, treading lightly, moving slick as a weasel through the thick undergrowth.

A thorn ripped her leg. Stumbling, she yelped.

"Are you okay?" Cloudtail crouched beside her.

"My paw's caught." A bramble was looped around it.

"Let me help." He pressed closer.

Dovewing could feel him trembling. "Are you okay?"

"Yes." He swallowed. "I never . . . I never expected *this*." He grabbed the bramble in his jaws. Twisting, he loosened its grip on her leg.

"What do you mean?" She pulled her paw free.

"Being attacked by dead cats."

Dovewing suddenly remembered that Cloudtail didn't believe in StarClan. It was the only part of his kittypet birth that he carried with him. "I don't think any cat expected this," she meowed.

As she spoke, paws skidded on the slope above. Someone had come back to find them.

"It's okay! We're comin—" Dovewing froze as she

recognized the black-and-silver pelt of Darkstripe from her vision of the Dark Forest. "Look out!" She screeched a warning to Cloudtail, but the white warrior was already on his hind legs, claws flashing.

Muscle thumped against muscle as the toms crashed together. Cloudtail staggered backward but stayed on his paws. "Darkstripe! I'm not surprised to see you're with the Dark Forest traitors," he snarled.

"So you believe in StarClan now?" Darkstripe challenged.

"I believe in evil!"

"At least you believe in something, kittypet!"

"I've always believed in the warrior code and I always will." Flattening his ears, Cloudtail swiped at Darkstripe. Blood spattered the brambles as he sliced the tom's nose. Darkstripe growled and charged Cloudtail like a badger, knocking him backward and leaping onto his exposed belly. Cloudtail struggled to find his paws. Dovewing sprang forward, hooking her claws into Darkstripe's pelt. Grunting with the effort, she heaved him off Cloudtail.

"Brave little warrior!" Darkstripe hissed and thrust out his hind legs. He pushed himself backward with such speed that he sent Dovewing flying. She landed, winded, and Darkstripe found his paws first. Flying at her, he caught her muzzle with a vicious kick.

Half-blind with pain, she glimpsed Cloudtail beside her. The white warrior bushed out his fur and curled his lip at Darkstripe. Darkstripe's pelt didn't even ripple. Smooth as a snake, he darted at Cloudtail, slithering beneath him and raking the warrior's belly. Blood sprayed the forest floor.

"Get off him!" Dovewing staggered to her paws and hurled herself at Darkstripe, throwing her paws around his shoulders and clinging on desperately. As he tried to shake her off, she hooked a hind paw beneath his and toppled him. Together they rolled down the slope till brambles snagged them.

Teeth ripped into her shoulder. Shocked, she let go and dragged herself free, digging her claws into the earth to stop herself from falling. Darkstripe slashed her cheek with a blow that sent her reeling. She staggered, looking for Cloudtail. She would never be able to beat this warrior single-pawed.

"Bad luck, mouse-heart." Darkstripe glanced up the slope. With a gasp, Dovewing saw Cloudtail shrieking with fury as a tabby held him fast, churning his hind paws against his spine. "Sparrowfeather's finishing him off." Darkstripe curled his lip. "Which means I get to kill you all by myself."

Warriors don't kill! Rage roared through Dovewing. *Fight like rogues!* Firestar's order rang in her head and she launched herself at Darkstripe. Snapping her jaws, she sunk her teeth into his foreleg. He yowled and tried to shake her off but she crunched harder, feeling bone. *Guard your throat!* She remembered Ivypool's training as teeth clamped her neck. Frantic with terror, she flipped her hind legs around and managed to gouge Darkstripe's belly. He let go with a snarl and Dovewing ducked away, brambles scraping her ears.

A yowl split her ear fur and she turned just in time to catch a mighty swipe from Sparrowfeather. Reeling, she fell and landed hard. Paws thumped into her flank as Sparrowfeather leaped on top of her. Digging his claws deep into her pelt, he held her down and raked her with his hind paws. Dovewing struggled for breath, the wind knocked from her. Terror flooded her as she tried to fight her way free. The Dark Forest tom raked harder and a yowl of agony rose in her throat.

"Come on, Sparrowfeather! Darkstripe!" A new voice sounded on the slope beside them. A Dark Forest warrior was charging past. "Those two are beaten. Leave them to bleed to death. We're attacking the camp."

Dovewing felt Sparrowfeather's claws rip free as he let go and raced after his Clanmates.

"Cloudtail?" Dovewing struggled to her paws, fighting for breath.

Cloudtail lay a few tail-lengths up the slope, his pelt slick with blood. She raced to him and crouched down, wincing with pain. "Cloudtail!"

He lifted his head, eyes dull.

"They're attacking the camp!"

Cloudtail hauled himself to his paws. "Come on!" he croaked. "We've got to stop them." He plunged down the slope, his front leg buckling beneath him.

"Are you okay?" Dovewing caught up to him in a couple of strides. Her pelt was fiery with pain.

"I have to be!" Cloudtail straightened up and pushed on.

Outside camp, Squirrelflight and Sandstorm were side by side, matching their blows as a patrol of Dark Forest warriors snapped at them like foxes. Sparrowfeather and Darkstripe barged through and joined the attack.

"We need backup!" Squirrelflight yowled.

Brambleclaw, Leafpool, Cinderheart, and Dustpelt raced from the entrance, but more ragged pelts swarmed from the trees and began to drive the Clan cats back against the thorn barrier. The ferns shivered on the far slope and Firestar and Lionblaze crashed out. Paw steps skidded behind Dovewing and she turned to see Snowbird and Graystripe race past her and leap into battle. Shaking the blood from his eyes, Cloudtail followed them.

Dovewing plunged in after him. She spotted Darkstripe's pelt and slashed at it. *Fight like a rogue.* She dropped the skillful swipes she'd been taught as an apprentice and instead dug her claws into whatever flesh she could reach. She spun around, raking warrior after warrior, pelts blurring before her eyes.

"Watch out!" Squirrelflight yelped beside her. Dovewing had accidentally scraped her Clanmate's flank.

"Sorry." Quickly, she turned back, aiming for a darker pelt, relieved as she sunk her teeth into foul-smelling flesh.

"They're in the camp!" Lionblaze's yowl split the air.

Dark pelts were streaming through the thorns, turning the narrow entrance into a ragged hole. Lionblaze flashed in after them.

"Cinderheart! Dustpelt! Graystripe! Go with Lionblaze and drive them out!" Firestar sent a Dark Forest warrior flying with a backward kick. "We'll hold the rest off here."

Dovewing heard Ferncloud shriek. *The kits!* She raced for the thorns but long claws hauled her back and sent her flying. She landed with a thump. Struggling to her paws, she suddenly spotted familiar pelts on the slope above camp. Warriors from RiverClan and WindClan had arrived. Dovewing just hoped they were on the right side.

The patrols thundered down the slope and Troutstream, Pebblefoot, and Mintfur hurled themselves into battle beside Dovewing. She watched them closely for a moment, then breathed out in relief when she realized they were aiming only for Dark Forest cats.

"There's more in camp!" Firestar screeched, batting away Darkstripe.

"We'll deal with them." Owlwhisker disappeared through the barrier with Whitetail and Boulderfur on his tail.

As screams sounded from the hollow, the RiverClan warriors turned tail-to-tail and began driving the Dark Forest warriors apart. Dovewing dived into a gap between two tabbies and, with whirling paws, began pushing them farther away. Within moments, the Dark Forest throng was split into much smaller groups.

Firestar lined up beside Bumblestripe and Poppyfrost and began herding a knot of warriors toward the trees. Dovewing joined Millie and Squirrelflight to push back another cluster. She reared and dived, sure of her movements, knowing exactly where to aim. She nipped at a tabby's hind legs while Millie batted his muzzle. Squirrelflight tripped another and Dovewing sliced his ear. The Dark Forest warriors jerked around, looking at their scattered allies with dismay before turning and running for the trees.

Dovewing spun around. Lionblaze was chasing a tabby up

the slope. Leafpool sent a black tom staggering backward. The Dark Forest cats had thinned to a few stragglers.

Firestar stood stiff-legged in front of them. "You can run or you can die," he offered in a low growl.

They froze, then turned and pelted for the forest.

"Cowards!" Ferncloud hissed from the entrance to the hollow.

Pebblefoot and Sandstorm exploded out from behind her, driving the last few Dark Forest warriors out of camp. As they hurtled past, Dovewing pricked her ears and followed the sound of their wailing back into the Dark Forest. Excitement rose in her chest. *We survived!*

Then she froze.

Beyond the wailing she heard fiercer yowls. Battle cries. Paws slapped against slimy earth. Not fleeing, but marching—heading this way. "There's more coming," she whispered.

"Cloudtail! Pebblefoot! Dustpelt!" The ThunderClan leader called to the bloodiest cats. "Medicine den! Now!"

They limped across the battered thorns, turning the branches red.

"Is anyone else badly hurt?" Firestar scanned the patrol. Millie rubbed at a torn ear. Graystripe pressed against her, his eye swollen. Poppyfrost licked a wrenched claw. Mintfur sniffed a scratch on Troutstream's flank while Smokefoot shook out his ragged pelt.

Leafpool wove between them, checking wounds. "Nothing dangerous," she meowed.

Brambleclaw ducked out of camp. "All clear," he reported. "The kits are safe."

"For now," Firestar answered darkly.

Dovewing stiffened as paw steps pounded beyond the rise.

Cloudtail arched his back. "Who is it?"

A young ShadowClan cat appeared at the top of the slope.

"Stoatpaw?" Brambleclaw padded forward. "How's ShadowClan?"

"Blackstar's losing a life!" Stoatpaw raced toward them, eyes wide. "We've been overrun! We need help!"

Smokefoot darted forward to meet the apprentice. Oakfur and Snowbird watched their Clanmates, panic lighting their eyes.

"Have you seen Cherrypaw?" Poppyfrost asked.

Stoatpaw blinked. "Isn't she here?"

Poppyfrost stiffened.

"Perhaps she's gone to WindClan to find Molepaw." Leafpool pressed against the tortoiseshell warrior. "Or she might be lying low until it's safe to travel."

Firestar looked at Dovewing. "How near is the next Dark Forest patrol?"

Dovewing listened, relieved to find that their paw steps were still muffled by Dark Forest mist. "They haven't broken through yet."

The ThunderClan leader lashed his tail. "Lionblaze, go to ShadowClan. You go too, Graystripe. We can manage here without you."

Can we? Dovewing trembled. The paw steps might still be far away, but they were approaching steadily, relentless as storm clouds.

"Smokefoot!" Firestar called to the ShadowClan warrior. "Take your patrol home. Your Clanmates need you more than we do."

As Smokefoot nodded, Brambleclaw weaved around Lionblaze. "Save them, Lionblaze." He touched his muzzle to the golden warrior's cheek as though they were still father and son. "I know you can."

Lionblaze gazed for a moment into Brambleclaw's eyes, then pulled away and raced into the forest. Graystripe and the ShadowClan patrol hurtled after him, Stoatpaw trailing behind on tired legs.

Dovewing's belly felt hollow as they disappeared. She glanced around at her Clanmates. Fear sparked in their eyes.

"The camp's been destroyed," Ferncloud growled.

"We've rebuilt it before." Firestar turned and headed through the ragged barrier. "We can rebuild it again."

Dovewing tried to block out the distant thrum of approaching paws. *Only if we survive the next attack.*

CHAPTER 24

❧

Lionblaze pounded toward the ShadowClan border. Ferns whipped the tips of his whiskers. Graystripe raced after him, Snowbird, Oakfur, and Smokefoot flashing through the trees alongside. The ground blurred beneath his paws.

"Oomph!" Graystripe stumbled behind him, falling with a grunt.

Lionblaze slewed around and raced back.

Graystripe was scrambling to his paws. "A bramble tripped me," he growled.

For a moment, Lionblaze saw frailty mist the old warrior's eyes. Suddenly he noticed the stark outline of bone showing along his spine.

Graystripe curled his lip. "Why are you looking at me like that? Come on! We've got a battle to fight." He hared after Smokefoot and Snowbird.

As they crossed the border, Lionblaze heard the screech of battle cries. Pelts writhed behind a low juniper bush.

"Crowfrost!" Snowbird screeched, and she sprang over the bush.

Two ShadowClan warriors thrashed in the claws of three

Dark Forest warriors. The Clan cats' pelts were ripped and bloody. Their eyes sparked with fear.

"Toadfoot, we're coming!" Oakfur followed Snowbird. He cleared the juniper and launched himself at the nearest Dark Forest tom, sending him tumbling while Snowbird hauled another away from Crowfrost.

Lionblaze slowed. Another knot of warriors clashed farther along the trail. He recognized the pelt of Snaketail writhing among the battling cats. *Snaketail's an elder! But we can't get distracted by skirmishes. Blackstar needs us.* "We have to get to the camp," he urged Graystripe.

"Snaketail needs help," Smokefoot called.

"Then help him." Lionblaze veered off the trail and cut through brambles, taking the straightest route. "Come on, Graystripe."

As the pines thickened, Lionblaze heard wailing. Brambles rose ahead. *The ShadowClan camp.* Holes had been torn in the boundary. Outside, the bracken was crushed and spattered with blood. Swallowing against the stench of fear and Dark Forest scent, Lionblaze ducked through a gap in the brambles.

Injured cats littered the clearing. Pinenose, a black queen, wailed over the small, lifeless body of a kit. Tawnypelt weaved around her Clanmate, her gaze sharp with horror. Four Dark Forest warriors paced at the far end of the camp, watching the Clan like foxes waiting for cornered prey to wear itself out.

A ragged line of ShadowClan warriors faced them. Emberfoot, Gorsetail, and Furzepelt of WindClan stood with Ratscar and Tawnypelt. Hollowflight, Robinwing, and

Petalfur swelled their ranks.

Graystripe scrambled to a halt beside Lionblaze. "Why isn't ShadowClan fighting back?" he panted.

"Do you want us to lose *more* warriors?" Littlecloud squeaked as he dashed past, darting from one wounded Clanmate to the next. "Blackstar's lost a life." The ShadowClan medicine cat paused beside Scorchfur, who was lying on his side, blood pooling at his belly. He pressed down on the wound, but blood bubbled around his paws. "I'm running out of supplies!" Panic edged his mew.

Graystripe strode forward. "You need moss." He beckoned to Kinkfur trembling at the edge of the clearing. "Go and find some!" he ordered. "As much as you can carry."

She darted away, her eyes lighting up as though she was relieved to know what to do.

"Cedarheart! Whitewater!" Graystripe called to the elders crouching beneath the battered brambles. "Find cobwebs! There are wounds to dress!"

An ominous growl sounded from the head of the clearing and Lionblaze saw a flash of fur. One of the Dark Forest warriors crashed through the ShadowClan line and hurled himself at Graystripe.

Graystripe met him with a swipe that slammed the tom backward. "You'd better wait for backup before you try taking us on," he growled.

The tom glared at him, but slunk back toward his Clanmates.

"They're waiting for the next wave to come." Lionblaze

leaned toward Littlecloud. "You need to patch up as many of these cats as you can. They have to keep fighting."

Scorchfur lifted his head weakly. "I'll fight to the death if I have to."

Lionblaze scanned the camp again. "Where's the ThunderClan patrol?" There was no sign of Sorreltail, Thornclaw, or Spiderleg.

Littlecloud didn't look up from his patient. "They must have chased Dark Forest warriors into the forest."

Cedarheart raced toward him, his forepaw wadded with cobweb. "Here!" He held it out for Littlecloud to unwrap. "Whitewater's bringing more. The hollow tree's thick with it."

Kinkfur ran across the clearing and dropped a bundle of dripping moss beside Littlecloud.

"Thanks." Littlecloud began wrapping cobweb over Scorchfur's wound, the tension in his shoulders easing as the blood stopped pulsing. "Get more."

As Kinkfur raced away Littlecloud pawed the moss closer; Scorchfur twisted and lapped at it thirstily.

Lionblaze scanned the camp. The panic that had frozen the Clan seemed to be fading. Cats were darting in and out through the ragged bramble wall, fetching moss and cobweb. Ratscar began to pace, his tail flicking menacingly. Lionblaze leaned closer to Graystripe. "Stay here and guard Littlecloud." He crossed to the warriors facing the DarkClan cats. "Move closer," he whispered to Ratscar. "Very slowly. One claw-length at a time."

Ratscar nodded, signaling to his patrol with a flick of his

ear before shuffling forward. The line moved with him, then moved again. The Dark Forest cats shifted uneasily. One of them eyed the camp wall hopefully, as though looking for reinforcements.

"Just keep creeping forward," Lionblaze whispered to Ratscar. "Not too close, just enough to distract them while I see how Blackstar is doing."

Ratscar nodded toward a gap in the brambles. "He's in there."

"Thanks." Lionblaze hurried toward it and ducked inside.

Rowanclaw met him, bristling. "You came."

"Of course." Lionblaze glimpsed Blackstar lying on the sandy floor behind the ShadowClan deputy. "How is he?"

"Recovering." Rowanclaw blocked Lionblaze's way. "He's not on his last life but he'll be weak for a while." His eyes flashed defensively. "ShadowClan's not beaten yet. We'll be fighting again in a heartbeat."

"Good." Lionblaze weaved around the ShadowClan deputy and crouched beside Blackstar. "We've come to help."

The ShadowClan leader's eyes were glazed, but his breathing was steady.

Rowanclaw leaned down and sniffed his leader. "He'll be on his paws soon." Blackstar's tail twitched as breath stirred his fur. "Where did these rogues come from?" Ratscar whispered. "I've seen cats I thought were dead!"

"Evil lives forever," Lionblaze murmured. "We were wrong to think that only StarClan could survive death. The Dark—"

A shriek from the clearing cut him off.

"Get him up!" Lionblaze ordered Rowanclaw. But the ShadowClan deputy was already nosing Blackstar onto his paws.

Lionblaze raced from the den. Dark Forest warriors streamed through the gaps at one side of the camp. "Ratscar! Get your warriors into groups. Try to force the enemy apart. Don't let them form a line!" He raced to Littlecloud. "We need to get the injured to shelter."

"Underneath the camp wall should do." Littlecloud flicked his tail toward the drooping brambles at the edge of the clearing. "Kinkfur! Whitewater! Help me!" He grabbed the scruff of an unconscious tom in his teeth and started to haul him toward the brambles.

"Tallpoppy!" Lionblaze beckoned the ShadowClan elder.

The long-legged she-cat raced across the clearing, dodging past a Dark Forest warrior, and picked the dead kit up in her jaws. Nudging Pinenose ahead of her, she bundled the grieving queen behind the trailing brambles and laid her kit at her paws. Emberfoot, Robinwing, and Ferretclaw clustered in the middle of the clearing, pressing their spines together and lashing out at the onslaught of Dark Forest warriors. Dawnpelt and Starlingwing stood side by side, keeping tight and slashing furiously against a river of stinking pelts.

"Hold your positions!" Lionblaze yowled.

Emberfoot's patrol disappeared beneath a wave of bristling warriors. Lionblaze leaped forward and started lashing out on all sides, feeling his paws connect with flesh and fur. It seemed as if there were no ShadowClan cats left on their feet.

Was this the end for the proud, battle-skilled Clan?

"They're overrunning us!" Graystripe shouldered past Lionblaze, throwing warriors aside with mighty swipes. He reached Emberfoot's patrol and hauled a matted tortoiseshell from the WindClan warrior's back.

Suddenly paw steps sounded beyond the camp wall. Lionblaze stiffened. *Another attack?* The camp was already overwhelmed.

The brambles trembled and collapsed as a patrol of bristling warriors burst through. Lionblaze stared at the newcomers. Their pelts were transparent, moving like shadows into battle. He could see trees and grass behind them, where he should only have seen fur and solid muscle. But when he looked closer, he knew he had seen these cats before. *The Ancient cats from the Cave!*

The ghostly warriors streamed among the Dark Forest cats. Eyes narrow, ears flat, they began to lunge with outstretched claws and snapping teeth, landing blows as real as any forest cat.

Rowanclaw darted to his side. "Who in the name of StarClan are they?"

A faded, mottled she-cat paused in front of the Shadow-Clan deputy. "We were here before StarClan, youngster!" She glanced at Lionblaze. "We meet again."

"Owl Feather!" A pale, ancient warrior called to her. "Help me finish this one off." The warrior was driving a Dark Forest tabby backward across the clearing.

"I'm coming, Half Moon!"

As Owl Feather darted away, a massive creature crashed through the remains of the camp wall. Its white, striped muzzle was as big as a dog's, its gray shoulders huge beside the battling cats.

"Midnight!" Graystripe called to the badger as she lumbered across the clearing. Dark Forest cats and ShadowClan warriors fled from her path, terror lighting their eyes. "It's okay!" he yowled. "The badger is an ally!"

With a roar, Midnight plucked a Dark Forest warrior by the back of his neck and lifted him high, then tossed him away like a piece of prey. Hope flaring, Lionblaze grabbed the nearest stinking tom and pinned him to the ground. He slashed his cheek and raked his flank, then kicked him away.

"Nice move." Half Moon fell in beside him, her pelt as pale as mist.

A Dark Forest tom lunged at her. She ripped her claws across his cheek. The tom snapped at her legs. Quick as a fox, Lionblaze slid under the tom and thrust upward, sending him flying. Half Moon leaped up and snatched him from the air as though she were plucking a bird from the sky.

"Help!"

Lionblaze jerked around as a shriek sounded beyond the brambles. He jumped over the remains of the camp wall and raced through the trees.

"You'll die like a traitor!" A vicious Dark Forest tom was pinning Ratscar between the roots of a pine.

"No, Shredtail! Please!" Ratscar struggled in terror as Shredtail curled his claws tighter around his throat.

Lionblaze skidded to a halt. "Let him go!"

Shredtail lifted his head. "Let him go?" He stared scornfully at Lionblaze. "But he betrayed his Dark Forest Clanmates."

Lionblaze stared at Ratscar. *"Clanmates?"*

"They never told me they were training me to destroy my own Clan!" Ratscar croaked.

Shredtail tightened his grip, making Ratscar's eyes bulge. "You knew what would happen if you disobeyed me!" He lifted a paw, claws flashing.

Ratscar writhed desperately.

"Get off him!" White fur streaked past Lionblaze and knocked Shredtail sideways. Snowbird landed hard on all four paws, back arched and spitting with fury. "Ratscar's my littermate!" she hissed as Shredtail recovered his balance. "He'd never betray his Clan." Behind her, Ratscar scrambled to his feet.

Shredtail glared at Snowbird. "Oh, really?" he sneered. "Then why has he been training in the Dark Forest?" He flicked his muzzle toward the camp. "And he's not the only one." His gaze fixed on a dappled ginger tom who was dragging Dawnpelt across the clearing by her scruff.

"Redwillow?" Snowbird stared in disbelief.

"Yes," Shredtail snarled. "Redwillow."

Redwillow spun around as he heard his name and let go of Dawnpelt.

The ShadowClan warrior leaped to her paws, eyes wild with fury. "What are you doing, mouse-brain? I'm not the enemy!"

"Come here, Redwillow!" Shredtail called.

"What is it?" Redwillow raced toward Shredtail, his eyes glittering with excitement.

"How's the battle going?" Shredtail tipped his head.

"Great!" The treacherous warrior glanced hungrily back at the action. "At last I can fight properly. You're right about the Clans being weak and lazy. This is easy. They're so obsessed with being honorable and sticking to the warrior code, I can pick them off like mice!"

Snowbird lunged at him. "The warrior code is more important than any cat's life!" She flung him backward and dug her claws into his throat. "I'm going to kill you."

"Stop, Snowbird." A voice trembled behind Lionblaze.

Blackstar was limping toward them, the scent of death still on him.

Snowbird backed away. "But he's a traitor!"

"I'm loyal to my *new* Clan!" Redwillow jumped to his paws and stood beside Shredtail. He glared at Blackstar. "Your time is over," he snarled. "You're nothing but an elder growing old over and over. Why don't you just give up and die?"

Blackstar padded closer to the young warrior. "I am still leader of this Clan," he growled. "And you have betrayed us all." Fast as a bird, his paw flew out and slashed deep into Redwillow's chest. Blood gushed from the wound, pulsing onto the forest floor. Redwillow stared in astonishment, then glanced down at the gash. Legs buckling, he collapsed. As his head thumped onto the pine needles, his eyes rolled and turned dull.

Shredtail turned on Blackstar. "You killed my loyal warrior!"

Blackstar met his gaze, unflinching. "I killed one traitor, and now I'm ready to kill another."

Shredtail's eyes lit. "You think you can kill me?"

"No!" Lionblaze sprang between them. "Fight me!" He narrowed his eyes at Shredtail. "Or are you afraid?"

"Nothing scares me." With a hiss, Shredtail leaped at him.

Lionblaze felt the thud of muscle against his chest, surprised for a moment by Shredtail's strength. He dug his hind claws hard into the needle-strewn earth and reared up, ready to swipe Shredtail's muzzle. But Shredtail backed away and crouched down, his eyes gleaming as if he knew every move that Lionblaze would make.

Lionblaze paused. *Shredtail thinks he can win.* Doubt pricked his belly. He batted it away and attacked. Hurling himself at Shredtail, he twisted and hooked a paw around Shredtail's forelegs.

Shredtail hopped backward. "You won't beat me fighting like a kit." He lunged for Lionblaze's throat. Lionblaze dodged just in time, flinching at the snap of empty jaws beside his ear. He stood up on his back legs, ready to slam Shredtail with his forepaws, but Shredtail spun away too quickly and thrust his hind paws into Lionblaze's belly so hard it sent him stumbling backward.

Shredtail lashed his tail. "When are you going to start fighting like a real warrior?"

"Now!" As Lionblaze leaped forward, claws grabbed him

from behind, fastening around his throat. He tried to struggle free, body thrashing, fighting for breath, scrabbling to find a grip on the slippery needles.

"Shall I let my Clanmates finish you off?" Shredtail gloated. Then he glanced past Lionblaze's shoulder and his gaze suddenly glittered with fear.

The paws gripping Lionblaze's throat dropped away. He smelled the scent of badger's breath as Midnight moved behind him. "Destiny is the choice of every cat," she rasped in his ear. "But some cats have destiny chosen for them." She turned and lumbered away.

I am going to kill this cat. Lionblaze saw what would happen next as clear as a star-specked sky. *I may not be able to match your fox-hearted tactics, Shredtail, but I can fight like the best warrior that ever lived.*

Shredtail lifted a paw and flexed his claws. "It's a shame your badger friend won't fight for you." He drew back his lips to reveal teeth already stained with blood.

Energy surged beneath Lionblaze's pelt. Exploding from the ground, he sunk his teeth deep into Shredtail's throat while pine needles showered around them. The softness of flesh in his mouth and the taste of blood made him gag, but he held on, tearing deeper and deeper until, gurgling and thrashing, Shredtail collapsed. Lionblaze clamped his jaws harder and the Dark Warrior fell limp.

Letting go, Lionblaze staggered back and watched Shredtail's body fade. Growing paler against the forest floor, it disappeared. He looked up, suddenly aware of the other cats watching, feeling his face wet with Shredtail's blood. The Dark Forest warriors began to back away, then turned and pelted back toward the camp.

"Lionblaze?" Blackstar stepped forward. "I'm proud to fight beside you." He nodded toward the battle. "Now shall we get rid of these other fox-hearts?"

"Lionblaze?"

Graystripe's mew took him by surprise. He turned and saw the gray warrior pushing through the bracken with the dark brown ancient on his tail.

"Half Moon says we should go home." Graystripe glanced over his shoulder toward the ShadowClan camp. "They don't need our help anymore."

Blackstar nodded. "Thanks to you. Go on, fight with your Clanmates now."

Lionblaze dipped his head to the ShadowClan leader. "Okay." He flicked his tail. "Let's go."

Chapter 25

❧

Ivypool crouched inside the dirtplace tunnel. She could hear Firestar in the clearing, ordering patrols. Yowls echoed above the hollow. The Dark Forest had reached the woods.

Ivypool bristled with frustration. Dovepaw had prodded her awake too soon. *I was trying to reach Blossomfall and Birchfall before the battle started!* Now it was too late. *I've got to find them.* She pricked her ears.

"Stay with Brambleclaw and guard the camp." Firestar gave a final order, then thundered out of camp.

Ivypool waited. *Where would Brokenstar send ThunderClan recruits?* Not to their own Clan, surely? They'd be more eager to fight other Clans. Ivypool crept deeper into the brambles and skirted the dirtplace, pushing through ferns until she was clear of the camp. The forest smelled dank as darkness swallowed it. Wind roared in the treetops.

"Ivypool?" Brambleclaw's mew took her by surprise. "Shouldn't you be on Firestar's patrol?"

She whipped around to see the ThunderClan deputy standing underneath a rowan tree. Brambleclaw knew she'd trained in the Dark Forest. What if he thought she was betraying her Clan? "I—I have to find Blossomfall and Birch-fall and Mousewhisker."

He padded closer. "Do you know where they are?"

"No! I wish I did. I want to stop them before . . ."

"Before they betray their Clan?" Brambleclaw narrowed his eyes.

"They wouldn't!" she gasped. "I *know* they wouldn't! But they'll be scared. Brokenstar has threatened to kill them if they don't fight alongside him."

Brambleclaw touched his muzzle to her head. "Go find them, Ivypool."

"Really?" She blinked. "It's okay?"

"I'm depending on you."

"Thank you!" Bursting with relief, Ivypool spun around and pounded toward WindClan territory. Screeches rang from the moorland and echoed across the water, but there was no sign of pelts. She pushed harder, paws skidding on the slippery grass as she neared the stream that marked the border.

"Ivypool." A growl took her by surprise. Amber eyes flashed in the darkness beyond the ditch.

Ivypool halted, unsheathing her claws. "Who is it?"

Tigerheart slid out of the bracken.

Ivypool narrowed her eyes. "Where are you heading?" She leaped the stream, keeping her distance from the dark warrior. "You know the battle's begun, don't you?"

Tigerheart glanced over his shoulder. "Hawkfrost told me to meet him here."

Ivypool shifted her paws. "Are you in his patrol?"

"Are you?" His gaze sparked with suspicion.

"I—I don't know yet. I haven't gotten my orders." Her mind whirled. Which side was Tigerheart on?

"Hawkfrost will tell you what to do when he gets here."

But I have to find my Clanmates! Ivypool began to push through the bracken.

"Where are you going?" Tigerheart challenged.

"I don't have time to wait!" Ivypool kept going. "The battle's begun!"

"But you don't know who to fight!"

Frustration raged through her. "Of course I know who to fight!" She turned on Tigerheart. "I'll fight any Dark Forest warrior I meet." She glared at him. "And any Clan cat who fights with them!"

"But I thought the Dark Forest warriors were your Clanmates now." Tigerheart took a step closer. There was menace in his mew. "Isn't this what you've been training for?"

Ivypool shook her head. "I know which cats deserve my loyalty. I'll die before I fight beside Brokenstar and Hawkfrost."

Tigerheart showed his teeth. "You may have to," he growled. "You heard what Brokenstar said he'd do if we betrayed him."

Ivypool met his gaze, anger surging beneath her pelt. "I don't care."

"You sound like your sister," Tigerheart spat back.

Ivypool frowned. "What's Dovewing got to do with this?"

"She put her Clan ahead of me."

"So?" Tigerheart's gaze darkened as Ivypool went on. "You

should put your Clan first, too! Have all these moons in the Dark Forest made you forget the warrior code?"

Tigerheart bared his teeth. "I haven't forgotten *anything*."

The bracken beside them rustled. Ivypool whipped around, her heart lurching. Hawkfrost emerged. "Ivypool." His eyes flashed. "Where have you been?"

"Looking for Blossomfall and Birchfall," Ivypool stammered.

Hawkfrost stretched his muzzle close. "Find them," he hissed. "Now. Then go straight to the WindClan camp. I want you with me in the second attack."

Ivypool nodded and raced away. She glanced back once to see Tigerheart leaning toward Hawkfrost's ear. Terror scoured her belly. *If he tells Hawkfrost I'm a traitor, I'm dead!* Her heart pounding, she ducked into the heather and fled. "Birchfall!" she yowled. "Blossomfall!"

"Ivypool!"

She skidded to a halt as she heard Birchfall's mew. Her Clanmate was crouching beneath a clump of wind-blown gorse. His pale tabby pelt glowed in the darkness. Blossomfall and Mousewhisker huddled at his side, their eyes glittering with fear. Suddenly there was an explosion of shrieks close by and two WindClan warriors streaked past, Dark Forest warriors on their tail. Farther up the slope, more warriors clashed, their yowls splitting the roar of the wind.

"What should we do?" Blossomfall whispered. "We can't attack Clan cats!"

Ivypool lifted her muzzle. "Of course we can't! We have to

defend the Clans against the Dark Forest."

Birchfall stared at her. "Did you know all along this is what they were planning?"

"Yes," Ivypool confessed.

Mousewhisker blinked at her. "Why didn't you tell us?"

"I was spying." She straightened up. "I didn't know who I could trust. I had to let you work it out for yourselves."

"She's right." Birchfall stepped forward. "We should have guessed earlier what was going on."

Mousewhisker glanced over his shoulder. "So what do we do?"

"We join the battle, just as Brokenstar ordered, but we fight for the Clans," Ivypool told him. "We've been trained by the Dark Forest, so we can use their own tricks against them." A familiar scent touched her nose. "Applefur?" she called warily as she smelled the ShadowClan she-cat. Would she have the courage to oppose the Dark Forest warriors?

As Applefur slid out from the heather, Breezepelt barged past her. Ivypool's fur lifted when she saw Thistleclaw and Snowtuft at his tail.

"There you are!" Breezepelt's eyes shone. "We're going to launch an attack on the camp."

"But Hawkfrost told us to meet him," Ivypool argued.

"You will," Thistleclaw growled. "He'll be attacking from the far side."

Ivypool blinked at the dark tabby. "Okay. Let's go." Her gaze flitted desperately to her Clanmates. *We have to play along for now!* She charged after Breezepelt's patrol as it sped toward the WindClan camp. "We don't have to attack WindClan cats once we're there," she hissed to Birchfall as he fell in beside her.

Heather brushed her pelt, its flowery scent smothered by the stench of decay. The peaty earth felt slimy beneath her paws. *The moor's turning into the Dark Forest!* Ivypool pushed the thought away. *It can't! I won't let it!*

"Hurry!" Mousewhisker dashed past her. "We can't let them get there first."

Scrabbling up between the bushes, her lungs aching, Ivypool followed Birchfall and Blossomfall. From the top she could see into the WindClan camp. The clearing teemed with shrieking cats. Emberfoot reared over a Dark Forest warrior who lunged, screeching, at the WindClan warrior's hind legs. Another Dark Forest tom slapped Crowfeather to the ground and began thrashing him with claw-spiked paws. Ivypool recognized Whitewing, Berrynose, and Hazeltail, broad-shouldered and sturdy among the lithe WindClan cats. Mallownose of RiverClan and Shrewfoot of ShadowClan fought beside them. A Dark Forest warrior batted Mallownose away with a vicious swipe. A tom clawed at Hazeltail's belly while another tore lumps from Whitewing's flank. The Clan warriors were outnumbered and fighting for their lives.

Breezepelt paced the top of the rise, tail lashing. Thistleclaw gazed down into the camp.

"When do we attack?" Applefur sounded scared.

"When the first patrol has weakened them," Thistleclaw told her.

Blossomfall shifted her paws. Ivypool could feel the tortoiseshell's pelt pricking with frustration. "Why don't we help them now?"

"Wait." Thistleclaw lifted his gaze to the far side of camp where Hawkfrost sat, silhouetted against the clouds. His patrol weaved impatiently beside him. Tigerstar's tabby pelt shone among them.

A wail flared below. Ivypool caught her breath as she saw a queen rearing up to grapple a Dark Forest tom away from a tiny kit shivering beside the frayed camp wall.

Hurry up! She fought to keep her paws rooted to the spot, then saw Hawkfrost lift his tail. Lashing it down, he gave the signal.

"Attack!" Thistleclaw yowled and charged down the slope, crashing through the heather wall into camp. Snowtuft charged after him, Blossomfall on his tail.

Ivypool blocked Applefur's way. "You're not going to fight on their side, are you?"

Applefur stared at Ivypool, her eyes wild with terror. "B-but I have to!"

"You have to defend the Clan!" Ivypool hissed. "Isn't *death* better than having Brokenstar as your leader?"

Applefur blinked.

"You are still a warrior," Ivypool reminded her. "And the warrior code says we should lay down our life for our Clanmates. They have never needed us more than they do now!"

Applefur nodded. "You're right," she whispered. "My life is a small price to pay, considering what I've done."

"There's no time for guilt now," Ivypool told her. "Fight loyally, and with courage. That is all your Clan asks of you."

"Then that is what I will give them!" Applefur sprang away toward the camp. Ivypool raced after her. She had to get to Breezepelt. She exploded through the heather and landed, skidding, on the peaty clearing. Cats grappled and yowled on every side. She scanned the camp. Breezepelt was chasing Thistleclaw through the throng. Ivypool snaked after him.

"No!" As Breezepelt reared up to attack a WindClan warrior, Ivypool launched herself at him. Smashing into Breezepelt's flank, she sent him flying. "You can't fight for the Dark Forest!"

"Are you crazy?" Breezepelt struggled free and stared at her. "This is what we've been training for!"

"But you can't believe that this is right!" Suddenly claws raked Ivypool's cheek. Pain shot through her and she staggered sideways.

Thistleclaw loomed over her, his lip curled to show long, yellow teeth. "Traitor!"

"I'm no traitor!" Ivypool hissed. "I've been loyal to my Clan all along! I only came to the Dark Forest to find out what you were planning!"

Her heart froze as Hawkfrost appeared behind Thistleclaw's shoulder. Then Snowtuft landed beside her, his eyes darkening with hate.

"We won't fight for you either!" Birchfall flung himself at a Dark Forest tabby.

Applefur lunged for a ragged tom. "I fight for the *Clans!*"

Rage flared in Hawkfrost's gaze. "Then we shall kill you first, before we destroy your wretched Clans!"

Ivypool braced herself, stiffening as fur flashed beside her. Claws pierced her flank. She spun around as the full weight of Snowtuft sent her sprawling. Jumping to her paws, she hurled herself at the skinny, white tom. She hooked her claws into his shoulders and hauled him backward, but he twisted and snapped at her throat. She dodged just in time and crashed into a dark tabby flank.

Tigerheart! She recognized his scent. "Do I have to fight you, too?" she snarled.

Tigerheart's eyes narrowed. "I'm a warrior," he growled. "I fight for the Clans." He turned and kicked out with his back legs, sending Thistleclaw sprawling. "Dark Forest warriors don't belong here. This is *Clan* territory!"

With hope flaring inside her, Ivypool thrust Snowtuft away. His fur ripped in her claws. "Then why were you in the Dark Forest?" she called to Tigerheart.

Tigerheart ducked under Thistleclaw's belly and shoved him off balance. "Same as you. I wanted to find out what they were up to."

Thistleclaw rounded on him. "But you're Tigerstar's kin!"

"That doesn't mean I have to be like him." Tigerheart swiped at Thistleclaw. "He almost destroyed ShadowClan once before. I wasn't going to let him do it again!"

Roaring, Hawkfrost barged past Thistleclaw. "I'll finish this traitor off." He hurled himself at Tigerheart. "You and Snowtuft deal with Ivypool."

Ivypool felt claws slice her shoulders. Legs buckling, she stumbled sideways. Snowtuft and Thistleclaw reared over her, side by side. Together they began to drive Ivypool back through the ragged camp wall, swinging blow after blow at her muzzle. Ivypool raised her forelegs, trying to fend off the strikes, but her hind paws slipped on the peaty floor. Heather snagged her pelt and she tripped and fell, finding her feet just in time to leap out of the way as Snowtuft lunged for her. Looking up, she realized she'd become separated from the Clan cats. She could see Tigerheart in the clearing, surrounded by Dark Forest warriors. Birchfall was defending a kit at the far side of the camp. Applefur and Blossomfall fought back to back, blood dripping from their whiskers, fending off blows from four Dark Forest toms.

StarClan, help me! Snowtuft and Thistleclaw kept forcing Ivypool back with stinging blows. The camp slid from view, swallowed by shadow as they drove her deeper and deeper into the heather. Then they paused. Snowtuft dropped onto all fours and stared at her. Thistleclaw stood panting beside him.

Ivypool whipped around, catching her breath as she looked for an escape route. Gorse, thick with thorns, crowded every side. Snowtuft and Thistleclaw blocked the only way out.

"We've trapped her!" Thistleclaw called over his shoulder.

Hawkfrost strode into the tiny clearing. "Did you really think you'd live after betraying me?" His blue eyes shone as he glanced at Thistleclaw and Snowtuft. "Let's make her death slow," he growled.

He lunged at Ivypool, throwing her backward with such force that it knocked the wind from her. Gasping for air, she felt claws rake her spine. Thistleclaw's pelt flashed at the edge of her vision. Snowtuft grabbed her from behind. Teeth and claws ripped her pelt. Pain seared her flesh. *I won't die easily!* Terror sent power surging through her. *And I'll take you with me, Hawkfrost!* With a roar, Ivypool reared up, strong as a badger, and sent her attackers flying.

Hawkfrost landed neatly on all four paws. "I trained you too well," he snarled. His gaze fixed on her throat.

Ivypool backed away. She twisted and ducked under him as he leaped, but his claws sank into her tail and pinned her to the ground. Thistleclaw and Snowtuft attacked from opposite sides, snarling, slicing her ears. She struggled away from them, crashing into hard muscle. Hawkfrost was behind her now. He stabbed his claws into her shoulders. With a gasp, Ivypool saw his teeth flashing beside her throat. Then a black pelt flashed over the top of the gorse. Paws landed with a thump beside her.

"Get off her!" Hollyleaf yowled.

Ivypool's world spun as the black warrior slammed into Hawkfrost and sent him reeling into the gorse. Free from Hawkfrost's claws, Ivypool turned on Thistleclaw and Snowtuft. She began slashing with her front paws, remembering in a crystalline moment every moon of training. Hollyleaf reared up beside her, matching her blow for blow, as though she instinctively knew where Ivypool would strike next. Blood sprayed the forest floor as Ivypool sliced Snowtuft's muzzle and tore Thistleclaw's nose. Turning, she kicked out with hind legs and knocked Thistleclaw backward, then sank her teeth into Snowtuft's neck.

The white warrior screeched and ripped free from her jaws. Ivypool tasted his blood as he hared away through the bracken. She met Thistleclaw's gaze. Fear sparked in his eyes as she spat out a bloody clump of Snowtuft's fur.

"Run," she hissed. "Because if you stay, I *will* kill you."

Mouth open, Thistleclaw fled, disappearing through the gorse. A shriek exploded behind Ivypool. She turned and saw Hollyleaf swipe at Hawkfrost's muzzle. The force of the blow sent the Dark Forest warrior crashing away. He dropped with a thump and scrabbled to his paws. Blood dripping from his cheek, one eye swollen shut, he glanced at Hollyleaf and tore his way through the gorse.

Ivypool stared at the black she-cat. "You saved my life!"

Hollyleaf staggered and fell to the ground.

"Hollyleaf!" Ivypool darted to her side and saw blood pulsing from a wound in her neck. Panic formed a hard lump in Ivypool's belly.

Grasping Hollyleaf's scruff in her teeth, she began to half drag, half carry her Clanmate toward the ThunderClan border. Jayfeather would know what to do.

"I'll get you home," Ivypool growled through gritted teeth. "I promise I'll get you home."

A tabby pelt crashed through the gorse toward them. Ivypool braced herself, ready to fight again.

"Let me help!" Tigerheart stopped beside her and shoved his

nose beneath Hollyleaf's shoulder. Taking half the weight, he pressed his flank against Ivypool. "We can do this together."

The screeches of the battle for WindClan faded behind them as they began to haul the injured warrior away.

CHAPTER 26

❧

Dovewing caught her breath. The Dark Forest warriors had gone but she could hear the paw steps of a second patrol pounding toward the camp. They'd break out of the Dark Forest soon, into the heart of ThunderClan. She blocked out the noise and tried to focus on the camp.

"They went straight for the kits." Leafpool stopped beside her and dropped a bundle of herbs. Her mew was shaky.

Shredded brambles hung from the nursery. Ferncloud paced outside, her claws unsheathed, her pelt streaked with blood.

Poppyfrost looked up from licking the scratches on her flank. "We saw them off, though."

"We did." Mousefur stood beside Purdy outside the elders' den. She lifted a paw, her stiffness apparently gone, and rubbed at a scratch on her nose.

I just hope we can do it again, Dovewing thought grimly.

She could see Brightheart through the torn nursery walls, clutching her kits to her belly and calming their frightened mewling with gentle strokes of her tongue. Her tail was wrapped tight around Lilykit and Seedkit, who peered from the nest beside her.

"We'd better fix what we can." Brackenfur was already hauling brambles from beside the medicine den. "Mintfur, Troutstream!" He called to the RiverClan warriors. "Can you help?"

They hurried to join Brackenfur in dragging brambles to patch the nursery. Dovewing wrinkled her nose at the scent of Leafpool's herbs, wondering what it felt like to be a warrior one moment, and a medicine cat the next. ThunderClan was lucky to have her. If they survived the next onslaught, they would need medicine cats more than anything. "How's Daisy?"

"She's got a nasty scratch on her muzzle, but she'll be fine." Leafpool picked up her leaf bundle and headed toward Mousefur. "Jayfeather's seeing to it now."

Dovewing licked her nose, washing away the herb smell. *Fresh blood!* She stiffened as the scent wafted from outside the hollow. Paws were staggering toward the camp, fur dragging behind. "Someone's coming! They're injured!" She raced across the clearing and barged out through a hole in the barrier.

Ivypool was lurching down the slope, Tigerheart at her side. Hollyleaf dangled limply between them.

"Jayfeather! Leafpool!" Dovewing yowled over her shoulder before racing to meet them. "Ivypool, are you hurt?" She circled the trio, looking for wounds. *So much blood!* She sniffed at Tigerheart. He smelled of Dark Forest cats. Had he done this? Was he fighting for Brokenstar? *He can't be!*

Dovewing hopped out of the way as Firestar raced from the camp, Jayfeather at his tail.

"Let me take her." The ThunderClan leader lifted the weight from Ivypool's shoulders, sharing the burden with Tigerheart. "Can you make it into camp?" he asked the ShadowClan tom.

"Yes," Tigerheart grunted.

Dovewing watched the ShadowClan warrior duck through the barrier. "What happened?" she asked her sister.

Ivypool gazed past her, eyes round with shock. "Hollyleaf saved my life."

You nearly died? Fighting to steady her breathing, Dovewing pressed against Ivypool and led her into the hollow.

Tigerheart and Firestar were gently rolling Hollyleaf onto the ground. Brambleclaw and Squirrelflight stared, frozen, at the edge of the clearing. Watery light shone on the she-cat's black pelt, glittering where blood welled through the fur.

Poppyfrost crept around the edge of the clearing and stopped beside Ivypool. "Have you seen Cherrypaw? Or Molepaw?"

Ivypool shrugged. "No. They could be anywhere," she murmured bleakly.

Leafpool crouched beside her daughter. "Hollyleaf?"

Hollyleaf half opened her eyes and moaned.

"It's okay." Leafpool lapped at her cheek as Jayfeather unrolled a leaf bundle beside her. He sniffed her pelt and began to press cobweb where there was blood.

"She's bleeding here!" Leafpool gasped in panic. Blood was

pooling around her paws. She grabbed a pawful of cobweb and stuffed it underneath Hollyleaf's neck.

"It's okay, Leafpool." Hollyleaf's eyes flickered open again. "I don't mind," she croaked. "I'm glad I came back to ThunderClan." Her chest fluttered as she fought for breath. "I couldn't bear to . . . to leave without getting to know my mother."

"Save her!" screeched Ivypool. "You have to save her! Hawkfrost tried to kill me, but Hollyleaf chased him away."

"Hawkfrost?" Brambleclaw looked up from beside Hollyleaf, his eyes darkening. "He did this?"

Ivypool nodded. "I was fighting Snowtuft and Thistleclaw. I couldn't help her."

Dovewing pressed against her sister. "You carried her home," she soothed. "You couldn't have done more." She pricked her ears as she heard the paw steps of the Dark Forest patrol crunch over leaves. "Firestar," she hissed. "They've reached the woods."

Firestar stiffened beside Leafpool.

"Hollyleaf." Leafpool pressed her muzzle against her daughter's cheek. "Hollyleaf?"

Hollyleaf's head fell back and her eyes dulled.

Leafpool turned frantically to Jayfeather. "She's not breathing!"

"She's lost too much blood," Jayfeather mewed gently. He touched Hollyleaf's pelt. His paw trembled. "We couldn't have saved her."

Paw steps sounded outside the hollow, determined and fast.

Firestar wrenched his gaze away from the still, black shape on the ground and straightened up. "Prepare for attack!"

Brambleclaw signaled to Squirrelflight and Sandstorm, sending them to guard the nursery, where Ferncloud was nosing Brightheart through the shredded brambles. The WindClan and RiverClan patrols spread out across the clearing. Mousefur and Purdy lined up outside their den. Leafpool dragged Hollyleaf's body to the edge of the hollow. As her Clanmates prepared for attack, she crouched over the motionless cat as if she could nurse her to life by the warmth of her fur.

The shredded barrier quivered as Birchfall leaped through it. He skidded into the clearing with Blossomfall just behind him. Shock pulsed through Dovewing. *Are they leading the attack?* Her own father, fighting for the Dark Forest!

Jayfeather raced for the medicine den and disappeared through the brambles. "Briarlight!" he yowled. "Get back in the herb store!"

Firestar met Birchfall's gaze. "How could you betray us?" He advanced on his Clanmate, his lip curled into a snarl.

Dovewing's paws turned cold. "I thought you'd choose to fight on our side."

"He did!" Ivypool shot forward. "He fought with me at the WindClan camp."

Birchfall lifted his tail. "We would never betray Thunder-Clan!"

Mousewhisker skidded into the camp. "We came to warn you!"

Blossomfall butted in. "We saw the Dark Forest patrol! They're coming!"

As she spoke, a huge gray-and-white tom crashed through the thorns. His muzzle was striped with wounds, one eye swollen, but hard muscle twitched beneath his pelt. "Traitors!" he snarled at Birchfall. "We lost the WindClan camp thanks to you!" His tail whipped behind him. "I'll save killing you till last."

"Not if I kill you first, Thistleclaw!" Birchfall hissed. "You tricked us!"

Dark Warriors began to flood the hollow. A tabby sent Bumblestripe flying with a powerful front-paw swipe. Two toms leaped on Tigerheart, hurling him to the ground. Squirrelflight disappeared under a wave of spitting warriors.

"Guard the nursery!" Firestar yowled.

Broad-shouldered warriors surged past Sandstorm. Brambleclaw launched himself across the clearing and began hauling them away. Tigerheart struggled free and rushed to help. Daisy shot out of the brambles and began slashing wildly at the wall of snapping jaws.

"Hide!" Ferncloud thrust Brightheart and the kits deep into their nest as a Dark Forest tom reached through the tattered den wall. She slashed his muzzle, then spun around and grabbed a bunch of bramble stems in her teeth. She dragged them across the top of the nest, covering the she-cat. "I won't let any cat near!"

Brightheart struggled up through the brambles. "I won't let you fight alone!" She straddled her nest and reared up beside Ferncloud.

"Darkstripe!" Mousefur's hiss sounded from outside the elders' den. "I hoped I'd never see you again." The old she-cat lashed out at a snarling tom.

Darkstripe hit back, sending Mousefur reeling.

Dovewing skidded across the clearing and knocked Darkstripe away. He turned to her, lips drawn to show bloodstained teeth.

"Go for his ears!" Cinderheart landed beside her. "I'll go for his legs."

Dovewing swiped at Darkstripe, her paws fast as birds. He stumbled as Cinderheart hooked his forepaws from under him. Dovewing battered his muzzle into the earth.

"Nice." Cinderheart sprang onto Darkstripe's back and began scrabbling at his spine with her hind claws.

More Dark Forest warriors streaked toward them.

"Ready, Mousefur?" Purdy nodded at his denmate and the two elders arched their backs against the honeysuckle den and began fighting.

Dovewing saw a ginger pelt flash at the top of the hollow. Cherrypaw was peering over the edge. Firestar signaled with his tail and she darted away to get help from any Clan patrol she could find.

Suddenly paws slammed into Dovewing's ribs. She staggered, turning.

"Why don't you just give up?" A tortoiseshell lunged at her, grabbing Dovewing's paw in her teeth.

"Because I'd rather die!" Dovewing hooked the tortoiseshell's lip with a claw and tugged hard. Squealing, the tortoiseshell raked her muzzle.

Pain seared her nose. Blood flooded her mouth. As Dovewing reared to strike back, claws hooked her neck. A tabby yanked her backward and pinned her to the ground.

"Get off my sister!" Ivypool flashed at the edge of Dovewing's vision. She sank her teeth deep into the tabby's shoulder. As he screeched with rage, Dovewing writhed free and sprang to her paws.

Ivypool flung the tabby backward. "We're outnumbered!"

Cinderheart barged between Ivypool and Dovewing. "Hold your ground!"

"What do we do?" Brambles stabbed Dovewing's spine. The wall of Dark Forest warriors was pressing them back toward the medicine den.

"Stay close and fight!" Cinderheart lunged forward and tore a lump from a Dark Forest warrior's cheek, sending blood spraying across his orange-and-black fur. "You fox-hearts killed my best friend!" Her gaze flicked toward Hollyleaf, a huddle of black fur at the edge of the clearing. "You'll pay for what you've done!"

Ivypool darted low and caught his paw in her teeth. Dovewing jumped and landed square on the warrior's back. Digging in with her claws, she hung on as he bucked beneath her. She could feel muscle hard as stone beneath his pelt. Hooking a hind leg around his, she managed to unbalance the tom. She let go as the tabby went staggering through the mass of Dark Forest pelts.

"Watch out!" Dovewing heard Cinderheart's warning

but dodged too late. A matted tom lunged from the side and caught her forepaw in his jaws. He bit down hard.

Pain scorched through her. As she flung the tom off, the thorn barrier rattled. Crowfeather leaped into the hollow, Breezepelt on his tail. As they dived into the throng, Dovewing stumbled. A paw was clutching her hind leg, clinging on with thorn-sharp claws. Kicking out, Dovewing knocked it away and turned back to check on Ivypool.

Ivypool was on her hind legs, her tail lashing to balance her. Paws swiping, she drove two toms back into the throng. Cinderheart pinned a tortoiseshell to the ground and paddled her hind paws against his spine. Dovewing caught her breath, scanning the battle for the pelts she recognized. Cloudtail writhed outside the nursery. Squirrelflight shook a warrior from her back while another lunged beneath her belly. Icecloud reared beside the beech tree, encircled by snapping jaws. Desperate shrieks echoed from the stone walls. Every Clan cat was locked in a battle for life.

Suddenly, Lionblaze appeared through the thorns. Graystripe landed a paw step behind him. Dovewing gasped as more cats streamed after them. She recognized none of them, and their pelts were oddly pale—almost transparent, with trees and grass clearly visible through them. These were no living cats; that was for sure. Had a new wave of Dark Forest warriors chased Lionblaze and Graystripe back to camp?

Cinderheart froze beside her. "Who are they?"

Outside the elders' den, Mousefur's eyes widened. Icecloud

hesitated midblow and was sent reeling by a Dark Forest tom.

"It's okay!" Lionblaze yowled. "They're Ancient allies, from before StarClan! They're on our side!"

A pale she-cat shot past him, her pelt no more than a shadow in the moonlight, and leaped for a Dark Forest tabby. The tabby screeched in surprise as the fading she-cat sent him bowling backward and lunged at him with a flurry of claws. A tom sprang after her, his orange-and-white pelt little more than a blur as he knocked a tattered tom to the ground.

Then a massive shape crashed through the entrance to the hollow.

"Badger!" Blossomfall shrieked.

"Midnight!" Firestar's eyes lit up. "It's okay! She's with us!"

The badger lumbered through the clearing. Cats scattered before her.

A snarl sounded in Dovewing's ear. "A badger and a bunch of fading elders won't save you." Thistleclaw loomed over her. Fast as a mouse, Dovewing slammed a paw into his swollen eye. Yowling, he spun away and Dovewing dodged around the edge of the clearing. She tripped over the orange-and-white tom as he whipped past and skidded to a halt beside Hollyleaf. Dovewing watched as the ghostly cat crouched beside the dead warrior.

"Fallen Leaves!" Another Ancient rushed to join him. "There's no time to grieve now."

Fallen Leaves lifted his head, his eyes filled with sadness. "She wasn't meant to die here, Broken Shadow. I . . . I promised I'd see her again."

"She died defending her Clan." Broken Shadow nudged the tom away. "Honor her memory by helping."

Dovewing whirled as brambles shifted behind her. Jayfeather slid out of the medicine den. His nose twitched. "Half Moon!" His cry was almost a wail. "Are you here?"

"Jay's Wing!" A smoke-gray Ancient ducked away from the battle and rushed to meet him. She touched her muzzle softly to his.

"You came," Jayfeather whispered.

"Of course, my love." Half Moon held her cheek against Jayfeather's, then broke away. "I must fight."

Jayfeather nodded. "Send any wounded to me." He nosed his way back into his den.

Half Moon glanced at Dovewing. "Come on," she meowed briskly.

Dovewing raced after the Ancient as she plunged back into battle. She could hardly see in the darkness. Cloud pressed down above the hollow, extinguishing the stars. Pelts writhed and tumbled around her. She could make out the huge shape of Midnight, but Dark Forest warriors were swarming over the badger's back. With a howl, Midnight fell, dragged down by countless claws.

Dovewing fought back panic.

"Fight beside me!" She recognized Lionblaze's growl and turned to see the golden warrior's eyes flashing at her.

"We're still outnumbered," she wailed.

"Then we need to fight harder."

"Look out!" Dovewing shrieked a warning as Breezepelt

flew from the edge of the clearing.

Lionblaze turned, caught off balance, and fell beneath the WindClan tom.

Breezepelt ripped his claws along Lionblaze's cheek. "You're not as strong as I expected," he gloated.

"Breezepelt, no!" Ivypool snaked through the throng. "Don't do it! Please! Do you really want to destroy the Clans for Brokenstar's sake?"

Breezepelt pulled back Lionblaze's head and smacked it hard against the ground. Growling, Lionblaze tried to shake him off, but Breezepelt held on tighter.

"This has nothing to do with Brokenstar." His gaze flashed at Ivypool. "Lionblaze should never have been born. None of them should." He flicked his tail triumphantly toward Hollyleaf's body. "She's dead; now it's your turn, Lionblaze." He bit into Lionblaze's neck.

"We're kin!" Lionblaze gasped.

"Never!" Fury blazed in Breezepelt's eyes.

A black pelt barged past Dovewing. *Crowfeather!* The Wind-Clan warrior sank his claws deep into Breezepelt's shoulders and hauled him back. Lionblaze scrambled to his paws.

"This has to stop!" Crowfeather pinned Breezepelt to the ground. "I will not watch you harm a whisker on that cat!"

Breezepelt writhed, snarling. "I always knew you hated me!"

"I never hated you!" Crowfeather growled. "That's just what you were determined to believe. And Nightcloud encouraged you."

"It's not her fault!" Breezepelt spat.

"No," Crowfeather hissed. "I should have done something much earlier. But now it's too late. You chose the Dark Forest." He hauled Breezepelt to his paws and flung him away. "Get out of here!"

Breezepelt stared at his father, eyes wide, then turned and raced from the camp.

"I'm so sorry!" Leafpool burst from the battle, her eyes clouded with grief. "I never meant for this to happen!"

"He's a warrior," Crowfeather hissed. "He's been making his own choices for a long time now."

Leafpool looked down at his paws. "Perhaps if we'd stayed together, things would be different."

Crowfeather's gaze sparked for a moment, then he sighed. "It was never meant to be." Leafpool flinched, but Crowfeather touched his tail to her flank. "I don't regret anything," he murmured. His gaze flicked toward Lionblaze. "Nothing at all." Ears twitching, he shouldered his way through the battle to the brambles sheltering Hollyleaf's body. He slid beneath them and touched his muzzle to her lifeless pelt.

A rough pelt jostled Dovewing and she stumbled into Ivypool. "What's happening?" Had more Dark Forest warriors arrived? She turned, blinking, as a massive white tom appeared at her side.

"Whitestorm!" Graystripe's yowl rang through the air and he came plunging toward them. "You're here!" Graystripe nudged the white warrior's shoulder warmly.

Whitestorm shouldered him away. "Move over, youngster,"

he growled. "This is a battle, not a reunion." He reared up and sent a Dark Forest warrior staggering back with a powerful front-paw swipe.

"Where's Mousefur?" A familiar voice sounded in Dovewing's ear.

"Longtail!" she gasped as her dead Clanmate squeezed past.

"Where is she?" Longtail demanded.

"Defending her den." Dovewing nodded toward the honeysuckle bush where Mousefur fought beside Purdy.

"Come on!" Longtail leaped away, knocking a Dark Forest warrior from his path.

Mousefur was hissing, a ragged tabby in her grip as she churned at his spine with vicious hind claws.

Longtail plucked the tabby away. "Let me help!" He sliced a gash in the tabby's flank, then flung him back toward his Clanmates.

"You took your time," Mousefur muttered. "Always late, that's your trouble."

"Not too late, I hope," Longtail retorted.

As he spoke, a Dark Forest tom lunged from behind. Knocking Longtail out of the way, he grabbed Mousefur in his jaws. Surprise lit Mousefur's gaze as she stumbled and fell.

"No!" Longtail dived for the tabby and bit down on his spine. The tabby gasped and let go, then fell twitching to the ground.

"Come on! Get up!" Longtail snatched Mousefur's scruff in his teeth and tried to drag her to her paws, but she slumped onto her side. Dovewing stared in horror. Mousefur's head was twisted strangely, her eyes dull.

"No!" Rage flared Longtail's gaze. Snarling, he turned and exploded into the battling cats.

Purdy appeared, his muzzle smeared with blood. He stopped when he saw Mousefur and dropped down beside her. His eyes glittered with grief. "You died a warrior's death after all." He sent Dovewing away with a flick of his tail. "Go back to the fight," he murmured. "I'll watch over her." He buried his nose in his denmate's pelt.

Dovewing reeled away, dizzy.

"Hey!"

She had stumbled into Bumblestripe.

"Are you okay?" The young tom lifted her muzzle with his and stared into her eyes.

"Mousefur's dead."

Bumblestripe's ears twitched, then he straightened up. "Come and fight with me." He turned her toward the battle. "We've trained together enough times."

Blindly, Dovewing followed him into the tangle of tails and claws.

A Dark Forest tom blocked their way. "I thought we'd picked off the weakest," he snarled. He darted for Dovewing's throat, but Bumblestripe caught him by his scruff and dragged him onto his back. Instinctively, Dovewing slashed at the tom's exposed belly till Bumblestripe let go, then together they drove him backward, matching blows, swipe for swipe.

As Bumblestripe knocked the tom sideways, she scooped the Dark Forest warrior's paws from under him. The tom crashed onto his side.

"Nice move," Bumblestripe puffed.

Together, they sprang onto the Dark Forest cat. Screeching with panic, he squirmed from under them and raced for the thorn barrier. He fled past two small figures who were bounding into the camp.

Molepaw! Cherrypaw! Dovewing nudged Bumblestripe. "They're safe."

Cherrypaw flicked her tail excitedly. "The other Clans are winning!" she announced.

"RiverClan has driven them right to the border!" Molepaw called breathlessly.

Dovewing scanned the clearing for Poppyfrost. Had she seen her kits arrive? The tortoiseshell was fighting beside a dappled tabby she-cat. *Honeyfern!* Together, the sisters were driving a Dark Forest tom toward the fallen beech. Taking it in turns, they jabbed and swiped as though they'd been training together for moons.

Poppyfrost paused, her tongue flicking out as she tasted the air. "Molepaw! Cherrypaw!" She turned, thrusting the Dark Forest warrior backward with a powerful hind kick, and raced to greet her kits. Honeyfern batted the tom to the ground with a final swipe and raced after her.

Dovewing jumped as orange fur flashed past her ear.

"Runningwind!" Firestar stopped beside a lithe brown tabby. "Are you still fast on your paws?"

"Of course!"

Firestar flicked his tail toward the entrance. Dark Forest

warriors were racing from the hollow. "Then take Dustpelt and make sure those fox-hearts flee all the way back to the Dark Forest!"

"I'll go with them." A handsome warrior clashed two Dark Forest heads together and stepped over the falling bodies. "It's been a long time since I've chased this kind of prey."

Firestar's eyes glowed. "Thanks, Lionheart!"

"Come on," Bumblestripe hissed in Dovewing's ear. "Let's make sure those Dark Forest cowards never come back."

Excited, Dovewing ran after Bumblestripe out of camp. She heard paw steps at her heels and turned to see Sandstorm.

"Firestar sent me too," Sandstorm panted. "In case it's a trap."

Bumblestripe pulled ahead, racing to catch up with the StarClan warriors as they pelted away through the trees.

Sandstorm suddenly skidded to a halt. "Look!"

"What?" Dovewing swerved and stopped.

Sandstorm was staring up through the trees. "I saw a claw-scratch of moonlight," she breathed. "That must be a good sign."

"Not for the Clans." A snarl sounded from the ferns.

Dovewing froze as she spotted a matted tortoiseshell pelt.

Sandstorm bristled. "Who are you?"

"You should *know* who I am," the cat hissed. "ThunderClan destroyed my life!"

Sandstorm frowned. "What's your name?"

The Dark Forest she-cat stepped out of the shadows. "My name's Mapleshade!" With a hiss, she sprang. She landed on

Sandstorm and pushed her muzzle into the earth.

"I'm going to make you pay for every blessing StarClan gave you!" Mapleshade growled in Sandstorm's ear. "And every blessing they stole from me!"

Dovewing raced to help but claws pinned her tail. She turned and swiped at the black tom who'd grabbed her. Her paw missed and the tom hit back, slicing Dovewing's cheek. Through searing pain, she heard Mapleshade's yowl.

"You have everything *I* wanted, Sandstorm! A mate that loved me, kits that I could watch grow up and have kits of their own, the respect of my Clanmates! I should have had all that!" Mapleshade's eyes shone with fury as she grasped Sandstorm's throat in her jaws.

"Let her go!" A star-flecked tortoiseshell cat darted from the ferns and ripped Mapleshade away from Sandstorm. As Sandstorm crouched, coughing, the tortoiseshell flung Mapleshade to the ground.

Mapleshade scrambled up and turned on the StarClan cat. "Spottedleaf!" she hissed. "Why didn't you let me kill her? She stole Firestar's love from you."

The hair rose on Spottedleaf's spine. "There was nothing to steal. Sandstorm made him happy!"

Mapleshade lunged at her. Spottedleaf rolled under the warrior's weight, paws flailing as she fell. With a snarl, Mapleshade sliced open the medicine cat's throat.

"No!" Firestar's screech ripped through the air. Exploding from the ferns, he grabbed Mapleshade's pelt in his claws and threw her backward. Sandstorm scrambled up and hurled herself at the matted she-cat, claws slashing, jaws tearing. Firestar sprang from the side, sending Mapleshade crashing to the ground. Sandstorm jumped on her and raked her belly with thorn-sharp claws. Shrieking with pain, Mapleshade struggled free and pelted up the slope. Sandstorm raced after her. Dovewing watched her orange pelt streak away into the trees.

In the deserted forest, Firestar crouched beside Spottedleaf's trembling body. Blood welled at her neck, soaking Firestar's cheek as he pressed against her. "Spottedleaf! Please don't go." Dovewing heard a sob in his mew. "You promised you'd be there to welcome me."

Spottedleaf gave a tiny shake of her head. "That was never going to happen, my love. I cannot journey with you anymore. I'm so sorry."

Firestar pawed at her. "No! I still need you!"

"Let her go." A she-cat shimmered into view, her gray fur long and matted.

"Yellowfang?" Firestar looked at her, his green eyes pleading. "Don't let her disappear. Please."

"This was her destiny." Yellowfang touched her muzzle to Firestar's head. "Let her follow it."

"But she said she'd wait for me in StarClan!" Firestar's mew caught in his throat.

Spottedleaf looked up at him and opened her mouth as if she wanted to say something. A small gasp escaped her; then she fell limp. Her fur started to blur, leaving a faint outline and then nothing but bloodstained grass. Firestar's head drooped.

The ferns rustled beside them and Sandstorm slid out. She crouched beside Firestar and nodded Dovewing away. Dovewing turned and headed for camp. Glancing over her shoulder, she saw Sandstorm press closer to Firestar.

She skidded into the clearing. Half the Dark Forest cats had gone, pursued by StarClan and Ancients and Midnight the badger, but the remains of Thistleclaw's patrol fought on, pelts bristling with rage. Sorreltail's patrol was back from ShadowClan's camp. Spiderleg grappled with Thistleclaw himself. Sorreltail pinned Darkstripe to the ground. Thornclaw launched himself, hissing, from the beech and landed on a muscled tabby while Midnight drove a gang of Dark Forest warriors shrieking into the brambles beside the medicine den.

A screech sounded from the nursery. Dovewing's pelt spiked as she saw Daisy slam a Dark Forest warrior onto the ground. Brightheart lunged for his throat, sinking her teeth in with a growl. *Who is guarding the kits?* Dovewing scanned the shattered den. Ferncloud straddled Brightheart's nest, slashing at a massive black tom. Spitting in fury, she darted for his throat. The warrior dodged and caught her scruff between his jaws. Snapping back his head, he dragged her from the den.

Ferncloud stared up at him in terror as he sank his teeth deep into her neck. With a grunt, she fell still.

"Ferncloud!" Firestar raced into the camp as the Dark Forest warrior crouched over the dead queen.

The warrior turned. "Too late, Firestar."

"Brokenstar!" Firestar showed his teeth.

Brokenstar glared at him, eyes bright with hatred. Firestar

sprang forward but when he crashed into the huge tom, he lost his footing and thumped to the ground.

"Firestar!" Sandstorm's terrified screech rang across the hollow as she followed him in. "You can't fight anymore. You only have one life left!"

"Every warrior here has only one life!" Firestar scrambled to his paws and faced Brokenstar again.

Brokenstar eyed him gleefully. "I'm going to shred you till there's nothing left to join StarClan," he growled.

A burst of starlight shone beside Firestar, and Dovewing recognized Yellowfang again. "Enough!" yowled the old she-cat. She dived at Brokenstar and grasped his throat in her jaws. Dovewing heard the crack of bone as she killed him. Yellowfang dropped her son's body, then watched it fade in the moonlight till no trace remained.

"Brokenstar's dead!" Thistleclaw stepped back from Spiderleg and stood stiff-legged with dismay.

"Brokenstar?" Darkstripe spun away from Sorreltail, ears flat.

"Retreat!" Thistleclaw stumbled for the entrance. Fear edged his cry. Pelts swooped past him like bats as the Dark Forest patrol fled.

Dovewing sank her claws into the earth, her pelt stinging, her paws as heavy as stone. All around her, shafts of moonlight streamed through the clouds. Was this really the end?

Lilykit and Seedkit peered up from their nest.

"Come here, my dears. It's safe now." Sorreltail beckoned them with a flick of her tail, and they slid from the nursery and hurried toward her, pressing hard against her blood-soaked fur.

Troutstream and Pebblefoot limped across the clearing. Whitestorm and Longtail stood panting with exhaustion, their tails drooping. And the brightest beam of moonlight landed on Ferncloud's body, lying motionless beside the nursery.

"Why is Ferncloud asleep?" Amberkit asked, popping her head up.

"She's tired after all the fighting, silly," mewed Dewkit beside her. He pricked his ears as Dustpelt pounded into camp. "Dustpelt will wake her up."

"Is it over?" The tabby warrior stumbled to a halt, following the gaze of his Clanmates toward his mate's body. "Ferncloud?" He stiffened. "Ferncloud!" He raced to her and tugged at her pelt with a frantic paw.

Birchfall and Icecloud joined him. Their eyes glistened as they gazed at their mother's body.

Dustpelt jerked around. "Don't just stare! Get Jayfeather."

Firestar dipped his head. "It's too late, Dustpelt."

Eyes bright with anger, Dustpelt curled his lip. "Why didn't you protect her?" His gaze flitted to Icecloud. "Where were you when she needed you?"

Firestar approached the tabby warrior. "No one could have saved her," he murmured. "Not even you."

Dustpelt looked up at the ThunderClan leader. "I could have," he insisted. "I *would* have. If I'd been here."

Firestar touched his muzzle to Dustpelt's shoulder. "She

saved the kits from Brokenstar."

The thorns at the entrance quivered again as a battered warrior staggered, bleeding, into camp. *Hawkfrost.*

"The battle's over," Firestar growled.

"Not for him." Brambleclaw followed Hawkfrost in. "I found him in the forest trying to run back to his Clanmates."

Hawkfrost glared at the ThunderClan deputy. "Let me return to my Clan."

Yellowfang stirred and lifted her head to watch the two warriors.

Ivypool darted forward, her eyes dark. "You killed Hollyleaf!" She sprang toward the gray tom. He slammed her away but she landed nimbly and turned on him again.

"No!" Dovewing raced to help but Firestar blocked her way.

"Let Ivypool settle this," the ThunderClan leader ordered.

"But he might kill her!" Dovewing's breath caught in her throat as she watched Ivypool fly at Hawkfrost, claws flashing.

"You murderer! Liar! Betrayer!" She gouged at his eyes and raked his belly with her hind claws. With a howl, Hawkfrost flung her off. Ivypool grunted as his powerful paws crushed her spine.

"You're the traitor." He pushed her muzzle into the earth. "And this time I'll kill you."

"No, you won't!" Brambleclaw flung himself at Hawkfrost and peeled him away. Before the Dark Forest warrior could twist free, Brambleclaw sunk his teeth into his neck. The snap of bone echoed through the hollow and Hawkfrost fell dead.

As Ivypool staggered to her feet, a deep growl sounded from beside the medicine den. Tigerstar stepped into the moonlight. "Well done, Brambleclaw."

Brambleclaw stared at his father in horror.

Tigerstar turned his amber gaze on Firestar as the ThunderClan leader unsheathed his claws. "Not yet," the Dark Forest cat snarled. "We *will* meet in battle. But not until you've watched every one of your Clan die."

Firestar lashed his tail. "The battle's over!"

"The Dark Forest is endless," Tigerstar hissed. "It has more warriors than you could ever imagine. The battle is just beginning."

Dovewing darted forward. "But Brokenstar and Hawkfrost are dead! Why would they fight now? They have no leader."

Tigerstar flexed his claws, holding them so they caught the moonlight. "They have me."

CHAPTER 27

♣

"You're no leader, Tigerstar." Firestar padded closer. "You never were."

Tigerstar snarled, "I'm a better leader than you could ever be."

"A leader puts his Clan first." Firestar lashed his tail. "Instead, your Clanmates are made to fight your battles, not theirs."

"Real warriors love battle," Tigerstar sneered. "I give them a chance to die for a cause."

Dovewing searched Tigerstar's gaze. Was he mad? Countless cats had died in his battles. Did he really believe he'd done them a favor?

Firestar's pelt rippled, his muscles twitching. "And what have all your battles been *for*, Tigerstar? What cause is worth the lives of so many warriors?"

Tigerstar's eyes burned. "Defeating you, of course."

Firestar met his gaze. "You haven't defeated me yet."

Dovewing held her breath. There was a wildness in the dark warrior's eyes that terrified her.

"That's why I'm here," Tigerstar growled.

"The Dark Forest cats won't follow you," Firestar told him.

"They know now that they can't beat the Clans. They won't try again."

"I don't need them." Tigerstar glanced at the cats bristling at the edge of the clearing. "I only have to beat you. Then I can pick off your Clanmates one by one, moon after moon, till there's no one left."

Firestar's gaze flitted from Ferncloud's body to Hollyleaf's. "I'm not going to let you harm another of my cats, not ever." His tail swished low over the ground.

"Then you're going to have to kill me."

Firestar narrowed his eyes. "Has it been worth it, Tigerstar? All the hate? All the death?"

Tigerstar flattened his ears. "Every moment." Eyes slitted, he attacked. Hooking his claws deep into Firestar's shoulder, he raked his spine with churning paws. "The moment Bluestar found you, I became nothing! I have waited all this time to have my revenge!"

Firestar twisted free and slashed at him. The dark warrior ducked back, head low, and grabbed Firestar's hind paw in his teeth. Biting hard, he dragged Firestar onto his belly, then reared up and slammed his forepaws onto Firestar's spine. "When you're dead, I can rule the Clans or kill them."

Graystripe darted forward, teeth bared. "Never."

Whitestorm blocked him. "No, Graystripe. This is Firestar's battle."

Firestar heaved himself to his paws and turned to face Tigerstar. "I will not die until the forest is safe from you." He leaped for the dark warrior. Swerving in midair, he landed a whisker away from Tigerstar's flank. As Tigerstar spun to defend himself, Firestar smashed his paws into the dark warrior's side. Unbalanced, Tigerstar staggered and fell. Firestar rained slashing blows onto Tigerstar's head.

Writhing away, Tigerstar struggled to his paws. He blinked blood from his eyes and lunged at Firestar's throat. The ThunderClan leader lurched backward. Tigerstar clung on, his claws spiking Firestar's neck.

Sandstorm leaped forward, hissing with rage, but Sorreltail reached out and heaved her back by her scruff. "You can't change his destiny, Sandstorm."

Firestar dug his hind claws into Tigerstar's belly and thrust him off. Fur ripped at the ThunderClan leader's throat.

No! Dovewing held her breath, waiting for blood to pulse from the wound. But only pale skin showed through. Tigerstar's clumsy grip had torn nothing but fur.

Firestar jumped to his paws. "You lived like a rogue. You can die like a rogue." Flashing like lightning across the clearing, he flew at Tigerstar, aiming for the dark warrior's throat. With a vicious snarl, he sank his teeth deep into Tigerstar's neck. He held on while Tigerstar thrashed and staggered and finally collapsed to the ground.

Firestar kept hold of the dark warrior as blood flowed over his paws. When Tigerstar finally stopped twitching, Firestar let go of his throat. He straightened up and watched Tigerstar fade away, his gaze blank.

Dovewing turned to Ivypool, shaking. "Tigerstar has gone!"

As she spoke, thunder cracked the sky. She looked up as a bolt of lightning struck the fallen beech beside Firestar. The tree exploded into flame. Smoke rolled over Firestar. Eyes streaming, chest burning, Dovewing struggled to see her Clan leader. As she peered through the smoke, the clouds opened. Rain pounded the hollow. The burning beech hissed and crackled as the fire faded and died.

Dovewing lifted her tail, relief flooding through her. "It's really over!" she gasped to Ivypool.

"Firestar!" Sandstorm's yowl sounded above the thrumming of the rain. She raced toward the place where Tigerstar had fallen. A body was lying on the ground. Dovewing frowned. Tigerstar had disappeared, right? Why was there still a huddled shape on the bloodstained grass?

No!

She pelted after Sandstorm. *He can't be dead!* She skidded to a halt and stared in horror at Firestar's body.

Sandstorm buried her nose deep into her mate's sodden fur. "I told you not to waste your final life," she whispered.

Brambleclaw crossed the clearing, rain streaming from his whiskers, and stood beside her. "He didn't waste it."

"Fire will save the Clan," Leafpool whispered.

Graystripe pushed past Tigerheart and Whitestorm and crouched beside his old friend. "I would have taken your place, if you had let me." His voice was hoarse with grief.

"Firestar!" Dustpelt called softly. "When you see her, tell Ferncloud I love her."

Purdy nosed past him. "Is he dead?"

"Yes." Bumblestripe wrapped his tail gently over the elder's back.

Tigerheart's ear twitched. "It was his last life?"

"Yes." Dovewing nodded toward Boulderfur and Trout-stream, who lingered uncertainly near the entrance with their patrols. "It's time for you to go home. The battle is won and I need to be with my Clanmates." *And yet it feels as if everything has been lost.* She drew in a breath, then slid quietly in beside Bumblestripe. Rain dripped into her eyes and she blinked it away. Bumblestripe shifted so that his pelt rested warmly against her. Dovewing felt his breath against her ear.

"You're safe now," he murmured.

She leaned her head on his shoulder. "I know." She didn't look around as she heard Tigerheart pad away.

Brambleclaw lifted his muzzle. "The battle is over. Our victory belongs to Firestar!"

The rain eased as he spoke and a shaft of moonlight sliced through the clouds and lit up the unmoving orange body. There was a faint noise at the camp entrance and Dovewing looked up to see a StarClan warrior glimmering beneath the ragged thorns, her blue eyes glowing like circles of sky.

"Bluestar?" Brambleclaw beckoned to her with his tail. With a nod, Bluestar stepped out from the shadows and walked across the clearing. A russet tom followed, his pelt glittering with stars. A silver she-cat padded after; a mottled gray tabby sparkled at her side. A black-and-white tom padded at the back, with Yellowfang tagging on behind.

As the Clan parted to let the cats pass, Runningwind and

Lionheart slipped out to join their starry Clanmates. Dovewing blinked up at the walls of the hollow. They rippled with light from StarClan pelts. The scent of wet stone, sharp and cold, bathed her tongue. *Is this what starlight tastes like?*

Jayfeather stepped forward as they circled Firestar's body. "These cats gave Firestar his nine lives," he explained to the Clan. "Redtail"—he nodded to the russet warrior—"gave a life for courage. Silverstream gave a life for loyalty."

Graystripe got to his paws and stared at the beautiful she-cat. "Silverstream!"

She gazed back at him, her blue eyes filled with longing. "I'll be waiting," she whispered.

"Brindleface." Jayfeather dipped his head to the mottled gray tabby. "The life you gave was for protection. And Swiftpaw"—his blind blue gaze drifted to the small black-and-white tom—"yours was for mentoring."

Brambleclaw nodded. "Firestar was the best mentor I could have had."

"Yellowfang gave compassion, Lionheart gave courage, and Runningwind gave tireless energy, which he used to serve his Clanmates through all his lives."

As Jayfeather paused, Bluestar stepped forward, her paws touching Firestar's pelt. "Spottedleaf isn't with StarClan anymore." Grief thickened her mew. "But she gave Firestar a life for love."

A sob shook Sandstorm's shoulders.

Bluestar went on. "I gave him a life for nobility, though he was born with more nobility than any warrior I ever knew."

Her blue eyes glazed with sorrow. "I knew that Firestar would save the Clan many moons ago. As fire, and then as the fourth cat in the oldest prophecy, he succeeded. He leaves Thunder-Clan in the paws of a new leader." She looked at Brambleclaw. "If you have half the courage and loyalty of Firestar, you will be a fine leader for ThunderClan."

As she spoke the StarClan cats drew closer around Fire-star's body. Touching pelts, they gazed down. A shadow stirred over the orange shape.

Dovewing gasped. Pale as moonlight, graceful as the wind, Firestar stood up.

"His spirit is leaving," Jayfeather murmured.

Firestar's gaze swept slowly over his Clan. Dovewing swallowed as it reached her, then relaxed. It felt warm like sunshine.

"It's time to go," Bluestar breathed.

Firestar dipped his head to Brambleclaw, then leaned down and touched his muzzle to Sandstorm's. She stared up at him, her eyes glistening with grief as he turned and followed the StarClan cats out of the hollow. Dovewing jerked her head around as a black pelt moved at the edge of her vision. Hol-lyleaf's spirit was padding after them.

"Look!" Sorreltail gasped.

Mousefur's spirit leaped up from her body and bounded like a kit across the clearing.

Purdy whisked his tail. "She'll get all the hunting she wants now."

"Ferncloud's awake!" Amberkit squeaked from the nursery.

Ferncloud's spirit rose and padded after Mousefur. It paused at the thorn barrier and turned, dipping its head to Dustpelt, then disappeared after the others. Dovewing stared at the gap in the brambles, her chest aching.

Sandstorm stood up. "Bramblestar!"

"Bramblestar!" Lionblaze lifted his muzzle to the clearing sky.

The Clan joined in. "Bramblestar! Bramblestar!"

As Bramblestar looked up, Dovewing followed his gaze. A new star was shining among the others. *Is Firestar there already?*

"I will honor my ancestors in StarClan," Bramblestar vowed, "but not those who have ever walked in the Dark Forest. Guide my steps wisely, warriors of the past." He lowered his head. "And warriors of now."

Jayfeather touched his tail to Bramblestar's spine. "It's time to choose a deputy," he prompted gently.

Dovewing glanced around her Clanmates. Surely, Bramblestar would choose Lionblaze? He was the only warrior who couldn't be beaten in battle. He'd make a powerful deputy and leader one day.

"Will you be my deputy, Squirrelflight?"

The she-cat stared at him, every hair on her pelt quivering. "Really?"

Bramblestar nodded. "There is no cat I trust more. Everything you do is for the best of reasons. I understand that now."

Squirrelflight dipped her head. "Then I accept."

A slender brown cat burst forward. It was Leafpool. "My sister," she murmured, pressing her head to Squirrelflight's.

"You deserve this honor, and more. Thank you, for everything."

Squirrelflight licked Leafpool's ear. "I would do it again in a heartbeat," she whispered.

Jayfeather padded forward to stand beside Dovewing. "An ending, and a beginning," he observed briskly.

Dovewing looked at Lionblaze. The golden warrior's gaze was heavy, his shoulders drooping with exhaustion. For a brief moment, they had held the power of the stars in their paws. And now it was over. Grief welled in Dovewing's throat. They'd saved the Clans, but Firestar was dead.

Jayfeather's tail brushed her shoulder. "He gave his life to save the thing that mattered most to him: his Clanmates," he meowed softly. "He truly has the stars at his paws now. You will see him again, when it is time."

A breeze stirred Dovewing's pelt, as if something had walked past. She lifted her head and saw two shapes standing just beyond her Clanmates, watching. One was a badger with a narrow, striped face and wise, kind eyes, and the other was a grotesque hairless cat with bulging eyes that saw nothing and everything. They met her gaze and nodded, just once. *Thank you,* Dovewing heard, quieter than a sigh.

There will be three cats, kin of your kin, with the power of the stars in their paws. They will find a fourth, and the battle between light and dark will be won. A new leader will rise from the shadows of his death, and the Clans will survive beyond the memories of his memories. This is how it has always been, and how it will always be.

ADVENTURE GAME

Visit www.warriorcats.com
*to download game rules, character sheets,
a practice mission, and more!*

Written by **Stan!** • Art by **James L. Barry**

LOOKING FOR NEWLEAF

Whatever the previous adventure you played, consider that enough moons have passed that the cats have gone through all of leaf-bare and it is now nearly newleaf. If the time of year hasn't been important in your other games, simply say that six moons have passed. Determine what age that makes all of the cat characters (including the one belonging to the person who will take the first turn as Narrator) and use the information found in the "Improving Your Cat" section in Chapter Four of the game rules to make the necessary improvements.

"Looking for Newleaf" is a very challenging adventure. If your group hasn't played this game before, you should probably try a more typical adventure (such as "Saving the Kits," which is available as a free download on www.warriorcats.com) first.

Unless you are the first person who will act as Narrator in this adventure, you should stop reading here. The information beginning in the next paragraph is for the Narrator only.

The Adventure Begins

Hello, Narrator! It's time to begin playing "Looking for Newleaf." Make sure all the players have their character sheets, the correct number of chips, a piece of paper, and a pencil. Remember that the point of the game is to have fun, so don't be afraid to go slow, keep the players involved, and refer to the rules if you aren't sure exactly what should happen next.

When you're ready, begin with **1** below.

1. Lean Times

Special Note: This adventure takes place at a very specific time of year—late in the season of leaf-bare. Snow has covered the Clan territories for many moons, and the Clan cats are anxiously awaiting the coming of newleaf. Help set the proper atmosphere before you begin playing by getting the players to think about how tough things are for the cats. The days are short and cold; the nights are long and even colder. If there is a bad time to be a Clan cat, this is it.

The players can role-play their cats however they see fit, but as Narrator you should make it clear that most of the cats are hungry, a little short-tempered, and very anxious for warmer weather to arrive.

Read Aloud: "No one can remember a leaf-bare that has lasted so long. It seems like snow has covered the Clan territories forever. Fresh-kill is scarce, the medicine cats are running low on herbs, and the elders are beginning to wonder if they'll ever see greenleaf again."

Narrator Tips: The situation for all the Clans is pretty desperate at the beginning of this adventure. After making do with dangerously little for more than a moon, the Clan leaders have gotten together and decided to send hunting parties beyond the Clan lands in search of food and any sign they can find that newleaf is coming.

The players' cats make up one of those hunting parties. They are being sent to the woods beyond the Moonpool. Have one of the Clan leaders speak to the players' cats to express how important this mission is. The cats aren't starving yet, but the kits and the elders have grown thin and dangerously weak. It won't be long before some of them join StarClan.

The plan is for the players' cats to catch as much fresh-kill as they can, eating enough to keep themselves going, but storing most of it under the snow as they continue to hunt. (Burying the fresh-kill will help it stay fresh for a longer period of time.) When they've gathered all they can carry—or all there is to find—the players' cats are to bring the rest of it back as quickly as possible.

As a secondary assignment, the Clan leader asks the players' cats to keep an eye out for signs that newleaf is coming. If they can bring back proof that things will change soon, it will improve everyone's spirit.

Let the players ask any questions they like, and answer from the Clan leader's perspective. No cat knows much—sometimes leaf-bare lasts longer than usual, and StarClan has not sent dreams to any of the medicine cats to explain the situation or offer a solution.

When that's done, briefly describe the first two days of the trip as the cats go through familiar territory that is almost unrecognizable because of all the snow. The scenes are beautiful, but desolate—there are no birds or squirrels or rabbits—and no tracks in the snow, other than those belonging to the players' cats.

On the morning of the third day, the players' cats must choose whether they are going to follow a path up to the highlands or one down to the valley. Both seem equally covered in snow and equally lacking in potential prey. If the players are having a difficult time making up their minds, ask them whether they think that it's more likely that prey animals (squirrels, rabbits, voles, etc.) would live in the valley or on the hillside. (There isn't a right answer, but that opinion is probably the best way for them to choose a course.)

What Happens Next: If the players' cats want to begin by looking for prey in the valley, continue with **4**.

If the players' cats want to begin by looking for prey in the highlands, continue with **7**.

2. Whiteout

Read Aloud: "The wind suddenly rises, sounding like a howling dog. The air around you is thick with snow. Before long, it's impossible to see anything but a solid wall of white blowing snow."

Narrator Tips: This is a whiteout. There's so much wind and snow that you can't see more than a few inches in front of your face. It's a real weather condition, and it's extremely dangerous—even more so for cats.

Describe the situation for the players and ask what their cats are going to do about it. Right now they cannot even see one another. If they want to move together and gather as a group, each cat must remember EXACTLY where the others were. To do that, each cat must make a Focus Check (it is possible to use the Alertness Knack with this Check) and get a total of 8 or higher. If any of the players' cats fail the Check, that cat has lost its way.

If all of the cats manage to gather together, they have two options: Huddle where they are and wait for the storm to end, or try to move to the shelter of the trees in the highlands.

Huddling where they are is a sure way for the group to stay together, but it means they will spend the whole time in dangerously cold weather. All of the cats suffer 2 chips' worth of damage from the experience. But when the whiteout ends, they have kept their bearings.

Trying to move to the trees (or any other location) is risky because the cats can no longer see anything through the blowing snow. If they want to move, they must pick one member of the group to lead the way. That cat must make a Ponder Check. If the total is 10 or higher, the group keeps their bearings and arrives at the place they were headed. If not, the group has lost its way.

What Happens Next: If any of the cats lost their way in the whiteout, continue with **5.**

If the cats were on the hilltop and they kept their bearings, this is the end of the chapter. Hand the adventure to the next Narrator and tell him or her to continue with **8**.

If the cats were in the valley and they kept their bearings, this is the end of the chapter. Hand the adventure to the next Narrator and tell him or her to continue with **13**.

3. Fresh Tracks

Read Aloud: "The trail seems to go cold momentarily. You can't see the tracks at all. But just when you're about to give up hope, you come across another collection of tracks—and they're still fresh!"

Narrator Tips: The players' cats have found a collection of tracks that seem to have been made today. Improvise a scene that lets the cats investigate these tracks, using Skills like Ponder, See, and Smell (and Knacks like Track, Animal Lore, and Alertness) to figure out which tracks to follow.

Tell them that there are tracks from lots of different animals, but only the rabbits are prey—the others are foxes, raccoons, and maybe even a bear (if you want to give the players a bit of a scare as they worry that their cats might have to fight such a huge animal). The problem is that the rabbits seem to have been chased out of this location and run in several directions at once. There's no easy way to tell where they might be now. It's also unclear which of the other animals might have been chasing them.

Have the players' cats all make Ponder or See Checks. (The Track Knack can be used with this attempt.) Then add their totals together to get a group total, which will determine the set of tracks they actually follow.

What Happens Next: If the group total is 20 or higher, continue with **10**.

If the group total is 19 or lower, continue with **13**.

4. Down in the Valley

Read Aloud: "In greenleaf this valley is full of grass and small streams—just the kind of place where prey can be found. It only makes sense that they would have their burrows here, too."

Narrator Tips: Tell the players that there are no immediate signs of prey—no tracks in the snow or obvious locations for burrows. Then ask them what their cats want to do next. How will they go about hunting for their prey? Based on their answer, decide what Skill (and perhaps an associated Knack) would be most appropriate for that activity. (It's likely that the See Skill and the Track Knack will be helpful, or perhaps Ponder and the Animal Lore Knack.) Tell the players that only one of them may attempt the Check—too many cats fussing about will scare away potential prey.

The result of the Check will determine the next scene of this adventure.

What Happens Next: If the Check had a total of 20 or higher, the cat has found many tracks to follow—continue with **13**.

If the Check had a total of between 15 and 19, the cat has found a few tracks to follow—continue with **11**.

If the Check had a total of between 10 and 15, the cat found no tracks. The cats must replay this scene again.

If the Check had a total of 9 or lower, continue with **2**.

5. Lost in the Snow

Read Aloud: "You wander through the blowing snow for a very long time. When the weather finally clears, you have no idea where you are."

Narrator Tips: The players' cats got so lost in the whiteout that they have left familiar territory entirely. The cats will have to find some kind of landmark they can use to guide their travels or they might never make it back to the Lake and their Clans.

Have each cat make a Ponder Check (adding in the Pathfinder Knack if they can and wish to) and add the results together to get a group total. If that group total is equal to 20 or less, the cats wander around for a very long time, and only find something familiar when they're already half-starved. They have no choice but to go straight back to the Clan territories and report their mission as having been a failure.

If the group total is 21 or higher, the mission is still a failure in that they did not accomplish what they'd intended. But as Narrator, you may want to give them a small story bonus for such a great effort. If so, run the group through scene 19, saying that in their search for familiar land, the cats came across a small warren of rabbits. Instead of ending the scene as described, though, have the players' cats suddenly see other Clan cats come into the clearing. The players' cats wandered so far off course that they have intruded on the area that another group of warriors was supposed to search. Although they will bring some fresh-kill back for the Clans, the mission was not a success, and the players' cats have to tell their leaders that the effort failed.

What Happens Next: The adventure is over. The players' cats do *not* get any Experience rewards for this adventure. The players' cats *can*, however, play the adventure again.

6. There They Are!

Read Aloud: "Look! Over there! Did you see that flash of fur? Are the foxes back?"

Narrator Tips: The players have just finished dealing with the foxes (in one way or another), so you can have some fun playing with their expectations at the beginning of this scene. You can ask them to make See Checks (even allowing the Track Knack) and if they don't have impressive totals, you can hint that what they saw *might* have been a fox.

Of course, if any of them get very good results (totals of 12 or higher), you should absolutely tell them the truth of the situation. (As Narrator, you sometimes get the fun of intentionally misleading the other players, but when the cats perform a task well, you should always reward them with useful results.)

In any case, the deception should be short lived. Tell the players that their cats see a group of rabbits—scrawny, skinny rabbits, but rabbits just the same. Half the rabbits scamper up a nearby hill; the other half run deeper into the valley. Almost immediately, the rabbits are out of sight. Perhaps they've gone over a rise or behind a snowdrift. Perhaps they've reached their burrows and gone underground. Perhaps they heard the cats approaching and have gone into hiding. There's no way for the cats to know without investigating further. But which group of rabbits will they follow?

What Happens Next: If the players' cats decide to follow the rabbits up the hillside, continue with **7**.

If the players' cats decide to follow the rabbits in the valley, continue with **21**.

7. High on the Hill

Read Aloud: "In greenleaf this hill is shaded by tall trees. Now, even with the trees bare, the snow is clearly less deep than it was in the valley. But as you step away from the trees, the wind becomes quite strong and the snow gathers in drifts."

Narrator Tips: Tell the players that there are no immediate signs of prey—no tracks in the snow or obvious locations for burrows. Then ask them what their cats want to do next. How will they go about hunting for their prey? Based on their answer, decide what Skill (and perhaps an associated Knack) would be most appropriate for that activity. (It's likely that the See Skill and the Track Knack will be helpful, or perhaps Ponder and the Animal Lore skill.) Let them all make Checks for their appropriate skills.

Any cat whose Check total was 13 or higher is thoroughly absorbed in the hunt. Tell their players that the cats are certain that there are no tracks or clues to be found here.

If a cat's total was 12 or less, tell that player the cat was distracted by the howling wind and drifting snow.

Then have all the cats make a Focus Check (with which the Alertness Knack can be used) and add all the cats' individual results together to create a group total. As a bonus to this total, add +2 for every cat that wasn't distracted by the winds on the earlier Check. If the group total (including the bonus) is equal to 20 or higher, they notice that the wind isn't just stronger on the hilltop, it's increasing because bad weather is about to blow in. It would be best for the cats if they found shelter somewhere.

There really are only three options open to the cats—try to press on despite the weather (which they automatically do if they failed to notice the coming storm), seek shelter under the tall trees, or try to outrun the storm and get down into the valley.

What Happens Next: If the cats press on or head toward the valley, continue with **2**.

If the cats decide not to seek shelter, continue with **8**.

8. Shelter from the Wind

Read Aloud: "The sound of the wind and the bite of the blowing snow only increase as night falls. Huddling together for warmth, hopefully you can dream of a beautiful, warm new-leaf."

Narrator Tips: Briefly describe what it is like for the cats, as they lay on top of one another, like they did when they were kits. When the weather turns this bad, it's the only thing you can do. And despite the terrible conditions, the familiarity of the situation provides a feeling of safety as they drift off to sleep.

Their dreams, however, are not of carefree days when they were kits. Instead, they each receive a message from StarClan. The details of each dream should be tailored to the individual cats—featuring cats and situations from their past (both past games, and the background story each player has created for his or her cat). This will require you, as Narrator, to improvise extensively but, since this is a dream, it also gives you the freedom to take a stronger hand in crafting the scene.

In dreams, things don't always happen in the logical way they do in real life—you can move the players' cats from place to place, or even time to time. You can make the situation as strange as you like, even put the cats in extremely dangerous situations since, no matter what happens, they will awake safe and sound when the dream is over.

Before beginning the dream, ask each player how many chips they have of each color. Although they may have to spend chips on actions in the dream, when they awaken they will get those chips back, plus the normal Healing a cat gets every morning. (See Chapter Five of the game rules.)

The dream should begin with a situation the cats know well, but someplace dangerous—perhaps a climactic scene from one of their previous adventures. Make them play through the scene as if it were real, except nothing they do succeeds, no matter what totals they achieve with their Checks. Things look bad for the cats, like they may actually fail or, worse, die. But just then, a bright light comes from behind them and the cats' enemies disappear like fog in a strong wind.

When the cats turn around, they see a member of StarClan that has some personal significance to them. Different cats may see different members of StarClan, but they each receive the same basic message: The cats of StarClan know that leaf-bare has been long and difficult, but the Clan cats must see it as a test, which, if they pass, will leave them even stronger in the future. "The test," the StarClan cat says, "is to find a green shoot in a white field and bring it back to your Clans. If you do this, newleaf will arrive before the next moon. If you fail, leaf-bare will continue for at least one moon more."

The StarClan cat will be willing to answer a few questions from the players' cats, but it cannot give any further instruction. (It can't, for example, tell the cats where to find this green shoot.) It can, though, answer personal questions from the cats' past, if you feel comfortable improvising such details.

When the dream ends, it ends abruptly—perhaps even in the middle of a sentence the StarClan cat is speaking—with all the players' cats waking up at the exact same minute. This happens when the time feels right to you, as the Narrator. Don't let this scene go on too long. Better to leave it with questions unanswered and mysteries still abounding.

Once the players' cats are awake, they must decide what to do next. Will they continue to hunt for prey (and now a "green shoot") here in the highlands, or has the dream made them think that the valley is a better place to look? Perhaps they think it's worth climbing even higher up the hill to search for clues.

What Happens Next: If the players' cats want to keep searching where they are, continue with **16**.

If the players' cats want to go down to the valley and they have not yet encountered any foxes, continue with **4**.

If the players' cats want to go down to the valley and they have already encountered foxes during this adventure, continue with **10**.

If the players' cats want to climb higher on the hillside, continue with **15**.

9. Fox Fight

Read Aloud: "Look out! Their teeth are small, but they're sharp—and so are their claws!"

Narrator Tips: Foxes are wily opponents and this is going to be a tough fight. Make sure you're as familiar as possible with the "Fighting" section in Chapter Five of the game rules before you begin. Remember that while you control the foxes that are fighting against the players' cats, you are not trying to "beat" the players—your job, as Narrator, is to make your decisions based on the best interest of the story.

As you narrate this scene, do your best to make the foxes act cleverly, while being careful not to make them act like they know everything you do (because as Narrator you will hear all of the players' cats' plans ahead of time). A good method is to write down a list of simple actions the foxes will attempt— which cats they will focus on first, whether or not they will use teamwork, and how. Then, if you're not sure what the foxes will do at a given moment, you can refer back to that list.

The foxes each have a Jump score of 10, a Pounce score of 7, a Swat score of 10, and a Bite score of 8. A fox has Ability chips just like the players' cats do, and spends them in the same way. Each fox has 5 Strength chips, 8 Intelligence chips, and 7 Spirit chips. For the purposes of this fight, a fox is treated just the same as a player's cat except that Narrator controls all its movements.

Each fox will fight until it loses half of its Health Chips. At that point, if there are more foxes in the fight than there are cats, the fox will continue fighting. Otherwise, it will flee. It is faster than the cats, so it can get away, but any cat that was fighting that fox can make one more attack before it gets away. **What Happens Next:** If the players' cats run away, this is the end of the chapter. Hand the adventure to the next Narrator and tell him or her to continue with **7**.

If any of the players' cats are knocked out, continue with **17**.

If the players' cats win the fight and chase away the foxes, this is the end of the chapter. Hand the adventure to the next Narrator and tell him or her to continue with **6**.

10. Sly Competition

Read Aloud: "Just beyond the snowdrift you catch a flash of brown fur. Peering carefully out, you see a fox. And then another!"

Narrator Tips: The cats are lucky in that they found the foxes rather than the other way around. If the foxes had snuck up on the players' cats, the first sign of trouble would have been the beasts charging to attack.

The number of foxes present depends on the number of players in your game (not counting the Narrator). If there are between three and five players, there are two foxes. If there are six or more players, there are three foxes. If there are only one or two players, there are at first two foxes, but as the players' cats watch, one of the pair runs off to hunt elsewhere, leaving just a single fox. Of course, one fox is nearly twice as big as a cat.

Armed with this information, the players' cats must again make a decision about how to proceed. To make matters more interesting, tell them that the foxes are sniffing around what seem to be very fresh rabbit tracks.

If the players ask for more information about the foxes, feel free to give them any of the information that they could have gotten in scene 13. In addition, allow the group to choose one cat to make a See Check (that can make use of the Animal Lore or Alertness Knack). If the total for this Check is 7 or higher, the cat notices that the foxes look thin and hungry. The long leaf-bare has been even tougher on them than it's been on the Clans.

In the end, the players' cats have three choices: attack the foxes, leave the valley and go to the highlands, or try to sneak around the foxes and keep hunting in the valley.

What Happens Next: If the players' cats attack the foxes, continue with **9**.

If the players' cats go into the highlands, this is the end of the chapter. Hand the adventure to the next Narrator and tell him or her to continue with **7**.

If the cats try to sneak around the foxes, continue with **12**.

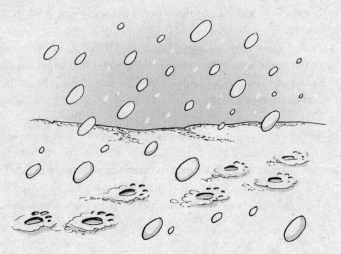

11. Misleading Tracks

Read Aloud: "Finally! Tracks! Quick, follow them—but which ones?"

Narrator Tips: The trail the players' cats are following intersects with a collection of tracks set in a small patch of ice. These are a mix of old and new tracks that were made on a warmer day and then frozen in place when night came and the temperature dropped again.

Mostly these appear to be rabbit tracks, but there are also squirrel, raccoon, and fox tracks. This must be a spot that different creatures pass on their way to and from different locations, because the tracks come in from various directions, mingle a bit in the center, and then head off in another wide variety of directions. Improvise a scene where the cats can investigate these tracks and try to figure out which tracks are most likely to lead them to prey animals now.

In order to figure out what set of tracks to follow, the cats should each make a Ponder Check (the Animal Lore Knack can be used with this attempt) and then add their totals together to get a group total to determine which tracks they chose.

What Happens Next: If the group total was 15 or higher, continue with **3**.

If the group total was 14 or lower, continue with **5**.

12. Outfoxing a Fox

Read Aloud: "Those foxes have such big ears! This isn't going to be easy."

Narrator Tips: Be sure to tell the players that this is a very difficult thing to do. The foxes are already on alert because they are hunting. The cats can see the foxes' ears twitching to hear every sound and see their noses twitch as they sniff every wind for a new scent. It's not too late for the players to choose a different course of action—heading to the highlands or attacking the foxes while they're still unaware of the cats' presence.

If the group wishes to attempt sneaking around the foxes, have the players' cats make a Sneak Check (which can be aided by use of the Stalk Knack). Each cat must have a total of 9 or higher in order for this plan to work. If any of the cats has a total of 8 or lower, the foxes hear the group.

What Happens Next: If the players' cats would rather strike first and attack the foxes, continue with **9**.

If the players' cats would rather go into the highlands, this is the end of the chapter. Hand the adventure to the next Narrator and tell him or her to continue with **7**.

If the players' cats successfully sneak around the foxes, continue with **6**.

If the players' cats are unsuccessful at sneaking around the foxes, continue with **9**.

13. Warning Signs

Read Aloud: "As you pass through an area of deeper snow, the tracks become clearer—but that's not necessarily a good thing."

Narrator Tips: Deeper snow means clearer tracks, which allows the players' cats to get a better idea who and what they're following. Have the group choose one cat to make a See Check (which may use the Animal Lore Knack). If that Check has a total of 7 or less, the cat can't tell what the tracks are. If the total is between 8 and 10, the cat can tell that there are rabbit tracks—and they were made today. If the total is 11 or higher, the cat can tell that there are fox tracks in the mix, too—and that the fox tracks are the freshest.

The players must now decide whether their cats are going to continue following these tracks—perhaps knowing that one or more foxes are on the trail, too—or if they are going to give up searching in the valley and instead head up to the highlands. This probably isn't going to be an easy decision. Foxes are dangerous. Any cat with Animal Lore can inform the group that foxes are clever, fast, and tough. A single fox can sometimes defeat up to four warriors in a single fight.

On the other hand, the valley has had fairly abundant signs of life (in particular, rabbits). Going to the highlands might lead the cats away from the foxes, but it might also lead them away from the prey animals they are looking for.

Help the players through their discussion, making sure they

consider their options and understand the potential consequences. When they've made their decision, continue below.

What Happens Next: If the players' cats decide to follow the tracks in the valley, continue with **10**.

If the players' cats decide to go into the highlands, this is the end of the chapter. Hand the adventure to the next Narrator and tell him or her to continue with **7**.

14. Snowbound

Read Aloud: "Cold. All you can think about is how cold it is. No matter how brave a warrior you are, you can't fight the cold."

Narrator Tips: If the adventure has reached this scene, it's because one or more of the cats failed to escape a snowy danger—either an avalanche or a perilously deep snowfield. Being buried in snow is very disorienting. It's dark, freezing, and in most cases difficult to even tell which way is up. It is hard to even move, let alone start digging yourself out of the predicament.

Improvise a very short scene based on the events as they played out in your game—let the players' cats have that brief moment of absolute panic as they realize they are trapped and there is little or nothing they can do about it. Meanwhile, ask the other players what their cats are doing. The snow is now perfectly safe to walk on, so they would be in no additional danger if they try to dig their friends out—if they can find them!

Have the searching cats make a few rounds' worth of appropriate Skill Checks (to dig, or hear the cries of their buried friends, or just remember where they were standing). Then, no matter what their totals, have them succeed in finding the buried cats. But these cats are no longer in any shape to continue the mission—they are cold through to the core, they may have broken bones, and they need some rest. The only real choice is to get them back to the Clan territories.

Hopefully, the other groups of warriors will be more

successful. Or perhaps, once the wounded cats are healed, the group can go out and try again.

What Happens Next: The adventure is over. The players' cats do *not* get any Experience rewards for this adventure. The players' cats *can*, however, play the adventure again.

15. Climb Higher

Read Aloud: "The hill is steep, and the snow is lightly packed. Pretty soon you find yourself up to your nose in snow."

Narrator Tips: Improvise a brief scene where the cats have to deal with traveling through snow that is deeper than they are tall. In order to move, they must leap out of the tiny "snow pit" they are in, and then immediately land in an identical situation.

This kind of travel is difficult. Ask each of the players how many Levels their cats have in the Jump Skill. Cats with 3 or more Levels can navigate this deep snow with no problem. Cats with 1 or 2 Levels can travel this way, but it's exhausting—they lose 1 chip from fatigue. If any of the cats have 0 Levels in Jump, traveling like this takes them extra time and they lose 2 chips from fatigue, plus they automatically fail the Focus Check discussed below.

After two jumps, the players' cats realize that because the snow is so lightly packed, jumping in it like this could shake the snow loose and cause it to slide down the hillside. If this possibility worries the cats, they can safely turn back and go lower on the hill (or even down to the valley). If they decide to proceed, have each cat make a Focus Check to try to jump carefully. If any of the cats have a total of 6 or lower, they have shaken the snowpack loose. If all the cats have totals of 7 or higher, they have successfully crossed the upper highlands.

What Happens Next: If the players' cats want to turn back and go to the part of the highlands they were in before, continue with **16**.

If the players' cats want to turn back and go to the valley and they have not yet encountered any foxes, continue with **4**.

If the players' cats want to turn back and go to the valley and they have already encountered foxes during this adventure, continue with **10**.

If the players' cats shake the snowpack loose, continue with **22**.

If the players' cats successfully cross the upper highlands, this is the end of the chapter. Hand the adventure to the next Narrator and tell him or her to continue with **21**.

16. Crossing the Deep

Read Aloud: "This is the deepest snow you've ever seen. You have to leap free of the snow even to move, but when you land you're once again surrounded—and it doesn't look well packed."

Narrator Tips: As in scene 15, the cats have to travel through snow that is deeper than they are tall—only this time the snow is even deeper. Plus, it's loosely packed, and threatens to collapse and bury them every time they land.

Have each cat make three Jump Checks (that can make use of the Dodge Knack) and add the three totals together. If a cat's grand total is 14 or lower, that cat has been trapped in a collapsing snow tunnel. The cat has one last chance to escape—a single Strength Check. If the total of this check is 8 or higher, the cat escapes.

What Happens Next: If all the players' cats get safely through or successfully escape the snowfield, this is the end of the chapter. Hand the adventure to the next Narrator and tell him or her to continue with **21**.

If any of the players' cats get trapped in the snowfield, continue with **14**.

17. Outfoxed

Read Aloud: "The claws that scratch. The teeth that bite. Even a warrior has limits."

Narrator Tips: If the adventure has reached this scene it is because one or more of the players' cats has been knocked out while fighting with the foxes. Improvise a short scene where the other cats get their friend back to the safety of the Clan territories. Let the players decide how they will get their unconscious friend home.

It's possible that the players may want to look for medicinal herbs and try to use those to heal their friend. With the Ponder

Skill and the Herb Lore Knack, that is possible, but it's very hard. A single cat must get a total of 20 or higher on the Check, and even that only brings the unconscious cat back to a single Health Chip. He or she still must go back home immediately to seek healing from a medicine cat.

When the cats get back, one of the Clan leaders will ask them what happened. Let the players tell their cats' tale. The leader will be impressed by their bravery, even though their mission ended badly. The leader will tell the cats that they acted as true warriors should, and they should be proud of themselves. But the leader will look a little dejected because there still is nothing to eat and no clue as to when newleaf will come.

What Happens Next: The adventure is over. The players' cats do *not* get any Experience rewards for this adventure. The players' cats *can*, however, play the adventure again.

18. Follow the Hare

Read Aloud: "You round a snowbank and see the hare dashing across an open field. Suddenly it turns to the left, kicking up snow as it does and revealing a single, green shoot poking through from below."

Narrator Tips: The cats must decide whether to follow the hare or dig up the shoot. Getting fresh-kill is important, but the Clan leaders also gave the cats a secondary mission to bring back any proof they can find that newleaf is coming soon (and cats who communicated with StarClan—from Scene 8—have an even clearer reason to do so). This shoot is the only green thing they've seen on the whole journey. The cats must choose which goal they will focus on, the hare or the shoot.

Ask the players what their cats want to do. If they want to follow the hare, improvise a brief chase scene with the hare getting farther and farther away each time it ducks around a snowbank. In fairly short order, it is gone entirely. If the cats then go back to the green shoot, they find only a rabbit-gnawed nub where the shoot once stood. The shoot is gone, and so is the chance to fulfill their secondary mission.

If the players want their cats to split up, with some of them following the hare and others trying to dig up the shoot, begin by following those chasing the hare. They have the same experience described above and will be gone long enough to miss the whole digging effort. By the time they get back, the situation will be resolved.

If all or some of the players' cats ignore the hare and try to dig up the shoot, it will require a team effort to succeed. As simple as that task sounds, it is actually fairly challenging. The shoot is small, young, and fragile. Digging it up improperly could destroy it.

Have each cat make a Focus Check and add them together to get a group total. If that group total is equal to or higher than the total number of players (not including the Narrator) times four, the cats have successfully dug up the shoot. If not, they just bit (or clawed) off a small piece of the shoot. They can try again, but next time the group total must equal the total number of players (not including the Narrator) times *five*. The group can try a number of times equal to the number of cats making Focus Checks. So, if there are three cats adding to the group total, they may try three times. If they have not succeeded by that point, the shoot is ruined and the mission cannot be fulfilled.

What Happens Next: If the players' cats succeed at digging up the shoot, continue with **20**.

If the players' cats failed to dig up the shoot, they will find that a field full of normal rabbits is still gathered in a nearby field (though the snow hare will *not* be there). Continue with **19**.

19. Fresh-Kill

Read Aloud: "The hunt is on!"

Narrator Tips: This scene begins as a great rabbit hunt. The players must come up with a strategy for hunting so that they can get as much fresh-kill as possible. There are a half dozen rabbits in the field digging in the snow looking for anything edible. They aren't having much luck, and they are on high alert for predators.

Hunting a rabbit first requires a Sneak Check with a total of 7 (the Stalk Knack can be used with this Check). If that fails, the rabbit is aware of your presence. For every point that a cat's total is below 7, another rabbit in addition to the target rabbit is aware of the cat's presence. For example, if a player's cat only managed a total of 4 on this Check, the target rabbit would know he or she was there, as would three other nearby rabbits (7-4 = 3). Once a rabbit knows there is a cat nearby, it immediately flees. On this snowy terrain, the rabbits are much faster than the players' cats, so there is no hope of catching them.

If a cat successfully sneaks up on a rabbit, he or she must make a Pounce Check with a total of 6, and a Bite Check with a total of 5. If either of these Checks fails, the rabbit gets away. However, if both the Checks succeed, the rabbit is now fresh-kill that the cat can bring back at the end of the day.

Use the Hunting rules (found in Chapter Five of the game

rules) to improvise a hunting scene based on the players' cats plans. Remember that as soon as one of the cats goes on the attack, all of the rabbits will have a chance to notice and then try to escape with their lives. With such a complicated situation, including so many different cats and rabbits, it may fall on you, as Narrator, to improvise a lot more than usual. When doing so, remember that this is the end of an adventure where the players' cats have faced great danger and come through like the heroic warriors they are. Plus, their opponents are only a group of half-starved rabbits, so it is a good rule of thumb to decide most questionable situations in the cats' favor.

When the hunt is done, narrate a brief scene describing the players' cats' journey home, followed by a more detailed scene describing their reception. The fresh-kill they bring—spare as the meat is—goes to feed a great many hungry cats, and probably saves a few of them from joining StarClan.

The players' cats are treated like heroes, and rightly so, but the truth is that they did not succeed in the task given to them by StarClan. They did not find the green shoot in a white field and bring it back to the Clans and, as the dream predicted, it is more than a moon later that leaf-bare finally loosens its grip. Don't let this knowledge ruin their thoughts about their other success—this is, after all, a successful conclusion to the adventure. It's just that there was an even better conclusion that could have been reached.

What Happens Next: The players' cats have succeeded in getting fresh-kill for the hungry Clan cats. They have earned Experience but their victory is incomplete, and so are the rewards that they can collect. See the "After the Adventure" section for details.

20. Shooting the Moon

Read Aloud: "With a pop, the shoot comes loose from the frozen ground and lays on the snow in front of you."

Narrator Tips: The players' cats have succeeded in fulfilling this part of their mission. Nothing happens immediately, though. They simply have a green shoot to carry with them back to the Clan lands. But the cats back there are still hungry. If the players ask what happened to the field full of rabbits, tell them that their cats must go back and look. If they do, they will find that the rabbits are there (although the snow hare no longer is). Let the cats hunt the rabbits, as described in Scene 19, but give each cat 5 bonus points they can spend on any Checks they want to during the hunt. (These points can be spent the same way that Ability chips are, and they always count as the right color chip for the action being taken.)

If the players do not think to ask about the rabbits, have them stumble across the field by accident as they start their journey home. Let them hunt as described above except that they do *not* get the bonus points.

If the players' cats had an earlier conversation with StarClan, on the first night of their journey home, they get another message in their dreams. In that dream, the same member of StarClan who spoke to the cat before appears and tells him or her what a good job the group has done. "When you deliver the shoot to the Clan leaders, give them this message: The warrior code is meant to bind the Clans together, but too often it is used as a reason for them to fight. As the moons pass, remember how much more you can accomplish when you work together. The Clans must *all* cooperate if any of them are going to survive."

When the players' cats return, bearing fresh-kill and the green shoot, they are treated as heroes. And when the Clan leaders hear what StarClan said, they all look a little shaken—but they promise to think about those words of wisdom and use them in the future.

If the cats come back with the shoot, but with no fresh-kill, their greeting is much less warm. Completing a mission from StarClan is certainly a good thing, but the Clan cats need food! The Clan leaders will listen to the message that StarClan sent, but will not be as receptive as described above. Their attitude will be one of disappointment that their Clanmates must suffer for such a simpleminded message.

Either way, true to StarClan's word, signs of newleaf begin to appear everywhere. Trees bud, prey animals come out of their leaf-bare slumbers, and the snow begins to melt. Well before the end of one moon, newleaf is in full bloom and the Clan cats are all on their way to regaining their strength and returning to life as normal.

What Happens Next: The players' cats have succeeded in getting fresh-kill for the hungry cats from all Clans, and they have fulfilled StarClan's mission. They truly have earned the Experience rewards that await them. See the "After the Adventure" section below for details.

21. Rabbit Run

Read Aloud: "At first you think the cold must be getting to you—the snowy field ahead seems more brown than white.

Then you realize it's not brown snow, it's brown rabbits—a field full of them!"

Narrator Tips: After a long, dangerous, and very uncomfortable hunt, the players' cats have found just what the Clan Leaders sent them to find—a glen full of prey animals to be hunted and brought back as fresh-kill. In truth this is just a half dozen or so rabbits that have woken up from hibernation thin and hungry. But for a cat that hasn't seen a live prey animal in nearly a moon, they would seem like a sumptuous feast.

Describe the scene in such a way that the players understand what a bounty they have found, and ask them how they are going to go about hunting the rabbits. While they are talking that over, have all of the cats make a See Check (to which the Alertness Knack may be applied). Any cat whose total is 10 or higher sees a strange sight. (This is crucial to the adventure, so if none of the cats have a total higher than 10, then the cat who got the highest total sees it instead.)

At the far end of the glen stands a single strong and healthy snow hare—its pure, white fur practically sparkling in the sunlight. Unlike the other rabbits, it does not look haggard and timid. It is strong, with lots of meat on its bones, and sits up proudly and defiantly. It stares directly at the players' cats with a strange glint in its eyes.

Have all the cats make a See Check. Anyone who has a total of 8 or higher notices that the glint was actually the image of a plant shoot sprouting up through the snow—defying the cold leaf-bare wind in the same way the hare seems to be defying the cats themselves.

Then the snow hare suddenly spins and runs away, disappearing behind a snowdrift.

The cats must make a split-second decision—will they stay here and hunt the rabbits or chase after the snow hare and risk scaring away the rabbits as they do?

What Happens Next: If the players' cats want to stay here and hunt rabbits, continue with **19**.

If the players' cats want to follow the snow hare, continue with **18**.

22. Avalanche!

Read Aloud: "You hear a sound like a thick tree branch snapping, and suddenly the top layer of snow on the hillside begins to slide down toward the valley—taking you with it!"

Narrator Tips: The players' cats have inadvertently caused an avalanche, and they are standing right in the middle of it. Suddenly the world around them disappears and they are tumbling down the hill completely surrounded by flowing powder. It's dark, cold, and hard to breathe. Ask the players what their cats are going to do to try to save themselves.

The best answer is for the cats to try to swim the way they would in a river. If the players come up with that answer on their own, give all of the cats a +2 bonus on the Swim Check. If they don't think of it, or if they seem to think a different solution is better, allow all of the cats to make a Ponder Check. If the total is 5 or higher, they know that swimming is the best solution (but they no longer get a bonus to the Check). If the Ponder Check has a total of 8 or higher, they know that no action other than swimming has any chance of success.

In the end, the cats can take any actions they prefer. If they get a total of 7 or higher on a Swim Check, they get out of the avalanche safely. Any cat that gets a total of 6 or lower, or tries any action other than swimming, is automatically buried by the avalanche.

What Happens Next: If the players' cats all escape the avalanche, continue with **16**.

If any of the players' cats are buried by the avalanche, continue with **14**.

AFTER THE ADVENTURE

After the last scene of the adventure has been played, the game itself is not necessarily over. There still are a few things you can do if the players want to keep at it.

Play It Again

If the players' cats made a quick path through the adventure, or if they failed in either or both of their missions, you may want to go back and play again so that the group can explore all of the options the adventure contains. Or perhaps you just want to go back and pick up the adventure again somewhere in the middle where it feels like things went wrong. In either case, your cat would be right back where he or she was and have another chance to find a more favorable outcome.

One of the great things about storytelling games is that you can always tell the story again. And, since there are many different ways to approach their goals, the story could unwind in a different way every time you play (particularly as different Narrators get to guide the storyline).

Experience

If the cats completed the adventure successfully, then they all get Experience rewards. There are two different sets of experience for this adventure, though—one for coming back with fresh-kill and the other for retrieving the green shoot. It is important to note, though, that each cat can only get each of these Experience rewards *once*! If you play through and successfully finish that section of the adventure several times, your cat only gains the rewards listed below after *first* time he or she does so.

If you use different cats each time, though, each one can get the Experience rewards. The rule is *not* that a player can only get experience once; it's that a cat can.

Bringing Fresh-kill

If the players' cats brought fresh-kill back for the hungry Clan cats, they get the following rewards:

Age: Although all the action in this adventure happens over the course of just a few days, the presumption is that this is the most interesting and exciting thing that happens to your cat during the whole of that moon. Increase your cat's age by 1 moon and make any appropriate improvements described in Chapter Four of the game rules.

Skill: On top of the improvements your cat gets from aging, he or she also can gain 1 level in two of the following skills: Focus, Jump, Ponder, or See.

Retrieving the Green Shoot

If the players' cats retrieved the green shoot and brought it back to the Clan leaders, they get the following rewards:

Spirit: On top of the improvements your cat gets from aging, he or she also increases his or her Spirit Ability Score by 1.

Knack: On top of the improvements your cat gets from aging, he or she also gains 1 level of the Animal Lore or Interpret Dreams Knack.

More adventures can be found at the back of each novel in the Omen of the Stars series, and you can find extra information at www.warriorcats.com.

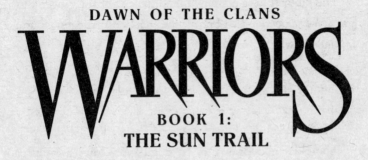

DON'T MISS

DAWN OF THE CLANS

WARRIORS

BOOK 1:
THE SUN TRAIL

Cold gray light rippled over the floor of a cave so vast that its roof was lost in shadows. An endless screen of water fell across the entrance, its sound echoing from the rocks.

Near the back of the cavern crouched a frail white she-cat. Despite her age, her green eyes were clear and deep with wisdom as her gaze traveled over the skinny cats swarming the cave floor, restlessly pacing in front of the shimmering waterfall: the elders huddled together in the sleeping hollows; the kits mewling desperately, demanding food from their exhausted mothers.

"We can't go on like this," the old she-cat whispered to herself.

A few tail-lengths away, several kits squabbled over an eagle carcass. Its flesh had been stripped away the day before as soon as their mothers had caught it. A big ginger kit shouldered a smaller tabby away from the bone she was gnawing at.

"I *need* this!" he announced.

The tabby sprang up and nipped the end of the ginger kit's tail. "We *all* need it, flea-brain!" she snapped as the ginger tom let out a yowl.

A gray-and-white elder, every one of her ribs showing through her pelt, tottered up to the kits and snatched the bone away.

"Hey!" the ginger kit protested.

The elder glared at him. "I caught prey for season after season," she snarled. "Don't you think I deserve one measly bone?" She turned and stalked off, the bone clamped firmly in her jaws.

The ginger kit stared after her for a heartbeat, then scampered, wailing, to his mother, who lay on a rock beside the cave wall. Instead of comforting him, his mother snapped something, angrily flicking her tail.

The old white she-cat was too far away to hear what the mother cat said, but she sighed.

Every cat is coming to the end of what they can bear, she thought.

She watched as the gray-and-white elder padded across the cave and dropped the eagle bone in front of an even older she-cat, who was crouching in a sleeping hollow with her nose resting on her front paws. Her dull gaze was fixed on the far wall of the cave.

"Here, Misty Water." The gray-and-white elder nudged the bone closer to her with one paw. "Eat. It's not much, but it might help."

Misty Water's indifferent gaze flickered over her friend

and away again. "No, thanks, Silver Frost. I have no appetite, not since Broken Feather died." Her voice throbbed with grief. "He would have lived, if there had been enough prey for him to eat." She sighed. "Now I'm just waiting to join him."

"Misty Water, you can't—"

The white she-cat was distracted from the elders' talk as a group of cats appeared at the entrance to the cave, shaking snow off their fur. Several other cats sprang up and ran to meet them.

"Did you catch anything?" one of them called out eagerly.

"Yes, where's your prey?" another demanded.

The leader of the newcomers shook his head sadly. "Sorry. There wasn't enough to bring back."

Hope melted from the cats in the cave like mist under strong sunlight. They glanced at one another, then trailed away, their heads drooping and their tails brushing the ground.

The white she-cat watched them, then turned her head as she realized that a cat was padding up to her. Though his muzzle was gray with age and his golden tabby fur thin and patchy, he walked with a confidence that showed he had once been a strong and noble cat.

"Half Moon," he greeted the white she-cat, settling down beside her and wrapping his tail over his paws.

The white she-cat let out a faint *mrrow* of amusement. "You shouldn't call me that, Lion's Roar," she protested. "I've been the Teller of the Pointed Stones for many seasons."

The golden tabby tom sniffed. "I don't care how long the

others have called you Stoneteller. You'll always be Half Moon to me."

Half Moon made no response, except to reach out her tail and rest it on her old friend's shoulder.

"I was born in this cave," Lion's Roar went on. "But my mother, Shy Fawn, told me about the time before we came here—when you lived beside a lake, sheltered beneath trees."

Half Moon sighed faintly. "I am the only cat left who remembers the lake, and the journey we made to come here. But I have lived three times as many moons here in the mountains than I did beside the lake, and the endless rushing of the waterfall now echoes in my heart." She paused, blinking, then asked, "Why are you telling me this now?"

Lion's Roar hesitated before replying. "Hunger might kill us all before the sun shines again, and there's no more room in the cave." He stretched out one paw and brushed Half Moon's shoulder fur. "Something must be done."

Half Moon's eyes stretched wide as she gazed at him. "But we can't leave the mountains!" she protested, her voice breathless with shock. "Jay's Wing promised; he made me the Teller of the Pointed Stones because this was our destined home."

Lion's Roar met her intense green gaze. "Are you sure Jay's Wing was right?" he asked. "How could he know what was going to happen in the future?"

"He had to be right," Half Moon murmured.

Her mind flew back to the ceremony, so many seasons before, when Jay's Wing had made her the Teller of the

Pointed Stones. She shivered as she heard his voice again, full of love for her and grief that her destiny meant they could never be together. "Others will come after you, moon upon moon. Choose them well, train them well—trust the future of your Tribe to them."

He would never have said that if he didn't mean for us to stay here.

Half Moon let her gaze drift over the other cats: her cats, now thin and hungry. She shook her head sadly. Lion's Roar was right: Something had to be done if they were to survive.

DOGS WILL RULE THE WILD IN

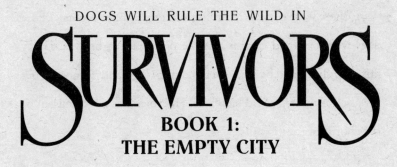

SURVIVORS

BOOK 1:
THE EMPTY CITY

Lucky startled awake, fear prickling in his bones and fur. He leaped to his feet, growling.

For an instant he'd thought he was tiny once more, safe in his Pup Pack and protected, but the comforting dream had already vanished. The air shivered with menace, tingling Lucky's skin. If only he could see what was coming, he could face it down—but the monster was invisible, scentless. He whined in terror. This was no sleep-time story: This fear was *real*.

The urge to run was almost unbearable; but he could only scrabble, snarl, and scratch in panic. There was nowhere to go: The wire of his cage hemmed him in on every side. His muzzle hurt when he tried to shove it through the gaps; when he backed away, snarling, the same wire bit into his haunches.

Others were close . . . familiar bodies, familiar scents. Those dogs were enclosed in this terrible place just as he was. Lucky raised his head and barked, over and over, high and desperate, but it was clear no dog could help him. His voice was drowned out by the chorus of frantic calls.

They were all *trapped*.

Dark panic overwhelmed him. His claws scrabbled at the earth floor, even though he knew it was hopeless.

He could smell the female swift-dog in the next cage, a friendly, comforting scent, overlaid now with the bitter tang of danger and fear. Yipping, he pressed closer to her, feeling the shivers in her muscles—but the wire still separated them.

"Sweet? Sweet, something's on its way. Something bad!"

"Yes, I feel it! What's happening?"

The longpaws—where were they? The longpaws held them captive in this Trap House but they had always seemed to care about the dogs. They brought food and water, they laid bedding, cleared the mess . . .

Surely the longpaws would come for them now.

The others barked and howled as one, and Lucky raised his voice with theirs.

Longpaws! Longpaws, it's COMING. . . .

Something shifted beneath him, making his cage tremble. In a sudden, terrible silence, Lucky crouched, frozen with horror.

Then, around and above him, chaos erupted.

The unseen monster was here . . . and its paws were right on the Trap House.

Lucky was flung back against the wire as the world heaved and tilted. For agonizing moments he didn't know which way was up or down. The monster tumbled him around, deafening him with the racket of falling rock and shattering clear-stone. His vision went dark as clouds of filth blinded him. The screaming, yelping howls of terrified dogs seemed to fill his skull. A great chunk of wall crashed off the wire in front of his nose, and Lucky leaped back. Was it the Earth-Dog, trying to take him?

Then, just as suddenly as the monster had come, it disappeared. One more wall crashed down in a cloud of choking dust. Torn wire screeched as a high cage toppled, then plummeted to the earth.

There was only silence and a dank metal scent.

Blood! thought Lucky. *Death* . . .

Panic stirred inside his belly again. He was lying on his side, the wire cage crumpled against him, and he thrashed his strong legs, trying to right himself. The cage rattled and rocked, but he couldn't get up. *No!* he thought. *I'm trapped!*

"Lucky! Lucky, are you all right?"

"Sweet? Where are you?"

Her long face pushed at his through the mangled wire. "My cage door—it broke when it fell! I thought I was dead. Lucky, I'm free—but you—"

"Help me, Sweet!"

The other faint whimpers had stopped. Did that mean the other dogs were . . . ? No. Lucky could not let himself think about that. He howled just to break the silence.

"I think I can pull the cage out a bit," said Sweet. "Your door's loose, too. We might be able to get it open." Seizing the wire with her teeth, she tugged.

Lucky fought to keep himself calm. All he wanted to do was fling himself against the cage until it broke. His hind legs kicked out wildly and he craned his head around, snapping at the wire. Sweet was gradually pulling the cage forward, stopping occasionally to scrabble at fallen stones with her paws.

"There. It's looser now. Wait while I—"

But Lucky could wait no longer. The cage door was torn at the upper corner, and he twisted until he could bite and claw at it. He worked his paw into the gap and pulled, hard.

The wire gave with a screech, just as Lucky felt a piercing stab in his paw pad—but the door now hung at an awkward angle. Wriggling and squirming, he pulled himself free and stood upright at last.

His tail was tight between his legs as tremors bolted through his skin and muscles. He and Sweet stared at the carnage and chaos around them. There were broken cages—and broken bodies. A small, smooth-coated dog lay on the ground nearby, lifeless, eyes dull. Beneath the last wall that had fallen, nothing stirred, but a limp paw poked out from between stones. The scent of death was already spreading through the Trap House air.

DON'T MISS

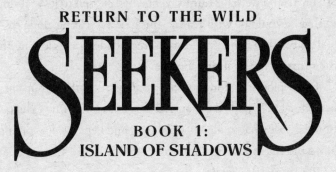

RETURN TO THE WILD

SEEKERS

BOOK 1:
ISLAND OF SHADOWS

Excitement tingled through Lusa's paws as she padded down the snow-covered beach. Ice stretched ahead of her, flat, sparkly white, unchanging as far as the horizon. She didn't belong here—no black bears did—yet here she was, walking confidently onto the frozen ocean beside a brown bear and two white bears. Ujurak had gone, but Yakone, a white bear from Star Island, had joined Lusa, Kallik, and Toklo. They were still four. And a new journey lay ahead: a journey that would take them back home.

Glancing over her shoulder, Lusa saw the low hills of Star Island looming dark beneath the mauve clouds. The outlines of the white bears who lived there were growing smaller with each pawstep. *Good-bye,* she thought, with a twinge of regret that she would never see them again. Her home lay among trees, green leaves, and sun-warmed grass, a long, long way from this place of ice and wind as sharp as claws.

Lusa wondered if Yakone was feeling regret, too. The bears of Star Island were his family, yet he had chosen to leave them so that he could be with Kallik. But he was striding along resolutely beside Kallik, his unusual red-shaded pelt glowing in the sunrise, and he didn't look back.

Toklo plodded along at the front of the little group, his head down. He looked exhausted, but Lusa knew that exhaustion was not what made his steps drag and kept his eyes on his paws and his shoulders hunched.

He's grieving for Ujurak.

Their friend had died saving them from an avalanche. Lusa grieved for him, too, but she clung to the certainty that it hadn't been the end of Ujurak's life, not really. The achingly familiar shape of the bear who had led them all the way to Star Island had returned with stars in his fur, skimming over the snow and soaring up into the sky with his mother, Silaluk. Two starry bears making patterns in the sky forever, following the endless circle of Arcturus, the constant star. Lusa knew that Ujurak would be with them always. But she wasn't sure if Toklo felt the same. A cold claw of pain seemed to close around her heart, and she wished that she could do something to help him.

Maybe if I distracted him. . . .

"Hey, Toklo!" Lusa called, bounding forward past Kallik and Yakone until she reached the grizzly's side. "Do you think we should hunt now?"

Toklo started, as if Lusa's voice had dragged him back from somewhere far away. "What?"

"I said, should we hunt now?" This close to shore, they might pick up a seal above the ice, or even a young walrus.

Toklo gave her a brief glance before trudging on. "No. It'll be dark soon. We need to travel while we can."

Then it'll be too dark to hunt. Lusa bit the words back. It wasn't the time to start arguing. But she wanted to help Toklo wrench his thoughts away from the friend he was convinced he had lost.

"Do you think geese ever come down to rest on the ice?" she asked.

This time Toklo didn't even look at her. "Don't be bee-brained," he said scathingly. "Why would they do that? Geese find their food on *land*." He quickened his pace to leave her behind.

Lusa gazed sadly after him. Most times when Toklo was in a grouchy mood, she would give as good as she got, or tease him out of his bad temper. But this time his pain was too deep to deal with lightly.

Best to leave him alone, she decided. *For now, anyway.*

As Star Island dwindled behind the bears, the short snow-sky day faded into shadows that seemed to grow up from the ice and reach down from the sky until the whole white world was swallowed in shades of gray and black. When Lusa looked back, the last traces of the hills that had become so familiar had vanished into the twilight. Star spirits began to appear overhead, and the silver moon hung close to the horizon like a shining claw. The bears trekked between snowbanks that glimmered in the pale light, reaching above their backs in strange shapes formed by the scouring wind.

"It's time we stopped for the night," Kallik announced, halting at the foot of a deep drift. "This looks like a good place to make a den."

"I'll help you dig," Yakone offered. He began to scrape at the bottom of the snowbank.

Lusa watched the two white bears as they burrowed vigorously into the snow. This would be Yakone's first night away from his family, away from the permanent den where he had been raised. Yet he seemed unfazed—enthusiastic, even, as he helped Kallik carve a shallow niche that would keep off the worst of the wind. The white bears' heads were close together now as they scraped at the harder, gritty snow underneath the fluffy top layer. Yakone said something that made Kallik huff with amusement, and she flicked a pawful of snow at him in response.

Lusa turned away, not wanting to eavesdrop. A pang of sorrow clawed once more at her heart when she spotted Toklo standing a little way off, watching the white bears without saying anything. After a moment he turned his back on Kallik and Yakone and raised his head to fix his gaze on the stars.

Looking up, Lusa made out the shining shape of Silaluk, the Great Bear, and close to her side the Little Bear, Ujurak. Seeing him there made her feel safe, because she knew that their friend was watching over them. It helped to comfort her grief.

But there was no comfort for Toklo. All he knew was that

his friend, the other brown bear on this strange and endless journey, had left them. His bleak gaze announced his loneliness to Lusa as clearly as if he had put it into words.

"We're here, Toklo," she murmured, too faintly for the brown bear to hear. "You're *not* alone."

She knew that Toklo had been closer to Ujurak than any of them; he had taken on the responsibility of protecting the smaller brown bear. *Toklo felt like he failed when Ujurak died,* Lusa thought. *He's wrong, but how can any bear make him understand that?*

ENTER THE WORLD OF
WARRIORS

Warriors

Sinister perils threaten the four warrior Clans. Into the midst of this turmoil comes Rusty, an ordinary housecat, who may just be the bravest of them all.

Download the free Warriors app at www.warriorcats.com

Warriors: The New Prophecy

Follow the next generation of heroic cats as they set off on a quest to save the Clans from destruction.

All Warriors, Seekers, and Survivors books are available as ebooks from HarperCollins.

Also available unabridged from HarperChildren's *Audio*

HARPER
An Imprint of HarperCollinsPublishers

Visit www.warriorcats.com for the free Warriors app, games, Clan lore, and much more!

Warriors: Power of Three

Firestar's grandchildren begin their training as warrior cats.
Prophecy foretells that they will hold more power than any cats before them.

Warriors: Omen of the Stars

Which ThunderClan apprentice will complete the prophecy that
foretells that three Clanmates hold the future of the Clans in their paws?

Also available unabridged from HarperChildren's *Audio*

Warriors: Dawn of the Clans

Discover how the warrior cat Clans came to be.

HARPER
An Imprint of HarperCollinsPublishers

Visit www.warriorcats.com for the free Warriors app, games, Clan lore, and much more!

Warrior Cats Come to Life in Manga!

HARPER
An Imprint of HarperCollinsPublishers

Visit www.warriorcats.com for the free Warriors app, games, Clan lore, and much more!

The *New York Times* bestselling series SEEKERS

Three young bears…one destiny. Discover the fate that awaits them on their adventure.

Seekers: Return to the Wild
The stakes are higher than ever as the bears search for a way home.

Available in Manga!

www.seekerbears.com

A new series from ERIN HUNTER

SURVIVORS

Survivors #1: The Empty City
www.survivorsdogs.com

When the Big Growl strikes, Lucky must decide: Is he a Lone Dog? Or does he belong with a Pack?

ERIN HUNTER

Also available unabridged from HarperChildren's*Audio*

HARPER
An Imprint of HarperCollinsPublishers